SHE'S OUT

Lynda La Plante was born in Liverpool. She trained for the stage at RADA and worked with the National Theatre and RDC before becoming a television actress. She then turned to writing—and made her breakthrough with the phenomenally successful TV series *Widows*. Her novels have all been international bestsellers.

Her original script for the much-acclaimed *Prime Suspect* won awards from BAFTA, Emmy, British Broadcasting and Royal Television Society, as well as the 1993 Edgar Allan Poe Award. Lynda has written and produced over 170 hours of international television.

Lynda is one of only three screenwriters to have been made an honorary fellow of the British Film Institute and was awarded the BAFTA Dennis Potter Best Writer Award in 2000. In 2008, she was awarded a CBE in the Queen's Birthday Honours List for services to Literature, Drama and Charity.

If you would like to hear from Lynda, please sign up at www.bit.ly/LyndaLaPlanteClub or you can visit www.lyndalaplante.com for further information. You can also follow Lynda on Facebook and Twitter @LaPlanteLynda.

Lynda La Plante

SHE'S OUT

ZAFFRE

Copyright © La Plante Global Limited, 1995, 2019

Typeset by Scribe Inc., Philadelphia, PA.

First published in Great Britain by Pan Books, 1995
First published by Simon & Schuster UK Ltd., 2012
This edition published in the United States of America in 2019 by Zaffre
Zaffre is an imprint of Bonnier Books UK
80–81 Wimpole Street, London W1G 9RE

10 9 8 7 6 5 4 3 2 1

Hardcover ISBN: 978-1-4998-6218-8
Trade paperback ISBN: 978-1-4998-6219-5
Digital ISBN: 978-1-4998-6220-1

For information, contact
251 Park Avenue South, Floor 12, New York, New York 10010
www.bonnierbooks.co.uk

CHAPTER 1

The date was ringed with a fine red biro circle, March 15, 1994. It was the only mark on the cheap calendar pinned to the wall in her cell. There were no photographs, no memorabilia, not even a picture cut out of a magazine. She had always been in a cell by herself. The prison authorities had discussed the possibility of her sharing with another inmate but it had been decided it was preferable to leave Dorothy Rawlins as she had requested—alone.

Rawlins had been a model prisoner from the day she had arrived. She seemed to settle into a solitary existence immediately. At first she spoke little and was always polite to both prisoners and prison officers. She rarely smiled, she never wrote letters, but read for hours on end alone in her cell, and ate alone. After six months she began to work in the prison library; a year later she became a trusty. Gradually the women began to refer to Rawlins during recreational periods, asking her opinion on their marriages, their relationships. They trusted her opinions and her advice but she made no one a close friend. She wrote their letters, she taught some of the inmates to read and write, she was always patient, always calm and, above all, she would always listen. If you had a problem, Dolly Rawlins would sort it out for you. Over the following years she became a dominant and highly respected figure within the prison hierarchy.

The women would often whisper about her to the new inmates, embroidering her past, which made her even more of a queen-like figurehead. Dorothy Rawlins was in Holloway for murder. She had shot her husband, the infamous Harry Rawlins, at point-blank range. The murder took on a macabre undertone as throughout the years the often repeated story was embellished, but no one ever discussed the murder to her face. It was as if she had an invisible barrier around her own emotions. Kindly toward anyone who needed comfort, she seemed never to need anything herself.

So the rumors continued: stories passed from one inmate to another that Rawlins had also been a part of a big diamond raid. Although she had never been charged and no evidence had ever been brought forward at her trial to implicate her, the idea that she had instigated the raid, and got away with it, accentuated her mystique. More important was the rumor that she had also got away with the diamonds. The diamonds, some said, were valued at one million, then two million. The robbery had been a terrifying, brutal raid and a young, beautiful girl called Shirley Miller had been shot and killed. It was never discovered that Shirley Miller had been one of the women who took part in the infamous robbery at the Strand underpass.

Four years into her sentence, Rawlins began to write letters to request a better baby wing at Holloway. She began to work with the young mothers and children. The result was that she became even more of a "Mama" figure. There was nothing she would not do for these young women, and it was on Rawlins's shoulders that they sobbed their hearts out when their babies were taken from them. Rawlins seemed to have an intuitive understanding, talking for hour upon hour with these distressed girls. She also had the same quiet patience with the drug offenders.

Five years into her sentence, Dolly Rawlins proved an invaluable inmate. She kept a photo album of the prisoners who had left, their letters to her, and especially the photographs of their children. But only the calendar was pinned to the chipboard on the wall of her cell. Nothing ever took precedence over the years of waiting.

She would always receive letters when the girls left Holloway. It was as if they needed her strength on the outside, but usually the letters came only for a couple of weeks then stopped. She was never hurt by the sudden silence, the lack of continued contact, because there were always the new inmates who needed her. She was a heroine, and the whispers about her criminal past only grew. Sometimes she would smile as if enjoying the notoriety, encouraging the stories with little hints that maybe, just maybe, she knew more about the diamond raid than she would ever admit. She was also aware by now that the mystery surrounding her past enhanced her position within the prison pecking order, allowing her to remain top dog without fighting or arguments.

After seven years, Rawlins was the "Big Mama"—and it was always Dolly who broke up the fights, Dolly who was called on to settle arguments, Dolly who received the small gifts, the extra cigarettes. The prison officers referred to her as a model prisoner, and she was consequently given a lot of freedom by the authorities. She organized and instigated further education, drug rehabilitation sessions and, with a year to go before she was released, Holloway opened an entire new mother-and-baby wing, with a bright, toy-filled nursery. This was where she spent most of her time, helping the staff care for the children. For Dolly, who had no visitors, no one on the outside to care for or about her, the babies became her main focus—and began to shape a future dream for when she would finally be free.

Dolly Rawlins did have those diamonds waiting and, if they had been worth two million when she was sentenced, she calculated they now had to be worth double. Alone in her cell she would dream about just what she was going to do with all that money. Fencing them would bring the value down to around two million. She would have to give a cut to Audrey, Shirley Miller's mother, and a cut to Jimmy Donaldson, the man holding them for her. She would then have enough to open some kind of home, buy a small terraced house for herself, maybe in Islington or an area close to the prison, so she could come and visit the girls she knew would still need her. She contemplated opening the home specifically for the children of pregnant prisoners, who, she knew, would have their babies taken away. Then they would at least know their babies were in good care, as many of the girls were single parents and their babies might otherwise be put up for adoption.

This daydreaming occupied Dolly for hours on end. She kept her idea to herself, afraid that if she mentioned it to anyone they would know for sure she had considerable finances. She did have several thousand pounds in a bank account set up for her by her lawyer and she calculated that with that, a government grant and the money from the gems the home could be up and running within a year of her release. She even thought about offering a sanctuary for some of the drug addicts who needed a secure place to stay when they were released. And, a number of the women inside were battered wives: perhaps she could allocate a couple of rooms for them. The daydreaming relieved the tension. It was like a comforter, a warm secret that enveloped her and helped her sleep. But the dream would soon be a reality as the months disappeared into weeks, and then days. As the ringed date was drawing closer and closer, she could hardly contain herself: at last she would have a reason to live. Being so close to newborn babies had opened up the terrible, secret pain of her own childlessness. But soon she would have a houseful of children who needed her. Then she could truly call herself "Mama."

They all knew she would soon be leaving. They whispered in corners as they made cards and small gifts. Even the prison officers were sad that they would lose such a valuable inmate, not that any of them had ever had much interaction with her on a personal level. She rarely made conversation with them unless it was strictly necessary, and some of them resented the fact that she seemed to have more power over the inmates than they did. A few years back, Rawlins had struck a prison officer, slapped her face, and warned her to stay away from a certain prisoner. She had been given extra days and been locked up in her cell. The result had been that Rawlins was fêted when she was eventually unlocked and the officer, a thickset, dark-haired woman called Barbara Hunter, never spoke to or looked at Rawlins again. The animosity between Hunter and Rawlins remained throughout the years. Hunter had tried on numerous occasions to needle Dolly, as if to prove to the Governor that the model prisoner 45688 was in reality an evil manipulator. But Dolly never rose to the bait, just looked at her with ice-cold eyes, and it was that blank-eyed stare that, Hunter suspected, concealed a deep hatred, not just of herself, but of all the prison officers.

Finally the day came, March 15, and Dolly carefully packed her few possessions from her cell. She had already given away all her personal effects: a radio, some tapes, skin cream, books and packets of cigarettes. She had lost a considerable amount of weight, and the suit she had worn the day she arrived hung on her like a rag as she waited for the call to the probation room for the usual chat with the Governor before she would finally be free. The years she had spent banged up had made her face sallow and drawn; her gray hair was cut short in an unflattering style.

As she sat, hands folded on her lap, until they called her to go into the first meeting, she appeared as calm as always but her heart was beating rapidly. She would soon be out. Soon be free. It would soon be over.

The old Victorian Grange Manor House was in a sorry state of disrepair, although at a distance it still looked impressive. The once splendid grounds, orchards and stables were all in need of serious attention. The grass was overgrown and weeds sprouted up through the gravel driveway. A swimming pool with a torn tarpaulin was filled with stagnant water, and even the old sign "Grange Health Farm" was broken and peeling like the paint on all the woodwork of the house. The once handsome stained-glass double-fronted door had boards covering the broken panes, many of the windows had cracks and some of the tiles from the roof lay shattered on the ground below. The double chimney-breasts were tilting dangerously. The house seemed fit only for demolition, while the once vast acreage that had belonged to the manor had been sold off years before to local farmers, and the dense, dark wood that fringed the lawns had begun to creep nearer with brambles and twisted shrubs.

A motorway had been built close to the edge of the lane leading to the manor, cutting off the house from the main road. Now the only access was down a small slip road that had been left, like the house, to rot, with deep potholes that made any journey hazardous. The rusted, wrought-iron gates were hanging off their hinges, and the chain threaded through them with the big padlock hung limply as if no one would want to enter anyway.

The Range Rover bumped and banged along the lane as it made its slow journey toward the house, the hedges either side hiding the fields and grazing cows.

Ester Freeman swore as the Range Rover hit a deep rut; it was even worse than the last time she'd been there. She was a handsome woman in her late forties. Five feet six and slender, she was a smart dresser, who always wore designer labels, and there was an elegance to her that belied the inner toughness that even her well-modulated voice sometimes couldn't disguise. Now, with her dark hair scraped back from her face and her teeth clenched, she looked anything but ladylike. She continued to swear as the Range Rover splashed through yet another water-filled pothole on its lurching course down the lane.

Sitting beside Ester, Julia Lawson looked equally unhappy. She was much younger than Ester and taller, almost six feet, with a strong, rangy body made to seem even more mannish by her jeans and leather jacket. She wore beat-up cowboy boots and a worn denim shirt, and there was an habitual arrogance to her expression that sometimes made her seem attractive, at other times plain. She had a deep, melodic, cultured voice, and was swearing fruitily as they bounced along. "Jesus Christ, Ester, slow down. You're chucking everything over the back of the car!"

Ester paid no attention as she heaved on the handbrake, jumped out and crossed to the wrought-iron gates. She didn't bother with a key to open the padlock—she just wrenched it loose and pushed back the old gates.

As they drove up the Manor House driveway, Julia laughed. "My God, I think it needs a demolition crew."

"Oh shut up," Ester snapped as they veered round a pothole.

"You know, I don't think they'll find it."

"They'll find it, I gave them each a map. Don't be so negative. She's out today, Julia. Come on, move it!"

Julia followed Ester slowly out of the car and looked around, shaking her head. She stepped back as a front doorstep crumbled beneath her boot. "You know, it looks unsafe."

"It's been standing for over a hundred years so it's not likely to fall down now. Get the bags out."

Julia looked back to the piles of suitcases and bulging black bin liners in the back of the Range Rover and ignored her request, following Ester into the manor.

The hallway was dark and forbidding: the William Morris wallpaper hung in damp speckled flaps from the carved cornices and there were stacks of old newspapers and broken bottles everywhere. The old wooden reception desk was dusty, the key-rack behind it devoid of keys.

Their feet echoed in the marble hall as Ester opened one door after another, the smell of must and mildew hanging in the air.

"You'll never get it ready in time, Ester."

Ester marched into the drawing room, shouting over her shoulder, "Oh yes I will, if everybody helps out."

Julia picked up the dust-covered telephone with a look of surprise. "Well I never. The phone's connected."

Ester stood looking around the drawing room: old-fashioned sofas and wing-backed chairs, threadbare carpet and china cabinets. The massive open stone fireplace was still filled with cinders. "I had it connected," she snapped as she began to draw back the draped velvet curtains, turning her face away as years of dust spiraled down. Even when Ester had occupied the place, no one had ever been that interested in dusting.

The Grange Health Farm had been defunct when Ester bought the manor with all its contents, but she had no plans to refurbish the old house as it was a perfect cover for her real profession. All Ester had done was spread a few floral displays around the main rooms and bring in fourteen girls, a chef, a domestic and two muscle-bound blokes in case of trouble. The Grange Health Farm reopened, catering to clients who wanted a massage and a sauna, but if they wanted a little bit more physical contact, Ester provided that too . . . at a price.

"We should have started weeks ago," Julia said as she lolled in the doorway, looking around with undisguised distaste.

"Well, I didn't, so we're gonna have to work like the clappers." Ester looked up to the chandelier, trying the light switch. Two of the eighteen bulbs flickered on.

"Bravo, the electricity's on as well," laughed Julia.

Ester glared around the room. "We'll clean this room, the dining room and a few bedrooms. Then that's it, we won't need to do any more."

"Really?" Julia smiled.

Ester pushed past her, wiping her dusty hands on a handkerchief, and Julia followed her back into the hall, watching as she banged open shutters.

The dining room was in the same condition but with empty bottles and glasses scattered on the table and smashed on the floor. Ester was flicking on lights, dragging back curtains with manic energy. But she seemed to deflate when she saw the wrecked kitchen, broken crockery and more smashed bottles. "Shit! I'd forgotten how bad it was."

"I hadn't. I told you this was a crazy idea from the start."

Ester crossed to the back door. She unlocked it, pushing it open to get the stench of old wine and rotten food out of the kitchen.

"Must have been some party," Julia mused.

"It was," Ester said, as she looked at the big black rubbish bags bursting at the seams.

"Surprised the rats haven't been in here."

"They have," Ester said as she spotted the droppings.

She hadn't realized just how bad the place was. When she and Julia had visited a few weeks earlier, there had been no electricity and they had arrived at dusk. Ester sighed: it had been some party all right. There used to be one every night but she had not been able to see the last one through to the end. She had been arrested along with her girls. She reckoned most of the damage had been done by the few who were left behind or who had come back when they knew she had been sentenced to grab whatever they could. A lot of the rooms looked as if they had been stripped of anything of value.

She had not bothered to come to see the damage before; she knew the bank held the deeds as collateral for her debts. She had dismissed the place from her mind until she got the news that Dolly Rawlins was going to be released. Then she had begun thinking—and thinking fast: just how could she use the old Grange Manor House to her benefit? But only if she could get it ready in time.

Julia strolled to the back door and looked out into the stable yard. The old doors were hanging off their hinges and even more rubbish and rubble had piled up.

Ester began banging open one bedroom door after another. Every room stank of mildew, and most of the beds hadn't been touched since the occupants had rolled out of them. In a few rooms clothes and dirty underwear lay discarded on the floor.

Julia started to walk up the old wide staircase, when Ester appeared at the top. "Go and get the cases."

"You're not serious, are you, Ester? This is madness."

"No, it isn't. I've already laid out cash for a bloody Roller and a chauffeur. There are caterers, florists . . . so we'll just have to get stuck in while we wait for the others to give us a hand."

Julia sat on the stairs and began to roll a cigarette. "So, you gonna tell me who you've invited to this celebration?"

Ester looked down at her. Sometimes she wanted to slap her—she could be so laid-back.

"You don't know them all. There's Connie Stevens, Kathleen O'Reilly, and I've asked that little black girl, Angela, to act as a maid."

Julia laughed. "She's gonna be wearing a pinny and a little hat, is she?"

Ester pursed her lips. "Don't start with the sarcasm. We need them, and they all knew Dolly."

Julia looked up at her. "They all inside with her like us?"

"Not Angela, but the others. And I don't want you to start yelling—but Gloria Radford's coming."

Julia stood up. "You joking?"

"No, I'm not."

"Well, count me out. I can't stand that demented cow. I spent two years in a cell with her and I'm not going to spend any more time with her if I can help it. What the hell did you rope her into it for?"

"Because we might need her, and she knows Dolly."

Julia turned and began to march down the stairs in a fury. "She reads aloud from the newspapers, she drove me crazy, I nearly killed her. I'm out of here."

"Fine, you go. I don't give a shit, but it's a long walk to the station."

Julia looked up. "Gloria Radford on board and this is a fiasco before we even start. She's cheap, she's coarse, she's got the mental age of a ten-year-old."

"What makes you so special, Doctor? We needed as many of us as I could get, Julia, especially ones that were as desperate as us. Now, are you staying or are you going?"

Julia lit her roll-up and shrugged. "I'm leaving."

Ester moved down the stairs. "Fine, you fuck off, then, and don't think you'll get a cut of anything I get. You walk out now, and I'll never see you again. I mean it, we're through."

Julia hesitated, looked back at Ester standing at the top of the stairs. Her face, her dark eyes, now blazing with anger, made her heart jump. Despite everything she'd said, she knew she'd be staying. She couldn't stand the thought of never seeing or touching Ester again.

She dropped her roll-up and ground it into the floor with her boot. "I'll get the cases but just don't ask me to be nice to that midget."

Ester smiled, and headed back to the bedroom. "The only person you've got to be nice to is Dolly Rawlins."

Julia got to the front door. "What if she doesn't come, Ester? *Ester?*"

Ester reappeared, leaning on the banister rail. "Oh, she'll come, Julia, I know it. She'll be here. She's got nobody else."

Julia gave a small nod and walked out to the car. She began to collect all the cases and bin liners, then paused a moment as she looked over the grounds. There was a sweet peacefulness to the place. She was suddenly reminded of her childhood, of the garden at her old family home. She had been given her own pony and suddenly she remembered cantering across the fields. She had been happy then . . . it seemed a lifetime ago.

The bedroom Ester chose for Dolly was spacious, with a double bed and white dressing table. Even though the carpet was stained, the curtains didn't look too bad, and with a good polish and hoover, a few bowls of flowers, it would be good enough. After all, she had spent the last eight years in a cell. This would be like a palace in comparison.

Julia appeared at the door. "You know, we could call the local job center if they've got one here, get a bunch of kids to start helping us. What do you think?"

Ester was dragging off the dirty bedlinen. "Go and call them. We'll have to pay them, though. How are you off for cash?"

"I've got a few quid."

Ester suddenly gave a beaming smile. "We'll be rich soon, Julia. We'll never have to scrabble around for another cent."

"You hope."

"Why are you always so negative? I know she's got those diamonds, I know it . . ."

"Maybe she has, maybe she hasn't. And maybe, just maybe, she won't want us to have a cut of them."

Ester gathered the dirty sheets in her arms. "There'll be no maybes. I've worked over more people than you've had hot dinners, and I'll work her over. I promise you, we'll get to those diamonds, two million quid's worth, Julia. Just thinking about it gives me an orgasm."

Julia laughed. "I'll go call a job center. This our bedroom, is it?"

"No, this one's for Dolly."

Ester patted the bed, then sat down and smiled, thinking of how rich she was going to be.

Mike Withey looked over the newspaper cuttings. They were yellow with age, some torn from constantly being unfolded, and one had a picture of Shirley Miller, Mike's sister. It was a photograph from some job she had done as a model, posed and airbrushed. The same photograph was in a big silver frame on the sideboard, this time in color. Blonde hair, wide blue eyes that always appeared to follow you around the room, as if she was trying to tell you something. She had been twenty-one years old when she had been shot, and even now Mike was still unable to believe that his little blue-eyed sweetheart sister had been involved in a robbery. He had been stationed in Germany when he received the hysterical call from his mother, Audrey. It had been hard to make out what she was saying, as she alternated between sobs and rantings, but there was one name he would never forget, one sentence. "It was Dolly Rawlins, it was her, it was all her fault."

The following year Mike married Susan, the daughter of a sergeant major. His mother was not invited to the wedding. Their first son was born before he left Germany and his second child was on the way when he was given a posting to Ireland. By this stage he was a sergeant, but he didn't tell Audrey about his promotion. Susan was worried about him being stationed in Ireland and since she was heavily pregnant with a toddler to look after and all her friends were in Germany, she persuaded Mike to quit the Army. He was reluctant at first, having signed up at seventeen: it was the only life he knew. It had been his salvation, it had educated him and, most importantly, given him a direction and discipline lacking in his own home.

Mike's second son was born on the day he found out that he had been accepted by the Metropolitan Police, and with an excellent recommendation from his CO, it was felt that Mike Withey was a recruit worth keeping an eye on. He proved them right: he was intelligent, hard-working, intuitive and well liked. Mike became a "high-flyer," never missing an opportunity to further his career prospects. No sooner was a new course pinned up on the board than he would be the first to apply. It was the many courses, the weekends away at special training colleges that made Susan, now coping with two toddlers, suggest that Mike should contact his mother again, not just for company but because she hoped Audrey could give her a hand or even babysit. Mike's refusal resulted in a big argument. Susie felt his boys had a right to know their grandmother as her own parents were still in Germany.

Mike took a few more weeks to mull it over. He supposed he could have been honest with Susan about his younger brother Gregg, who had been in trouble with the law, but he didn't want her knowing that his sister was Shirley Ann Miller, killed in an abortive robbery. It had been easy for him to conceal it because they all had different fathers, different surnames, though he was unsure if his mother had actually ever been married.

Audrey was working on the fruit and veg stall when Mike turned up as a customer, asking for a pound of Granny Smiths. She was just as he remembered her, all wrapped up, fur-lined boots, headscarf, woolen mittens with their fingers cut off.

"Well, hello, stranger. You want three or four? If it's four it'll be over the pound." She took each apple, dropping it into the open brown-paper bag, trying not to cry, not to show Mike how desperately pleased she was to see him. She wanted to shout out to the other stallholders, "This is my son. I told yer he'd come back, didn't I?" but she had always been a tough one, and never showed her feelings. It had taken years of practice—but get kicked hard enough and in the end it comes naturally. She didn't even touch his hand, just twisted the paper bag at the corners. "There you go, love. Fancy a cuppa, do you?"

He had not expected to feel so much, to hurt inside so much as he followed her into the same council flat in which he had been brought up. No recriminations, no questions, talking nineteen to the dozen about people she thought he might remember: who had died on the market stalls, who had got married, who had been banged up. She never stopped talking as she chucked off her coat, kicked off the boots and busied herself making tea.

She still chattered on, shouting to him from the kitchen, as he saw all his postcards, the photo of his wedding, his boys, laid out on top of the mantelshelf, pinned into the sides of the fake gilt mirror. There had been a few changes: new furniture, curtains, wallpaper and some awful pictures from one of the stalls.

"Gregg's doin' a stint on one of the oil rigs," Audrey shouted. "He's trying to go on the straight an' narrow, there's a postcard from him on the mantel."

Mike picked up the card of two kittens in a basket and turned it over. His brother's childish scrawl said he was having a great time and earning a fortune, saving up for a motorbike. The postmark was dated more than eight months ago. He replaced the card and stared at himself in the mirror.

It was then that he saw her. The thick silver frame, placed in the center of the sideboard, a small posy of flowers in a tiny vase in front of it. She was even more beautiful than he remembered. It was one of the pictures taken when she was trying to be a model, very glamorous. Shirley's smile went straight to his heart.

"It's her birthday tomorrow," said Audrey, "and you've not seen her grave."

"I'm on duty tomorrow, Mum."

She held on to his hand. "We can go now."

Audrey hung on to his arm. It was dusk, the graveyard empty. Shirley was buried alongside her husband Terry Miller. The white stone was plain and simple, but the ornate flowers in a green vase were still fresh. "Tomorrow she'll have a bouquet. They do it up for me on the flower stall, never charge me neither." Her voice was soft as she stared at the headstone. "She came to me straight after it had happened."

"I'm sorry, what did you say?"

She remained focused on her daughter's name. "That bitch—that bitch Dolly Rawlins came to see me and I've never forgiven myself for letting her take me in her arms."

"We should go, Mum."

She turned on him, hands clenched at her sides. "She was behind that robbery, she organized the whole thing. They never got the diamonds . . ."

Mike stepped forward, not wanting to hear any more, but there was no stopping her. "No, you listen. That bitch held me in her arms and I let her, let her use me just like she used my Shirley. She had them, she had the bloody things."

"What?"

"The diamonds! She had them—got me to—she got me to give 'em to a fence, said she would see I was looked after, see I'd never want for anythin'."

Mike's heart began to thud. He was unable to comprehend what he was hearing, as Audrey's voice became twisted with bitterness. "I *did it*, I bloody did it. She got me so I couldn't say nothin', couldn't do anything, and then . . . she fuckin' shot her husband."

Mike took her to a pub, gave her a brandy, and watched as she chain-smoked one cigarette after another. "No mention of the diamonds at her trial—they never had any evidence that put her in the frame. She got done for manslaughter."

Mike was sweating. "You ever tell anybody what you did?"

"What you think?" she snapped back at him. "She got me involved, didn't she? I could have been done for fencin' them, helpin' her. No, I never told anybody."

"Did you get paid?"

She stubbed out her cigarette. "No. Payday is when the bitch comes out. Bitch thinks she's gonna walk out to a fortune."

Mike gripped Audrey's hand. "Listen to me! *Look at me!* You know what I am. You know what it means for you to tell me all this?"

Audrey lit another cigarette. "What you gonna do, Mike, arrest your own mother?"

He ran his fingers through his hair; he could feel the sweat trickling down from his armpits. "You got to promise me you will never, *never* tell a soul about those diamonds. You got to swear on my kids' lives. You don't touch them—don't even think about them."

"She'll be out one day. Then what?"

Mike licked his lips.

"She as good as killed Shirley," Audrey continued. "I had to identify her, watch them pull the sheet down from her face."

"*Stop it!* Look, I promise I'll take care of you. You won't need any more dough—but I'm asking you, Mum, don't screw it up for me, please."

She stared at him, then leaned forward and touched his blond hair—the same texture, same color as Shirley's. "I'll make a deal with you, love. If you make that bitch pay for what she done to my baby, you get her locked up—"

"Mum, she *is* away, she's in the nick right now."

Audrey prodded his hand with her finger. "But when she comes out she'll be rich and free. I don't care about the money, all I want is . . ."

Audrey never said the word "revenge" but it hung in the air between them. So Mike made a promise. It felt empty to him but he had no option. He promised that, when Dolly Rawlins came out of Holloway, he would get her back for her part in the diamond robbery.

Five years later, the promise came back to haunt him, because his mother had never forgotten it. She called him and asked him to come round. As if unconcerned, Audrey was tut-tutting over some character's downfall on the TV, then offhandedly suggested he look in the left-hand drawer of the side table. Every single newspaper article about the diamond robbery was there, along with calendars with dates marked one year, two years, three years in thick red-tipped pen. He flicked through the news-clippings and his eye was drawn to a photograph, taken at some West End nightclub. He had never seen Dolly Rawlins, wouldn't know her if he was to come face to face with her in the street, but he instantly knew which one she was: she had to be the blonde, hard-faced woman sitting at the center of the large round table. She had a champagne glass in her hand, a half-smile on her face, but there was something about her eyes: unsmiling, hard, cold eyes . . . The handsome man seated next to her had an almost angry expression, as if annoyed by the intrusion of the photographer. Mike recognized his brother-in-law, dead before Shirley. Terry Miller had always looked like he never had a care in the world: his wide smile was relaxed, one arm resting along the cushioned booth seat as if protecting his pretty, innocent, child-like wife. Shirley Miller.

The TV was turned off and Audrey turned to Mike. She was crying, clutching a sodden tissue in her hand. She pointed to the photo of Dorothy Rawlins. "You never seen her, have you, love?"

Beneath her picture was a smaller one with the heading: "Gangland Boss Murdered by his Wife." Harry Rawlins had been a handsome, elegant, if cruel-faced man, and his picture made him look like a movie star. Dolly's hard gaze made them seem an unlikely couple but they had been married twenty years none the less. Harry Rawlins was one of the most notorious gangsters in London, a man who had never been caught, never spent a day behind bars, and yet had been questioned by the police so many times he was a familiar face to most of the Met officers. He had lived a charmed life until his wife shot him. The newspaper article stated that Dorothy Rawlins had shot and killed her husband when she had discovered that he had a mistress and a child. There was no mention that he had planned a robbery in which Shirley Miller's husband had been burned to death. They had nicknamed Dolly the "Black Widow" because throughout her trial she had always been dressed in black.

Audrey prodded Dolly's face in the paper. "Nine years. Nine years. Well, she'll be out any day now," she said, wiping her eyes.

Audrey had never told Mike that she had been pregnant when Dolly had come to see her and had lost the baby. She blamed that on Dolly Rawlins as well. Dolly had not sat down but stood in the small hallway, her head slightly bowed, her voice a low whisper. "I'm sorry about Shirley. I am deeply sorry for Shirley."

Audrey had been unable to reply, she was in such a state.

"Nothing will make up to you for her loss, I know that."

Still Audrey couldn't speak. Then Dolly had lifted her head, her pale washed-out eyes brimming with tears. "You'll get a cut of the diamonds, that I promise you. Just hand them over to Jimmy Donaldson. Jimmy'll keep them safe. When this is all over, I'll see you're taken care of, Audrey."

But that hadn't been the end of it. Everything had changed when Audrey read in the paper that a small-time fence called Jimmy Donaldson had been arrested for dealing in stolen property. Audrey had then done something she would never have believed herself capable of. She had done it all by herself and, having done it, she had been terrified. But the weeks passed and gradually she grew more and more confident that what she had done was right.

But now she was scared, really scared, and she didn't know if she should tell Mike or not, because Dolly Rawlins was coming out and she would come out looking for her, Audrey was sure of that.

Mike was feeling uneasy. It was back again, that constant undercurrent of guilt whenever he was with his mother. He had made that promise, but how could he keep it? He held on to his temper. "Mum, there is nothing I can do—"

"You're a ruddy police officer, aren't you? Re-arrest her. She did that robbery, Mike—I know it, you know it. She as good as killed our Shirley, never mind her bloody husband."

The tears started again. He was due at his station in half an hour; he wished he'd never called in. "Look, Mum, the problem will be if it implicates you—and it could."

Audrey clung to him. "I've got an offer. Friend's got a villa in Spain. I can stay as long as I like. That way I can keep out of it."

"Look, I'll see what I can do, okay?"

Audrey kissed him. "Just let her sleep in peace, let my little girl sleep in peace."

Mike turned on the ignition of the car but the last thing he felt like doing was going into the station. He checked his watch again and then drove to Thornton Avenue in Chiswick. He worried that he was making a mistake, this was a stupid move, but he needed to get his head straightened out. He parked the car and walked up the scruffy path. He was about to ring the front doorbell when he heard someone calling his name.

Angela was running up the road, waving, with a big wide smile. "Mike, Mike . . ."

Mike turned as she threw herself into his arms.

"I knew you'd come and see me again, I just knew it."

He walked hand in hand with her to his car, already wanting to kick himself for coming to her place.

"I've missed you," she said, hanging on to his arm.

Mike released his hand. "Look, I shouldn't have come, Angela. It was just . . . I'm sorry."

"Oh, please stay, please. Me mum's down at the center, there's no one in the house, and, please, I got something to tell you, please . . ."

Mike locked the car and followed Angela into her mother's ground-floor flat. It was dark and scruffy and kids' pushchairs and toys littered every inch of the floor. Angela guided him toward the small back bedroom, and all the time he kept on saying to himself that he was dumb, he was stupid to start this up again. Angela began to undress as soon as she shut the door but he shook his head. "No, I can't stay, Angela, I'm on duty in an hour. I just . . ."

She slumped onto the bed. "I been waitin' for you to call for weeks. You know the way I feel about you. Why did you come here, then?"

He shook his head. He was feeling even worse. "I dunno, I was over at my mum's place and she starts doing my head in over my sister, and I just . . ." She wrapped her arms around him, kissing his face. "No, don't, Angela, I shouldn't have come."

She broke away. "Well, get out, I don't care, I'm goin' away anyway."

"Where you goin'?"

"Friend's place, just a few days, bit of work."

Mike looked at her, shaking his head. "What kind of work?"

Angela plucked at her short skirt.

"You're not going back on the game, are you?"

"*No, I am not,*" she shrieked.

Mike sat on the bed and rested his head against the wall. He closed his eyes.

"I was never on the game and you know it. You of all people should know it. I just worked as her maid, Mike."

"This Ester Freeman, is it?" he asked.

Angela crawled onto the bed to sit next to him. Mike had been on the Vice Squad when Ester Freeman had been busted for running a brothel.

Angela was one of the girls who had been arrested along with twelve other women but they had all, including Ester, insisted that little Angela was not on the game, just serving drinks. Mike and Angela, who was then only fifteen, had begun an affair, a stupid, on-off scene that he constantly tried to break. He never saw her more than once a month, sometimes twice, over the years, but he was very fond of her. He even gave her money sometimes but he had no intention of ever leaving his wife. If it hadn't been for him, she might have been sent to an approved school, but that was just an excuse. The sex was good and he simply refused to admit that that was what he used Angela for.

"Ester called yesterday. Wants me to go to her old manor house."

"Oh yeah? She back running another brothel?"

"No way. She's holding some kind of party, for a woman called . . ."

Angela frowned as she tried to remember, and then grinned. "Oh, I dunno, but she was in Holloway wiv her, shot her old man, you know. She was famous. He was a big-time villain. Anyway, she's comin' out of the nick and Ester is arranging a group of old friends to sort of welcome her, you know, give a party, and she wants me to act as a waitress."

Mike fingered the knot in his tie. His mouth was dry. It couldn't be, could it? "Dolly Rawlins? Is that who it is?"

"Yeah, she was in Holloway with Ester."

Mike started undoing the buttons of her shirt. "Who else is going?"

"I dunno, but it'll be some kind of scam, you can bet on it. I got to wear a black dress an' apron. Ester never did nothin' for nobody without there being something in it for her. She's a hard cow but I need the cash. Said she'll pay me fifty quid."

Mike eased off Angela's shirt, reaching round to the clasp of her lacey bra. "She say anything else about Dolly Rawlins?"

Two young prisoners peeked into Dolly Rawlins's cell, looking at the small neatly packed brown suitcase, a coat placed alongside it. Apart from these two items the cell was empty.

Footsteps echoed on the stone-flagged floor. The two girls scuttled back down the corridor as Rawlins, with a prison officer, walked toward her cell. But whatever they were expecting to see, they were disappointed. The infamous Dolly Rawlins seemed pale and worn out. The officer stood outside the cell waiting for Dolly to get her case and coat.

The corridors were strangely silent. Nearly all of the women were waiting, hiding, whispering.

The tannoy repeated a message that Rawlins, prisoner 45688, was to go to landing B. They all knew that was the check-out landing. She was almost out.

The coat was too large now she had lost so much weight, but it was good quality and she had always liked the best. She did up each button slowly and then reached for her case. None of the girls had spoken to her or said goodbye, but she refused to show that she was hurt. She looked to the officer and gave a brief nod. She was ready.

As Dolly headed toward landing B, the singing began, low at first, then rising to a bellow as every woman joined in.

"Goodbye, Dolly!"

They bellowed and stamped their feet, they called out her name and clapped their hands. "Goodbye, Dolly, you must leave us . . ." They screeched out their thank yous for the cigarettes, for her radio, her cassettes, for every item she had passed around. Some of the girls were sobbing, openly showing how much they would miss "Big Mama." One old prisoner shouted at the top of her voice, "Don't turn back, Dolly, don't look back, keep on walking out, gel . . ."

She could feel the tears welling up, her mouth trembling, but she held on, waving like the Queen as they walked onto the landings. They continued to sing, their voices echoing as she was ushered along the corridor toward the Governor's office. It wouldn't be long now.

Mike thumbed through the files and then sat, drumming his fingers on the mug shot of Dorothy Rawlins. He had read enough about Dolly Rawlins and her husband to know that if the diamonds existed she would go after them. He thought about Angela on her way to Ester Freeman. He wondered about a lot of things, trying to think if there was any possibility of doing something for his sister, for his mother—if he could get Dolly Rawlins back inside.

Mike was just starting to go through Harry Rawlins's files when he received a phone call—nothing to do with Dolly Rawlins, nothing to do with his mother or his sister. It was from Brixton Prison: a boy called Francis Lloyd wanted to give some information.

A lot of police officers had their private snitches in the prisons. Lloyd was a youngster Mike had arrested during a burglary eighteen months ago. He had been sentenced to two years because of a previous conviction. He was a likable kid, and Mike had even got to know his mum and dad, so he returned the call—and for the second time in one day he heard the name Dolly Rawlins. Francis had some information but he didn't want to talk about it over the phone.

Governor Ellis rose to her feet from behind the desk as Dolly Rawlins was ushered into her bright, friendly office. She offered tea, a usual ritual when a long-serving prisoner was leaving. Mrs. Ellis was a good governor, well-liked by the inmates for her fairness and, in many instances, even for her kindness and understanding. Rawlins, however, seemed never to have needed her kindness and, as she passed Dolly her tea in a floral china cup, Mrs. Ellis couldn't help but detect an open antagonism.

She eased the conversation round, discussing openings and contacts should Dolly feel in need of assistance outside, making sure she was fully aware that she would, because of the nature of her crime, be on parole for the rest of her life. When she asked if Dolly had any plans for the future she received only a quiet, "Yes, I have plans, thank you."

"Well, rest assured there is a network of people who will give you every assistance to readjust to being outside. Eight years—it should have been nine but as you know, you're being released early for good behavior—is a long time, and you will find many changes."

"I'm sure I will," Dolly replied, returning the half-empty cup to the tray.

Barbara Hunter remained with her back to the door, staring at Rawlins, whose calm composure annoyed the hell out of her. She listened as Mrs. Ellis passed over leaflets and phone numbers should Rawlins require them. She kept her eyes on Rawlins's face, wanting to see some kind of reaction, but Dolly remained impassive.

"You have been of invaluable help with many of the young offenders and especially with the mother-and-baby wing. I really appreciate all your hard work and I wish you every success in the future."

Dolly leaned forward and asked, bluntly, if she could leave.

"Why, of course you can, Dorothy." Mrs. Ellis smiled.

"Anything I say now, it can't change that, can it?" Dolly seemed tense.

"No, Dorothy, you are free to go."

"Good. Well, there is something I would like to say. That woman . . ." Dolly turned an icy stare on Barbara Hunter who straightened quickly. "You know what she is. I've got no quarrel with anyone's sexual preferences so don't get me wrong, Mrs. Ellis, but that woman should not be allowed near the young girls comin' in. She shouldn't be allowed to get her dirty hands on any single kid in this place, but she does, and you all know it. She messes with the most vulnerable, especially when they've just had their babies taken from them. You got any decency inside you, Mrs. Ellis, you should get rid of her."

Mrs. Ellis stood up, flushing, as Dolly sprang to her feet, adding, "I know where she lives."

Mrs. Ellis snapped, "Are you making threats, Mrs. Rawlins?"

"No, just stating a fact. I'll be sending her a postcard. Can I go now?"

Mrs. Ellis pursed her lips and gave a nod as Hunter opened the office door. Dolly walked out, past Hunter, and never looked back. Two more officers were waiting outside for her as the door closed.

Mrs. Ellis sat down and drew the file of prisoner 45688, Dorothy Rawlins, toward her. She opened it and stared at the police file photographs, then slapped the file closed. "I think we'll be seeing Dorothy Rawlins again before too long."

Hunter agreed. "I've never trusted her. She's devious, and a liar."

Mrs. Ellis stared at Hunter. "Is she?" she said softly.

"Jimmy Donaldson was in the canteen two nights ago and I was next to him, I couldn't help but hear." Francis Lloyd looked right and left, lowering his voice. "He said that he was holding diamonds for Rawlins, that you lot copped him for peanuts compared to what he'd got stashed at his place. Diamonds . . ."

Mike leaned back in the chair. "You sure about this, Francis?"

"Yes, on my life. Diamonds, he was braggin' about them, honest. Said he'd held on to them for eight years—diamond robbery, I swear that's what he said."

Mike leaned forward and pushed two packs of Silk Cut cigarettes forward. They'd been opened and there was a ten quid note tucked in each of them.

"Thanks, thanks a lot."

On his way back to the station, Mike went over everything he had picked up and started to piece it together. By the time he'd parked his car in the underground car park at the station he was feeling more positive, and even thinking that maybe, just maybe, he would be able to get Dolly Rawlins put back inside. He couldn't wait to see his mother's face when he told her, but he had to go by the book and first run it by his governor.

Detective Chief Inspector Ronald Craigh was a sharp officer, a high-flyer with a good team around him. His other sidekick was Detective Inspector John Palmer, steady, cool-headed and a personal friend. The pair of them often joked about Mike being over-eager but that was not a stroke against him—far from it. Craigh listened attentively as Mike discussed the information he had received that day.

"I have a good reliable informant who told me Rawlins is going to a big manor house. There's a bunch of ex-cons waiting for her. I then get a tip-off from my informant in Brixton nick."

Craigh leaned forward. "Hang about, son, this informant . . . are they in my file?"

"Yes, it's Francis Lloyd—he's in Brixton." Mike made no mention of Angela. She was not on the governor's informant list. He presented the old files on the diamond robbery, explaining how Dorothy Rawlins would be out any minute and would, he estimated, go for the diamonds.

"Well, that'll be tough, won't it?" Craigh smiled. "If Jimmy Donaldson is holdin' them for her and he's banged up, how's she gonna get to them?"

Mike paced up and down. "What if we were to bring him out, talk it over with him, see what he has to say? I mean, we might be able to have a word with his probation officer or the Governor at Brixton, see if we couldn't get him shipped to a cushy open prison."

"No way," Craigh said.

Palmer held up his hand. "We might be able to swing something that'll make him play ball with us."

Craigh shook his head again. "Come on, you know we got no pull to move any friggin' prisoner anywhere—and if we get him out, then what?"

"We get the diamonds," Mike said, grinning like a Cheshire cat. "One, there's still a whopper of a reward out for them, two, we clean up that robbery—nobody was pulled in for it. What if it was Rawlins all along? We'll find out if she contacts Donaldson. It'll be proof she knows about the diamonds."

Craigh was still iffy about it. "According to the old files, it was suspected that Harry Rawlins was behind it—"

"She shot him," Mike interrupted.

"I know she did. What I'm saying is there was never any evidence to connect her to that blag."

"There will be if she goes for those diamonds."

Craigh sucked on his teeth and then picked up all the old files. "Okay, I'll run it by the Super, see what he's got to say about it."

Mike followed him to the door. "She's out today, Gov."

Craigh opened his office door. "I know that, son, just don't start jumping over hurdles until we know what the fuck we're gonna do."

Mike looked glumly at Palmer as Craigh slammed the door. "It's just that she's out, and she might call Donaldson, find out he's in the nick and . . ."

"Maybe she knows already," Palmer said, doodling on a notepad.

"Just sit tight. If the Super gives the go-ahead, we'll see what they decide. In the meantime . . ."

Mike sighed. He had a load of reports to complete so he took himself off to the incident room. As he reached his desk, his phone rang. It was Craigh. They were going to talk to Donaldson, if he wanted to come along. Mike grinned; it was going down faster than he'd thought.

Ester ordered the six boys from the job center to collect every bottle and piece of broken glass before they started to hoover and dust. A florist's van had arrived with two massive floral displays that were propped up in the hall. Julia was using a stiff brush to sweep the front steps when she saw the taxi at the open manor gates. "Someone's coming now," she called out.

The taxi drove slowly down the drive, skirted the deep hole in the gravel and stopped by the front steps. Kathleen O'Reilly peered from the back seat. She had boxes and cases and numerous plastic bags. "Hi. You moving in or on the move, Kathleen?" asked Julia.

Kathleen opened the car door. "They're all me worldly possessions. I had to do a bit of a moonlight but Ester said I could doss down here for a few days. Will you give the driver a fiver? I'm flat broke."

Kathleen: overweight, wearing a dreadful assortment of ill-matched clothes—a cotton skirt with two hand-knitted sweaters on top of a bright yellow blouse. She had red hair spilling over a wide moon face and her false teeth, yellow with tobacco stains, needed bleaching. But she had a marvelous, generous feel to her, an open Irish nature. Julia delved into her pocket to pay off the driver as Kathleen hauled out her belongings. "They said this was closed down," she bellowed as she staggered into the hallway. Kathleen dumped her bags in the hall and looked around. "Holy Mother of God, what a dump! Is that chandelier safe, Julia?"

Julia dropped one of Kathleen's cases. "Ask Ester—she's running the show."

At that moment Ester came down the stairs. "You made it here, then?"

"Well, of course I did." Kathleen embraced her. "I was glad you called, darlin'. I was in shit up to me armpits, I can tell you, with not a roof over my head. So . . . is she here, then?"

Julia turned, listening.

"Not yet, and I hope she won't be for a few hours. We've got to get the place ready."

Kathleen plodded to the stairs. "Well, let me unpack me gear, darlin', and I'll give you a hand."

Ester instructed Kathleen to use one of the second-landing bedrooms and went into the kitchen, squeezing past the boys as they scrubbed the floor. Julia picked up the broom again, trying to remember what Kathleen had been in prison for, but her attention was diverted by yet another car making its slow progress down the driveway.

Connie Stevens sat next to the railway-station attendant, a nice man who, seeing Connie outside the small local station waiting for a taxi, had offered her a lift. Men did that kind of thing for Connie: she had such a helpless Marilyn Monroe quality to her, they went weak at the knees. She even had a soft breathy voice, hair dyed blonde to match her heroine's, and recent plastic surgery that gave a dimple to her chin, tightened her jaw and removed the lines from her baby eyes. She worked hard to retain her curvaceous figure as she was already in her mid-thirties—not that she ever admitted it to anyone: she had been twenty-five for the past ten years.

Julia watched as the man, red-faced, struggled to remove an enormous case on wheels from the boot of his car.

"Thank you, I really appreciate this so much," Connie cooed. The station attendant returned to his car, and, embarrassed by Julia's obvious amusement, drove out as fast as he could, crashing into the pothole as he went.

Ester leaned out of an upstairs window. "Hi, Connie, come on in. Kathleen's already arrived."

Connie dragged her case toward the steps. Julia tossed away the broom and took her case by the handle. "Here, lemme help, Princess."

Connie gave a breathy "aweee" as she looked at the hall. "It's changed so much since I was last here."

Ester jumped down the stairs and embraced Connie warmly, then held her at arm's length to admire her new face. "You look good—*really* good. Just drag your case upstairs and get into some old gear. We've got to clear the place up and make it ready for Dolly."

"How many more are coming?" asked Kathleen. "I mean, are we gonna cut it between us all?"

"I don't know. Like I said, Ester's in charge, ask her. She hasn't told me what she plans on doing."

Kathleen moved closer. "They're worth millions, the diamonds, everyone used to talk about them. Are you certain she'll be coming?"

Julia picked up the broom and started sweeping the steps again. "Ester seems to think so, that's why she's got us all here."

Kathleen started hoovering with venom. She certainly hoped this wasn't all a waste of time. She was in deep trouble: her three kids had been taken into care and she needed money, a lot of it, and fast. Dolly Rawlins's diamonds would be her only way out of the mess she had got herself into.

Way down the lane, Gloria Radford threw up her hands in fury. She'd been down one dead end after another, up onto the motorway three times, and still not found the Manor House. She got out of her dilapidated Mini Traveller and headed toward a man on a tractor in the middle of a field. "Oi, mate, can you direct me to the Grange Manor House?"

The old farmhand turned in surprise as Gloria, small, plump and wearing spike-heeled shoes and skin-tight black pants, waved from the field gates. Her make-up was plastered on thick: lip gloss-smudged teeth, mascara-clogged lashes with bright blue eye-shadow on the lids—she was like someone from the late Sixties stuck in a time-warp. Gloria Radford waved the hand-drawn map Ester had sent her. The old boy wheeled his tractor toward her.

"Down there." He pointed.

"I been down there and I been back up there and I keep gettin' back on the bleedin' motorway."

"Ay, yes, they cut off the access road. Just keep on this slip road and you'll get to it. The manor's off to the right."

Gloria stepped over the clods of earth and headed back to her Mini. The farmhand remained watching as she reversed straight into a pothole and let rip with a stream of expletives.

Ester was now checking the cutlery. Some of it was quite good but it all needed cleaning, as did every plate and cup and saucer. Kathleen was on duty in the dining room, dusting the chairs, when the crate of wine was delivered. She was ready for a drink and about to open a bottle when they all heard the tooting of a car horn and the sound of Gloria Radford arriving, towed in by a tractor.

They all stood crowded on the doorstep, watching the spectacle. Julia turned to Ester. "Subtle as ever. I suppose you wanted the entire village to know we were here."

"Me bleedin' back end's fucked!" yelled Gloria, as she heaved out a case.

Julia winced as Gloria negotiated some complicated financial arrangement with the old man on his tractor to tow the car to the nearest garage. She was so loud and brassy that she was almost comical: her fake-fur leopard coat slung round her shoulders, her too-tight puce wrap-around skirt. "Er, Ester, you got a few quid I can bung 'im?"

Julia saw Ester purse her lips and join Gloria at the tractor.

Ester paid ten quid to the tractor driver and directed him to the nearest garage that would be able to repair the Mini.

Gloria banged into the hallway. "Cor blimey, this is the old doss-house, is it? Hey, Kathleen, how are you doin', kid?" Kathleen said she was doing fine, then Gloria pointed at Connie. "I know you, don't I?"

Connie shook her head. "I don't think so, I'm Connie."

"You one of Ester's tarts, then, are you?"

Connie's jaw dropped. "No, I am not."

Gloria seemed unaware of how furious Connie was. She turned to Julia. "I didn't know you was on this caper, Doc."

"Likewise," said Julia sarcastically.

"You sure you got Dolly comin'? I mean, I come a hell of a long way to get here, you know." Julia had to turn away because she wanted to laugh out loud.

Ester clenched her fists: Gloria had only been there two minutes and she was getting under her skin already. "She'll be here, Gloria. Just get some old gear on and start helping us, we've got a lot to do."

"Right, you tell me what you want done, sweet face. I'm ready, I'm willin' and nobody ever said Gloria Radford wasn't able."

Ester looked at her watch. She thought she should have received a call from Dolly by now but she said nothing, just hoped to God she had played her cards right. She had laid out a lot of cash already and if wily old Dolly Rawlins copped out, she was in trouble. All the women she had chosen were desperate for cash, but Ester more than any of them.

* * *

Dolly was out. She had walked out a free woman two hours ago. The fear crept up unexpectedly. Suddenly she felt alone. She stood on the pavement as her heart began to race and her mouth went bone dry. She was out—and there was no one to meet her, no one to wrap their arms around her, no place to go. She saw the white Rolls Corniche; it was hard to miss, parked outside the prison gates. She stepped back, afraid for a moment, when a uniformed chauffeur got out and looked over.

"Excuse me, are you Mrs. Rawlins, Mrs. Dolly Rawlins?"

Dolly frowned, gave a small nod, and he smiled warmly, walking toward her. "Your car, Mrs. Rawlins."

"I never ordered it."

He touched her elbow gently. "Well, my docket says you did, Mrs. Rawlins, so, where would you like to go?"

Nonplussed, she allowed herself to be ushered toward the Rolls. He opened the door with a flourish. "Anywhere you want. It's hired for the entire day, Mrs. Rawlins."

"Who by?" she asked suspiciously.

"You, and it's paid for, so why not? Get in, Mrs. Rawlins." Dolly looked at the prison, then back to the car. On the back seat was a small bouquet of roses, a bottle of champagne, and an invitation. "I don't understand, who did this?"

The chauffeur eased her in and shut the door. Dolly opened the invitation.

Dear Dolly,

Some of your friends have arranged a "SHE'S OUT" party. Take a drive around London and then call us. Here's to your successful future, and hoping you will join us for a slap-up dinner and a knees-up,

Ester

Dolly read and reread the invitation. She knew Ester Freeman but she'd not been that friendly with her.

"Where would you like to go, Mrs. Rawlins?"

She leaned back, still nonplussed. "Oh, just drive around, will you? So I can see the sights."

"Right you are."

She saw the portable phone positioned by his seat. She leaned forward and picked up the phone.

"Call any place you want, Mrs. Rawlins."

She turned the phone over in her hand, never having seen one before, and then she smiled softly. "My husband would have loved one of these," she whispered.

CHAPTER 2

James "Jimmy" Donaldson was a small, sandy-haired man. With his trim physique and thick hair with a deep widow's peak at the temple, he looked younger than his fifty-five years. He was exceedingly nervous, having been brought from a woodwork class to be confronted by DCI Craigh and DS Mike Withey. The prison officers left the three men alone, which seemed to unnerve Donaldson even more, and his eyes darted nervously from one man to the other.

Craigh asked quietly if he knew a woman called Dorothy Rawlins. Donaldson shook his head, then shifted his buttocks on the chair to sit on his hands, as if afraid they would give him away because they were shaking.

"You sure about that, Jimmy?"

He nodded, blinking rapidly, as Craigh, still speaking softly, asked him about the diamonds.

"I d-d-don't know anything about them," he stuttered.

"She's out today, Jimmy. Dolly Rawlins is out."

Donaldson went white.

Craigh spoke soothingly. "No need to worry, Jimmy. If you help us, then maybe we can make things easier for you, maybe even get the authorities to move you to a nice, cushy open prison."

Two hours later, Donaldson was taken from Brixton Prison to their local nick. It was done fast and Craigh made sure that it was put out that Donaldson required a small operation, so that when and if they sent him back he wouldn't be subjected to threats for grassing. All he had admitted so far was that he might know about the diamonds but he refused to say anything more unless he was taken out of the jail.

On the journey he brightened up at the prospect of being moved, even going home to visit his wife. Craigh had laughed. "Don't get too excited, Jimmy, because we'll need to know more—a lot more. You're doing time for fencing hot gear right now and we've not got much sway with the prison authorities. All we do is catch 'em, the rest is not down to us unless you have some very good information."

It was almost six thirty by the time Donaldson was taken into the station, and he was given some dinner before they really began to pressure him. He admitted that he knew Dolly Rawlins but he had known her husband better, and had held the stones for her as a favor. When asked if Rawlins instigated the diamond raid, he swore he didn't know and he was certain that Mrs. Rawlins couldn't have done it because she was a woman. He knew she had killed her husband but word was he'd been fooling around with a young bit of fluff who'd had a kid by him. At the time of the shooting, there were many rumors around as to what had happened, but the truth had always been shrouded in mystery—and fear, because Harry Rawlins was a formidable and exceptionally dangerous man, nicknamed the "Octopus" because he seemed to have so many arms in so many different businesses. A lot of men known to have crossed him had disappeared.

Harry Rawlins had masterminded a raid on an armored truck. The plan had been to ram it inside the Strand underpass but the raid had gone disastrously wrong. The explosives used by his team had blown their own truck to smithereens; four men inside had died, their charred bodies unrecognizable. Dolly Rawlins had been given a watch, a gold Rolex from the blackened wrist of one of the dead men. She had buried his remains, the funeral an ornate affair, with wreaths from every main criminal in England. In many instances they were sent not out of sympathy, but relief.

Dolly had been in deep shock. The husband she had worshipped for twenty years was gone, her loss made worse by the pressure from villains trying to take over her husband's manor. Her grief had turned to anger when they approached her at his graveside, and then to icy fury. When she found Harry's detailed plans for the abortive robbery, Dolly drew together the widows of the men who had died alongside Harry in the truck. She manipulated and cajoled them into repeating the raid that had taken their men. Always a strong-minded woman, Dolly grew more confident and arrogant each day. Her belief that they could handle it quelled their fears, and her constant encouragement and furious determination ensured that they not only succeeded in pulling off one of the most daring armed robberies ever, but she also made sure they got away with it. She had been doing it for Harry, using his carefully crafted plans. Never for one moment had she believed or even contemplated his betrayal.

Harry Rawlins was alive. He had been the only one to escape from the nightmare raid that killed his men. Rawlins had arranged that when the raid was over he would never return to his wife, and would leave Dolly for his twenty-five-year-old mistress. To his amazement, Harry Rawlins had found himself watching as Dolly went ahead with the raid, and then laughed because he knew that if she succeeded he would take the money. Her audacity amused him. Safe in his girlfriend's apartment, he had watched and waited, had played with his baby boy, the child Dolly had been desperate to give him.

But Harry Rawlins had underestimated his wife.

Dolly succeeded in the raid and she also found out the terrible truth. She never confronted him—it would have been too dangerous, not for herself but for the other women concerned. Instead she planned their escape from England, leaving him penniless and desperate.

For a while the widows had lived high but the bulk of the money became a monster they could not control. Dolly had chosen to hide out in Rio, not only for safety, but because she knew Harry had a bank account there with over fifty thousand in it, and as she had his death certificate she knew she would be able to claim it. Their sojourn in Rio did not last long, though, as Dolly discovered Harry had arrived there and when he found out she had cleaned out his bank account, he would come after her. She was able to move the money from the security raid from a convent where she had worked to beneath the stage of the local church hall. She also discovered that Harry, desperate to track her down, was organizing a jewelry raid. As she recalled the women back to London, her plan was to tip off the police about the diamond heist, but tragically, not everything had gone according to plan. One of them, Linda Pirelli, was killed in a car accident, a second, the young beautiful Shirley Miller, who had unwittingly become involved as a catwalk model wearing some of the diamonds, was shot during the robbery.

Dolly got away with a large portion of the diamonds, but the police net was drawing in.

Yet again she reacted as her husband would have. She knew Jimmy Donaldson could be trusted; small-time he might be but he had done a lot of work for Harry in the past and had never been charged so she used that as a lever to ensure that he would keep the diamonds safe. She could have got away with it but something was more important than the diamonds: her guilt about little Shirley. She went to Audrey, Shirley's mother, because she felt she owed her a debt. Audrey would also be unlikely to go the police, because Dolly had used Audrey in the first raid when they had escaped from England. Dolly was hoping the promise of a cut of the diamonds would atone for Shirley's death. All Dolly had asked Audrey to do was wait, and in time she would get her share. Audrey wept but had delivered the diamonds to Jimmy that same night, as Dolly had instructed, agreeing that they would have no further contact until Dolly gave the word. Neither Jimmy nor Audrey knew that while they were organizing a hiding place for the diamonds, Dolly had arranged a meeting with her husband and was waiting for him with a .22 handgun. Harry had been sure as soon as she saw him that he would be able to talk her round, make her believe that he'd had to lie low because he would have been arrested. He had allowed her to go through the charade of a funeral because if he hadn't, the filth would have known he was still alive. So he had waited, confident he could manipulate her. Never had he properly considered the pain he had caused her, the terrible grief he had put her through—the wife who had stood by him for twenty years.

Harry had smiled when Dolly approached and had taken a few steps toward her. He had still been smiling when she fired at point-blank range into his heart.

Dolly Rawlins was arrested and charged with manslaughter, a nine-year sentence to be served at Holloway Prison. She had never stopped loving him and the pain never did go away, but the years eased it. In prison she embraced the hurt inside her, like the child she was never able to conceive.

Even after Harry's death, Jimmy Donaldson's fear of Harry Rawlins remained. All he had admitted to was having received a package from Dolly Rawlins. Even after his subsequent arrest for fencing, he had remained silent about the diamonds. In reality, he had been too scared to fence them or mention them to anyone else. But now he began to talk.

"She's a tough bitch, you know, hard as nails. Everyone knew how much her old man depended on her—gave him more alibis than you've had hot dinners, mate."

Donaldson became quite cocky as he told them how Dolly had promised he'd get a nice reward for keeping her property safe.

"So where are they, Jimmy?" asked Craigh.

Donaldson pursed his lips. "Well, that would be telling. I mean, you gonna let me see my wife?"

Craigh became tougher, prodding him with his finger. "We make the deals, Jimmy, not you. You're lucky we're not gonna slap more years on for not coming out with this at your trial."

"Fuckin' hell, you bastards, you just been stringing me along. Well, no more, no way, I retract everythin' I said, I dunno anythin'."

The truth was that Craigh was in no position to offer a deal until he had spoken to the prison authorities and to Donaldson's parole officer to see if they could get him moved. Mike was eager for them to make any promise and he was the one who asked Donaldson if Dolly Rawlins had contacted him since she had been in Holloway.

"No, never—she's not stupid. But a few times I sort of felt a finger on the back of the neck, so to speak."

Donaldson never divulged that Dolly Rawlins had quite a hold over him because of all the other times he had fenced stolen gear for her husband, knowing he could be put away for a lot longer than five years. Now he felt a bit of relief because they seemed to want to put her away again and it would mean he was free of her.

Mike Withey was also relieved. At no point had Donaldson mentioned the part his own mother, Audrey, had played.

"How is she going to collect the diamonds?"

"Well, she'll call me. She was never arrested or charged for that gig, was she? I mean, nobody knows she's got them, do they?" Still not knowing the location of the diamonds, Craigh and Palmer talked it over with the Super and decided to take Donaldson to his home and give it a few days to see if Rawlins made contact.

Once Donaldson knew he was going home to see his wife—even if a police officer would be with him at all times—he told them where the stones were hidden. His wife still ran his junk and antique shop and the main wall had a four-brick hideaway; if they removed the bricks, they would find the gems.

Craigh and Palmer high-fived each other, thinking of the big reward for the return of the stones. Mike was more pleased about the fact that, if Donaldson handed the diamonds over to Dolly, they could send her straight back to prison. Rest in peace, Shirley Miller.

Dolly stood outside her old house in Totteridge. She stared at the new curtains, the fresh paint. For the twenty years of her marriage this was where she had lived. She had always been house-proud, and had done her best to make it into a place Harry would be proud of. Harry entertained regularly and she had always set a nice table with good, home-cooked food. She had thought she was happy, had believed he was too. As she stood there now, thinking of his betrayal, she clenched her hands, trying not to break down, refusing to after all these years. He had forced her into a grief-driven fury—she had even buried him when all the time he had been alive. Alive and cheating on her. It was so bizarre, so insane what she had done, what she had become. And even when he had faced her, knowing that she knew everything, he had still been so sure of her love that he had opened his arms and said, "I love you, Doll."

She had pulled the trigger then, almost nine years ago. She had served the sentence for his murder and now she was free. She walked back to the waiting chauffeur and he opened the car door. Dolly had sold the house and all its contents for a lot of money through her lawyers, and now wanted to go to the bank to collect enough to buy herself a small flat.

"That was my home," she said softly.

He helped her inside the car.

"Now it's someone else's." She sounded so sad, but she suddenly gave him a sweet smile.

"Can I use this portable phone, then?"

Ester grabbed the phone after two rings, knowing it had to be Dolly. She'd got a new number when the phone had been reconnected and only Dolly knew it. She listened for a moment, then put the phone down. Dolly was on her way. Ester sighed with relief and then hurried into the dining room.

The table was almost ready but Gloria and Kathleen were having a go at each other. "She's drinking, Ester. I keep telling her not to get pissed."

Ester snatched up one of the bottles, recorked it and banged it onto the table as Kathleen shouted that all she was doing was getting them ready for the decanters. "She's on her way, and as soon as those lads are finished we'd all better have a talk, get sorted. She's not stupid so we got to make this look good. Where's Connie?"

"I'm here. I've been repairing my nails. I've chipped two already—they're not supposed to be in too much water, you know."

Gloria raised her eyes to heaven as Connie showed off her false-tipped nails. Ester told her to start bringing up extra chairs from the basement. She had to show her the way and as they walked down the hall, Connie pulled her to one side. "What were they in prison for?"

Ester told her that Gloria had been in for a long stretch for fencing stolen guns and Kathleen was in for forgery and kiting.

"And what about Julia? What was she in for?"

Gloria appeared. "The Doc was in for sellin' prescriptions. She was a junkie."

Connie flushed with embarrassment.

"I heard you, Ester. I wasn't done for the guns, that was a total frame-up. I was stitched up," Gloria said.

Ester sighed, already sick and tired of Gloria. She ushered Connie to the cellar door, which led down to the sauna, the steam room and the old laundry. There was also a gymnasium, and there were showers and changing cubicles, all from the days when the manor had been a health farm.

Connie went down to inspect the chairs as most of the ones in the dining room were broken. Confronted by banks of mirrors, she couldn't resist looking at herself and pouting, then jumped when Julia asked what she was doing in her droll voice. Connie squinted in the semi-darkness, looking over the stack of chairs. "I love to work out, I do it whenever I can—it's like a fix." She put her hand to her mouth. "Oh, I'm sorry, I didn't mean that the way it came out . . ."

"I know what you meant," Julia said. "You worked for Ester, right? What were you, then?"

"I'm a model. I don't do any of that kind of thing now, not anymore."

Julia smiled. "Well, I don't use drugs, and you're not selling that lovely body, so we both seem to have improved our lives, don't we?"

Julia turned and left and Connie sighed. She hated it when anyone assumed she had been a prostitute. But that was what she had been, like it or not. Then when Lennie, who she had trusted, who she believed had loved her, had tried to make her go back on the game it had really hurt because she had dreamed of one day being a model, a proper one, one that kept her clothes on. She had written to agents and now, with all the work done on her face, she reckoned she might even get a TV commercial. She had big plans for herself: she would have a big-time photographer do a good contact sheet, send out a portfolio. She was sure she had a chance. Lennie had laughed and told her she was too old, told her that was the reason he had paid for her surgery, so she could make some money on her back, but she had refused.

Connie sat down on one of the dusty chairs and started to cry. He never touched her face, at least he didn't ruin that, but her body was still covered in bruises. She had said she would do whatever he wanted, if he just left her alone. The following morning Ester had called, not to ask her to go on the game as she had first thought, but to give her a chance of making a lot of money. Connie had immediately thrown a few things into a case and done a runner. She knew Lennie would be going crazy, knew he would be out looking for her: he'd want his money back for the surgery at the very least, but Ester had said that she'd have more money than she would know what to do with. She hoped Ester was right. Connie had never really met Dolly Rawlins.

"What the hell are you doin' down here?" Gloria suddenly yelled.

Connie picked up the chair and brushed past her.

"You see any big trays around here? Ester said we need one," Gloria added.

Connie hadn't, so Gloria began to sort through the odd bits and pieces of furniture in the gym. She sighed when she caught her dirt-streaked reflection. Then she inspected the black roots of her hair. She needed a tint badly; she had to have it done before she went to see Eddie.

Eddie Radford was serving eighteen years for arms dealing and armed robbery. He was going to be away for so long that sometimes Gloria wondered if it was worth going back and forth to the prisons. He'd spent most of their marriage in one or another. To be honest, they were two bad pennies, as she had been in and out for this and that since she was a teenager. But Eddie was trouble—she'd known it when she first met him. He was even worse than her first husband. Now he'd got a stash of weapons hidden at their old house with two of his bastard friends trying to get them. She had no money but Eddie kept telling her he'd arrange a deal, that she just had to sit tight and wait until he'd made the contact. Gloria was behind with the rent, and the council had told her to leave. It seemed like everyone was always telling her what to do and it always ended up a mess. She was scared of sitting on such a big stash of guns, scared of his so-called contacts and she was sick to death of always being on the move, always looking over her shoulder in case one of Eddie's friends tracked her down.

When Ester had called, it had been like a breath of fresh air. The thought of getting away from that pressure, away from Eddie's bloody heavies, was intoxicating. And with the promise of big money tied in with it, who could refuse?

Ester checked the table. It was looking good. As it grew darker it got harder to see the dilapidation, and she had bought boxes of candles and incense sticks, plus room sprays, so gradually the stench of mildew was disappearing. Gloria said it smelt like someone had farted in a pine forest.

The food had been delivered on big oval throwaway platters, and all they had to do was heat it up. The Aga was on, the boiler was working and fires were lit in the dining room and drawing room. Julia had cut logs and carried them in, and slowly the firelight and the candlelight had given warmth to the old house. The kids from the job center had gone and only the women remained. Ester shouted for them all to meet up and have a confab as Dolly would be arriving in a couple of hours.

The doorbell rang and Ester swore, looking at her watch. It couldn't be her yet . . . Then she remembered Angela.

"You took your bloody time getting here. I said this afternoon. It's almost six," she snapped.

Angela dumped her overnight bag. "I had to bleedin' walk all the way from the station, it took hours. And I missed the train so I had to wait . . ." She looked at the bank of candles. "Eh, this looks great, I thought it was wrecked."

"It was, it is, we've done a good bandage job."

Angela hadn't seen the old house for years, not since it was busted, so she was impressed by the big floral displays in the hall, the banisters gleaming from the hours Kathleen had spent polishing.

Gloria walked out from the dining room and glared at Angela. "Who's this? What're you doing?"

Ester said that Angela was a friend who had come to serve the dinner.

"Oh yeah? We cut this any more ways and there's not gonna be much to go round, you know."

Ester pushed Gloria against the wall. "She doesn't know anything, she doesn't know Dolly and she's not in for a cut. She gets fifty quid to wait on us at dinner. Now will you get the others in the dining room so we can have a talk?"

Angela went into the kitchen. Ester pointed to what food needed heating, what was to be served cold and showed her the low oven of the Aga for the plates to be heated. Angela looked around, nodding, then trailed after Ester to the dining room.

"There's a room ready for you. Dump your bag. Did you bring a black dress and an apron?"

"Yes, ma'am," said Angela with a little curtsy.

"Okay, all of you read these." Ester handed round old newspaper clippings she had Xeroxed about the diamond raid: there were photographs of Dolly Rawlins after the shooting of her husband and several of Shirley Miller.

"Holy shit, you read this?" said Gloria. "'Diamonds worth more than five million were last night stolen in a daring raid.'"

Julia grabbed the clippings. "Gloria, we can read it for ourselves, okay?"

Gloria picked up another. "Fuckin' hell, listen to this, 'Harry Rawlins was last night shot at point-blank range by his wife. His body was discovered in a lake in—'"

Julia snatched it from her. "Shut up, just shut up."

Kathleen looked at Ester. "This was some raid. Did she set it up? Dolly?"

"She was never shopped for it if she did."

Gloria frowned. "This was no doodle at Woolworth's. Look at the gear they got away with, and guns. See this?" She held up a cutting. "'Shirley Miller, aged twenty-one, was shot and killed during a terrifying armed raid that took place at a fashion show last night. The models were wearing *over ten million pounds' worth of diamonds . . .'*"

Julia glanced at Ester in exasperation. She had had to put up with Gloria reading aloud when they had shared the same prison cell and she was about to make her shut up when Ester stopped them all short.

"If they were worth ten million nearly nine years ago, you can double the value now. Even if Dolly didn't get the motherload."

Kathleen whistled in awe. Gloria's face was puckered in concentration. "I mean, I know there were rumors, Ester, but, like, she might have started them. How can you be sure she's really got these diamonds?"

"Because nobody ever found them after the raid."

"That don't mean she got 'em," said Gloria.

Julia sighed. "Let's take it that she does have them."

"Okay, she's got them, and now she's out and she's coming here tonight."

"Right. She's coming here, to be with friends, and that's what we are going to be for her, dear old friends," said Ester.

Gloria shook her head. "You must be joking. She don't know the meaning of the word."

"Gloria, will you keep it shut for ten minutes and *fucking listen to me*?" Ester ran her hands through her hair. "I know she has no one, had no visitors. She's going to be very lonely, even frightened, so we make her welcome, we make her have a great night . . ."

Gloria nodded. "Then what? When do we get our hands on the stones?"

"None of you, not one of you, mentions diamonds. We just want her to feel like we're her friends, that she can trust us. She might need a good fence— Kathleen knows plenty. She might have trouble getting the stones—Gloria's got contacts. She will need us, you understand? Above all, we make her trust us. When she tells us about the diamonds, we go for them, we take them if we feel like it, and we share them between us."

"The five of us?" asked Gloria.

"Yes, Gloria, the five of us, or six—"

"Who's the sixth, then? Not that little black chick you got in for the nosh?"

"No, Gloria, Angela is not the sixth, but I reckon Dolly might want a cut of her own gear."

"Well, if I was her I'd just say piss off. I mean, why give us a cut?"

Ester sighed, beginning to think the whole thing was turning into a fiasco, when Connie suddenly giggled. "Five million! Oh, *yes!*"

They all started to laugh and Ester decided it was time to break it up and told them to start getting changed: Dolly was on her way and would be there within the hour. Like kids they trooped out.

Julia began to rub Ester's neck, feeling the tension. "I hope to God this works, Julia, and works fast, because I don't think I could stand more than a few hours cooped up with that bloody Gloria Radford."

Julia cupped Ester's face in her hands and kissed her lips. "Don't say I didn't warn you. If anyone can pull it off, you can. I just hope there really are diamonds. It could all be a fantasy—you know that, don't you, darling?"

Ester gripped her wrists. "No. There's diamonds, believe me, I know it. And I know that bitch has got them somewhere . . . and we'll get them away from her and then . . ."

Julia stepped back. "Then?" she said softly.

"I'm free, Julia. I'll be free. No bastard trying to slit my throat. I'll even airmail their wretched tape back to them. With all those millions I won't need to grovel or beg from anyone. I don't reckon in all honesty I've ever in my life been free but this time I will be."

"I hope for your sake you get them, then. I love you, Ester."

Ester was already walking out of the room. She didn't hear or if she did she pretended not to. Alone, Julia looked round the once magnificent room. Maybe Dolly would be taken in if she didn't look too carefully, if she didn't see the cracks, if she believed that Ester was her friend, all of them were her friends. Julia sighed. In some ways she felt sorry for Dolly Rawlins because she was walking into a snake pit and she was ashamed to be a part of it.

The candles threw shadows on the wall and she raised her hand to make a silhouette of a bird flying, flapping its wings. Dolly Rawlins's first day of freedom in eight years. Julia watched the shadow bird flutter and then broke the shadow as she moved her hands away from the candle. Ester had planned this evening carefully, each one of them chosen because they were desperate, herself included. She was desperate not to lose Ester, desperate to safeguard the lies she had told her ailing elderly mother, lies she had spun round her arrest and prison sentence. Julia's mother didn't know her daughter the doctor was an ex-drug addict, that she had been struck off and for the last four years had been in prison. She had arranged an elaborate charade via friends who passed Julia's letters written in Holloway to look as if they were sent from abroad. Julia's mother had never suspected her daughter was leading a double life, just as she had no notion that her daughter could or would be deeply in love with another woman. It was beyond her comprehension, and Julia was determined her mother would never know. Keeping up the pretense had taken money, and still took every penny she could lay hands on, as she paid all her mother's bills. Julia needed those diamonds just like the rest of them. The only difference was, she was ashamed of the awful con they were all about to begin on Dolly Rawlins.

CHAPTER 3

Jimmy Donaldson's wife had been informed that her husband was return-ing home on a "special leave" from prison. She was asked not to mention the visit to anyone and to remain in the house until he was brought home. When he did arrive, in the company of two plainclothes officers, they had only one or two moments alone before he was taken into their sitting room. One officer placed a tape recorder and bugging device on their telephone in the hope that Dolly Rawlins made contact. The small antique shop was already being searched. DCI Craigh arranged for a rota of officers to remain in the house and keep an eye on Jimmy. Mike Withey was to take the following morning shift. Mike couldn't wait to see his mother and tell her what was happening.

At the same time Dolly Rawlins was about to arrive at Grange Manor House. The women had all changed into cocktail dresses. Ester had laid out one of her own dresses for Dolly to change into and, as she saw the headlamps of the Corniche turning into the driveway, she gave hurried orders for the women to remain in the dining room and stay silent. Next she briefed Angela that when the doorbell rang she was to open the front door and welcome Dolly into the house. Ester would then make her appearance.

Dolly stepped out of the car. She looked around, feeling unsure, even more so than when she'd been driving down the dark, potholed lane leading to the house. Now that she was here, it was difficult to see what state it was in. The chauffeur guided her toward the front steps. She stopped.

"Are you staying?"

"If you would like me to, Mrs. Rawlins. It's entirely up to you." He rang the bell. Some of the stained glass was broken but Dolly wasn't paying much attention; she was feeling edgy.

Angela opened the door, wearing a neat black dress and white apron.

"Good evening, Mrs. Rawlins. Welcome to the Grange."

Dolly hesitated and then saw Ester, elegant as ever, standing with her arms wide. "Dolly. Come on in."

She walked into the hall.

"What's going on?"

"It's a welcome-out party for you. All your old mates, Dolly, from Holloway."

She watched as Angela closed the door, taking Dolly's small case from the chauffeur, and then Ester embraced her warmly, kissing her on both cheeks.

"Come on, let me show you around. You'll want a bath, won't you?"

Dolly looked at the banks of flickering candles, still nonplussed as Ester guided her up the stairs. She stopped. "Why are you doing this?"

Ester continued up the stairs. "We all know what it feels like, coming out to nothing and no one, Dolly. We wanted to make sure you got a special party, to sort of start you off in the right direction."

Dolly followed Ester up the stairs, impressed by the state of the house, then the clean room with the black lace dress laid out on the bed. There were stockings and clean underwear, even a couple of pairs of high-heeled shoes.

"You did all this for me?" Dolly said, still nonplussed.

"It's not a new dress but it is a Valentino. Would you like me to run a bath for you? Wash your hair?"

Angela slipped in with Dolly's suitcase and placed it by the bed. She was out again before Dolly could say a word. "Who's that?"

"Oh, she's just a kid that used to work for me."

"A tart, is she?"

"No, she's just here to serve us so we don't have to do anything but enjoy ourselves."

Dolly wandered around the room. "Who else is here?"

Ester went into the ensuite, turned on the taps, felt the hot water—it wasn't what you'd call *hot* hot—and poured in bath salts.

"Kathleen O'Reilly, you remember her?" Ester told her the other names.

Dolly sat on the bed. "Well, I wouldn't call any of them friends, Ester. They all here, are they?"

"Yes, well, I tried to get as many women as I thought you knew so it'd be a bit of a knees-up."

"I'm not sure what to say."

Ester smiled. "Just have a nice bath. I'll go and tell them you'll be down soon, okay?"

Dolly slowly took off her coat, and then smiled. "Yeah, why not? I could do with a drink."

They all looked toward the double doors as Ester came into the dining room. "She's getting ready, won't be long."

"I hope not, I'm starving," Gloria muttered.

Julia lolled in her chair. "She knows who's down here?"

"Yes, she does," Esther said, looking round the room. "Please don't drink any more, Kathleen. We've got to work her over and if you get pissed you'll open that yapping mouth. That goes for you too, Gloria."

She glanced over the table and then went to the kitchen. Angela had her feet up and was reading a magazine. "We'll have the first course, then I'll ring for you."

"Yeah, you told me that before."

"When she's ready to come down, I want you to bring her in. Go up to her room when I tell you. I don't want her wandering around."

"You told me that as well."

Ester walked out. Angela waited a moment, then followed. As soon as she saw her heading up the stairs she crept to the phone, eased it off the hook, and dialed. She waited, eyes on the dark, candlelit hallway.

Susan was dishing up dinner and Mike answered the phone. He spoke softly and then replaced the receiver. He was smiling like he'd just been given good news.

"Who was that?"

"Mum. I said I'd go over later after dinner."

"Oh, I'd liked to have come with you. Why didn't you tell me? I could ask the girl next door to babysit."

"I'm only going for a few minutes."

Mike sat down as Susan passed him a plate of stew. She had long blonde hair, like Mike's sister Shirley, and was almost as pretty. Their two boys had already been put to bed and she'd half-hoped they could have an evening together.

"Is your mum still planning to go to Spain?"

Mike nodded, his mouth full. "Yeah, that's why I said I'd drop in, see if she needed me to do anything."

"Funny time to go, isn't it, winter?"

Mike shrugged, forking in another mouthful. "Got some friend there with a villa, be good for her, she needs to get away."

"Don't we all. It's been ages since we had a holiday—be nice to get away."

"We will," he said, eyes on the clock, wondering if they'd found the diamonds yet.

Susan watched him: he'd been very distracted of late, moody and snapping at the kids. "Everything all right at work, is it?"

"Yep." He pushed the plate aside, only half finished, and wiped his mouth with a napkin. "I'll shove off. Sooner I go, sooner I'll be home."

He leaned over and kissed her forehead.

"There's nobody else, is there, Mike?"

"What?"

"It's just I hardly have time to talk to you, you're always out, and most weekends you've been on duty. If there is somebody else . . ."

He sat down again. "There isn't anyone else, Sue, okay? It's been a bit heavy lately, I've got a lot on and . . ."

"Yes?"

"Well, it's to do with Shirley. The woman Mum blames for her being killed, Dolly Rawlins, got released today, so Mum's been a bit hysterical, you know the way she always harps on about it."

"Well, you can't blame her. If one of our boys was killed I'd feel the same."

"I won't be long, I promise, okay?"

Once he'd gone, Susan tried to finish her supper but she wasn't hungry anymore. She was sure Mike was seeing someone else—she'd even searched his suit pockets, looking for evidence. She hadn't found anything but that didn't prove anything because he was a detective so he wouldn't be stupid enough to leave anything incriminating, would he? She told herself to stop it: it was just as he said, overwork, he was tired and she was reading more into his moods than she should. She pushed her plate away, muttering to herself. What about *her* moods? Nobody ever seemed concerned about her or the way she felt.

Ester cocked her head to one side, sprayed lacquer over Dolly's hair and stepped back. "That's much nicer, softer round your face with a bit of a wave. So, we all set to go down?" Dolly stood up and admired herself in the wardrobe mirror. "This is a lovely frock."

Ester opened the bedroom door. "It was a lovely price, too, a few years back, Dolly. Come on, they're all starving down there."

They walked down the stairs together, Angela waiting at the bottom.

"No men invited, then?" Dolly asked.

Ester laughed. "Well, we could always get the chauffeur back."

"Couldn't you get the Chippendales? They're all the rage in the nick—girls have got their posters on the walls. Good-looking lads, they do dances just for women."

"I know who they are, Dolly, but they're a bit passé now. That's always the problem in the nick. Years behind what's going on."

Angela opened the dining-room doors wider and Ester stepped back to allow Dolly to walk in ahead of her.

The women all rose to their feet and began to sing. "Good luck, God bless you . . ."

The banks of candles, their dresses and the beautifully laid table made Dolly gasp: it seemed almost magical. The room with its ornately carved ceiling, the huge stone hearth with a blazing log fire, the women all raising their glasses in a toast.

"To Dolly Rawlins. She's out!"

Dolly slowly moved from one woman to the next. Like a princess, she touched their shoulders or kissed their cheeks.

Ester drew out the carved chair at the head of the table. "Sit down, Dolly. This is your night, one we won't let you forget."

Dolly sat down, seeming near to tears. She accepted a glass of champagne and lifted it. "God bless us all."

In the soft firelight with the flickering candles, they looked almost surreal: six women enjoying a celebration dinner. No one caught the strange glint behind the star guest's eyes because she was smiling, seemingly enjoying every precious moment. In reality she was waiting, knowing they wanted something, and she had a pretty good idea what it was. But she could wait. She was used to waiting.

The officers found it difficult to search the dark, poky little antique shop. There was a lot of junk and clutter to be moved aside and Donaldson had said the diamonds were hidden in a wall recess, but by ten o'clock they still had not been found. The men decided to call it quits for the night and to start again early the following morning.

Audrey was in her dressing gown when she opened the door to Mike. He beamed as he hugged her. "Have I got news for you."

She shut the door, a look of anticipation on her face.

"She's out, Mum, and, I know exactly where she is, and . . ."

Audrey sat on the settee as Mike gave her all the details about what had gone down that day, ending by clapping his hands together and laughing. "Right now we got blokes searching for the diamonds, right? When they find them, we'll have Jimmy Donaldson wired up. If she calls, and she will, she'll go straight for them. We'll be ready and waiting. She's going to go right back inside, Mum, just what you wanted."

Audrey had gone pale. "You should have warned me, told me what you were doing."

"How could I? It all happened today. It was such a bloody coincidence I couldn't believe it. First Angela—"

"You're not still messing around with that little tart, are you?"

"For Chrissakes, Mum, she's very useful. Because of her, right now I know where Dolly Rawlins is. Then I got a tip-off about Jimmy Donaldson. It was beautiful, just beautiful, I got my governor jumping around. You know there was a reward for those stones and—"

"You got to stop this, Mike," Audrey said sharply.

"Why? It's what you've been bleatin' on about for the past eight years, isn't it? Well, I'm going to have Dolly Rawlins put back inside for that robbery. She's going to be copped for those diamonds."

"No, she isn't, love."

"What are you talking about?"

"The diamonds."

"Yeah, we got blokes stripping Donaldson's place for them."

"They won't find them."

"Why not?"

"Because they're not there."

"How do you know?"

"Because I took them."

Mike's jaw dropped. He couldn't take it in.

Audrey started to cry. "When I read about Jimmy being arrested, I . . . You see, she always said I'd get a cut. I couldn't risk him telling the police where they were."

"Jesus Christ, I don't believe this."

"So I went round to his shop. I've known his wife for years and, well, she asked if I wanted a coffee, then she went round to a café to bring it back and I knew where he'd stashed them, so I took them."

"You've got them?"

"No, I had them."

"So what the fuck have you done with them?"

"Sold them."

Mike stood up. He was shaking. "You sold them?"

Audrey took out a tissue and blew her nose. "Yes. God help me, I didn't know what to do with them once I'd got them here and I was scared. I mean, they just sat there and I got more and more scared having something worth that much in the flat."

Mike slumped into a chair, his head in his hands. "Holy shit, you've really landed me in it. Who's got them now?"

Audrey twisted the tissue. "Well, I couldn't really shop around, could I? I knew this dealer, Frank Richmond. He's dodgy but I took them to him and he said he'd get what he could for them. But you know, they weren't easy because they were still hot. Well, that's what he said."

"He paid you for them?"

"He gave me four hundred and fifty grand."

Mike leaned back, his eyes closed.

"They were worth millions, I knew that, but I wasn't gonna start pushing for more money, was I? I was desperate—I knew she'd be out, knew she'd go to Jimmy and then come here."

Mike jumped to his feet. "You've been bullshitting me, haven't you? All that crap about Shirley. You've lied to me."

"*No, I haven't!*"

"Yes, you bloody have. This wasn't for Shirley. It was for you, *you*, and now you've got me caught up in it."

Audrey sobbed as he paced up and down the room.

"Where's the money?" Mike demanded.

"Well, some of it's in my bank, some's in a building society but the bulk of it's in Spain."

"*Spain?*" Mike wanted to shake or slap her, he didn't know which. "Is that why you're going there?"

She sniffed. "Yes. Wally Simmonds bought a villa for me."

Mike gaped. "A villa?"

She nodded. "It was ever such a good buy and we did a cash deal. I'm leaving for good. I was gonna tell you when I'd sorted myself out."

Mike swallowed. It was getting worse by the second. He could feel the floor shifting under his feet.

"What am I going to do, Mike?"

"I don't know."

"Do you want a cup of tea?"

He turned on her in a fury. "*No, I bloody don't.* Just shut up and let me think this one out."

She sat snuffling as he sat with his head in his hands. Eventually he asked flatly, "Do you know anyone who could make us up some dud stones that'd look like the real things?"

Audrey licked her lips, trying to think.

Mike continued, "I could stash them at Donaldson's. It could still work but we'd only have a few hours, a day maybe, to get the stuff ready. Do you know anyone?"

"I'm sorry I've done this to you, love. Will you get into trouble?"

He stared at his mother. "I could lose my fucking job—that good enough for you? Now, do you know anyone?"

Audrey took a worn address book from her handbag. "There's Tommy Malin—he's probably the best—and if we said we'd pay cash for it he might do us a favor."

"Us now, is it?"

"Well, I'll just do whatever you tell me to." Her brain was a jumbled mess of questions. Why, why had she been so stupid? Why had she done it? Was it because she just wanted to get back at Dolly? Was that it? But there was another element: greed. Audrey wanted money. She had always wanted it but it had always been out of her reach. When she read about Jimmy's arrest, all the waiting seemed to have been for nothing and it was her fury at being cheated that pushed her into getting the diamonds. She had not foreseen how deeply she would bring her son into it all. Somehow she had thought he'd just arrest the bitch and put her away, out of reach.

"I'm so scared of her, Mike. I know she'll come after me. She won't understand what it was like having them stones in the flat, why I just had to . . ."

Mike sighed as she started crying again. "Mum, you're up to your neck in it, whatever excuses you make. Gimme the address book. I'll call this fence bloke but I can only do so much. Then I gotta walk away from it—and from you if necessary."

They had all had a considerable amount to drink: champagne, white and red wine. The booze had eased the tension and now they were all talking freely. Kathleen, well away, was telling an elaborate story about how she found her ex-husband in bed with a lodger and how she'd locked him in a coal hole. Connie was sketching the details of her plastic surgery operations on a paper napkin. Gloria was having a heated argument with Julia about body fat. Their voices were like music to Dolly. She didn't listen to whatever anyone was saying: it was the freedom, the roaring laughs, and the relaxed atmosphere. Ester did not drink as much as the others but watched Dolly throughout, noting how often her glass was refilled, waiting for the right moment to start a conversation about Dolly's future arrangements.

Angela carried in a tray and said that coffee and brandy would now be served in the drawing room.

Ester saw Dolly stumble slightly as she pushed back her chair. She was obviously enjoying herself and even took hold of Gloria's hand as they wove their way into the drawing room, where there were more candles and another big blazing fire, the perfumed incense disguising the damp smell, the gentle light hiding the darkened patches on the wallpaper.

Julia whispered to Ester to keep her eye on Kathleen as she started thumping out a song on the piano, having a ball, almost forgetting why she was there. Julia handed out the drinks as Gloria picked up the box of After Eight mints. "Here you go, Dolly love. Have a mint and tell us what you're gonna be up to now you're out?"

Ester edged closer, wanting Gloria to shut up. Not subtle at the best of times, Gloria now plunged right in. "So you got yourself a nice nest egg, have you, Dolly?"

Dolly laughed as she sipped her brandy. "I might have."

"I bet that old man left you a few quid, didn't he?" Gloria continued, and then grimaced as Ester stood firmly on her foot.

"He left me comfortable." Dolly shrugged, moving toward the mantelpiece. Then she turned to face them all as Kathleen staggered away from the piano stool to slump into a big winged chair.

"So, why don't you all come clean? What you all after?" Dolly said it calmly but there was an edge to her voice.

Ester sounded convincingly bemused. "After? What's that supposed to mean?"

"Well, this is all very nice but none of us were what you would call friends. So I just wondered what you wanted."

Ester stood up, a furious look on her face. "Oh, thanks a lot, Dolly. We all worked our butts off today to get this place ready for you. You think we did it for what? What you got that any of us would want? We did it, I arranged it, because in the nick you belted that cow Barbara Hunter. I admired that, we all admired that, but if you think we've all come here for some ulterior motive, then screw you. We only wanted you to come out to friends, to have one night to find your feet." She marched angrily toward the door as if about to make an exit.

"I'm sorry," Dolly said quietly.

"So you bloody should be. I know it's hard to trust people inside but we're not inside. We're all out. All we wanted was to give you a bit of a party."

"I said I'm sorry. Come on, sit down."

Ester gave a tiny wink to Julia as she grudgingly sat on the arm of the easy chair, close to Gloria so she could keep a watchful eye on her.

Dolly turned toward the fire. "Truth is, I do have a few quid put by."

A low murmur from them all, and sly glances flashed between them.

"Well, that's good to know," said Connie. "I hope you have a secure and successful future."

They all raised their glasses and toasted Dolly yet again.

"So how much you got, then?" asked Gloria, getting an immediate dig in the ribs from Ester.

"It's not a fortune but . . . I'm all right, comfortable."

They waited with bated breath as Dolly drained her glass and placed it on the tray. "I'm going to tell you something."

They all leaned forward, listening attentively, hoping she was now about to say "diamonds."

"For eight years, I've been sort of planning it, in my head. It's my dream, my future."

A row of expectant faces waited.

"I want to put back something into society. It might sound crazy, but I really want to do something useful with the rest of my life."

No one spoke. They felt a trifle uneasy, though—she was coming on like something from *The Sound of Music*.

Dolly took a deep breath. "I want to buy a house and I want to open it up as a home, a foster home for kids, battered wives, a home run by me, for all those less fortunate than me."

None of them could speak. They looked at Dolly as if she had two heads. She had taken the carpet from beneath every one of them.

Tommy Malin agreed that he could make up a bag of fake stones, using some real settings and some fake ones. He could do it for two grand cash and have it ready by the following afternoon. Mike tried to push him to have them done by the following morning but he refused, saying if they wanted the stuff to look good, really good, they'd have to wait. He'd have to shop around for some good cut-glass fakes, maybe throw in a couple of zircons, and that took time. Mike agreed and said Audrey would collect them as soon as he called to say they were ready.

By the time Mike got home it was after twelve and he was exhausted. Susan heard the front door shut and turned over to her side of the bed, not wanting to speak to him or confront him. She was sure now he had another woman and it was breaking her heart.

Mike cleaned his teeth. His eyes were red-rimmed, his face chalk white; he was in it up to his neck now, just like Audrey. He had to find some way of stashing the fakes in Jimmy Donaldson's place. He splashed cold water over his face, half hoping that Dolly Rawlins would never make contact about the bloody diamonds.

Susan heard him undressing and then he got into bed beside her, turning his back to her. Neither said a word, Susan because she was sure he was cheating on her, Mike hearing his own heart thudding as he went over the mess he had got himself caught up in. Whatever excuses he tried to make for Audrey, the fact was that she had dragged him back into the world he had tried so hard all his life to escape. Shirley had been well caught up in it, together with her husband, and she had ended up getting shot. In the end, though, it all came back to Dolly Rawlins. If he could get her put away, it would get them all out of trouble. And even if he had to frame her, she still deserved everything she got.

Ester had a mink coat slung round her shoulders and Dolly wore Gloria's fluffy wrap as they walked toward the stables. "I mean, look at this place, Dolly. You could have ten, twelve kids here, get a horse even. And there's a swimming pool, needs a bit of work, the whole house does, but it's crying out for kids. It'd be perfect."

Dolly looked back at the vast house. "I dunno, Ester. I was sort of thinking about a small terraced job, near Holloway."

"No. This is much better. Country air, grounds, and it'd be cheaper than any terraced house. I'll even throw in all the linen, crockery and furniture. I put it on the market for two hundred and fifty grand, but you can have the lot for two hundred. I've got the surveyors' reports. But if it's out of your league . . ."

It wasn't out of her league—in fact it was smack in it: she'd got two hundred and fifty grand to be exact but after shelling out here and there it'd be around the two hundred mark.

They walked on round the stables to the front of the house, Ester pointing over toward the swimming pool. "There's an orchard, vegetable patch. You could grow your own veg, be self-sufficient. It's a dream place for kids, Dolly."

Dolly sighed. "I dunno, Ester, it's an awfully big house."

"All the better. And we can all give you a hand, stay on and work it up for you, get the place shipshape. Hell, none of us have got anythin' better going for us. We'd be your helpers, it's a brilliant idea."

The women watched from the slit in the curtains. Kathleen turned away. "Home for battered wives! She's out of her mind. I've been one most of me life and I'm not about to start livin' with a bunch of them. She's got a screw loose."

Gloria kicked at the dying embers of the fire. "Well, I'm pissed off. I think this was all Ester was after from the start. She wanted us to break our backs cleaning the fuckin' place up so she can flog it to Dolly. That's what she got us here for—she's used the lot of us to sell this bleedin' place."

Julia poured another brandy and swirled it in her glass. "No, she hasn't, she's just being clever."

"You can say that again. We all done it up and she's the only one that's gonna make any dough out of it," Gloria retorted.

Connie joined in. "I didn't even know she was selling this place, she never told me."

Julia shook her head. "You really are dumb, all of you, aren't you? Dolly has got to have a lot of money. Well, this place will swallow that right away so where's she going to get the money to get this place up and running as a kids' home?" She drained her glass. "She'll have to go for those diamonds. Ester knows it. Can't you see what she's doing? She's creaming her, you stupid cows."

They looked at each other and then Kathleen yawned. "Well, in that case I'm staying on."

The rest of them quickly agreed it was the best thing to do.

* * *

Ester showed Dolly all the estate agents', valuers' and solicitors' letters, and all the old surveys of the Manor House. "Two hundred's a bargain, Dolly."

Dolly frowned. "That wipes me out, Ester."

Ester felt her belly tighten: she'd guessed right. It tickled her that she could always suss out people's cash-flow. It came with dealing for the girls, pushing the punters to the limit. She gave a wide smile. "But you'll get big grants for the kids."

Dolly looked over the documents again. "I dunno, Ester. What if the others won't stay on? I can't run this place on my own."

"Listen, none of them have got a place to go. They'll stay on, believe you me. And then we got Julia, she's a doctor, just what you need."

Dolly was still unsure.

"Look, don't do anything right away," Ester said breezily. "Think about it, take your time. If you're not interested, fine, I'll sell it to someone else. No skin off my back . . ."

Dolly suddenly took out her checkbook. "You're on. Here, I'll give you a check right now."

Ester put a hand on her arm. "Now don't do anything you're going to be sorry for. Maybe you should sleep on it. I don't want you thinking I bamboozled you into this. It's your choice. The only thing that might be a problem is the other offer that I got but it can wait at least until tomorrow."

Dolly wrote out the check there and then, still heady from the wine. She insisted Ester take it and she did, pocketing it quickly.

"Where's the phone?" Dolly asked.

"In the hall."

Ester slipped out of the kitchen, leaving Dolly looking over the papers. The women had all gone up to bed, the fires were dead, the candles burned out. She went upstairs to her own bedroom where Julia was waiting, lying on the bed with her hands behind her head. Ester showed her the check. "I'll put this in the bank first thing tomorrow before the old cow changes her mind. Not that she will, because we're going to work that woman over, every one of us. We'll make her believe we love the idea, want the home to be up and running. We all egg her on and keep it going until she . . ."

"Goes for the diamonds."

Ester smiled. "Right, and then . . ." She made a plucking motion with her fingers.

Julia stared at the check for two hundred thousand pounds. "You could do okay on this, you know."

Ester sighed. "I got debts that'd eat up more than two hundred grand. We need those diamonds—two, three million quid's worth, Julia, and we're going to have them."

"I love you when you're like this," Julia whispered.

"Like what?"

"Cruel. Come to bed."

Ester gave a soft sexy laugh as she sidled toward Julia and then froze halfway and turned to listen at the door.

Dolly stood in the marbled hall, the phone in her hand. "Jimmy, is that you?"

Jimmy Donaldson was in his pajamas, his hand shaking, as DI Palmer gestured for him to keep talking.

"Yes, this is Jimmy Donaldson. Who's this? You know what time it is?"

"Oh, I'm sorry to ring so late. It's Dolly, Dolly Rawlins."

Palmer leaned forward, hardly able to contain himself. It was going down even faster than any one of them had thought. Mike Withey had been right. Dolly Rawlins was going for the diamonds. Again he gestured for Donaldson to keep talking.

"I need to see you," Dolly said softly. "Tomorrow. I'm out, Jimmy. Have you got my things for me?"

"Yes, yes, I've got them."

"Well, what say we meet up tomorrow, about noon?"

Jimmy looked to Palmer. They still didn't have the stones but he reckoned they would by the following day. He wrote on a notepad. Jimmy nodded. "Can you make it later—like late afternoon?"

"They are safe, aren't they, Jimmy?"

"Yes, of course."

"Fine, I'll call you tomorrow, then."

Dolly hung up.

Donaldson looked at Palmer. "She's gonna call me tomorrow. She hung up before I could say anythin' different."

Frowning, Palmer drummed his fingers on the telephone table. "We better find those diamonds, then, Jimmy. You sure they're where you said they are?"

"If they're not, then some bastard's nicked them."

Palmer jerked his head for Donaldson to return to his bed. He checked the time and replayed the message. Dolly Rawlins had carefully not said the word "diamonds" but she certainly hadn't wasted much time. She'd only been released that afternoon. She was out all right.

CHAPTER 4

Dolly woke with a start, unable for a moment to orientate herself, and it scared her. Her heart thudded, she started to pant, then realized it was the sound of birds, rooks cawing from the woods, a sound she had not heard for a long, long time.

She got up and drew the curtains, then looked out of the window. "Holy shit." In the harsh light of day, for the first time she saw the derelict gardens, the dank, dark poolside. "Oh my God, what have you got yourself into, gel?"

She listened at her door, could hear no sound of movement so she went out onto the landing. In the cold light of morning, she moved silently round the old manor, peeking into each unoccupied room, from the attic to the ground floor, her heart sinking at every turn as she realized what she had let herself in for. The rundown state of the house was obvious, from the peeling wallpaper to the cracked ceilings and crumbling woodwork. The banister rail was fine, thick mahogany, but many of the pegs were missing and the carpets worn and dangerous on the old wide stairs. The smell of mold, damp and mildew made her nostrils flare but she kept on moving from room to room until she finally entered the old kitchen, easing back the bolts from the back door to walk outside into the stable yard.

She inspected the pool, the woods, the neglected orchard, and the wild, overgrown mess of brambles and throttling weeds that was the vegetable garden. She returned to the kitchen, her shoes covered in mud, her legs scratched from the brambles, and the hem of her coat sodden. No one was up so she put on the kettle, working out how to use the big lidded Aga, fetching a mug and making a cup of tea, her mind working overtime.

The house was a dog, she knew that, but she couldn't help liking it all the same. Perhaps it was fate; it was meant to be. Dolly sat with her hands cupping the chipped mug. From what she could see, the place could certainly accommodate at least ten, fifteen kids with ease, and she hadn't even been down to the basement. She went over the survey reports, all a few years out of date. She started to calculate on the back of an envelope just how much money it would take to get a place this size back into order. All her cash would go with the one check to Ester so it would mean she was dependent on the sale of the diamonds. Although she knew she hadn't got all of the stolen gems, she calculated that what she had would be valued at two or three million. The need to fence them quickly would bring the price down, but if she was able to work with Jimmy Donaldson she reckoned she would probably clear one to two million cash. The house would need a hell of a lot of money spent on it but she could use ex-prisoners to help her, perhaps even the women from last night.

Dolly spent over an hour making notes and working out costs and then went down to the basement. There was a sauna, a steam room, an old gym and a large laundry room. None of the machines appeared to be in working order and the stench of damp was even worse down there. She looked over the old boilers and knew they'd all have to be replaced. Maybe it really was all too much . . .

By the time she returned to the kitchen, Gloria was up and Ester and Julia were washing dishes in the big stone sink. Angela was clearing the debris in the dining room and came in carrying a tray filled with dirty glasses. "Good morning, you're up bright and early, Mrs. Rawlins."

Dolly gave a brittle smile. "Yes. Is everyone else up yet?"

"No, not yet. Do you want breakfast?"

"Yes."

"Eggs and bacon coming up."

Dolly opened the front door to look down the big wide drive.

"Good morning, Dolly." Connie beamed, wrapping a silk kimono round herself.

Dolly turned round as Kathleen appeared. "My God, I've got a bastard of a headache. How about you, Dolly?"

Watching the women coming and going made Dolly feel a bit better. "Get some coffee down you," she said to Kathleen, and then walked behind the old reception desk to look for a telephone directory.

Ester appeared at the kitchen door. "Good morning, Dolly. You looking for something?"

"Directories."

Ester wandered to the desk. "Be out of date, get the operator. Who are you calling?"

Dolly sighed. "Well, I should have a word with the local social services, just to see about the possibilities of opening this place up as a home."

"You don't waste much time, do you?"

"Nor do you, Ester. You did a good job hustling me into buying this place."

"What? Look, it was up to you, love. I mean, I'm not forcing you into anything you don't want to do."

Dolly raised an eyebrow. "Fine, just don't bank the check until I'm sure."

Ester moved into action, instructing the women to get the breakfast on the table and to look as if they loved the place. By the time Dolly joined them, the kitchen was filled with the smell of sizzling bacon and eggs, hot toast and coffee, all laid out ready and waiting. Their smiling faces greeted Dolly warmly as she sat down.

"I been all round the grounds. Place is in a terrible state."

"Get a few locals to clear the gardens. It used to be beautiful, in the summer especially." Ester continued to sell the manor, hinting time and again what a wonderful place it would be for children.

Angela gave Dolly the number for the social services but it was almost nine thirty when Dolly put in a call and arranged for a meeting at the town hall. She was still unsure and not giving much away. She had only the few things she had brought with her so she would need to do some shopping, but it would be a good opportunity to see what the local village was like.

As soon as Dolly was out of earshot, they started whispering about the diamonds. Ester hissed at them to keep their mouths shut.

"Yeah, well, that's why we're all here, Ester, and so far she's not said a dickie about them. All that's gone down is you're two hundred grand up. What if they don't exist?" Gloria muttered irritably.

"Oh they exist," snapped Ester. She crossed the kitchen and looked out into the hallway, drawing the door shut. "Make her think we're all behind the project, right? Offer to stay and help out, start clearing the place up. She's gonna need hard cash to get this place up and rolling so we watch her like a hawk and—"

Dolly called from the stairs, asking if the boiler was working as she wanted to have a bath before she left. Ester opened the door and shouted that the water was on and hot. She waited until she could hear the thud of the old pipes before she went to give the women more instructions. She then paid off Angela and said that when they went into the village she could catch the next train home.

"I got to go and see Eddie," Gloria said tetchily.

"Fine, you go," said Ester.

"I need my gear." Connie pouted.

Ester sighed. "Look, you all do what you have to but, whatever you do, keep your mouths shut about being here and especially about the diamonds. Is that clear?"

By eleven they were all waiting for Dolly, Ester out in the yard in her Range Rover. Julia was looking into the stables. "You know, this place must have been something," she said.

"It was. What the hell is she doing in there?"

Ester paced up and down, impatient to go into Aylesbury to bank the check.

Julia came close. "You going to be okay?"

Ester nodded. "Yeah. Nobody knows I'm here and besides, I got to bank the check and get her the deeds of the house."

Julia cocked her head to one side. "Well, you take care."

Gloria teetered out with Connie behind her. "I'm off to see Eddie. I'm givin' Connie a lift in. Can you take us to the garage to see if me car's ready?"

Connie put her bag into the back of the Range Rover. "I won't even see Lennie. He always leaves by twelve so I'll just get my stuff and come straight back."

Kathleen wandered out. "Where you all going?"

Ester sighed. "Into Aylesbury. Where's Dolly?"

"She's on the phone, the social services again, asking what they want her to bring in."

"Are you stopping, then?" Ester demanded.

"Yeah, I got nowhere else to go, have I?" muttered Kathleen.

Angela joined them, followed by Dolly, so they all squashed into the Range Rover and drove off, leaving Kathleen alone.

Gloria's car wasn't ready so Connie and Angela were dropped off at the local railway station. Ester took Dolly on to Aylesbury town hall. "I'll wait here for you." She smiled.

Dolly nodded but seemed ill at ease. "I'll just see what they say. I shouldn't be too long, then I'll need to do a bit of shopping, tights and stuff like that."

As soon as Dolly walked into the town hall, Ester drove straight to the bank. She kept a good lookout for anyone following her and hurried inside.

Dolly waited in the anteroom and eventually a pleasant-faced woman called Deirdre Bull asked if she would come into her office. Dolly was offered a seat and coffee as Deirdre sat down behind her cluttered desk. The walls were lined with posters for foster carers and adoption societies.

"Now, it's Mrs. Rawlins, isn't it?"

"Yes, Dorothy Rawlins. I've come to ask you about opening a foster home. I've done a bit of research with a probation officer but I thought I'd just run a few things by you."

Deirdre nodded and began opening drawers. "First there are some forms you'll need to look over and fill in. Have you ever been a foster carer before?"

"No, I haven't, but I'm buying a big house and I could accommodate up to ten or twelve kids easily."

Deirdre was so relaxed and friendly that Dolly began to ease up, as Deirdre patiently passed her one form after another to look over.

"Are you married?"

"I'm a widow."

"Do you have children?"

"No, but I have worked with a lot of babies recently, and I have some letters from . . ."

Ester finally handed the check to the cashier. Impatient, her eyes on the clock, she'd had to stand in a queue for ten minutes. The cashier took his time, working methodically, which Ester found infuriating. He looked first at the check, then at Ester's paying-in slip.

"There's nothing wrong, is there?" Ester asked sharply, leaning closer into the counter. "I'm in rather a hurry and I have someone waiting."

The cashier peered at Ester. "It's Miss Freeman, isn't it? Could you wait one moment?"

"Why? All I want are the documents I've listed. Can't you just get them for me? I'm in a hurry."

"The manager will need to speak to you, Miss Freeman," the cashier said pleasantly.

"But there's nothing wrong with the check, is there?"

"No, not that I can see, but he will need to talk to you. Your account has been frozen."

"I know that," Ester retorted. It was impossible to forget what her financial situation was. She was in debt up to her eyeballs, tax inspectors breathing down her neck, and the only asset she had was the manor—and that was frozen, like her accounts.

She tried a different approach. "I just want the deeds to Grange Manor House." She gave a soft smile. "I have a cash buyer, so part of the overdraft could be paid off. If the bank tried to sell the house, they'd not get as good a price. And I'm sure I'll be able to cover any further outstanding debts within a few weeks."

She was sure she sounded entirely convincing. The cashier looked up and gave her a tight nod: he was going to release the deeds of the house. He excused himself and left Ester waiting. She checked her watch again, willing him to move his arse.

Deirdre looked through Dolly's forms, and showed not a flicker when she read that she had only just been released from prison.

"The house is well situated, with gardens and a swimming pool. It will need a lot of work and I don't know how I apply for grants and allowances—or if I am acceptable as a foster carer," Dolly said.

Deirdre nodded. "Well, you'll have to go before a board of committee members—I can't say whether or not you'll be acceptable, Mrs. Rawlins. All this takes considerable time and your property will have to be reviewed and assessed by the committee."

"But you don't think it's out of the question?"

"I can't say. If you like, I can ask my superior, Mrs. Tilly, to come and talk to you."

Dolly leaned closer. "I would be grateful if you would. I don't want to go ahead with buying the house if I don't stand a chance with my application—if my background goes against me, you understand?"

Deirdre smiled warmly. "Mrs. Rawlins, there are so many children in need. Obviously your background will be taken into consideration but, that said, there are so many ways we can approach the board. If you can give me ten minutes I'll go up and have a word with Mrs. Tilly, see if she can tell you the best way."

"I'll wait," Dolly said, becoming more confident by the second. As soon as the door closed behind Deirdre, Dolly inched round the desk and drew the telephone closer. She looked to the door a moment before she dialed.

* * *

Jimmy Donaldson was sitting with a mug of tea. It was almost twelve and there had not been any further contact from Dolly Rawlins. DI Palmer was sitting reading the morning paper. In the hall another officer sat on duty. Mrs. Donaldson was confused about what was going on, especially as she had had little time alone with her husband. Even when they slept, an officer sat outside their bedroom. Jimmy was nervous and twitchy, but said with a bit of luck he'd be home for good sooner than they had anticipated. The police told her to speak to no one, to remain at home and continue with her housework as if they weren't there, which was easier said than done. Right now she was preparing lunch in the kitchen, trying to pretend the house wasn't full of cops.

The phone rang and she turned from the sink. The door to the sitting room was closed, the officer in the hallway giving her a pleasant smile. With a sigh, she went back to making lunch.

In the sitting room, Palmer gave a brisk nod for Donaldson to pick up the phone as he slipped on his headphones to listen to the call.

"Jimmy? It's Dolly."

Jimmy looked nervously at Palmer who gestured for him to continue the call.

"Hello, Dolly. How are you?"

"I'm fine. I'd like to collect."

Palmer nodded and Donaldson hesitated. "Okay. When do you want to come over?"

"I won't come to your place, you bring them to me. You know Thorpe Park?"

"What?"

"It's a big amusement park. About four o'clock this afternoon. I'll see you there."

She hung up before Donaldson could reply. He sat looking at the receiver in his hand. Palmer swore, told him to hang up and then put a trace on the call.

"Have they found them yet?" Donaldson asked.

Palmer said nothing as he waited for the results of the trace. DCI Craigh came in as Palmer was jotting something down. He passed the note to Craigh. "She made contact from Aylesbury town hall, social services. She's asked for a meet. You want to hear the call?"

Craigh nodded. "What the hell is she doing at the town hall? She's moving fast, isn't she? We've still not found the stones. They're ripping his entire shop apart because it was so long ago he can't remember which wall he hid the stones behind."

"Shit."

"Yeah, well, we'll just have to stall her, or Jimmy will."

Palmer looked back to the closed door. "You think he's spinnin' yarns? If we've not found the ruddy diamonds maybe they're not there."

Craigh sighed. This wasn't working out the way he'd hoped. Now they'd have to drag Donaldson out to Thorpe Park, and they'd be screwed if they didn't find the stones by four o'clock.

"Look, see if you can get his wife shipped out—to a relative or something. I don't like her being around. Meanwhile I'll go and see what I can work up for the four o'clock meet. Why Thorpe Park?"

Palmer shrugged. "I dunno. She said it, then hung up."

Tommy Malin had worked until late the previous night and went straight back to it in the morning. He reset the stones one by one, using a lot of settings from a previous little job he'd done, only then they had contained some beautiful emeralds and diamonds. He had never been asked to make up a whole bag of glass before but he wasn't going to turn his nose up at an easy two grand cash. Audrey called to ask if they were ready and he said they'd be finished later on in the afternoon. He had some business to attend to at lunchtime.

"They're not ready yet," Audrey said to her son as he paced up and down the living room. "Has she called? Do you know if she's talked to Jimmy yet?"

"No, I'm going over there now. I'll come back later and pick them up. And for Chrissakes don't tell anyone about this."

"Who'd I tell? I've got the cash ready," Audrey said nervously.

Mike stared at her, his anger at what she had got him involved with still close to the surface. "Just get the stones, Mum, and as soon as you've got them, call me on my bleeper."

Mike walked out of the flat and hurried to his patrol car as his bleeper went off. When he managed to call in, he was instructed to meet DCI Craigh at the station and not, as he had previously been told, at Donaldson's house.

Mrs. Tilly looked over Dolly's forms. She then stacked them in a neat pile. "Well, I think you stand a good chance but you'll have to be interviewed by the board and have your details assessed. It will take time for us to give you a positive answer and you'll obviously require grants, which is another area where you'll need to be instructed. There are so many different sections and application forms."

Dolly was feeling good, her dream already turning into reality. Mrs. Tilly frowned as she reread the top form.

"Grange Manor House? It had a bad reputation, you know."

Dolly looked confused. "I'm sorry? I don't understand. It was a health farm, wasn't it?"

"It used to belong to an Ester Freeman. Oh, I'm going back maybe five or six years. It's been closed—I thought it had been demolished, to tell you the truth, not just because the motorway was built across the main access, but because it was such a scandal—"

"I'm sorry, I don't know what you mean," Dolly interrupted.

"Grange Manor House was run as a brothel. The police arrested, oh, fourteen women, I think. It was run by Ester Freeman. I think she went to prison." Suddenly Mrs. Tilly flushed. "Did you buy it from Miss Freeman?"

"No I did not," Dolly lied, her hands clenched tightly. "Thank you for all your help." She managed to keep a smile on her face but she was so angry she could have screamed. This was all she needed. Trying to open a foster home as an ex-prisoner was one hurdle to get over, but now she knew that the place had been run as a brothel any association with Ester would obviously go against her.

Dolly stormed out of the town hall. Ester was not waiting as she had promised. Dolly forced herself to remain calm. She'd have to get out of this, and fast. She'd do a bit of shopping, get the next train to London, collect the diamonds and do just as she had planned: buy a small terraced house near Holloway and screw that bitch Ester Freeman.

Ester faced the bank manager, a dapper little man with a faint blond mustache. He shuffled Ester's thick file of documents. The check from Mrs. Rawlins, he assured Ester, was cleared or would be soon as he had already contacted Mrs. Rawlins's bank, but this still left Ester three hundred thousand pounds in debt. She would be declared bankrupt unless she had means to cover the outstanding balance.

"But I've just paid in a check for two hundred thousand."

The manager nodded patiently. "Yes, I know, Miss Freeman, but the bank are holding the house as collateral for the outstanding monies. I cannot release the property deeds."

"Fine. Then I'll withdraw the check. The money is for the sale of the manor and you know that it won't get that price on the open market. You sell it and the bank'll lose out. This way, at least I've paid off some of it and I give you my word you'll get the rest within a few weeks."

He sighed. What she was saying made sense. "So, Miss Freeman, is this check from Mrs. Rawlins for the sale of the property?"

"Yes. That's why I've got to have the deeds returned to me. If you refuse, there will be no sale. You then have to put it on the market and—"

He interrupted, drawing back his chair, "Fine. I will, however, have to wait for the check to be cleared, Miss Freeman. That still leaves your balance over three hundred thousand pounds in the red, and unless this situation is rectified we have no alternative but to begin proceedings against you."

She leaned on his desk. "Give me just one more month—you'll get the money. I am waiting to be paid a considerable amount, more than enough to cover my overdraft."

Ester would have liked to scream at him "Try three million quid's worth of diamonds, you fuckin' little prat," but instead she smiled sweetly as he flipped through her bank statements.

"Well, we'll give it three weeks, Miss Freeman, but then—"

"You'll get me the deeds? Yes?"

He nodded. "Yes. I'm prepared to trust you, Miss Freeman."

"You won't regret it," she said softly, having no intention whatsoever of paying in another penny. She was going to skip the country and fast, just as soon as she laid her hands on Dolly Rawlins's diamonds.

Mike met up with DCI Craigh in the station corridor. "She only called from the Aylesbury social services and you won't believe where she's asked Donaldson to meet her."

"Oh, they find the diamonds?" Mike asked casually, knowing it was an impossibility.

Craigh shook his head. "I'm gonna need extra men, sort this out at the bloody theme park, and we'll get Donaldson wired up. He'll just have to stall her or get her to implicate herself. I'm beginning to wish we'd never started this whole thing."

Craigh had no idea just how much Mike wished he had never mentioned Dolly Rawlins's name, let alone the diamonds.

* * *

Gloria eased her way round the visitor tables, crowded with the wives and mothers, girlfriends, kids. It never ceased to amaze her how many women were always there every visiting day. Never as many men—they were all banged up like her old man.

Eddie Radford was staring at his folded hands, a glum expression on his Elvis Presley lookalike features. Eight years younger than Gloria, he'd never even bought an Elvis record but she had. She'd been a great fan and the first time she'd set eyes on Eddie she'd seen the similarity, with his slicked-back hair. If he'd had sideburns he'd have been the spitting image.

"You're bleedin' late," he muttered.

"I had to get a train, missed the tube, waited fifteen minutes."

"Oh shuddup. Every time you come I got to listen to a bleedin' travelogue of how you got here. You get me some fags?"

"Yes."

"Books? Any cash?"

"Yeah, in me left sleeve, can you feel it?"

Eddie leaned over and kissed her as he slipped his hand up her sleeve and palmed the money. "How much?"

"Sixty quid, and that's cleaned me out. I got to pick up me giro."

"Where've you been? I called the house three times." Eddie opened the cigarettes and lit one, looking around the room at the men and their visitors. The racket was deafening.

"The council have given me my marching orders for non-payment of rent."

"Oh, great! What you let them do that for?"

"Could be because I've not got any cash and that Mrs. Rheece downstairs is a bloody moron. She let them in, found that bloke kipping down and so they said I was sublettin'."

"What bloke?"

"You know, him with the squint, friend of your brother's. I asked him to leave an' all but he wouldn't. Pain in the arse, he is."

"So where've you been stayin'?"

"I'm near Aylesbury, with some friends. You don't know them, Eddie. I wish you wouldn't grill me every time I come, it gets on my nerves."

"Who you staying with then?"

She sighed. "Ester Freeman, you don't know her. She did time with me. Julia Lawson, she was also in Holloway, Kathleen O'Reilly, a stupid cow called Connie and—"

"Ester Freeman? They all tarts then, are they?"

"No, they're not. Dolly Rawlins, she's there."

"Oh yeah, Dolly Rawlins, yeah, I remember Harry. So what you all there for?"

"For God's sake, I needed a place to doss down, all right? So we're all sort of helping Dolly out until—"

"Until what?"

Gloria flushed. "I always get a headache in here. They should keep the kids to another section."

Eddie reached out and gripped her wrist. "I said, *what are you doing there*?"

She wrenched her wrist free and rubbed it. "Word is, she's got some diamonds stashed and we're, well, we're waiting for her to get them."

"And then what?"

She smiled. "Well, we want a cut and if she doesn't like it, we're gonna take it. But you keep your mouth shut about it."

"Who would I tell?" he said bitterly.

She touched his hand. "You'll have some nice things, I'll get you anything you want, Eddie."

He pulled his hand away. "Who's looking after my guns?"

Gloria looked round nervously, then leaned close to whisper, "They're still out in the coal hut. I ain't touched them."

Eddie closed his eyes. "Brilliant! You're not even at the fuckin' house, that idiot bloke is hanging around and I got thirty grand's worth of gear stashed out back. You fuckin' out of your mind, Gloria?"

"I don't want anythin' to do with them. I get picked up again and that's me for ten years, Eddie. It's too dangerous."

"You listen to me, slag, you move them out of that place. I'll get you a decent contact, you'll flog them when I say so, understand me? You move them, you do that, Gloria. Get the gear, stash it where you're staying with all the tarts, then I'll get my friends to contact you. Gimme the number there."

"I can't, the phone's not connected, Eddie, on my mother's life."

He swore and then the bell rang for the first section of visitors to move out. He gripped her hand tightly. "Just get them. Then next time you come I'll arrange for you to meet someone. You do it, Gloria, they're all I got left in the world, them and you, so I'm depending on you, understand me?"

He drew her toward him and they kissed. She always felt like crying when he did that but this afternoon she was too much on edge, having gone and told him about Dolly Rawlins. For a second she hoped he'd forgotten but he suddenly smiled. "And if that cow don't want to part with her diamonds, you got the gear to make her, haven't you? Use them, sweetheart. You get me some dough and we'll go abroad, have a nice holiday when I get out."

The officers were pointing for him to go back to the corridor outside and be returned to his cell.

"I love you, Eddie," she said softly.

"I should hope so, Gloria. Ta-ra, see you next week."

He smiled wryly as he walked after the prison officer. He'd got eighteen years and there he was talking about when they would go on a bloody holiday together. She'd be in a Zimmer frame by the time he got out.

Dolly paid off the taxi and carried her purchases inside the manor. Ester's Range Rover was nowhere to be seen. She went straight to her bedroom and sorted out what she would wear for the afternoon, then started to pack her few things. She would leave without a goodbye and then get the check stopped. She swore at herself: she should have done that as soon as she came home. Dolly headed down the stairs as Ester breezed in, waving a big brown envelope.

"Hi! They said you'd left when I went to the town hall so I did a grocery shop. Here you go, Dolly, the lease all signed, and now the place is really all yours."

"Oh, is it? Well, you can take it and stuff it. I don't want this place, I don't want anything to do with you and I'm gonna stop that check."

"What?"

Dolly glared at Ester. "You really did me in, didn't you? Never thought to mention this place was a brothel."

Ester tossed the envelope down. "You knew what I was."

"I didn't know you ran a whorehouse from here, though, did I?"

"All you had to do was ask."

"They all know about this place, they told me at the social services."

"So what?"

"This place has got such a bad reputation. What with that and my record, you think they'll give us the go-ahead?"

Dolly was about to walk back up the stairs when Ester yelled, "They'll be more likely to give you the go-ahead on a place like this that's crying out for kids than any terraced place in fucking Islington or Holloway—and they cost, Dolly. You've been away a long time, any house in that area's gonna cost you at least a hundred and fifty grand. Here you got beds, furniture, linen, all thrown in, but if you don't want it, then that's up to you . . ."

Julia walked out and leaned on the kitchen door. "She's right, you know, Dolly. This is a fabulous place for kids."

Dolly hesitated. Julia's soft voice seemed to calm her. "The orchard and the gardens, the pool doesn't need much doing to it, then you can even get a horse for the stables . . ."

Ester winked at Julia. "She's right, Dolly. I mean, each kid would bring in about two hundred a week. I'm right, aren't I, Julia?"

"Yep, and then you'd get grants to rebuild and convert . . ."

Dolly sat down on the stairs, more confused than ever. Ester glanced at her watch. All she needed was a few more hours for the check to go into the system then Dolly couldn't stop it.

Dolly frowned. "I got to go to London, let me think about it."

"You want a lift, do you? To the station?"

Dolly nodded, then got up and went to her room.

"By tomorrow the check will have gone through," Ester said quietly to Julia. "Where do you think she's going?"

"I don't know, do I?"

Ester pulled her into the kitchen. "What if she's going for the diamonds?" She thought for a moment. "You make some excuse, say you got to go to London as well, see where she goes and who she talks to."

"Oh, for Chrissakes, Ester, that's ridiculous. You mean follow her around?"

"What the hell do you think I mean?"

By the time Dolly came back downstairs, Julia was already sitting in the Range Rover.

"Julia's got to go and see her mother so she'll catch the train with you," Ester explained as Dolly followed her out.

"She's still being kept in the lap of luxury by her beloved daughter. She has no idea Julia was even picked up and put in the slammer, never mind that she was a junkie. Julia's been paying for her for years, she's in a wheelchair or somethin', so that's housekeepers and cleaners and . . . you name it. That's why Julia's broke."

As soon as Dolly got into the car, she started asking Julia about her mother. "She's very old, Dolly. I don't want her to know what a mess I've made of my life. It would devastate her."

"Where does she think you are, then?" Dolly asked.

"Well, when I was in Holloway I got friends to send postcards from Malta. She thought I was working over there with the Red Cross."

"And now?" Dolly asked.

"Well, since my release, I told her I've been looking for a new practice. She doesn't know I was struck off—she doesn't know anything about my life, really."

Dolly nodded and looked at her watch: she was going to be late for the meeting with Jimmy Donaldson. She didn't know how she was going to get all the way to the theme park on time. Well, if he left, he left. She'd just have to rearrange the meeting.

Connie had asked the cab driver to wait while she hurried into the mansion block. Lennie always left just before lunch, did the rounds of his girls, then checked his club for the previous night's takings. He would then come home, change and have something to eat. Connie usually cooked him a light meal before running his bath. He would change and leave the flat between eight and eight thirty in the evening, rarely returning until the early morning.

For Lennie his girls, his club, his Porsche and his well-furnished flat came before any love or relationship. Connie knew that now. She had been with him for three years, cooking, cleaning, keeping his flat spotless. Occasionally she went to the club and they dined out frequently, but then he had started knocking her around and a few times told her to be "very nice" to friends of his. When that became a regular weekly session, she knew that it was all over between them, she was no longer "special." He was getting ready for a change, as if she was part of the fixtures and fittings.

He had beaten her up so badly one night, breaking her nose, that he had arranged for her to have plastic surgery. She had her eyes done, her nose remodeled, a cheek implant and a breast implant. At first she had felt wonderful. He had visited her in the clinic and been kind to her when she came home in the bandages. She had believed he'd changed, that perhaps he really did care for her, but when the bandages came off and she admired herself in front of him as he lay in bed, he had said, lighting a cigarette, "Well, now, girl, you can make up the money, seven grand you owe. I reckon you've a few more years in you now so you're going to share with Carol and Leslie."

Connie couldn't believe it. They were two of his girls and he was moving her out and in with them, as if there had been nothing between them. "But,

Lennie, I want to try going straight. You know, get a proper agent and do some modeling."

He had laughed. "No way. You can earn more for me on your back than doing any bleedin' cereal advert . . ."

She hadn't said anything, hadn't argued back, afraid he'd maybe whack her. She had simply waited for him to leave at his usual time, then Ester had called her and said she would be free to come to the manor. She had packed fast and run off. Now Connie was back, she let herself in and went straight to the kitchen. She began unplugging all the movable stuff she could lay her hands on. She then went into the bedroom and cleared out her side of the wardrobe. At least she was alone; he hadn't moved anyone else in yet.

Lennie's portable phone was on the stand, recharging. She was so busy filling the suitcase that she didn't notice it. Lennie never went anywhere without his portable. At that moment he was swearing as he realized he'd forgotten to put it in his pocket, right now doing a U-turn and heading back to the flat to pick it up.

The cab driver watched the metallic blue Porsche park, and saw the dapper West Indian straighten his draped suit as he headed toward the mansion block. He went back to reading the *Sun*, after a quick look at the meter. The girl had said she'd be ten minutes but she'd already been gone that. He swore, wondering for a moment if she'd just done a Marquess of Blandford on him and wouldn't be coming out, but then he saw she had left a bag on the back seat.

Connie had filled two cases when she heard the front door slam and instantly backed away in terror. He kicked open the bedroom door and looked at her.

"Hello, Lennie," she said in a trembling voice. "I was just packing me gear."

"I can see that. You missed anything? Like the light fittings?"

"I've not taken anything that wasn't mine, Lennie."

"I gave you the cash for everything you're standing up in, sweetheart. Now what the fuck do you think you're doing and where've you been?"

"Near Aylesbury . . . with some friends." He came closer. "Don't hurt me, please don't."

He laughed. "Aylesbury? You kiddin'? Who you staying there with?"

"Dolly Rawlins, you don't know her, but listen, Lennie, I might be onto a good thing. She's got diamonds, a lot of diamonds and—" Connie panicked, trying anything to stop him coming closer, pressing herself against the wardrobe, bracing herself for what she knew was coming. She raised her hands in a feeble gesture. "Please don't hit me in the face, Lennie."

The cab driver saw the West Indian guy walk out quickly and roar off in his Porsche. Then Connie came out, waking unsteadily as she carried a suitcase. She was wearing dark glasses and a headscarf. He took the case from her. "You all right, love?"

"Take me to Marylebone Station, please," she said, getting into the back seat.

"Right, the station . . ." He looked at her in the mirror. She had a blood-soaked handkerchief pressed to her face. "You sure you're okay, love?"

"Yes, yes, I'm fine, thank you." She could feel the swelling coming up under her eyes. Her nose was bleeding, but she didn't think he'd broken it, though her neck was covered in dark red bruises. She thought he was going to kill her, and he had only stopped when she had pretended to be unconscious.

"Kathleen? *Kathleen?*" Ester shouted. Kathleen was on her bed. She'd had a few drinks earlier and was now sleeping it off. Ester barged into the room. "Didn't you hear me calling you?"

"What do you want?"

Ester shut the door. "I think she might be going for the diamonds today. Who do you know that we could trust to fence them?"

Kathleen lifted her head a little. "Well, it depends, doesn't it? I mean, they're still hot but I've got a few people I'd trust."

Ester was pacing up and down. "If they were valued at God knows how many million when they were nicked almost nine years ago, what do you reckon they're worth now?"

"Could be double, it all depends on the quality. Soon as I see them I'll be able to tell you the best man. When do you reckon that's going to be, Ester?"

"I think she's maybe doing something about them this afternoon."

Kathleen sat up, rubbing her head. "Well, shouldn't someone be with her?"

"Julia's on her, I hope."

"Have you told Dolly you know about them?"

Ester shook her head. "No. Let's just take it one step at a time."

"Fine by me, but she's such a wily old cow she might pick them up and that's the last we see of her."

"No, she'll be back. All her gear's still in her room."

"Ah, she might be back, but will she be bringin' back the diamonds?"

"I bloody hope so. And in the meantime, you just stop nicking the booze," she added, walking out.

Kathleen slowly got off the bed. She splashed her face with cold water then patted it dry. The photographs of her three daughters were on the dressing table, positioned so she could see them from her bed. They were the last thing she saw at night and the first in the morning: the nine-year-old twins, Kate and Mary, and five-year-old Sheena. They were in care, a convent home, but how long they would remain together Kathleen couldn't be sure. All she knew was that when she got the cut of the diamonds they were going home, all of them, going back to Dublin. She'd be safe, the cops wouldn't find her there. "You get the diamonds, Dolly, love," she whispered to herself. "Pray God you get them before the cops find me."

Kathleen, like every one of them, was in trouble. But Kathleen's problem was not some bloke out to make her a punchbag: a warrant was out for her arrest on two charges of check-card fraud. She had simply not turned up for the hearing and Ester's invitation to come to the manor not only gave her hope for a lot of cash, but also a safe place to hide.

Dolly finally found a taxi for the last stage of the journey to Thorpe Park, and Julia was right on her heels, grabbing the next cab in the rank.

At the theme park Julia concentrated on keeping Dolly in sight, keeping her distance until she saw Dolly heading toward the funfair section.

What Julia didn't know was that she wasn't the only one watching Dolly. Far from it. Unmarked patrol cars and plainclothes officers were positioned at each exit, while a moody Jimmy Donaldson sat in another one. They had arrived at three fifteen and he'd been in the car for over an hour and a half. They were all almost giving up when they got the contact. "Suspect has entered gate C, over."

Donaldson was wired up, instructed to move slowly, and told not to approach any of the officers. He would be monitored at all times. He was still fuming that they had not found the diamonds because it meant that some other bugger had, and he spent his time trying to think who could have shifted them. Only Audrey and Dolly had known where they were—and maybe his wife. Could she have moved them? He wished he'd never agreed to the whole thing. It would only be worth it if they got him transferred to a nice, cushy open prison. He'd be safe there. It was, after all, nearly nine bloody years ago, and there'd been renovations in his back yard, so some bastard could have come across the diamonds, he supposed. Dolly Rawlins was a hard-nosed cow but, without her old man, just how much of a threat could she be? It was Harry who had had enough on him to put him behind bars for years. And now he was dead. On the other hand, Dolly was the one who had shot him, so she might decide to have a pop at him, too. Jimmy Donaldson was not a happy man, and getting more and more pissed off by the minute.

DCI Craigh beckoned him out of the car, pressing his earpiece into his ear, listening. "Okay, Jimmy. She moved to the hoopla stand or something, so you start walking in by gate B, the one closest to us. Just act nice and casual, and don't keep looking round. Off you go."

Donaldson shook his head. "She's not gonna like it, me not having them with me."

Craigh sighed. None of them liked it, but they couldn't do anything about it. "Just do the business. Tell her to meet you back at your place, it was unsafe to bring them here—tell her anything."

"This is entrapment, you know," Donaldson whined.

"You fuckin' do the business, Jimmy, or you'll be trapped all right, and for longer than you got in the first place."

He moved off with a scowl. When he got to the hoopla stand he couldn't see Dolly so he went over to the shooting arcade and handed over two quid for three shots. "Let her find me," he said to himself as he took aim. "Let her bloody find me."

Dolly walked casually around, enjoying the stands, marveling at the amazing rides. It was all beyond anything they had when she was a kid, and it all cost a hell of a lot more, too. She fingered the hoops, fifty pence a throw. In her day it had been threepence but she paid over her money and took aim with the wooden hoop.

"Rawlins is at the hoopla stand. She's throwing hoops now." Palmer wandered past, not even looking at Dolly as she threw her third hoop and was presented with a goldfish in a plastic bag. As she reached for the fish, she caught sight of Julia, hovering at another stand. She did a double-take.

Julia sighed. No matter how hard she tried to stay in the background she was so tall she stuck out like a sore thumb. As Dolly walked toward her, she smiled weakly.

"Hello, Julia. You just won yourself a prize," said Dolly, handing over the bag. "Here, take it back to the manor." As Julia took the goldfish bag, Dolly looked up at her. "So why you following me?"

"Ester told me to."

"Oh, I see, and what she tells you to do, you do, right?"

"Yeah. Well, now you've caught me at it, I'll push off."

"You do that, love. I'm only here for a bit of fun."

Julia couldn't help but smile but Dolly remained poker-faced, watching the tall woman as she threaded her way out of the area. Dolly was piecing it all together: they were definitely after her diamonds. Well, they were going to be in for a shock. As soon as she had them, she would be on her way and they could all rot in hell as far as she was concerned. Apart from Angela: she liked that little kid.

Dolly wondered if she'd missed Jimmy Donaldson—maybe he'd got tired of waiting.

"She's looking around now, handed a fish to a woman who's walked out. Should be coming through exit E. Check her out."

Julia made her way to the courtesy bus stop, thinking she would go and see her mother. It had been a long time.

Dolly finally spotted Donaldson and walked off in the opposite direction toward a Ferris wheel.

"I think she saw him but she's walked off, straight past him. Now at the Ferris wheel. She's talking to the boy on the ticket box."

Dolly smiled at the spotty young kid and slipped him a tenner. "I'll be back for a ride in a bit and you'll get another tenner if you make sure I get a nice view from the top of the wheel. Say about five minutes' worth of view, all right, love?"

He grinned. It was not unusual to get requests like that, and for twenty quid, why not? He watched as she strolled back into the crowd.

Donaldson had another three shots. On his last he got a bull's-eye and the stall owner begrudgingly handed over a stuffed white rabbit. He turned to see Dolly standing directly in front of him.

"Okay, they're together. He's just won a white rabbit so we can't miss them. He's walking off with her to the other stands."

"You're looking well, Dolly. Long time no see."

"I am well, Jimmy, very well. How's your wife?"

"Oh, she's her usual. Gone to see her sister in Brighton."

"That's nice for her. Would you like a ride?"

He looked at the Ferris wheel. "No. Can't stand those things."

"Oh, come on, it'll be fun. Might as well enjoy ourselves now we're here. I saw an article saying Princess Diana brings the princes here. Did you know that?"

He nodded. "That's the big theme rides over the other side. This is just the fairground. It's not part of the main park."

"I fancied that water ride, down a chute. I saw it in the paper. Never mind, we'll make do with this."

Dolly winked at the spotty boy and slipped him another tenner. He unbuckled the seat bar and helped her sit down.

"Dolly, I've not got a head for heights."

"Oh, get in, Jimmy, I want to see the view."

Donaldson was ushered into the seat and locked into his safety harness; below, the static interference was breaking up on the radios. Jimmy's and Dolly's voices were coming and going with a crackle and a buzz.

"They're on the Ferris wheel," an officer said into his radio.

"We can see that," DCI Craigh muttered back. They could hear them too, just about, but so far not one word about the diamonds. Mike was in the car, listening on the radio, clocking the time, wondering if his mother had picked up the fakes yet, getting more and more agitated. He hadn't even seen Dolly Rawlins yet, and he didn't know how he'd deal with it if he did.

"They're on the ride," crackled his radio.

Mike pushed his earpiece further into his ear, wincing as the static caused by the steel girders on the Ferris wheel deafened him.

Donaldson clung to the safety bar as the wheel turned slowly. "There's nobody else getting on," he panted.

"Oh, there will be," she said, smiling.

"Why are they doing it so slowly?" he gasped as they inched higher.

"They got to allow for the punters to get on. So, have you got them for me?"

She said it so casually, he felt even sicker. "Er, not with me, it's too dangerous."

She stared ahead, and the wheel turned higher until they were almost at the top.

"You've not got them at all, is that right?"

"Yes—no—I've got them but not on me. You crazy? I couldn't carry them around . . . Oh, oh, holy shit, is this bleedin' thing safe?"

They remained poised at the top of the wheel and Dolly leaned forward, looking around at the views. "Isn't it lovely, Jimmy?"

"No, I'm gonna be sick."

She faced him, her eyes hard. "You will be sick, Jimmy, if you're trying it on. Are you trying it on with me, Jimmy?"

"No, no, I swear. Listen, is there an alarm? I'm feeling sick, really I am. I hate swings, I hate heights, I'm dying, Dolly."

She pushed at the seat with her feet. It swung backward and forward. "Where are they?"

"*At home! I got them at home!*" He was shaking in terror, his knuckles white from gripping the safety bar.

She looked down, waving to the boy, and the wheel began to move down. "I'll come for them tomorrow, then. I'll call you."

"All right, all right, anythin' you say . . ."

She nodded, and then leaned closer. "Life is too short to mess around. You won't mess with me, will you, Jimmy? I've been waiting eight years."

"Yeah, well, I got to get a good fence. I mean, you're talking millions so you'll need the very best."

"No, love, you don't need to get anything but what belongs to me. I'll do the rest and then you'll get your cut."

DCI Craigh was ripping his hair out. They still hadn't mentioned the word "diamonds." "Jesus Christ, say it, woman, *say* it."

Dolly left a white-faced Jimmy Donaldson leaning against the fence, throwing up, as she went out of the exit, carrying the white rabbit. They could follow her all day, but she hadn't said the word "diamonds," and neither had the stupid bastard Jimmy Donaldson.

Julia arrived at the station and put in a call to Ester, who instantly went into a screaming fit. Julia yelled back, saying she should have followed Dolly herself. "I'm going to see my mother, okay?" Then she slammed down the phone, picked up the bag with the goldfish and walked onto the platform to wait for the train. She wished she'd never agreed to the Dolly Rawlins business. She wished she'd never met Ester, she wished she hadn't fucked herself up so badly, she wished she could start her life over again. She was such an idiot, such a stupid bitch to have got herself into such a mess.

It was after eight by the time Gloria arrived at her old place, which looked even more rundown in the dark. Mrs. Rheece was coming out of the front door. Gloria ran up the path. "Mrs. Rheece, it's me, Gloria Radford. I just come to pick up my stuff. Is that okay?"

"You can do what you like, no business of mine. I don't give a shit what anyone does. The council have been round askin' after you and that bloke was here last night again, the one with the squint. I said to him you wasn't here and he was fuckin' abusive."

"Oh, I'm sorry. You tell him to sod off the next time."

"There won't be a next time, Mrs. Radford, 'cos I'll call the law on him."

The old woman went off with her shopping trolley down the road, still muttering to herself about the council, as Gloria slipped round the back of the house to the old coal hut. It had been used as a bike shed, and rubbish bins were stacked up inside and out. She shone a torch round and began to move aside all the junk, swearing as she ripped her tights in the process. She squeezed her way into the back of the hut and then eased away some old wooden boards. Scared of being disturbed, she switched off the torch and fumbled around in the inky darkness. Soon she felt the big canvas bag and began to heave with all her might. It was very heavy, but she finally managed to drag it out. She went back for two more bags before she shut the coal-hut door. She dragged each bag out to the Mini Traveller and hauled it inside, terrified that someone would see her. Then she went up into her old flat, washed her hands and face, and collected a suitcase full of clothes.

She drove slowly, frightened of every passing police car. She knew that if she was stopped and the car was searched, she'd be arrested. Eddie's stash, Eddie's retirement money, was all in the back of the Mini: thirty thousand pounds' worth of weapons.

She got onto the motorway toward Aylesbury, her hands gripping the wheel tightly, her whole body tense. "Please God, nobody stop me, please God, don't break down, please God, let me get to the manor."

Ester heard the front door slam and looked over the banisters. Connie, still wearing her dark glasses and headscarf, was dragging in her case.

"Where the hell have you been all day?"

"I need a fiver for the taxi, Ester."

Ester thudded down the stairs. "I'm not a bloody charity, you know. I paid for everyone's taxi yesterday." Ester stopped in her tracks as she saw Connie's face. "What the hell happened to you?"

Audrey was in a right state. She had twice paged Mike on his mobile and he'd not returned her call. She now had the fake diamonds from Tommy and just having them in the flat made her freak. She kept on opening the pouch and looking at them. She'd never seen the original diamonds properly, but Jimmy had seen right away they were in gold or platinum settings, some from around 1920. She closed the pouch up again, and stood over the telephone. "Ring, come on, ring me. I've got them, I've got them."

Mike didn't call until after ten, saying he was just coming off duty and he'd come round to collect them. As he put the phone down, Angela paged him. He arranged to meet her outside Edgware Road tube station, then called his wife to tell her he would be late home. He had just finished the call when DCI Craigh wandered over to his desk.

"We've got Donaldson back at his place. He says that maybe we should take him over to his shop, maybe they've not been looking in the right place. I said to him, 'You drew the map, Jimmy, we're looking just where you told us to look.'" Jimmy got very evasive and described in detail how he'd removed the bricks from one of the walls, scraped out the cement and stuffed the jewelry bag inside. He replaced the bricks and cemented them in.

Mike could feel the sweat trickle under his armpits. "You want me to go over there and have a look?"

Craigh rubbed his nose. "Yeah, okay, I'm taking myself off home. We've been over all the tapes from the fairground. Useless. They could have been talking about anything. He's a smart-arsed prick, you know, Donaldson."

Mike nodded. "Yeah, well, we know what she meant though, don't we?"

"Yeah, we know, but it wouldn't stand up in court. Still, we'll see what we get tomorrow—she's calling him again then."

Mike put his coat on. It was another hour, sitting in traffic, before he picked up Angela. She told him as far as she knew the women were all still together at the manor; Dolly had bought it from Ester, paid her by check. She hadn't heard any mention of diamonds but they were all edgy, especially Ester.

Mike paid her a tenner. She wanted him to take her out for a burger, but he said he didn't have the time. "When will I see you again, then?" she asked him.

Mike cleared his throat. "Soon as I get some free time. It's getting a bit heavy with Susan right now—she's asking a lot of questions about where I am. We just have to cool it for a bit."

She started to sniffle and he hugged her. "Come on, now, don't start. I've got to be on duty in half an hour."

"You just used me."

He turned away from her. "I'm sorry if it feels that way but you knew I was married right from the start, Angela, I got kids."

She sniffed again and opened the car door. "All the same, you used me, Mike. I give you all that information and you can't spare ten minutes for me. How do you think that makes me feel?"

"Look, let me get this Rawlins business sorted, then I promise I'll call you, okay?"

He reached over and squeezed her hand and she watched as he drove off. She felt cheated but also slightly guilty. Mrs. Rawlins had seemed quite nice, not like the others. She hunched her shoulders and went back into the tube station, heading for her mother's place.

Audrey showed Mike the fake diamonds. "Two grand, I paid. Tommy's a real professional. What do you think?"

Mike was tired out. He stuffed the bag into his pocket without looking inside it. "Okay. Now you should get packed and out of here as soon as you can. I'll stash these tonight."

"Did she meet up with Jimmy, then, today?"

"Yeah, but they played games."

"She's clever, Mike. Don't trust her."

He looked at his mother. "You mean like I trusted you?"

"How can you say that? You know why I did it! You *know* why!"

He pursed his lips. "You did it for the money so don't give me the sob story about Shirley because it won't wash anymore. I'm doing this tonight and then that's it, you hear me? I want you out of here, out of my life."

"You don't mean that, do you?"

"Yes, I do."

"But the villa! You and the kids can come for holidays."

"No, Mum, I don't want to know about the fucking villa. You got it, you stay in it. Now pack your bags."

Audrey burst into tears and started talking about how she had every right to do what she did, how Dolly had killed Shirley. Mike couldn't take any more.

"You lost that baby because you downed a bottle of gin every night, so don't give me that crap. I'm only doing this for Shirley and I never want to see you again."

He ran down the stone steps, his mother's screeching voice in his ear, and he hated her. At that moment, he even hated his sister. But there was one person he hated even more. If he was caught replacing the stones at Jimmy Donaldson's antique shop he'd be arrested and it would all be Dolly Rawlins's fault!

Crashing the gears, he sped off down the road, the pouch of fake diamonds feeling like a red-hot coal in his jacket pocket.

CHAPTER 5

Julia kissed her mother's soft powdery cheek and then stepped back, holding up the goldfish. "I got you a present."

Mrs. Lawson smiled, gently stroking Bates the cat, who eyed the bag hungrily. "Well, I'll have my work cut out watching Bates to make sure he doesn't eat it."

"We used to have a fish bowl somewhere, didn't we? I remember it." Julia searched in the kitchen and eventually found it, filled it with water and tipped in the fish. Then she carried it into the drawing room. Her mother was still stroking Bates, sitting in her wheelchair, a cashmere shawl wrapped round her knees. The room was oppressively hot, the gas fire turned on full.

"So, how are you?" Julia said as she sat down, peeling off her sweater.

"Oh, Mrs. Dowey takes good care of me and her husband still looks after the garden."

Julia could think of nothing to say so she got up and looked over a stack of bills placed in a wooden tea-caddy on the sideboard. "Are these for me?"

"Yes, dear. I was going to send them to your accountant as I always do, but as you're here . . ."

They were the usual telephone, gas and electricity bills, Mrs. Dowey's and her husband's wages, and bills for repairs and maintenance to the house. Julia even paid for the groceries.

"You know, dear, if this is too much for you . . ."

Julia turned the wheelchair round to face her. "If it was I'd say so. Besides, who else have I got to look after?"

"I always hope you'll meet someone nice, marry and settle down. It would be nice to have a grandchild before I die."

Julia smiled, touching her mother's wrinkled hand. "I am trying, Mother, but you know my job—it's always taken precedence over my personal life."

"You look very well, dear." Mrs. Lawson smiled, changing the subject. "Will you be staying tonight?"

"No, sadly I can't. I've got surgery this evening."

"Ah, yes, of course. Perhaps a cup of tea?"

Julia nodded and stood up. She was so tall that the low ceiling felt as if it was pressing on her head. "I'll put the kettle on."

"That would be nice, dear, thank you."

Julia stood at the window, wanting to cry. Everything was exactly as she remembered it. Nothing had changed for years. Only her mother had got older and more frail, her voice light and quavery. It always seemed so strange that her mother never noticed how different she was. Couldn't she tell?

"I'll make the tea." Julia left the room and Mrs. Lawson turned to stare at the solitary goldfish swimming round and round in the empty glass bowl.

"We should get some green things for the fish, shouldn't we, Bates? He seems very lonely."

Mrs. Lawson continued to stare as if hypnotized while the fish went round and round. "Poor little soul," she whispered.

Angela let herself in, hating the smell that always hung in the air—babies' vomit and urine. "I'm back, Mum," she yelled, dropping her bag.

Mrs. Dunn was making a half-hearted attempt to iron, feed the two kids and cook all at once. Everything about her looked tired—her face, her hair, her clothes and, worst of all, her eyes. They seemed devoid of any expression.

"Where've you been?" It came out as a single sigh, the iron thudding over the drip-dry shirt that always creased.

"Working."

Mrs. Dunn thumped the iron back on its stand. She pulled more semi-damp clothes from the wooden rail, tossed them into an already laden basket, switched off a steaming kettle and took an empty Mars Bar paper out of her youngest son's mouth, all in one slow, tired swing.

"Here's a tenner for you."

"Put it in the tin on the sideboard. Eric's going crazy—you don't pay any rent or anything toward the food, we don't know where you are, when you're coming in, you treat this place like it was a hotel. There's been call after call for you."

"Who from?"

"I don't know, that girl Sherry? John at the ice rink? I'm not your social secretary. Where've you been?"

Angela sat down, kicking her heels against the table leg. "Ester Freeman gimme a job for a night—*just* waitressin'."

Mrs. Dunn moved slowly back to the ironing. "I've told you not to mix with her, she's no good, she'll have you on the game next. Eric said he wouldn't be surprised if you're not on it anyway."

"Eric would know, wouldn't he? He's a pest, a dirty-minded, two-faced shit. This is your house and he has no right to ask me to pay rent in it."

"He does if he's paying the bills, love, and he is. And don't speak about him like that."

"He's not my dad."

"No, he isn't, thank Christ, or we'd have no roof over our heads. Eric's taken you on."

Angela snorted, looking around the dank kitchen. "Yeah, I'm sure. This is a dump, it always was, and it's got worse over the years. You should complain to the council—you got every right, you know. There's empty flats either side, they're moving everyone else round here. You'd be up for a new place, five kids, no husband."

Mrs. Dunn banged down the iron. "Now, don't start. Just because you've got nothing in your life you got to have a go at me! Well, just stop it or you're out on your ear."

Angela sighed. She hated being home—hated everything about it—even more since Eric had taken over as "man of the house." He was half her mother's age and constantly made moves on Angela, but her mother refused to believe it, fearful that if Eric was confronted he would walk out on her.

"So, where have you been?"

"I just told you. You don't listen to what I say. I went to Aylesbury."

"Oh, yes, Ester Freeman." Mrs. Dunn suddenly sagged into a chair. "Don't go back to working for her, Angela, she's no good. I just don't know what to do about you, I really don't."

Angela got up and slipped her arms around her mother. "Mum, I've got a boyfriend, I was sort of working for him in a way. He's asked me to go and live with him. He's got a nice house and—"

"Oh, just stop it, Angela, you make up stories all the time. What man is this now? That copper?"

Mrs. Dunn put her head in her hands. "I don't know what to do with you. You won't go back to school, you got no qualifications. How you gonna get a job with no qualifications? You tell me that."

Angela stuck out her lower lip. Since she'd been picked up after the bust at Ester's, she'd had a string of part-time jobs. Nothing kept her interested for more than a few weeks and the pay was bad in all of them. She'd been a waitress, a barmaid, a clerk, a trainee at two hair salons, part-time sales girl in numerous boutiques and she'd even helped out a few market-stall owners at Camden Lock. But in reality she was just drifting around and she knew it. She didn't know how to stop it and she'd hoped Mike would help her—but he just fucked her, like everyone else.

"I dunno what to do, Mum. Nothin' seems to work out for me."

Mrs. Dunn kissed her daughter. She was such a pretty girl: her thick hair hung in a marvelous Afro spiral cascade and she was a pale tawny color with big, wide, amber eyes. "I want you to go and talk to your old teachers, see what they say, maybe get on some government training course. You can't just live your life wanderin' from one part-time job to another, you got to have a purpose."

"You mean like you?" Angela said sarcastically, and saw the pain flash across her mother's face.

"No, what I don't want is for you to have a life like mine, I wouldn't want it for my worst enemy."

Angela started to cry. She just felt so screwed up, with nothing in the future. She knew Mike didn't want to see her anymore—he hadn't for a while now. "I'll go and see them tomorrow, okay?"

Mrs. Dunn smiled and suddenly all the tiredness evaporated. "Just stay away from Ester, that woman's a bad influence."

Angela nodded and went upstairs. She packed her bag, stuffing anything that came to hand into it. She'd had enough; there was nothing to do but leave. She heard Eric come in and start shouting and yelling at her mother in the kitchen, so she never even said goodbye.

She had no place to go, so she called Mike at home but his wife answered and she put the phone down. She had no place to go but back to the Grange. She just needed somewhere to stay until she sorted herself out. Maybe when she told Mike he would help her, find a job for her. Then she'd come back to London.

By the time Dolly returned it was after eleven and she was still carrying the white rabbit. Ester had seen Dolly's arrival from the bedroom window and was waiting in the hall.

"Did you have a nice day?"

"Didn't Julia tell you? Here, she got the fish, you get the rabbit." Dolly threw the fluffy toy at her and walked slowly up the stairs as Connie wandered out of the kitchen.

"I got some stew on."

Dolly looked at her. She had cotton wool stuffed up her swollen nose, both eyes were black and she was crying. "What the hell happened to you?"

Connie sniveled and went back into the kitchen just as Kathleen was coming down the stairs. "Boyfriend, if you can call him that, whacked her one."

Kathleen passed Dolly, raising an eyebrow at Ester. "Nice bunny. Where'd you get it?"

Dolly washed her face and hands. She heard the doorbell ring and went downstairs, thinking it must be Julia. Ester came hurrying out from the kitchen. "I'll get it. You go on in and sit down and have your dinner, Dolly." She pulled open the front door to see Angela huddled on the doorstep.

"What do you want?" Ester snapped.

"Oh, please, Ester, I've had to leave me mum's house and I had no other place to go."

"Well, you can't stay here."

Dolly walked further down into the hall. "What's this?"

"It's Angela. I said we don't want her here."

"Well, she can't go back at this hour. Let her in, we've got enough room."

Ester stepped aside. "Thank you very much, Mrs. Rawlins," Angela said, giving Ester a superior look.

"There's some stew on so put your bag in a room and come into the kitchen," Dolly said, smiling. She headed into the kitchen.

Julia was already sitting at the table, helping a still tearful Connie serve up the stew, when Gloria banged in from the back yard. She went straight to wash her hands. "I brought me gear from the house."

Dolly cleared her throat. "Right. Things have changed since last night. I'm not taking on this house. I'm sorry, but I've had time to think and I reckon it'll be too expensive to do up, so I'm going back to my original plan and opening up a smaller place back in town." She placed her knife and fork together.

"You should have told me this morning, Dolly," Ester said.

"I'm telling you now. I want my money back, Ester."

"Well, if you'd told me this morning that might have been possible but you're too late now. I put it in the bank."

"You can take it out again, can't you?"

"No. I'm bankrupt. I've still got about three hundred grand to pay off, and they won't cash a check for a tenner right now." Ester looked dutifully crestfallen and her voice took on an apologetic tone. "I'm really sorry, Dolly. Like I said, you should have told me this morning."

Dolly's face tightened. "If you'd told me you were bankrupt I'd never have walked out without getting my money."

"But you did and now there's nothing I can do about it. The house is yours, Dolly, lock, stock and barrel."

Dolly pursed her lips. "You really stitched me up, didn't you, Ester? I really walked into this one, didn't I?"

"With your eyes open, Dolly, I never pushed you. I told you to think about it, if you recall. Now there's nothing I can do. But we're all here, we can all lend a hand, get this place up and rolling."

Dolly clenched her hands. "You any idea how much this will cost to get fixed up?"

"No, but we can start getting estimates in tomorrow. Local builders are cheaper than up in London."

"And how do I pay them?" Dolly said quietly.

Ester flicked a look at Julia. "Well, they give you grants, don't they? Unless you've got more dough stashed away."

Dolly got up and fetched a glass. "Any wine left from last night?"

Ester sent Angela to get a bottle from the dining room. All the women were looking at Ester, then back to Dolly as if at a tennis match.

Dolly went into the drawing room, where Angela was at the desk, reading a stack of newspaper cuttings. When she saw Dolly, she tried to stuff them back into the drawer. "I couldn't find any wine, Mrs. Rawlins."

"It wouldn't be in a drawer, would it, love?" She pushed past Angela and opened the drawer as Angela backed away from her. She flicked through the cuttings, headlines about the murder of her husband, headlines about the shooting of Shirley Miller—and the diamond raid, then folded them and picked up her handbag.

"What you staring at me like that for?" she demanded.

Angela stuttered, "I'm not, I just—just didn't know about all that."

"What? That I'd been in prison? You knew, they all know. Now go and get the bottle. Try the dining room, dear."

Angela scuttled out, and Dolly, taking a deep breath, walked back into the kitchen. The room fell silent.

Angela uncorked the wine as Dolly sat waiting, her hands clenched over her handbag. As soon as the wine was poured, Ester lifted her glass. "Well, here's to the Grange Foster Home." Dolly took only a small mouthful before she put her glass down.

"Isn't it about time you all cut the pretense and came clean?"

"About what, Dolly?" Ester asked innocently.

"Why you're all here," Dolly replied calmly.

Again they looked at Ester to take the lead. She smiled sweetly. "You know why. We were all at a bit of a loose end and thought it would be nice, you know, to have a little welcome-out party, that's all. As it turned out, you bought the place."

"No other reason?" said Dolly.

"I don't know what you mean, Dolly," Gloria said.

"Don't you?" Dolly threw the newspaper cuttings onto the table. "Not too clever leaving them lying around, was it? That's why you're all here. That's what you're all after, isn't it?"

"The diamonds?" Connie asked, and received a kick under the table from Ester.

"Yes. The bloody diamonds." Dolly rarely swore.

Mike drew up outside Jimmy Donaldson's rundown antique shop. The lights were on and a patrol car was parked outside. He patted his pocket, felt the pouch, and walked into the shop.

Arc-lights were turned on and three uniformed officers were searching the place. It was a tough job as furniture, junk and bric-a-brac were crowded into every inch of the shop space. An officer looked up at Mike as he entered. "There's another floor even more stuffed than down here, plus a back yard crammed full, and an outside lav."

"You not found them, then?" Mike asked.

"No. According to Donaldson, they were hidden behind a wall. Well, we've nearly had the place come down on us, we've pulled out so many bricks, but we've come to the conclusion he's playing silly buggers."

Mike eased his way round a Victorian washstand. "Well, carry on. I was just passing so I'll give you a hand for an hour or so."

The officer nodded. "You want a cup of tea? We're about to brew up out back."

"Yeah, milk, one sugar."

Left alone, Mike looked round the shop. He could see the wall where they had been removing bricks and he inched toward it. He had to be fast as the men were within yards of him. He pulled back two bricks and stuffed in the pouch, then shoved the bricks back into place. When the officer returned with two mugs of tea, Mike was standing by the opposite wall. He was inspecting the brickwork. "Go over every inch of all the walls again. Donaldson is still insisting it's behind the brickwork."

Mike stayed for another half-hour, helping move furniture around but keeping well away from where he had stashed the pouch, concentrating on the opposite wall. As he left, he suggested they stay at it.

He got home after twelve. His wife was already in bed and when he got in beside her, she didn't move.

"You awake?"

"Yes."

"Sorry I'm so late. It's this bloke we brought out of the nick, taking up a lot of extra time."

"Phone call for you."

"Oh yeah, who?"

"I don't know. She put the phone down."

Susan turned to face him. He sighed. "If whoever it was put the phone down, how do you know it was a she?"

"I can tell. And that's what I'm asking you to do, Mike. Tell me if there's somebody else, just tell me."

"There isn't, Sue, honestly, there's no one. This is starting to get on my nerves, you know."

She turned over again, and lay awake for about ten minutes, crying silently, until she couldn't stand it any longer and turned back to him, but he was fast asleep. She'd been through his pockets earlier and this time she'd found a crumpled half-page torn from an old diary. There was a phone number and a name. Angela. She'd called the number, asked to speak to Angela, but a woman had said she no longer lived there, had no idea where she was, and slammed down the receiver. Susan realized she should have said that the girl on the phone had said her name was Angela. She punched the pillow. Nothing in the world was worse than lying next to someone who was sleeping soundly, when you couldn't. She lay on her back and stared at the ceiling with tears in her eyes.

The bottle was empty. The women sat listening to Dolly as she twisted the wine glass round by the stem. "There were the four of us, all widows, Linda Pirelli, Bella, Shirley Miller and me. They're all dead."

Angela stared. She knew the name Shirley Miller, knew it very well, because Mike was always talking about her: his sister.

"Anyway, when it was over, I knew it would be just a matter of time before they picked me up so I left the stones with a friend of mine, someone I knew I could trust."

"You left them with someone for eight years?" Ester asked uneasily.

"Yes, but, like I said, I knew he wouldn't try anything because I had so much on him. Well, my husband did."

"Harry," Gloria said eagerly.

"You've read about him, have you?" Dolly looked at the old newspaper cuttings, the photocopies. One had his face on the front page: "Harry Rawlins Murdered," screamed the headline. "I know what I did was wrong," Dolly said softly. "I killed him. And I paid the price. And probably I'm the only person who still mourns him. I always will. In some ways I tried to be him, before I knew what he'd done to me, before I knew he had a cheap little tart of a girlfriend, before I knew she'd had his kid. I tried to be him, keeping him alive inside me, but the laugh was on me because he really was alive."

No one spoke, watching and listening intently as Dolly bared her soul.

"I'm serious about putting something back into society. He just took, for years and years, and I want to make up for it. I really do want to open a foster home . . . I want to have a purpose for the rest of my life."

Ester nodded. "Yeah, well, we all agree it's a great idea, and I know you may regret buying this place now, but when you've done it up, Dolly, think how many kids you can give a place to."

Dolly sighed. "Yeah, it's just the finances, isn't it? And that's what I'm going to use the diamonds for. Now, if any of you have any thoughts about getting a cut, then let me tell you, you've not got a hope in hell. They are mine, all mine, and I'll need every penny."

"But we know that. All we're doing is offering to help you run this place," Ester said warmly. The other women muttered in agreement.

Julia leaned forward. "Will you need any help in getting the diamonds back from this guy? Any help fencing them? Surely we can help you there."

"For what? A cut?" Dolly asked.

"Hell, no, just to show you how we all feel," Ester said, beaming. She could almost feel the money in her hands, she was so close.

Dolly leaned back. "Well, maybe I will need some help. I've been away a long time, and I'm not sure who to fence them to."

Kathleen received a nudge beneath the table. "Eh, Dolly, leave that to me, I know the best. You get them and we'll soon have them sorted out, and cash in your hand. How much you reckon they're worth?"

Dolly paused before she answered. "Maybe three and a half million . . . I doubt if I'll see more than one, maybe one and a quarter back."

There was a lot of murmuring and quiet sneaky looks as they each suddenly felt rich. Then Dolly stood up. "I'm collecting them tomorrow so we'll soon see what the value is. Now I'm off to bed, maybe just have a walk around. Goodnight."

They all chorused goodnight, as Dolly fetched her coat, refusing everyone's offer to join her.

As soon as the door closed behind her, Ester put out her hand. "Put it there. What did I tell you?"

A few slapped Ester's hand, but Julia rocked in her chair. "She doesn't seem eager to give us a cut, Ester. Maybe you're starting to celebrate a bit too early."

Ester gazed at her. "She brings them here and we don't get a cut, we don't wait for her to fence them, we simply take them! Agreed?"

They all nodded. They seemed to have forgotten Angela who had not said a word throughout. Ester reached out to prod her. "You just got lucky, darlin', but open your mouth to her about this and you'll be sorry, very sorry."

Angela hunched her shoulders. "I won't say anything to anyone." But her mind was buzzing. Mike would definitely talk to her if she told him about the diamonds.

Ester pulled back her bedroom curtains an inch, the room in darkness. "She's still out there, Julia, looking at the house, as if she's checking us out."

"Try just checking out what you lumbered her with," Julia drawled from the bed.

Ester jumped on the bed, crawling toward Julia on her hands and knees.

"Can I ask you something?" Julia said as Ester nuzzled her neck. "Would you kill her for them?"

Ester lay back against the pillows. "No. Let me ask *you* something. If she caught us taking them, do you think Dolly would kill us?"

Julia thought for a moment and then said, very quietly, "I'm sure of it."

Dolly paced round the garden. The night was chilly and she was cold, but she didn't want to go inside. It was talking about him; it brought it all back.

She walked slowly toward the swimming pool: the dank, dark water made her remember even more clearly. The way he smiled at her, waiting there by the lake. She would never forget the look of utter surprise on his face when she brought out the gun and fired: a half-mocking smile, then that moment of fear. And then he was dead, his body falling backward into the water.

She rubbed her arms, turning back to the house. She was going to make her dream come true, on a bigger scale than she had ever hoped for—with or without that bunch of slags.

CHAPTER 6

Dolly was up at six. She went through the *Yellow Pages* and earmarked the local building companies. She couldn't wait to get started. At nine, she had Angela sitting at the reception desk, calling all the companies and asking for them to come and give estimates. She gave the women orders to list what they felt needed to be done in different parts of the house, and they all went about the delegated duties with a zest and energy that sparkled like the diamonds they all expected to get a slice of.

By ten o'clock, the drive was filled with an odd assortment of trucks as builders arrived and started looking over the house, all vying with each other to win the business. Mrs. Rawlins wanted an immediate verbal estimate, and she wanted the work to start immediately, that afternoon if possible.

Dolly felt more alive than she had for years. She drove into the village in Gloria's Mini and bought provisions, wellington boots, sweaters and jeans. If the women weren't genuine, she'd soon find out. She then went into the town hall to speak to Mrs. Tilly again, feeling more confident than the last time, asking if there was any possibility of being interviewed by the board before she gave the go-ahead for structural work to begin on the house.

Mrs. Tilly liked Dolly, her forthrightness, her eagerness and, above all, her genuineness. When she went to see the chairman of the board, she would ask if there was any possibility of moving Mrs. Rawlins's application forward.

Back at the house, Dolly handed out the wellington boots, sweaters and jeans and asked for the groceries to be unloaded. She had ordered a giant deep freeze, plus a new fridge. The women looked on as trucks delivered wheelbarrows, spades, brooms and cleaning equipment. It was still only twelve o'clock when the builders began to ask to speak to Dolly about their estimates, and she sat in the dining room listening to each man. She eventually chose John Maynard, Builder and Carpenter. He was a one-man business that hired in workmen. His yard was only a mile from the manor and his estimates were lower than any of the others. The reason she hired "Big John" was not only because his estimates were low; she reckoned that as he was a one-man show she could make a cash deal and cut down on the VAT payments.

Working from the top of the house down to the cellars, he pointed out what structural work was required. Firstly the roof needed to be replaced and the chimneys were also dangerous. Every window sash had to be renewed, and all the plumbing in every bathroom, as well as the boilers; and ceilings had to be re-plastered. In other words, the manor needed to be stripped back to the bare boards and rebuilt. He said it would cost between sixty and seventy thousand pounds, and that excluded fixtures and fittings; with those it would come to at least a hundred and fifty thousand. And that was without taking into consideration the gardens, stables, swimming pool and orchard. But even with the extra work that would mean, his charges were still way under any of the larger firms'.

"How long will it all take?" Dolly asked.

"Six months at least."

Dolly frowned: she would have to have that meeting at the town hall to find out what grants she would be entitled to because it was now obvious that Ester's big deal about all the furnishing being part of the sale meant nothing. Everything needed to be replaced—cutlery, linen, beds, mattresses, carpets. She knew she was looking at around half a million to get the manor back into shape—and that was for only the bare necessities because she would still have to install fire alarms and child safety equipment. Even so, she couldn't help feeling excited. She felt confident she could finance the place and still come out with money in the bank for emergencies, perhaps schooling and further education for the kids, home helps, nannies.

Big John agreed to cut out the VAT for cash payment and departed a happy man to begin hiring workmen, plumbers, carpenters, and brickies.

The women, in wellington boots, jeans and sweaters, began to "look busy," with a lot of comings and goings, without actually over-exerting themselves. They were more intent on keeping an eye on Dolly, but monitoring her phone calls was difficult as Angela was constantly on the phone making calls for her.

Ester passed Angela twice. "You're not still on the phone, are you, Angela? Maybe Dolly wants to call somebody."

"I'm calling people for her. She's given me a list."

Angela was telephoning the social services, trying to find out what the building requirements and stipulations were, but she kept on being switched from one department to another.

Out in the stables, the women were half-heartedly clearing away years of rubbish, old wine crates and bottles.

Ester marched out. "That bloody Angela is *still* on the phone. It's crazy, she's been on it all morning."

"I thought Dolly was gonna call about the diamonds," bellowed Gloria.

"Can you say that any louder, Gloria? Maybe the station attendant didn't pick it up!"

Kathleen hurled a crate down from the loft. "Well, get her off the bloody phone." She climbed down the ladder as Ester started pacing up and down. "If she's paying cash to that builder, she's either got to have more than she let on or she's going for them later today."

Kathleen began to load the wheelbarrow and yelled that somebody else should also look as if they were working apart from her. Ester climbed up the ladder and began to kick down crates as Gloria dragged out an old table with three legs.

"Gloria, come up here. *Gloria!*"

"*What do you want?*" she yelled back, and then looked up at Ester as she peered down from the loft.

"You come up here, Gloria!" Gloria sighed and went up the ladder. As her nose appeared at the top, Ester pointed to some old straw covering several large canvas bags. "Are these yours?"

Gloria shrugged. "Maybe. What's your problem?"

Ester knelt down and dragged forward one of the open bags. "They're full of guns, Gloria."

"So bleedin' what? What's that got to do with you?"

"A lot. There's gonna be builders coming back this afternoon, and they'll be swarming all over the place. If they find them, they'll think the bloody IRA have taken up residence. Move them."

"Where to, for Chrissakes?"

"Somewhere out of sight, not left up here for anyone to find."

"I'll move 'em but I'll need you to help. They weigh a ton."

Dolly was reading the leaflets from the social services when she heard a yell from below. She crossed to the window to see Gloria staggering toward the house with Ester, carrying what looked like a body bag.

They stumbled through the kitchen, all the guns wrapped in an old piece of carpet. As they went into the hall, they found Angela on the phone.

"Well, I have to see you, it's important."

"Get off the phone," Ester snapped.

Angela whipped round. "I'm still calling for Dolly," she lied, and began to redial.

The two women continued on toward the cellar door and down into the sauna. Dolly watched from the landing, wondering what they were taking down there. She moved slowly down the stairs as Angela hurriedly dialed again. "Keep getting put onto different departments, Mrs. Rawlins."

Dolly pressed her finger over the button and then lifted it up. She asked Angela to dial a number for her and ask for Jimmy. Angela did as she was told. Dolly leaned forward, listening. "Ask him if he's got them," she whispered, as Angela held her hand over the phone.

"Got what?"

Dolly gave her one of her strange, sweet smiles. "I'll maybe tell you about it later but just do as I say, love."

Angela hesitated and then spoke into the phone. "Have you got them?" she stammered.

Donaldson looked at Palmer. They still hadn't found the stones but Palmer nodded for him to say that he had them, and to stall for time. "Yes, I've got them, but not here."

Dolly wrote on a notepad and passed it to Angela. She read it and then said into the phone, "I'll collect them at two o'clock tomorrow afternoon."

Dolly pressed on the button to cut off the call, and told Angela to carry on chasing the social services, as Ester and Gloria came up from the cellars. "Still clearing the junk from the stable, Dolly," Ester told her.

"Good, keep at it. We'll have some skips delivered soon so a lot of it can be chucked into them. I'm going to London tomorrow afternoon."

They went out smiling, and reported to the women outside that it looked like Dolly was going to pick up the diamonds the following afternoon. They all started clearing the rubbish with renewed vigor.

Dolly waited until Angela had started telephoning again before she slipped down into the basement to see what Gloria and Ester had been carrying. She went into the old sauna locker room. Some of the cupboards were dented and hanging open but a row of three was locked, dusty fingerprints showing they had been opened and used recently. Dolly looked around and found an old screwdriver left on a bench. She pried open a locker and found herself looking at a thick canvas bag. She swore, and then sighed, leaning against the old locker. "Stupid, stupid, stupid . . ."

At seven the workmen erecting scaffolding finally left. The women sat watching TV, all of them knackered, apart from Dolly who remained at the kitchen table making notes, and all went up to bed early. She was fast asleep when Ester suddenly sat bolt upright, nudging Julia. "Somebody's downstairs, can you hear?"

Julia listened, and then crept to the doorway. She couldn't hear anything. Ester looked out of the window and whispered, "She's out there again—look, up by the woods."

Dolly was standing, staring at the manor, looking from one window to the next. She wore wellington boots and a raincoat she had found in a closet, a man's raincoat, stained and torn.

"What's she doing out there?"

"Who cares? Come back to bed," Julia yawned.

"I don't trust her one bit," Ester said, reluctantly returning to bed. A couple of hours later she woke again as she heard someone on the stairs. She listened and then heard Dolly's bedroom door opening and closing.

"I don't trust her," she murmured, falling back into a troubled sleep.

The workmen arrived at six the next morning. They were still putting up the scaffolding, but they had also begun to clear out old carpets and broken furniture, lay down planks for wheelbarrow access into the hallway, and put bags of cement by the open front door. Dolly was up and having breakfast when Big John tapped on the door. "Scaffolding should be up by this afternoon and we'll start clearing out anything you don't want, and get ready for the roof. Er, I've hired eight men, so . . ."

"You'll get the first payment end of the week, if that's okay, just a couple of days."

"Oh, fine. It's just I'm laying out cash for all the tiles and the men'll want wages come Friday."

"I know, John, but I have to go to London to get the cash. You'll have it, don't worry."

"Okay, Mrs. Rawlins."

"Thank you, John." She sat a moment, tapping her teeth with a pencil, as one by one the women drifted down for breakfast.

"Will you all start clearing the vegetable patch? I got bags and bags of seeds we can start planting," Dolly said, as they started frying bacon and eggs.

Julia walked in, face flushed. "You know, those old stables are in quite good nick—be nice to get a horse. I used to have one when I was a kid. They're not that expensive to keep, you'd be surprised."

Dolly paid no attention, concentrating on her notes.

"Did you hear what I said, Dolly?" Julia said as she threw off her jacket.

"Last thing we need right now, love, is a horse. Let's get the garden in order first. We can start that while the house is being done over, no need to fork out for gardeners."

The women looked at one another, having no desire to "shift" anything but the eggs and bacon.

"I'm going up to London this afternoon. I'll take Angela with me." Dolly left the kitchen and went to the yard.

Ester closed the door behind her. "Told you, she's going for them this afternoon. Get Angela in here, go on."

Gloria caught Angela dialing. She crooked her finger. "Who you callin'?"

"My mum, let her know where I am."

"Well, do it later. Come in here, we want to talk to you."

It was a beautiful clear day and Dolly was walking up to the woods. She stopped as she heard the sound of a train, and looked over to see the level-crossing gates open and close. A square-faced boy was sitting on a stool, obviously a trainspotter. He was making copious notes in a black schoolbook, checking his watch, face set in concentration. Dolly strolled down onto the narrow lane by the crossing.

"Good morning," she said cheerfully.

The boy looked up: his face was even squarer close up and his thick black hair stuck up in spikes. "Good morning. My name is Raymond Dewey," he said loudly. "I'm here every day, checking on the trains. I'm the time-keeper. That was the nine o'clock express, on time, always on time."

"Really? You have an important job then, don't you? Raymond, was it?"

"That is correct, Raymond Dewey of fourteen Cottage Lane. Who are you?"

"Well, Raymond, I'm Dolly, Dolly Rawlins."

"Hello, Dolly, very nice to meet you."

She smiled at his over-serious face. Bright button eyes glinted back as he licked his pencil tip and returned to his work.

"Well," Dolly said, "I won't disturb you. Bye-bye."

He stuck out his stubby-fingered hand and she shook it. His grasp was strong, almost pulling her off her feet. Close to, he looked much older than at first sight but she thought no more of him as she wandered back up to the woods.

Mrs. Tilly replaced the receiver and checked her watch. She thought it was probably best to discuss what she'd just heard with Mrs. Rawlins personally, so she left her office.

The women were grouped around the vegetable patch. Connie was peering at seed packets as Julia dug the soil, turning it over. Two wheelbarrows were filled with weeds and rubbish.

"Should these be goin' in now?" Gloria asked, as she opened another packet.

Julia began to stick in rods. "Bit late, but if the weather keeps fine it'll be okay."

Gloria sprayed out the contents of the packet.

"*Not there!* Over here, what do you think I'm putting the rods in for?" Julia shouted.

"Well, I didn't know. What you got in your packet, Connie?"

Connie pulled at the top to open it and the seeds all fell out.

"Pick them up," said Julia, bad-tempered.

"What, all of them?" asked Connie. "There's hundreds!"

Gloria laughed and kicked at the seeds. "Who gives a bugger?"

They saw a Mini Metro pull up by the front path. "Who's that?" Julia asked.

"I dunno, she's driving this way now."

Mrs. Tilly wound down the window. "I'm looking for Mrs. Rawlins."

"Try the back door," said Gloria. "Round the back, past the stables. She was in the kitchen."

Mrs. Tilly smiled her thanks and pulled away.

Connie, on her hands and knees, was picking up one seed at a time. "Ugh, the dirt's gettin' under my nails."

"Take them off, then," said Gloria as she kicked more soil over a mound of seeds.

"No chance—do you know what they cost?"

Gloria peered down at her. "With a bit of luck, you'll soon be able to buy all the nails you want. Come on, let's go and see what the Metro lady wanted."

Mrs. Tilly tooted the horn and stepped out of the car as Dolly hurried out from the kitchen.

"Mrs. Tilly, good morning."

"Good morning, Mrs. Rawlins. I can't stop but I wanted to tell you personally. We had a cancelation for this afternoon so the board are reviewing your case and, if you're available, they can see you at four thirty. I'm sorry it's such short notice but as they're all gathered, it seemed a shame not to jump the queue, so to speak."

Dolly beamed. "Is there any advice you can give me, anything I should take with me?"

Mrs. Tilly smiled. "My advice to everyone applying for foster caring is always tell the truth because everything is always checked and double-checked."

"Thank you very much, Mrs. Tilly. Are you sure you won't come in for a cup of tea?"

"No, I shouldn't have really left the office unattended."

"I'll see you later then."

Angela had been listening. She came to the kitchen door. "Mrs. Rawlins, about this afternoon—"

Dolly turned and frowned at Angela to shut her up, then turned back to Mrs. Tilly. "Four thirty, then, Mrs. Tilly. Should I wear a suit, do you think?"

"You'll be asked a lot of questions, some very personal, so wear whatever you feel most confident and relaxed in. Goodbye."

Dolly felt like skipping—everything was coming together so fast. She waited until Mrs. Tilly's car had disappeared before she clapped her hands. "Did you hear, Angela? I've got a meeting with the social services board this afternoon!"

Angela wrinkled her nose. "But what about that Jimmy bloke? You said you'd see him this afternoon. I phoned him yesterday, remember? You can't go to London for two and be back by four thirty. It's after eleven now."

Dolly's face fell. How could she have forgotten? It was the excitement. She'd not felt like this since she was a kid. She hugged her arms tightly around herself. "Get the others in. Tell them we need to talk."

Dolly hurried up to her room to sort out what she would wear for the afternoon's meeting.

Sitting on the dressing-table stool, Dolly started brushing her hair, talking to herself, trying to sort out exactly what she should do. She didn't like leaving Jimmy Donaldson holding the stones for too long. He could get itchy fingers and she'd kind of given him an ultimatum. She didn't like going back on that as it made her look weak, as if she didn't mean business. Harry had something on Donaldson but without him, Donaldson might just try it on.

* * *

They were sitting at the table in the big kitchen, obviously waiting. As soon as she walked in, she could feel the tension. "Okay, this is how we work it. One of you will have to collect the stones for me. I can't risk losing this opportunity with the board members. They're doing me a big favor as it is. So . . ."

"What do you want us to do?" Ester asked.

Dolly sat down. "Jimmy's waiting for me to come at two o'clock. One of you'll have to go and do it for me."

There was a unanimous "I'll do it" but Dolly shook her head.

"What, don't you trust us?" Julia asked.

"No, if you want my honest opinion, but if I say I'll give you each a cut, then whoever picks them up better not do a runner or she'll do every one of you in. So that's a bit of an incentive to come back, isn't it?" Dolly's mind was racing. She'd never said how much of a cut but they could fight that out later, when she'd fenced the diamonds.

She looked them all over: Ester was Julia's partner, so it wouldn't do to put them together; Kathleen she wouldn't trust with a loaf of bread, or Gloria for that matter.

"Okay, Ester, you go."

Ester couldn't hide her smile.

"You sure, Dolly? I mean, what do you think, Ester?" Julia said, and Ester could have smacked her.

"I'll do it. Don't be stupid," she said quickly.

Julia shrugged her shoulders. She knew that Ester had people after her. "Okay, if you say so."

"Take Angela with you, the pair of you do it. Ester collects, you drive, Angela."

Angela seemed too scared to speak, looking from one to the other.

"Why Angela?" Ester demanded.

Dolly gave an icy smile. "I trust her."

"And you don't trust me?"

"No, but I don't think you'd leave Julia in the lurch—leave us all in the lurch—would you?"

They glared at Ester, warning her that she'd better not try anything.

"So get yourselves together, take the Range Rover and get moving."

Julia walked in as Ester was changing, and shut the door. "You're coming back, aren't you?"

Ester snapped, "Of course I am. She's not as dumb as you think. She knows I've got people after me. I'm not likely to fence the gear all by myself in one afternoon, am I?"

Julia sat on the bed. "I dunno. Just seems odd she'd choose you, not me."

"Why would she choose you?"

"Because she knows I'd come back if you were here, whereas I don't know if you would—that answer your question?"

Ester leaned over Julia. "She's tied me to Miss Goody-Two-Shoes, so she'll be watching me like a hawk. I'll be back, Julia, don't you worry about that."

"Then what?"

Ester clenched her fists. "Well, you said it the other night. You reckoned Dolly would kill for those diamonds. Maybe, just maybe, I would too."

"What about the others?"

"Fuck 'em. Now, how do I look?"

"Great, but then I'm biased." Julia smiled: Ester always turned her on when she was hard like this. Dangerous.

Dolly spoke softly, and Angela had to listen closely to hear every word. "You watch her all the time. You see her collect, then you put your foot down and come straight back here. This is the address, twenty-one Ladbroke Grove Estate. You all right?"

"I wish you'd ask one of the others."

"No, love, you're the only one who hasn't been inside. You've still got some honesty about you, some integrity none of the others has left. They'd have 'em and be away, I know it."

Angela was in turmoil but couldn't see any way out of it. She was still shaking as Ester walked in, dangling the car keys. "Okay, we're all set, sweet-face, let's go and collect."

Gloria looked at the clock. "Well, you got plenty of time."

"Maybe we'll stop off for lunch."

"Just as long as you don't stop off anywhere after you've picked them up."

Ester laughed, unaware that Dolly had already searched her room and pocketed her passport.

Ester gave Julia a little wink as they climbed into the Range Rover. "Right, might as well get on with it then."

Julia banged on the side of the door. "Take care, Ester, see you later."

Gloria, leaning on a rake, watched the Land Rover drive away. "Well, if she doesn't show, I'll shove this up her arse."

Dolly dialed and waited. She recognized Tommy's labored breathing immediately. "Hello, Tommy, it's Dolly, Harry Rawlins's widow."

"Good God, you're out then, are you, gel?"

"Yeah, I'm out, but I need a favor."

"You know old Tommy, lovey, if he can do you one, he will."

"Just so long as you get paid for it, right?" Dolly chuckled.

"On the nail. So what can I do you for?"

Dolly lowered her voice. "I've got a few things I want to run by Jimmy Donaldson, then maybe bring to you."

"Jimmy Donaldson?" Tommy wheezed.

"Yeah, you know him?"

"Course I do. Runs a gig over in Hackney, or he did. You know he's been away for a few years—still is as far as I know."

"Away? Where?"

"Banged up. Got pinched for floggin' some stolen Georgian silver. Didn't you know?"

"You sayin' he's still in the nick? You sure?"

"Yeah, a few days back someone was asking after him and . . . hello? Hello?"

Dolly felt cold, her hand still gripping the receiver. If Donaldson was nicked, how come he was answering his phone? She sat down and ran her hands through her hair, trying to remember everything he had said at the fairground. The more she thought about it, the more she began to think that maybe she was being set up.

The women turned as they heard Dolly calling for Ester. "She's gone. Dolly?"

Dolly ran toward them. "They've gone already? But why . . . ?"

"Well, they couldn't wait." Gloria started to laugh, but seeing Dolly's expression quickly became serious. "What is it?"

"I'm being set up. Jimmy Donaldson's supposed to be in the nick."

Julia looked distraught.

Gloria hurled aside her rake. "Get me car—we can catch them up. Come on!"

Julia ran after her, Dolly following close behind. Kathleen looked at

Connie, who was still half-heartedly digging a drainage trench. "What did you make of that?"

"I don't know. What do you think?"

Kathleen gazed down at the trench. She rammed in her spade. "Keep digging. This looks like a grave, and maybe we'll be putting somebody in it . . ."

CHAPTER 7

The Mini backfired again and this time Dolly hit the dashboard. "Next turning there's a hire firm. Pull in and get a car with something under the bonnet."

"Who's paying for it?" Gloria grumbled.

"I will! Just do it!" Julia shouted. Gloria turned left toward Rodway Motors.

"They should have waited!" Dolly seethed, as Gloria pulled onto the forecourt and went to reception. "If they'd just waited I'd have told them not to go."

"Well, they didn't," said Julia, looking at her watch, "but we can still be there in plenty of time."

Dolly was clenching and unclenching her hands. "If I miss this board meeting, I'll—I'll—"

Julia glanced at Dolly curiously. She didn't seem to care about the diamonds, only that she had been set up. "What about the diamonds, Dolly?" she said.

"If Jimmy has done me over, he'll regret it. I'll take everything he's got, then I'll have him taken out. I might even do it myself."

Julia blinked, and then heard the *toot-toot* of a horn as Gloria drove up in a red Volvo. "Right," said Dolly, getting out of the Mini, "move over, I'm driving."

At twelve fifteen, one of the officers at long last returned to the wall they had first checked, but it wasn't until almost one o'clock that they found the pouch of diamonds. It was driven at top speed to Donaldson's house on the Ladbroke estate and handed over to DI Palmer, who snatched it unceremoniously.

"I've not logged it yet, Gov," the officer told him.

"I'll do it, thanks."

DCI Craigh was standing in the hall. "They got them," Palmer gasped.

Craigh grinned. "Talk about cutting it fine. Let's have a look at them."

"They've not put it on record yet."

"I'll do it when I go in," Craigh said as he eased open the velvet pouch. "Holy shit, look at the size of some of those stones," he said in awe, then pulled the drawstring tight. "Look, we don't let these out of our sight—that's your job and yours only, you watch these babies, okay?"

Craigh walked into the living room and held up the bag to Jimmy Donaldson. "Saved by the bell, Sunny Jim, we got them."

Donaldson looked over with baleful eyes. "Just so long as you put her away. She plugged her old man and I don't want her going after me."

Craigh smirked. "That's the whole point of the exercise, Jimmy. We want her back inside for nicking these."

Mike stared blankly from his position by the window. He'd just about given up on them finding the stones in time but knew he couldn't risk going back to Donaldson's shop or it would look suspicious. All that had to happen now was for Rawlins to arrive and get nicked, and him and his bloody mother would be in the clear.

"What time is it?" he asked. Everyone looked at their watches, including Donaldson.

"We've almost an hour to go until she collects."

Ester liked driving fast, and they were in London with time to spare. They were parked close to Ladbroke Grove tube station, eating burgers. At least, Ester was; Angela couldn't stomach anything. She was a bag of nerves, wondering if she would have to face Mike.

"I don't drive."

Ester turned to her with her mouth full. "What did you say?"

"I said I don't drive. Well, I do, but not very well. I never passed my driving test and now, with my nerves I—I just don't think I'll be able to drive."

Ester tossed the half-eaten hamburger out of the window. "Well, it's a fucking brilliant time to tell me."

"I'm sorry."

Ester sighed. "Okay, we switch. You collect, I'll drive."

Angela chewed at her nails. "I don't think we should do this, Ester. I'm scared. What if we get arrested?"

"For Chrissakes, stop bleatin'. It's one thirty—we can start to head up the road soon."

* * *

"It's one thirty," squawked Gloria.

"You tell me the time just once more . . ." snarled Julia, and then looked at the road ahead. "Oh shit, look at the traffic! It's jammed solid."

Dolly slowed down, and glanced at the clock on the dashboard. "We can still make it. We get onto the flyover, it's only about fifteen minutes from there."

"We're nowhere near the bloody flyover!" yelled Gloria, and Julia reached over and whacked her one. Dolly pulled out and drove alongside the rows of orange cones and roadworks signs. "Fuckin' hell, you'll get us arrested next," Gloria screeched. But they made it to the front of the traffic jam, and nudged into the line of cars while an irate driver gave them a V sign and a flow of verbals. Gloria wound down her window. "We got a pregnant woman here on the way to the hospital, you prick, so *fuck off.*"

The man stared open-mouthed as Dolly pressed on, horn blaring as she bullied her way through the traffic and accelerated toward the Edgware Road.

Ester checked her watch. It was ten minutes to two. She put the car into gear. "Let's go for it. We wait any longer and you'll have chewed down to your knuckles."

They drove down Ladbroke Grove, passing the police station on the right. "Police station," Angela whispered.

"Thank you, I might not have noticed it," Ester said, but she drove carefully all the same, not wanting any aggro.

Driving fast from the opposite direction, turning off the Harrow Road, came Dolly.

"It's off to the right," said Julia. "If they keep to two o'clock, we'll just catch them."

Craigh looked at the clock. It was nine minutes to two. Donaldson was sweating now. "When she rings the doorbell," Craigh told him, "you answer it, bring her in here, the bag is open, and all she's got to do is . . ."

Mike turned from the window. He pressed his radio earpiece closer. "Nothing yet, road's still clear."

The two officers outside waited, scanning the road in front of them and checking their wing and rear-view mirrors. But the road was empty.

Then it happened. The Range Rover was coming toward them just as the red Volvo raced in from the opposite direction. They saw the Range Rover stop and Angela get out and then all hell broke loose as the Volvo mounted the pavement, Gloria hanging out of the window. "*Get back, get out of here!*"

The door opened and Angela was hauled bodily into the Volvo, while Julia leaped out, ran toward the Range Rover and jumped aboard. The two cars then roared away. The two officers got out of the patrol car, staring down the road in disbelief as DCI Craigh hurtled out of the house.

"What the fuck is going on?"

"We dunno. Woman ran from one car, driven off in another."

Craigh clenched his fists in frustration. "Was it her? *Was it Dolly Rawlins?*"

Mike was at the window. "What the hell is going on? It was her—it was Dolly Rawlins, for Chrissakes. Why aren't they going after the goddamned car?"

Palmer turned on Mike. "What the fuck for? Speeding? We dunno if it was her or not."

Mike ran out of the house. It was a total cock-up and it was at this moment Jimmy Donaldson saw his chance. He saw the stones, he saw Palmer with his back to him, and he was alone. He picked up the heavy glass ashtray, whacked Palmer over the back of the head, picked up the bag of diamonds and then he was out, closing the door behind him. He let himself out the back, leapt over a fence and took off down the narrow alley running between the houses.

Craigh leaned into the patrol car. He couldn't believe what had happened. They had three digits of the number plate, but the two officers were confused as to what they'd seen.

"We saw a Range Rover, right? Cruised up behind us, I mean, it wasn't a blonde at the wheel, right? It was a brunette. We saw it stop, young kid gets out, sort of walks a few paces, next minute this other fucking car screams up."

Craigh rubbed his head. "You see the driver at all?"

The officer pulled at his collar. "Yeah, it looked like a friggin' car full of women, but one was blonde."

The second officer peered at the sweating Craigh. "No, there were two blondes. There was one hanging out the window doin' all the screamin'."

Craigh breathed in, then told them to see if there was a police car in the vicinity.

"What you want, Gov?"

Craigh turned on him in a fury. "Not this fuckin' mess for starters. Just see if we can get a full reg on the car."

"Which one? One with the blondes or the Range Rover?"

* * *

The Range Rover was already at the Shepherd's Bush flyover, Julia panting with fear as Ester put her foot down. "Not too fast, keep in the near lane."

"What the fuck happened?" Ester bellowed.

Julia was white-faced with fear, hearing sirens now. "Dolly sussed she was being set up, that's all I know."

"You're out of your mind!" Gloria screamed, as Dolly drove all the way round the Shepherd's Bush roundabout and started to head back the way they had come. "You're driving us right back to Ladbroke Grove—you should have gone up on the motorway."

Dolly said nothing. She turned left onto Ladbroke Grove again and then onto a side street.

"*What* are you *doing?*"

"If they're trying to find us, they won't be looking for us right on his bloody doorstep, will they? I'm going back onto the Harrow Road and then to the station. There's a train at three and I'm gonna be on it."

Palmer was sitting dabbing his neck with a handkerchief. DCI Craigh was out in one of the cars searching for Donaldson while Mike sat on the stairs, shaking his head in disbelief. Things were now bordering on farce and they knew they were all in deep trouble.

Jimmy Donaldson had no idea he'd risked everything for a bag of glass as he dodged down the alleyways, hugging the pouch bag to his chest. He reached the end of Ladbroke Grove and took a quick look round to see if he was still in the clear. He jogged down Portobello Road, weaving in and out of the stallholders, catching his breath in antique shops. He was making his way toward a cut-through that led onto Harrow Road, where he knew he'd be able to nick a motor easy. They were sometimes being worked on by blokes he knew so he reckoned if he made it there he'd be away.

Dolly pushed Gloria into the back seat of the Volvo as she knew they'd be looking for a middle-aged blonde. Then she dragged Angela out of the car and shoved her into the driving seat. "Get in and drive."

Angela had never driven an automatic in her life. Dolly made herself small in the back seat with Gloria. "Just put the gear into 'Drive,' Angela, and take it nice and easy. Go up to the end and take a right onto the Harrow Road."

Dolly sat back, feeling things were going to be all right—until Angela took a left instead of a right, then she almost punched the back of Angela's head.

Donaldson was panting now, feeling like he was going to throw up, having run himself into the ground as he picked his way in and out of the parked cabs and trucks. He saw the car, the door open with the keys inside, and a surge of adrenalin gave him new strength.

As he made for the car, Angela careered down the alley, terrified that she couldn't control the Volvo, shouting to Dolly that she had never driven an automatic and hadn't even passed her test on an ordinary car.

"Stay fucking calm!" Gloria shouted back. "Where the hell are we? It's a dead end, Dolly."

Dolly knew exactly where they were and told Angela to keep going straight ahead. Either side of the road were garages, some with their doors open, mechanics working on vehicles, and no one was paying them any attention. By now they were moving more slowly. As they neared the end of the narrow road and Dolly told Angela to put her foot down, Jimmy Donaldson suddenly appeared from behind a truck. He was looking back over his shoulder, and ran out straight into the Volvo.

The car hit him side on, tossing him up into the air. He rolled across the bonnet and slithered to the ground with a sickening thump. Angela slammed on the brakes, throwing Gloria and Dolly forward in their seats. "What the bloody hell was that?" Angela wailed.

"You've gone an' hit a bloke, for Chrissakes!" bellowed Gloria. She then screamed as Donaldson, pushing himself to his knees, pressed his face to the window, while clawing at the door.

"Back up," shouted Dolly. Angela shoved the car into reverse with a shaking hand and, as the car lurched backward, Donaldson's body disappeared.

"He's under the fucking car," shrieked Gloria. She leaned over and rammed the car into "Drive." Angela started sobbing hysterically as the car lurched forward. They all felt the hideous bump and heard the crunching sound beneath the wheels.

Hearing the women screaming, two mechanics from a nearby garage looked over. Donaldson lay unmoving in the gutter, his chest crushed.

Dolly leaped out of the car and almost fainted when she recognized Jimmy Donaldson. As she felt his pulse, she saw the black velvet pouch still clutched in his hand. Without missing a beat she snatched it, stuffed it into her pocket, and got back in the car. Neither Gloria nor Angela saw her do it. Both were in a state of shock.

"Get out of here and fast. *Move it, Angela!*" Dolly shouted.

The Volvo's tires screeched as it hurtled round the corner and disappeared.

By the time DCI Craigh arrived at the scene, Donaldson's body was being lifted onto a stretcher. He quickly ascertained that the bag of diamonds was nowhere to be seen. All he had were useless witnesses who couldn't tell him the make of the car or give a description of the driver. What he did know was that Jimmy Donaldson was dead and no one had seen Dolly Rawlins anywhere near his home. If she had been in the car that killed Jimmy, they had no evidence. They had, as he put it to DI Palmer, fuck all.

Dolly made it to the train just in time. She had to run along the platform and opened one of the doors as the train was moving off. She scrambled on, ignoring the shouts of the guards, and hauled Angela after her. They slumped into two vacant seats, heaving for breath. Dolly felt the pouch in her pocket pressing into her stomach. She leaned back, closing her eyes.

"We made it."

Angela was still panting, scared to death. "That—that man I ran over."

Dolly opened her eyes. "Not your fault—you couldn't stop. Anyway, we've got other things to worry about; this is where we both get arrested for not having tickets."

She smiled, trying to lighten the mood, but Angela couldn't stop thinking about the collision. She kept seeing that big gray object as it hit the windshield, kept feeling that hideous bump as she ran over him, not once but twice. She started to cry.

"Pull yourself together, Angela, we don't want anyone to . . . remember us. So I'll sit up front, away from you, all right, love?"

Dolly made her way up the train, slipped into the toilet and held the bag of diamonds tightly to her chest. Whatever else had happened, she'd got them and she'd still make the meeting.

Gloria took a scenic route back to the rental garage, after stopping at a car wash to check for any signs of damage or blood on the bumpers—but the car didn't even have a dent. The windshield wasn't cracked either. The Volvo was a solid piece of machinery, she thought, but her feelings of relief were soon punctured by the realization that they hadn't got the diamonds. By the time she collected her Mini and drove back to the manor, she was feeling thoroughly depressed. She knew she should have stuck with what she knew, and not allowed herself to be swayed by Ester Freeman and her big ideas—especially not with her luck.

At the town hall, Dolly told Angela to see which room the meeting was in while she went into the ladies' and carefully stashed the bag of diamonds on top of one of the old toilet cisterns. If some bastard had set her up, they were bound to come sniffing around at the manor.

She turned as Angela slipped in and whispered, "They said they're running a bit behind and for you to go into the waiting room outside the boardroom."

Dolly examined her face in the mirror. Not too bad, she thought. It was only when she tried to put on some lipstick that she realized she was shaking.

Angela was biting her nails as she sat next to Dolly in the waiting room. Ten minutes ticked by, during which two women came in and walked out again, Dolly making a point each time of politely saying, "Good afternoon."

Angela suddenly started to cry again.

"I think he was dead, Dolly. I'm sure I killed him."

Dolly squeezed her hand tightly. "Yes, I think you did, love," she said, just as the boardroom doors opened and Mrs. Tilly walked out.

"I'm so sorry to have kept you waiting, Mrs. Rawlins. Please do come in."

As the door closed behind them, Angela sniffed and pressed her hand to her mouth. She'd killed that poor man, she'd killed him and she couldn't face it. She pressed her hands to her mouth, then got up and hurried out.

Mike's wife picked up the phone. She could hear someone sobbing on the other end of the line. "Look, whoever this is, don't keep calling here, do you hear me? Leave us alone."

"No, please," Angela begged, "I've got to talk to Mike—it's urgent." There was something in her terrified voice that stopped Susan from putting down the receiver. "Do you have a number he can contact you on? What's your name?"

"It's Angela, it's—" Susan couldn't make out any more because of the sobbing, and then the phone went dead. She called the office but they said Mike was out. Then she called her mother-in-law.

"Is Mike there, Mum?"

"No, love, I'm waiting for him to call. Did he tell you? I'm going to Spain."

Susan asked Audrey to get Mike to phone her straight away if he called.

"Are you all right, Susan?" Audrey asked, hearing the tension in her voice.

"No, Mum, I'm not. If I ask you something, will you be honest? I mean it, Audrey, I don't want you to lie to me."

"I won't, love." Audrey had never heard Susan so agitated.

"I think Mike is seeing someone else. I'm getting hysterical phone calls and then sometimes they just put the receiver down on me."

"Oh, Mike wouldn't, love. It'll be somethin' to do with his work; he wouldn't carry on."

Susan clutched the receiver tighter. "You ever heard him mention a girl called Angela?"

Audrey sighed. The fact was, he'd called an Angela a couple of times from her flat. When she'd asked about her, he'd said she was just a kid he was trying to help out. Maybe he'd been doing a bit more than helping her out. "Look, I'll talk to him, don't you worry about it. But I think you've got it wrong—I've got to go now, love, but don't you worry."

Audrey could hear Susan crying and then the phone went dead. She replaced the receiver, feeling guilty, but the truth was, she had more important things on her mind. She looked at the clock: it was almost five. She crossed her fingers. Dolly Rawlins should have been arrested by now. She went back to packing her clothes, half an ear listening for the phone, while the face of her dead daughter Shirley looked on with that sweet, vague smile from the picture frame.

The women were huddled in the kitchen as Gloria told her side of it, then Ester hers. Julia said nothing. Kathleen looked glum and Connie wanted to cry. "So, there's no diamonds?" she said.

Ester gave a slow, burning stare. "That's fucking bright of you to fathom out, Connie. What the hell do you think we've been talking about, a box of Smarties?"

Mr. Arthur Crow, the chairman of the board, looked over Dolly Rawlins's forms and listened intently to her answers. She seemed nervous but that was only to be expected. She described the manor and her intentions, how many staff she felt would be required, how many children she could easily accommodate. That section was impressive: she was concise and to the point, saying the grounds were ample, there were stables and a swimming pool, but truthfully that the house was in a poor state of repair.

They now turned to her criminal record and she quickly made it clear that, as she had been convicted of murder, she would be on parole for the rest of her life. She said quietly that she had never been involved in any criminal activity before the shooting of her husband and that it had been at a time when she was emotionally unstable, having been told he was dead, then discovering he was alive and living with another woman who had borne his child. She spoke candidly about the therapy sessions she had been given at Holloway but said she had required no therapy for the past five and a half years.

"I found great solace in working with the young female offenders, especially in the maternity section of the prison. I developed an interest in the group-therapy sessions for the inmates and became a trusty, working with probation officers and therapists, but not as a patient."

Deirdre gave Dolly small encouraging nods and Mrs. Tilly was a constant source of encouragement. The men, however, were offhand and cool, showing much more restraint.

Dolly was asked further questions about whether she would be prepared to work with a foster carer and resident-home advisory officers, and she agreed to be available and prepared to do anything the board suggested that would enable her to open the manor as a home.

"Mrs. Rawlins, how are you at this present moment financing the running of the Grange?"

Dolly explained that she had a considerable private income that had enabled her to purchase the manor.

"Do you know the previous owner?" It was slipped in fast.

"No, I do not. I believe her name was Ester Freeman and the place had a very bad reputation. Perhaps that is why I think, and my lawyers agree, I paid a fair price for such a substantial property."

Eventually, after over an hour and a half of questions and answers with Dolly maintaining her composure, she was asked if she would allow a visit within the next few days to assess the property. She said they were free to come at any time—in fact, the sooner the better. Mr. Crow ended the meeting by saying that everything she had said would be assessed and obviously her past checked into in some detail. They thanked her for her honesty and wished her every success.

She walked out confidently, and was further gratified by Mrs. Tilly's light touch on her arm as she left. "Thank you so much for coming in to see us at such short notice, and sorry again for keeping you waiting."

Dolly returned to the manor by taxi. At the level crossing they were held up for almost ten minutes. The cab driver shook his head and turned to the back seat. "Sorry about this, it's the mail train. Holds us up for sometimes ten, twelve minutes. One night it was fifteen." The gates opened, and they drove on down the narrow country lane back to the manor.

Dolly breezed in, all smiles, saying how well the meeting had gone, trailed by a downcast Angela. She shut the back door and tossed her handbag onto the table. "I don't know about anyone else but I'm starving. Who's on the dinner tonight?"

Ester stared at her in disbelief. "Is that all you've got to say? I'm glad everything went well for *you!*"

The police cars moved silently up the driveway, two officers from Thames Valley in front, followed by DCI Craigh, accompanied by DS Mike Withey with one uniformed driver. Craigh was first out. He walked up the manor steps, sidestepping the sacks of cement, and waited as more local police moved around to the back yard to enter from there. Then he radioed in that he was about to enter.

He gave one soft knock and murmured it was the police and that they had a warrant to search the premises. He then stepped back as the two Thames Valley officers banged on the door. They didn't need much force as it was only on the latch, and they burst into the hallway, Craigh holding up the warrant.

"We have a warrant to search the premises. This is the police."

Kathleen ran up the stairs onto the first landing and legged it out onto a low roof at the back. The other women ran in all directions, only Dolly remaining unflustered as she picked up the kettle to put it on the stove. Angela curled into a ball, making herself as small as she could, terrified that they had come to arrest her for the hit-and-run.

Dolly put a firm hand on her shoulder. "Angela, keep your mouth shut. Just give them your name, nothing more. Understand me?"

Gloria pulled at Ester's arm. "What the fuck do we do?"

Ester shrugged her away. "Nothing. There's nothing here."

Gloria was white-faced. "Yes, there is," she hissed. "We put the bloody guns in the cellar."

Ester froze, but could do nothing as they were surrounded by police and herded into the drawing room.

Craigh looked at Dolly as she calmly opened a tea caddy. "I am Detective Chief Inspector Craigh."

Dolly smiled. "Dorothy Rawlins." She held out her hand for him to shake.

"Do you mind if I talk to you first? Do you want to see the warrant?"

"Of course. I'd also like to know what this is about."

Craigh passed her the warrant and watched her study it. He looked into the hallway toward Mike. "I'll take Mrs. Rawlins's statement first, then the others'. Get their names, addresses, you know the drill."

He looked back at Dolly. "My men will begin searching the entire house and outbuildings."

She nodded, seemingly still carefully reading the warrant. He waited patiently.

The women wandered around the drawing room; Gloria was now crying along with Angela. Julia nudged Ester. "What the hell are they getting so upset about?"

Ester's face was tight with anger. "There's an arsenal of weapons down in the sauna. Gloria's husband's guns, three bags full of them."

Julia looked at Gloria, stunned. "Are you serious?" But before Ester could say anything more Mike Withey walked in.

"I'll need all your names, dates of birth, present and past addresses."

Behind Mike, the women could see the officers moving up the stairs, while others headed down to the cellar. No one spoke. All they could do now was wait for the police to find the weapons.

CHAPTER 8

Craigh sat with his notebook open as Dolly drank a cup of tea. She hadn't offered him one. She had admitted that she knew James "Jimmy" Donaldson, and seemed shocked when told he was dead.

"Dead? But he can't be. I only spoke to him yesterday. I met up with him a few days ago." She sat down with a heavy sigh.

"Would you mind telling me why you met Mr. Donaldson?"

"He was keeping something for me. I've been in prison, you see, and, oh, this is a shock . . ."

Craigh tapped his pen on the table. "What was he holding for you, Mrs. Rawlins?"

"Well, they were nothing to look at, really. You wouldn't even think they were valuable, but they are, they're worth a lot of money."

He leaned close. "What exactly, Mrs. Rawlins?"

"They used to be in my front garden at Totteridge. Gnomes—two Victorian garden gnomes. Not the bright plastic things but proper old carved stone ones. Jimmy was holding them for me until I got out. I called to see if he still had them and we arranged for me to collect them today, as a matter of fact."

Craigh wrote down every word, gritting his teeth. "Did you in fact collect them from Mr. Donaldson?"

"I couldn't get away because I had a very important meeting at the town hall."

"What time?"

Dolly said she'd been at the town hall from three fifteen until after five—shortly before they had arrived, in fact: she had been there for an assessment interview.

"Can anyone verify that, Mrs. Rawlins?"

"Oh yes."

Craigh dug the pen in deeply as he wrote one name after the other. He had a terrible sinking feeling in the pit of his stomach that he had been well and truly stitched up.

The officers searched every room, lifted the floorboards, opened cupboards and cases. They went into the attic, they were out in the stables. Kathleen remained stuck on the roof, half hidden by the gables, not moving a muscle. For eight hours, fifteen men searched the grounds, the swimming pool and the cellars.

Finally Kathleen crawled back into the room she'd escaped from and fell asleep under the bed. The police were now concentrating on the sauna and steam room. The women waited, expecting any moment for the shout to go up but it never came. They smelt bacon being cooked and, to their amazement, Dolly walked in with a tray of bacon butties. Gloria was about to blurt out to Dolly how much trouble they were in, but Dolly shoved a sandwich into her hand. "Eat it and say nothing."

Gloria stuffed a big bite of the sandwich into her mouth and sat down.

Craigh was picking through the sauna when Mike joined him. "They're searching the grounds now, but so far nothing."

Craigh felt knackered and, even worse, foolish. "She's got about eight or nine people giving her alibis. She was at the ruddy social services."

Mike was as tired out as Craigh and couldn't work out if this was good news or bad.

"This all stinks, you know that, don't you?" Craigh started pacing up and down. "The Super's gonna have a seizure about the whole cock-up— Donaldson was in our custody."

"I'm sorry," Mike muttered.

"You're sorry. Jesus Christ, *sorry*? Have you any idea what kind of a mess we're in? Donaldson dead, no sign of the diamonds . . ." Craigh hesitated and then licked his lips. "Look, until we've sorted this, keep schtum about those stones. I never put it in the record sheets so maybe we can—"

"Fine by me."

Mike nodded, his brain ticking away. He concentrated on looking as glum as Craigh obviously felt, while he thanked God nothing had been found. He was off the hook.

* * *

Dolly watched the London mob, as she referred to Craigh and Withey, leaving, then let the curtain fall back into place. "Right," she yawned. "I'm off to bed."

"How the hell can you sleep?" Ester said.

Dolly shrugged. "I've got a lot of thinking to do."

Gloria was pulling at a piece of sodden tissue. "Did you move them, Dolly? Did you?"

She gave her a hard look. "What the hell do you think, you stupid idiot? Of course I bloody moved them—and a good thing too or we'd all have been arrested. I've been waiting for you to mention them."

"I got nothing to do with them," said Ester.

"But you bloody knew they was in the house."

Ester turned away. It was always the same: instead of being grateful to Dolly, she just said nothing, whereas Gloria would have kissed her feet. But none of them was prepared for Dolly's next admission, dropping the line in quietly, with a little smile. "I also got the diamonds but I'm not talking about it yet. Like I said, I need to sleep, get my head straight."

"You got them?" Ester said in wonder.

"Yes, Ester, I got them but they're not here. What is here smells, because someone tipped off the police. Somebody here's grassing on me—*one of you*. One of you hates me enough to get me put back inside and I'm going to find out which one of you it is."

She walked out, slamming the door. No one spoke, not quite believing what they had heard her say, hardly daring to believe they still had a chance of a cut of the diamonds. Then Gloria said, "Grassin'? What she friggin' talkin' about? None of us'd do it, I mean, we want them diamonds as much as she does. She's nuts if she thinks it's one of us!"

Angela started to cry again and ran out of the room before anyone could tell her off, bumping into Kathleen, who was creeping down the stairs as the last of the Thames Valley police drove away. They all looked as she walked into the drawing room.

"Where the hell have you been?" asked Ester.

Dolly couldn't sleep. She stared at a stain on the wall, wondering. Who would hate her enough to want to put her back inside? Because that's what it came down to. If she'd been picked up with the diamonds, virtually holding Donaldson's hand, the cops would have had her. Even if they couldn't pin the old robbery on her, they'd have had her for fencing the stolen diamonds. Either way, with her out on parole, she'd have been back in a cell straight away and with no hope of bail. Was it just that dirty little conman, Jimmy? If it was, then he'd got his just desserts, but something inside her said there had to be more to it than that. Harry had taught her, "Always remember, sweetheart, it takes two to tango. One leads, the other follows." So who was Jimmy's dance partner? If it was one of the women she would find out and God help them.

The next morning Dolly left the house and drove straight to the town hall. She hurried into the ladies' and found the pouch bag exactly where she had left it. She kissed it with relief. She then got down, straightened her skirt and slipped out, bumping into a surprised Mrs. Tilly in the corridor.

"Mrs. Rawlins?"

"I was just passing. I know there's no possibility of you having any answers for me yet but I just wanted to ask you how I did. Was I all right?"

"Yes, you were. I thought you handled yourself very well but it'll be some time before we have any definite news. I'll let you know as soon as I hear anything."

"Thank you. I really appreciate all your help."

As Dolly hurried out, Mrs. Tilly went in to speak to Mr. Crow.

"You know, Mrs. Rawlins is so keen, I think we should push forward an on-site visit. I worry she may spend too much money without approval and I don't want her to waste her savings."

He looked up from his diary. "Well, we'll have to get some appraisals from her probation officer and the prison authorities. And we're nowhere near ready even to discuss the project yet."

"Well, I would just like us to inspect the Manor House. She was so enthusiastic."

He smiled, flattening down his few strands of hair. "I'll see what I can do. If we're visiting anyone near the location we can possibly have a look over the place as well. I was also impressed by her. I very much doubt if she will ever be allowed access to very young children—not enough experience—but she might be good with the older children, the problem ones particularly. Leave it with me."

Mrs. Tilly smiled and left the office. She doubted if Mr. Crow would show Dolly Rawlins any favors. He was a stickler for rules and regulations, after all.

But if he was going to make an exception for anyone, she thought it might be Dolly.

Dolly stopped at a phone booth and called Tommy Malin. She asked if he was still in business—unlike Jimmy Donaldson. They had a few laughs, and she said she would be around later in the afternoon as she had something that might interest him. She then returned to the manor. As she came in she saw Angela on the telephone. "Who you calling, love?"

Angela spun round. "Oh—my mum. I've not told her where I am."

"Well don't, and don't make private calls—that goes for all of you. Fewer people who know what's going on here the better."

"Okay."

"I'm going to London. You want to come with me?" Angela nodded. "Good, in about an hour, then."

The others, who had overheard the conversation from the kitchen, whispered and nudged each other, sure that Dolly was off to fence the stones. Ester gave them all a quiet talking-to: they were to show a lot more willing, they were to get out to that vegetable patch and look like they were working and loving every minute of it. They got to their feet, went out and began to trudge around with wheelbarrows, spades and rakes. When Dolly and Angela left in the local taxi, they appeared to be too intent on their labor even to notice them go.

As the cab passed them, Dolly laughed. "Amazing what a bit of incentive can do, isn't it?"

"I don't understand," Angela said.

"Well, they all know I'm going to fence the diamonds this morning and they all want a slice so 'Let's show Dolly how hard we're working!'"

Angela very nearly smiled. "Oh, yes, I see what you mean."

Mike had waited after Angela put down the receiver. He was hoping she would call back right away but after half an hour he gave up. It had unnerved him to be told that Dolly Rawlins had the diamonds but there was nothing he could do about it. If he told Craigh, he could just feel himself sinking deeper into the hole he'd dug for himself.

Susan walked in with a bag of groceries. "Hi, I didn't wake you when I went out, did I?"

"No, I'm up. I've had something to eat. I was just going to go, actually."

"Oh, were you? You stayed out all night. Surely they can't expect you to work today?"

He sighed. "Yes, they can."

"There was another call from your girlfriend yesterday—I tried to contact you, she seemed upset."

"What?"

"She was crying, in a terrible state." She stared at him, waiting. "She said her name was Angela."

"I heard you," he snapped.

"What's going on with her, then?"

He took a deep breath. "She's a tart, sweetheart, a young kid I helped out a while back when I was on Vice. Now sometimes she acts as an informant. There is nothing going on between us, it's business, all right? *Is that all right with you?*"

"I don't like tarts having your home phone number or ringing me up screaming and yelling. *Is that all right with you?*" Susan went into the kitchen. He dithered, knowing he should talk to her, try and straighten things out, but instead he grabbed his car keys and left without a word.

Sitting in the back of a taxi heading for Tommy Malin's address, Dolly took Angela's hand. "Don't you worry about that hit-and-run. Gloria said there wasn't a mark on the car and if they'd got anything on you—on any of us—we'd have been pulled in last night." Angela clutched Dolly's hand tightly, desperate to believe her. "Will you want to stay on and help me?" Angela nodded. "I'll be able to pay you a decent wage and you could even have cookery classes. Would you like that?"

Angela sniffed. "Yes, I would."

She wanted to tell Dolly about Mike, about everything. She liked her so much, felt protected by her—but how *could* she tell her? And now, with that poor man she'd run over, it was all so complicated. She wanted to talk to Mike, needed to ask his advice.

The cab headed toward Elephant and Castle and then turned off down a small one-way road, stopping outside a paint yard. Dolly got out, saying, "You wait here, love, I shouldn't be too long."

Angela watched as Dolly knocked on the door and disappeared inside the yard.

A young kid in filthy overalls pointed Dolly toward the office and then re-joined his colleagues stripping down some pine furniture.

"Dolly Rawlins," wheezed Tommy Malin, leaning against the doorframe.

"Hello, Tommy." They shook hands and he gestured for her to go in ahead of him. He waved at the workmen and closed the door.

"I'll put the kettle on."

"That'd be nice," she said, taking in the cheap desk, rows of bulging and dented filing cabinets and the massive cast-iron safe. Dolly eased herself onto a newspaper-filled chair. She looked over the equally cluttered desk: the scales, the rows of diamond cutters and pinchers, and rolls of velvet cloth, the only indication that perhaps Mr. Malin's paint and pine-stripping factory was also used for other purposes. Tommy Malin would deal in literally anything he could turn round fast. He was famous for his high percentage and his "no risk" attitude. He would deal in hot stuff but always insisted on a long chilling period. That was why he was so wealthy and had so far avoided arrest. He was very, very careful.

The women had done a half-day's work. Rods had been fixed up, more seeds sown, and the rubbish was now tipped into a skip left for them by the builder. Big John was getting a bit edgy; it was almost payday, he'd used up all his savings to buy the materials, and still Mrs. Rawlins hadn't given him the down payment. He'd seen all the women working out in the garden but Mrs. Rawlins wasn't among them. He'd even looked for her inside the house, but she wasn't there, either.

Connie was testing the sauna temperature when he asked if he could have a word. She turned and gave him a wonderful smile that made him flush.

"I'm sorry to bother you but is Mrs. Rawlins around?"

"No, I'm sorry, she's gone into London. Can I help at all?"

He could feel his cheeks burning. "Well, it was just we had an arrangement and Mrs. Rawlins is a bit behind with the first installment, you see, and I have to pay the men, pay for the materials and—"

"Oh, she's gone to get some money this afternoon." Connie gave another beaming smile. "You couldn't have a look at the sauna for me, could you? I think I've got it working but I'm not sure."

She brushed against him as they went into the small Swedish sauna hut. John checked the temperature dials and the coals. "Do you like it hot?" he asked seriously.

"Oh yes, as hot as you can give it to me." He flushed again but she seemed to be concentrating on the temperature gauge. "Do you work out?"

He stepped back—he couldn't deal with her closeness. She was the most glamorous woman he had ever been this close to in his entire life. "Yes, there's a good local gym, very well equipped."

"Ah, I thought you did, I can always tell. You've got marvelous shoulders."

Now the heat of the sauna was making him sweat but he didn't want to go. He found himself automatically flexing everything, even tightening his bum cheeks.

John breathed in gratefully as she opened the sauna door. He was getting dizzy.

"Thanks for your help, John."

When Connie joined the others, they were sweating and filthy. "Sauna's working, it's really hot. Do any of you want to work out first?"

She received a barrage of abuse in reply—as if after all the digging and wheeling stuff in barrows they needed to work out! All they wanted was a cold drink and a long afternoon in the sauna.

Tommy's wheezing breath and halitosis were overpowering. The drawn blinds, the bolted door and the hissing gas fire made Dolly feel light-headed. She took off her coat. Tommy's thick stubby fingers began to unfurl the cord round the pouch bag. He pulled it open and laid it out flat.

"Is this some kind of joke?"

"No. Why?"

"I just made these up for somebody."

"What?"

He turned his lamp out and pushed his eye-glass onto his forehead. "You didn't pay a bundle for these, did you, sweetheart?"

"What are you talking about?"

"I made them up. They're glass, good settings . . . I mean, I did spend quite a few hours—"

"*You made these?*"

Tommy stared at Dolly, whose face was now chalk white.

"Who for, Tommy?"

He wouldn't usually have said—clients are clients, and he was always a man to keep his mouth shut—but he had a feeling she wasn't going to leave his office until he told her.

"I nearly went back inside for this crap, Tommy, so you tell me who ordered you to make them up."

* * *

Mike knew something was up the moment the message came over the tannoy for him to go into DCI Craigh's office. Craigh looked up at him as he knocked sheepishly and entered. He pointed to the chair in front of his desk and told Mike to sit down. Mike could see a stack of files on his desk, including one with Dolly Rawlins's name printed across it. "Right, let's go from the top and don't bullshit me."

"I don't follow."

"I think you do. I am in it right up to my fucking ears over this Donaldson business. I've got the Super, the prison authorities, Donaldson's wife, his parole officer, all breathing fire all over me so let's start at the beginning, shall we? How did you know that Rawlins had bought the Manor House?"

"My informant."

"Oh yeah? Which one?"

Mike explained about Angela, how he'd busted her along with Ester Freeman.

"You booked her, did you?"

"No, she was never charged. She wasn't on the game, she was just serving drinks at the house for the tarts and their punters."

"So she told you all about Rawlins, and her buying the manor?"

"Yes."

"So what about the diamonds? Same source? You said it was a kid in Brixton with Donaldson. That's the only name I've got down as an informant."

"Yes, that's true. When he told me, I contacted Angela and that's how I knew all the women were staying there."

Craigh pushed his chair back and walked around the office, hands stuffed in his pockets. "Anything else? I mean, is there anything else you've not told me?" Mike licked his lips nervously as Craigh leaned down so his face was almost touching Mike's. "What about that diamond robbery, Mike? You want to tell me about that? Better still, tell me about Shirley Miller." Mike closed his eyes. Craigh prodded him and he flinched. "This was personal, wasn't it?" Mike nodded. "Your sister was killed on that diamond raid."

"Yes."

"Not on your original application form, Mike. There is no mention that you even had a fucking sister."

Mike gave a half-smile. "I didn't reckon it'd look good on my CV, Gov."

"Don't you fucking joke with me, this isn't funny. Let's go from the top again. Your sister worked with Dolly Rawlins and—"

Mike interrupted. "She used her, she manipulated her, she was only twenty-one, a beauty queen and . . ."

Craigh returned to his desk. Mike was close to breaking down, his voice faltering. "I didn't have all that much to do with Shirley. I was in the Army, stationed in Germany, when she was killed. Then when I joined the Met it was, like, all in the past, but my mum, er . . ." He was floundering, trying not to implicate Audrey. The sweat was pouring off him. "I saw her grave, right? And I felt guilty that I'd never come home, never even sent flowers, and . . . my mum was always on and on about Dolly Rawlins. I'm sorry, I am really sorry . . ."

Mike sniffed, trying to hold on to his emotions because he wasn't acting anymore. The more he tried to explain about Shirley, the more her face kept flashing into his mind and in the end he bowed his head. "I loved her a lot. She was a lovely kid." Craigh remained silent, staring at him. "I know Rawlins instigated that robbery, I know it."

"Mike, son, Rawlins was sent down for murder, she killed her husband. It was never proved that she had anything to do with that diamond heist."

"But she had."

"You don't have any proof." Craigh pursed his lips. "Listen to what I'm saying, Mike. Dolly Rawlins was *never* charged with anything to do with that heist. There was never a shred of evidence to link her to it. But your sister was no angel, her husband was a known villain, so don't give me all this whiter-than-white Mother Teresa stuff. All I know is you instigated a full-scale operation from personal motives, drawing me, DI Palmer, the whole team in on a crazy caper that has landed us in shit, making us all look like prize fucking idiots."

"I know she was going for those diamonds," Mike insisted.

"*No, you don't.* You don't know anything. It's all been supposition because *you* had a personal grudge against Rawlins."

"She got away with murder."

"No she didn't. She served her sentence, and as far as being implicated in the Donaldson business is concerned, she has an alibi, and a very strong one, saying she wasn't anywhere near Ladbroke Grove the day he was run over."

Mike frowned. "We had any joy tracing the car?"

"What car? How many red Rovers or Volvos are there in London?"

Mike remained silent as Craigh jangled the change in his pockets.

"We've got Traffic running around like blue-arsed flies—they always love a challenge. But we got nothing from the road where Donaldson got hit, we've not got one decent eyewitness. In fact we've got bugger all. But we do have a nasty, dirty mess that I've got to clear up."

"I'm sorry."

"I hope to Christ you are. And from now on you stay clear of this Rawlins bitch or I'll have you back to wearing a big hat in seconds flat, understand me?"

"Yes, sir."

"Now piss off and I'll see if I can iron all this out."

Craigh watched Mike walk out with his head bent. Picking up Rawlins's file, he stared at her harsh expression in the mug shots and began to flick through her record sheet. He put in a call to the Aylesbury social services to double-check one more time that Rawlins was, as she had stated, being interviewed by the board members.

Angela knew something was very wrong when Dolly walked stiffly back to the taxi. She opened the door and got in. "Go back to the manor—get the train home."

"Aren't you coming with me?"

"No. Just get on your way. I've got someone to see."

"Well, don't you need a lift?"

"No, I want to be on my own for a while."

Dolly passed over a ten-pound note and walked off down the road as Angela directed the cab driver to take her to Marylebone Station.

Mike let himself in and called out to Susan, but the house was silent. He checked the time, assuming she was collecting the kids. He sat down in the hall, knowing he'd had a narrow escape. The phone rang and he jumped.

Angela was at the station in a phone booth. She was relieved when Mike answered but shocked when he yelled at her never to call his home again.

"Well, I needed to speak to you. I'm in London, I came here with Dolly. She got the diamonds, Mike, she had them with her."

Mike stood up, trying to keep his voice calm. "You sure? Where is she now?"

Angela told him where she had been, and then Mike said he had to go, he couldn't talk any more. His head felt as if it was blowing apart. If Dolly

Rawlins had the diamonds then she had to have run over Jimmy Donald-son, and she had to know by now the diamonds were fakes. It seemed that any way he moved he just sank in deeper and deeper into the mud. There was one thing in his favor: she wouldn't go to the law. But he knew one place she would go and his panic went into overdrive. He hoped to Christ his mother was out of the country. He grabbed the phone and dialed her number.

Angela sat on the station platform. She had tried to call Mike again but the number was engaged. She kept trying but it was constantly busy. She was near to tears, sure he'd taken it off the hook. There was something else she had to tell him: she'd missed two periods.

Audrey picked up the phone and Mike started yelling before she'd even said hello. "She knows about Tommy. She's been to see him about the diamonds this afternoon."

"Who?"

"Who the hell do you think? Dolly Rawlins. She got the diamonds then went to Tommy Malin."

Audrey's legs were like jelly. "I've got me ticket, but I don't leave until tomorrow."

Mike rubbed his chin. "You'd better go tonight."

"You think she'll come here?"

He closed his eyes. "Look, the best thing you can do is go away, just clear out."

Audrey burst into tears and he yelled at her to pull herself together. He said he'd see if he could come round later, and hung up.

She sat for a moment, still cradling the phone before shakily going back to her packing. Half an hour later the doorbell rang shrilly and Audrey dropped her case as she ran to the door. She thought it would be Mike but when she swung the door open she froze.

"Hello, Audrey. It's Dolly—Dolly Rawlins."

Audrey forced a smile. "Good heavens! So you're out then, are you?"

"Yes. You going to ask me in?"

Audrey swallowed and held the door wider.

Dolly walked past her, straight into the sitting room. The first thing she saw was the big eight-by-ten color photograph of Shirley. She reached out, touched it, and laid it face down on the sideboard. Then she spotted the passport and plane ticket. "Going away?"

Audrey could hardly breathe. She gestured to the half-packed suitcases in her bedroom. "Just to Brighton, to see a friend for the weekend."

"Taking a lot of gear for just a weekend, aren't you?" Audrey flushed as Dolly held up her passport. "Won't be needing this then, will you?"

Audrey's eyes almost popped out of her head as Dolly slipped it into her pocket. "Why did you do that?"

Dolly sat down on the settee, unbuttoning her coat. "Because, Audrey, we've got to talk. Sit down."

Audrey moved to a hard-backed chair and perched on the edge of the seat. "How long have you been out?"

Dolly gave an icy smile. "I bet you know the exact minute. Come on, Audrey, how much did you get for the diamonds?"

She knew it was pointless to deny she'd taken them. "It's not the way it looks."

"I'm all ears."

Audrey gulped. "Well, when I read that Jimmy Donaldson had been arrested—"

Dolly interrupted, "You went round and collected. But you never thought to contact me, did you?"

"Well, it was too risky, wasn't it?"

"How much did you get?"

"Not a lot." Audrey cleared her throat.

"How much?"

"Four hundred and fifty thousand."

Dolly leaned back and gave a short humorless laugh. "Don't mess me around. *How much?*"

Audrey began to blubber, swearing on her life that was all she got, and said Dolly could even check it out with Frank Richmond.

"Frank Richmond? You fenced them through him, that cheap bastard? Why didn't you fence them with Tommy?"

"I didn't think— I was scared—I mean, they were here in the flat."

Dolly leaned back and closed her eyes. "Eight years I waited, Audrey, eight years . . ."

"Shirley's been dead eight years," Audrey said. Then she got even more scared as Dolly went rigid, her eyes shut tight, hands clenched. "I've only got a few thousand cash I can give you. I put the bulk of it in Spain."

"Spain?"

"I bought a villa and . . . it was all done in such a hurry because I was terrified I'd be nicked."

"I was, Audrey. I did almost nine years for killing Harry and right now I'd do ten for you. You get me my share and I want it by tomorrow."

"But I haven't got it."

"*Then get it!* And when you have, call me. This is my number." Dolly opened her bag and scrawled her phone number. She stood up to pass it to her, leaning in close, her face almost touching Audrey's. "Until I get it, I'll hold your passport. You call me by tomorrow or, like I said, I'll shop you, go down for you and don't think for a second I don't mean it."

Mike listened in stunned silence as Audrey told him about Dolly's visit. "I got to get money, Mike, or she'll shop me."

Mike could feel that mud turning into cement round his ankles now. "Does she know about me?"

"She thinks it was just me. Mike, I got until tomorrow to get the money."

"What the fuck do you want me to do?"

"I'll need the money I put in the kids' building society savings accounts."

"*What?* Are you telling me some of that cash is in *my kids' accounts*?" Audrey started sobbing. He couldn't make any sense of what she was saying. "Mum, get in a cab and come round. Now."

Mr. Crow looked out of the window as he drove up the Manor House driveway. Mrs. Tilly sat in the back seat with Mr. Simms, another member of the board.

"There's a lot of land. A wonderful place for kids," he observed.

They drove slowly up to the front door, where workmen's tools were lying around.

"Looks like work has already started," mused Mr. Crow, looking up at the scaffolding.

They got out and looked over the grounds again before walking to the front door. Mrs. Tilly had wanted to warn Dolly of their arrival, but they had been to visit another foster family and only just decided to make an on-site visit to the manor.

As the door was open they all entered the house. Mrs. Tilly called out for Dolly and, receiving no reply, peered into the lounge. "It's huge. I had no idea it was such a big property," she said.

"Hello? Anyone at home?" Mr. Crow called as he looked into the kitchen. The others followed him and stood in the doorway, impressed by the size of the old-fashioned kitchen. They were about to leave the leaflets and documents they had brought on the hall table when they heard the screams and laughter from the cellar.

Kathleen tried the first shower but nothing came out except a low rumbling from the pipes. She banged the pipes with a shoe as Gloria came out of the sauna. "Showers aren't working," Kathleen said, grinning when she saw the hosepipe. "How about bein' hosed down, shall we try that?"

Gloria pulled a face. "Forget it. I'm gonna have a bath in me own room." She hitched a towel round her and wandered out, heading up the cellar stairs. Mr. Crow and his party were just coming out of the dining room when she appeared. She took one look, shrieked and dived back down to the cellar.

"Was that Mrs. Rawlins?" Mr. Crow asked.

Mrs. Tilly shook her head on her way to the cellar door. She called again for Dolly but could hear only more shrieks from below.

Connie, stark naked, had her hands up as Kathleen turned the hosepipe on her full blast. Gloria yelled for her to switch it off but Kathleen pointed the hose at her just as the three visitors appeared in the doorway, spraying them with water as the women screamed and yelled like schoolgirls. There was a lot of fumbling for towels as Gloria shot out past them.

Mrs. Tilly was red-faced with embarrassment as she opened the sauna door. She gasped and slammed it shut.

"I think we should leave." She hurried out, appalled at what she had just seen: Ester and Julia, both naked, locked in each other's arms.

Ester grabbed her towel and ran out after them as they disappeared up the cellar stairs. "Just a minute! *Wait!* Wait a minute."

But they couldn't get out fast enough.

Esther called down the stairs to Julia, "I think they were from the social services. Better not mention this to Dolly."

It was getting dark when Angela appeared. When they saw her alone the women downed tools and asked her where Dolly was.

"I don't know, she sent me home."

"Shit!" Ester marched over. "Where did she go? She's coming back, isn't she?" she demanded, her heart sinking. Would Dolly just up, take the cash and leave them all here? She went into Dolly's room. All her belongings were there, including the deeds of the house, so she felt a little easier.

By the time Dolly did come back, a few hours later, the women were all having supper. When she walked in, they all started talking at once about how much work they had been doing, how they loved the house, but slowly their conversation petered out as Dolly chucked the pouch onto the table.

"Take a look. They're worthless, glass, all of them."

They fingered the glittering stones, before looking at Dolly in confusion.

"There's no money, so you all get a cut of nothing."

Kathleen picked up one of the biggest stones, holding it in her pudgy hand, then pressed it against her cheek. It felt cold but quickly warmed up. She hurled it against the side of the Aga where it shattered into tiny fragments. "Fucking glass, all right."

Each one of them would have liked to smash something, anything, as their initial confusion turned to anger, their dreams shattered just like the fake diamond. Gradually their anger subsided and a dark depression hung in the air. Dolly slowly sat down and picked up a piece of bread, picking bits off it as she looked from one crestfallen face to another. "So, will you be staying on, Ester?"

"Well, I've got to admit it, Dolly, I've never been one for kids so I guess I'm out of here."

"What about you, Julia?"

Julia shrugged her shoulders, then looked at Ester. "I guess I'll leave with Ester. That's not to say I don't love this place because I do but—"

Dolly interrupted, looking at Connie. "What about you?"

Connie flushed. "Well, to be honest, I know I've got this problem with Lennie and I need a place to lie low for a while, but as a long-term thing I want to start off my career proper, you know, get an agent and . . ." She trailed off, head bent, not able to meet Dolly's eyes.

Kathleen coughed. "I'll stay put with you, love. I need a place, I got nowhere else."

Angela reached out and touched Dolly's hand. "I'll stay too. I'm sure we can . . ."

Dolly held Angela's hand tightly, as Gloria pushed back her chair. "I'll be here for a few weeks." Dolly looked up at her, surprised. "You got Eddie's gear someplace and we'll have to sort something out about that."

"I see," Dolly said quietly. "Well, at least I know where I stand. So, those of you that are going, pack up and leave. It'll save on food bills. Goodnight."

* * *

Dolly stared at her reflection in the dressing-table mirror. She calculated that with the money from Audrey she might still be able to pull off something. It might even be better that it had worked out this way—at least she knew who she could trust, now that she'd found out it was Audrey, poor Shirley Miller's mother, who'd grassed on her.

CHAPTER 9

Dolly had only just come down to breakfast when John asked to speak to her. He was obviously angry: the men wanted paying; he wanted paying. She had successfully put off the first installment but now it was Friday and there was still no cash.

Guiltily, Dolly said she was having problems releasing the cash but assured him that he would have it by the following morning.

John didn't like the sound of it, but what could he do? His workers were less stoical about it, immediately downing tools and walking off the site, saying they would come back when he paid up.

The house, with the scaffolding and debris surrounding the grounds, looked in an even more dilapidated condition than before. Loose tiles had been thrown from the roof, the chimneys were still at a dangerous angle, windows were out in some rooms, sections of the front of the house had no plaster, leaving the rough old bricks exposed. It was a depressing sight, but Dolly didn't let it dampen her spirits: not only was some money coming her way, but she had impressed the social services.

Audrey, in a state of nerves matched only by her son's, gathered all the money she could lay her hands on. At least Dolly still had no knowledge of Mike's part and, thankfully for him, neither did the police. DCI Craigh had played down Mike's part to the Chief and the fact that the police had succeeded in tracing the stolen gems at Donaldson's antique shop had been swept under the carpet.

Traffic, however, had been pressured to trace the car that killed Donaldson and now, with the incentive to pull out all stops, they really went to work. They had only a part registration and a vague description of the vehicle, but they checked on paint color co-ordination with both Rover and Volvo companies, their computers triggering further developments as they began slowly to narrow down the make and year of the vehicle. All they required was time.

Julia knew that she would be in deep trouble if she returned to London. But Ester was set on leaving: "You do what the hell you like."

Julia had flounced out of the house and taken herself off to the local pub. She ordered a double Scotch on the rocks and leaned on the bar. Across the room, seated at one of the bay windows, was Norma Hastings, wearing jodhpurs and a hacking jacket. She looked at her curiously from behind her newspaper. Norma was an attractive woman, thick red hair, a pleasant round face and obviously fit: her cheeks had that ruddy glow. In comparison, Julia looked pale, her skinny frame mannish and her long, wiry brown hair like an unruly mop-head. Norma continued to watch her, pretending to read the paper, until she could not be bothered to hide her interest any longer and tossed the paper aside. She reckoned she was right about the gangly woman at the bar—it was rare that she wasn't. It was also clear she was unhappy, ordering one double Scotch after another, knocking them back in one gulp, then staring at the polished wood counter. As she dug into her pockets to count out the cash to pay the barman, Norma also couldn't help noticing her perfect, tight arse in her skin-tight trousers.

As Julia's boots were mud-spattered, Norma reckoned it would be a good opener to ask if she liked to ride—horses, of course, not herself; at least not yet. She wasn't often so blatant about it—in her job she couldn't be. If the Metropolitan Police knew that one of their mounted officers was gay . . . she could only imagine the snide cracks. She'd had enough of them just being a woman, without them knowing she was a lesbian as well.

Norma decided to go for it and walked toward the bar, but her confidence slipped as Julia turned to her. She had not expected such dark, angry eyes. "Hello, I'm Norma Hastings." She put out her hand.

"Are you now. Good for you," said Julia sarcastically.

Norma was undeterred. "Can I buy you a drink?"

"Why not? Double Scotch."

An hour later, Julia's cheeks were as flushed as Norma's, not from fresh air but from all the alcohol. She felt really very tipsy as the two climbed over a gate and into a field with a couple of grazing horses.

"She's called Helen of Troy and if you can stable her, I'll provide the feed. It's just that I've got Caper and he's a bit of a handful." Norma pointed to a three-year-old stallion and then smiled at the quietly grazing Helen of Troy.

Julia pressed her cheek against Helen's nose. "She's beautiful," she whispered.

"Well, I even put an advert in the local papers but I've had no offers yet. I was going to let the local riding school have her—she's still got a lot of life in her."

Julia was still plastered as she wove her way along the manor's drive. She wasn't alone. Dolly looked out from the drawing-room window. "Oh my Gawd!" she exclaimed.

"What?" asked Kathleen, trying to remove a bursting hoover bag.

"Julia's only gone and got a horse."

Gloria peered up into Helen's face. "Cor blimey, it's enormous this, isn't it?"

Connie reached out to stroke the horse and then stepped back as Norma drove up in a clapped-out Land Rover. "I've brought her tack and feed. Is that the stable?" she asked, hopping down.

The women looked at one another, not sure what was going on, as now Dolly and Kathleen came to the kitchen door.

"Hi, Dolly. This is Norma and this is Helen of Troy." Julia grinned like a schoolgirl. "She's been given to us, for free."

"Oh, yeah . . ." Dolly looked on as Angela squeezed out, running over to the horse.

Norma walked over and gave Dolly a bone-crushing handshake. "She'll be marvelous with kids. She's thirteen years old, retired now, but if you're opening this as a children's home she'll be ideal. You can drop a bomb in front of her and she won't even flinch. She can walk through a band or a riot and she's as cool as a cucumber."

Julia looked pleadingly at Dolly. "She's a police horse, Dolly."

Kathleen flinched as if the horse was about to arrest her.

"A minute, love," Dolly said, and went back into the kitchen, followed by a flushed Julia.

"She's beautiful, isn't she? And free! We don't even have to pay for her feed."

Dolly folded her arms. "Really? And Norma's a policewoman, is she?"

Julia nodded, grinning inanely. She reeked of booze.

Dolly sighed. "I don't like the filth, mounted or otherwise, poking their noses around."

Julia looked crestfallen. "Oh, well, I can take it back. I just thought . . ."

"You thought what? I don't ride, there's no kids here yet and you're leaving, so what the hell am I gonna do with a horse?"

Julia gripped the back of the chair. "I want to stay on, Dolly. I'll groom her, feed her . . . You wouldn't have to do a single thing, and I'll make sure Norma keeps her distance."

"You better. We got an arsenal of guns on the property and none of us are what you might call upright citizens."

Julia was about to return to the yard when Dolly put her hand on her arm. "Ester's gone."

Julia was stunned. "Gone?"

"About fifteen minutes ago. And if you don't mind me saying so, it's good riddance."

Julia couldn't believe Ester had walked out without even saying goodbye. She had to check that all her belongings had gone from their bedroom before finally accepting it. She slipped downstairs for a bottle of vodka, and started drinking it straight from the bottle. Ester had left her without so much as a note. Julia rested back against the pillow that still smelt of her perfume and started to cry, those awful, silent tears she had learned to cry in prison. Ester had chosen Julia, walked straight up to her. The other girls sitting with their dinner trays had moved away from the table, but Julia had said nothing, just continued to eat, her eyes down, afraid of what Ester wanted.

"You shooting up?" Ester had said.

Julia had swallowed, still unable to look at her.

"Bad stuff in here. You'd better go cold turkey. I'll take care of you."

Julia reached for the bottle, wanting to pass out. She didn't want to hear that wonderful gravelly voice in her head, smell that thick sweet-scented perfume. Ester was the love of Julia's life and without her the fear returned, her confidence dwindled and her deep-seated guilt and shame threatened to overwhelm her.

"I'm at the station," Audrey said.

"I'll be there, just wait in the car park." Dolly put down the phone and went out to find Gloria. She was with Kathleen, hanging over the stable door. Dolly held up the keys to Gloria's Mini. "I won't be long, just getting some groceries."

Gloria rushed over. "I need Eddie's guns, Dolly. I got to get some cash."

Dolly opened the Mini and got inside. "We'll talk about them later."

"They're worth nearly thirty grand, Eddie said."

Dolly wound down the window. "And they could have got us arrested. When I come back we'll talk."

"I'll cut you in, Dolly, that's only fair." Dolly started the engine and backed the Mini down the drive, Gloria still following her. "Say twenty percent?"

Gloria watched the car disappear down the drive.

Audrey was standing in the center of the car park clutching her handbag when Dolly pulled up. Audrey climbed into the Mini. The level-crossing gates were closed. "What's up?" Audrey asked, staring at the railway crossing.

"Must be a train due."

Raymond Dewey saw Dolly and waved. She lowered the window. "Hello, Raymond, you on duty, are you?" He came over to the car and shook her hand, then introduced himself to Audrey. She pressed herself back in her seat as his square head poked through the window. "How long will we have to wait?" Dolly asked.

"Oh, might be a few minutes. Not like the mail train, always a long delay every Thursday. This is the three twenty, local." He returned to his stool to jot down more notes in his precious book as Audrey and Dolly sat in silence. They watched the train chugging past them before the gates slowly lifted.

"Bloody nutter," said Audrey as they passed him, now waving them on like a traffic controller.

They went into the local pub and Audrey took a corner seat at the bay window as Dolly got the drinks. When Dolly put a large gin and tonic down in front of her she knocked it back in two gulps to try to calm her nerves. "Right, I've got you all I could. Twenty grand."

Dolly sipped her drink. "I hope you're joking."

"No, I'm not. I brought bank statements, everything, you can see for yourself that's all I could get. The rest, like I told you, went into the villa. I'll sell it, split the profits, but it'll take a while." Audrey opened her bag and took out a thick envelope. She was about to pass it to Dolly when Norma walked over.

"Hello, Mrs. Rawlins."

Dolly gave a tight, brittle smile. "Hello, Norma. I'd offer to buy you a drink but we're just leaving. Audrey, this is Norma. She's a mounted police officer."

Audrey gaped in horror. "Oh, nice to meet you."

Dolly waved at Raymond as they passed him again and drove into the station car park. Audrey still clutched her bag tightly, sweating with nerves and wishing Dolly would say something to break the tension. But she drove in tight-lipped silence.

"I'll need my passport, Dolly, and me ticket for Spain."

Dolly engaged the handbrake and leaned over to open the glove compartment. "Here, take them. Just give me the money." Audrey passed her the envelope. She shoved it into her pocket without counting it. "I don't want to see you or hear from you again, Audrey. Just get out of my sight."

Audrey fumbled with the door handle in her haste to get away. She ran into the station, still afraid Dolly might get out and attack her—she'd turned those chipped-ice eyes on her with such hatred. Dolly sat in the car and watched her go. Twenty thousand pounds! And she'd thought she would have millions. How was she going to make things work now?

Gloria and Connie were sitting at the kitchen table playing noughts and crosses when Dolly got back. "Did you get milk?" Connie asked.

"No. Shops were closed, wasted journey."

Gloria screwed up the paper. "About Eddie's guns, Dolly."

Dolly took off her coat. "We'll go and get them when it's dark but right now I'd like a cup of tea, if that's all right with you—even if we haven't got any milk."

Julia was lying face down on the bed. She didn't look up when Dolly tapped on the door and walked in. "I need a hand, Julia. We're going to get the guns and—" Julia tried to sit up then flopped down again. Dolly saw the empty bottle on the floor. "You'd better sleep it off, we'll manage without you."

"We'll need spades and a wheelbarrow," Dolly said to Gloria and then, as Connie, all dressed up, walked into the kitchen, "You leaving too, are you?"

Connie shook her head. "No, I'm going out with that builder bloke."

Gloria nudged Dolly. "I told her earlier to get the old leg over and he'd maybe work for nothin'."

Dolly shook her head at Gloria, as if she was a naughty kid, and then asked Connie to come into the room she now used as an office. She handed over an envelope with ten thousand pounds cash inside. "Give this to him, will you? Tell him he'll get the rest next week and if he could get the men back to work over the weekend, I'd be grateful."

"Okay." Connie slipped the envelope into her pocket.

Dolly hesitated, then patted Connie's arm. "Be nice to him. Be a help to me, know what I mean?"

Connie bit her lip. "Sure, pay my way, so to speak."

Dolly nodded. "Good. You have a nice evening, then."

Connie met John outside the manor gates. He'd changed into a suit and Connie was touched by the effort he'd made. "Sorry about the state of the van," he said nervously as they drove off. "Do you like Chinese?"

Connie hated Chinese. She flashed him a beaming smile. "That would be lovely."

"God, I'm hungry," complained Gloria as she trundled the wheelbarrow through the woods.

Kathleen trudged along behind with two spades. "Got to hand it to you, Dolly, if you hadn't stashed them, we'd be in a right old mess."

Gloria scowled, all the time wondering just how much Dolly would squeeze her for Eddie's guns, but she couldn't help being impressed by the fact she'd hidden them so far from the house and done it all on her own. As if she was reading her mind, Dolly looked at her. "I did it in three trips, Gloria, took half the night."

Julia woke up, her dulled senses finally making out the sound of the telephone ringing and ringing. She stumbled out of her room and almost fell down the stairs.

She lurched toward it, snatching it up. "Ester? Is that you?"

"Is Connie there?" said a man's voice.

Julia swung round and looked into the kitchen. "Connie? *Connie?*"

"She . . . she's not here," Julia slurred.

"Okay. I'm coming to meet her but I seem to be in a dead end road. How do I get to the Grange?"

Julia began to give him directions, assuming Connie had arranged for Lennie to collect her. She was too drunk to remember that Connie was terrified of him.

Lennie slipped the portable back into the glove compartment of his shining Porsche and started to reverse. He swore when the car sank into a pothole, the mud splashing the gleaming paintwork. Then he drove slowly down the lane.

Connie giggled as the waiter presented John with the bill and his eyes almost popped out of his head. But he paid up, digging into the envelope Connie had given him. She felt a bit bad about ordering champagne and pressed her leg against his under the table. He flushed as she kicked off her shoe and let her toes stroke his crotch. He had never before come across a woman like Connie and felt excited and terrified at the same time.

"Do you think she'll be able to pay the rest?" he asked, trying to appear nonchalant as Connie's toes stroked the fly of his trousers.

"Oh, so you asked me out to find out about Mrs. Rawlins?"

"No, no! It's just that I'm a one-man firm and I could go broke over this. I've ordered a lot of equipment."

"If Mrs. Rawlins says she'll pay you, then she will," Connie purred, leaning toward him over the table as her toes did all the walking below.

"I'd better get you home," he gulped.

Gloria had taken over the digging as Kathleen heaved the first bag onto the wheelbarrow. "You're stronger than you look, Dolly Rawlins. These weigh a ton."

Angela pulled the brambles away from the third hiding place as Gloria stuck in the spade. They were on the brow of a small hill just outside the wooded perimeter of the manor's land, and could see clearly the signal box below.

"Who's at the gates?" Kathleen pointed.

Dolly looked up. She could see the flashing signal lights, the barred gates, and the stationary builder's van.

Gloria prodded her in the ribs. "You think he's givin' her one or is it just light relief?"

Dolly grimaced. Sometimes Gloria's crudeness really irritated her but she couldn't help taking another look to see what was going on in the van.

John had Connie's top undone and was nuzzling her breasts as she kept one eye on the signal lights.

"Train's coming," she whispered.

He moaned, and for a moment she thought he was coming too but then he sat back. "I'm sorry."

She buttoned her blouse and snuggled up to him. "Are you married?"

"No, but I live with someone."

"And where does she think you are tonight?"

"At the gym."

She grinned. "Can I work out with you one day? I love doing weights."

The train thundered past and the gates slowly opened. "Anytime you like." John put the van into gear and they headed down the narrow lane back toward the manor.

Lennie reversed into a field through an open gate. He'd already driven past the manor, taken a quick look and decided that the element of surprise would be more beneficial. He was just about to get out when the van passed him. He waited until it parked by the manor, then followed on foot, keeping close to the overhanging hedgerow.

They'd finally loaded the wheelbarrow and were pushing it back toward the manor. Dolly walked ahead, her arm slung around Angela's shoulder. "You know you can go on special government courses, get further education, proper training in something. You're welcome to stay on here for as long as you like, you know that, but you should think about it. Do you like kids?"

"Oh yeah, and I'm used to them. I've got younger brothers still at school."

Connie leaned in to John and gave him a long, lingering kiss. "You'd better check your face before you go in. Lipstick!" She giggled as he wiped his mouth. "I'll see you tomorrow?"

He watched her wiggle and sashay her way to the front door, then turn and do her Marilyn Monroe pout. He blew her a kiss, felt stupid and quickly put the van into reverse. He drove past Lennie, waiting in the shadows, without seeing him.

"Connie!"

She knew his voice immediately. "Lennie?"

He stepped forward. "Surprise, surprise!"

She began to shake with terror. "You stay away from me, Lennie. Don't hurt me!"

He walked toward her, his arms out wide, smiling. "I'm not going to hurt you, Connie. Why would I do that? I've just come to take you home."

"I'm not coming with you, Lennie. You got to leave me alone."

He came closer and now he wasn't playing games. "You owe me, Connie, and you're gonna pay it off or work it off. Suit yourself."

"I won't go anywhere with you."

He lunged for her but she kicked out, screaming, catching him in the groin. He lost his footing, tripping over a plank left by the builders, while clutching his balls. "Don't you dare fuck with me!" he snarled through grit-ted teeth.

She was running in no particular direction, anywhere to get away from him, sobbing with fear. He started after her, yelling with rage, as she ran on, weaving her way erratically toward the woods.

Dolly went rigid as the sound of screaming made them stop in their tracks.

Gloria let go of the handles of the wheelbarrow. "It's Connie." She ran toward the manor.

Dolly started to follow and then turned to Kathleen and Angela. "You stay put, the pair of you, until I come back and get you." She tore after Gloria through the woods, hearing another high-pitched scream.

Connie had run straight into Gloria and Gloria had to slap Connie's face. "It's me, Connie, it's me, Gloria."

Connie clung to her. "He's here. Oh God, Gloria, he's here and he's gonna kill me. He was chasing me, he's going to kill—"

"Connie, listen to me." Gloria smacked her hard again. "Nobody is going to touch you, all right? We're all here."

Dolly was breathless when she reached them. "What's going on?"

"It's that bloke, her pimp. He's come after her."

Dolly gripped Connie's arm. "We won't let him lay a finger on you. Gloria, go and get the other two. I'll take Connie back to the house with me."

A terrified Connie clung to Dolly as they made their way cautiously, then ran the last few yards past the stables and into the safety of the house. Dolly quickly latched the door behind them but Connie still didn't feel safe. "What if he's here, in the house?"

Gloria, Kathleen and Angela wheeled the rest of the guns into the stable yard and then carried them inside. Connie was sitting with a large brandy, her eyes red-rimmed from crying, as Julia sat with her head in her hands, so hungover she could hardly speak.

Gloria held up a shotgun. "Right, we got enough of these. If that prick shows his face, I'll blow it off."

"We'll search the house," Dolly said. "Some of the windows are out so if he's here, we'd better find him. We'll have a good look round, then, Connie, you lock yourself in a room with Angela."

Connie began to sob again and Dolly lost her patience. "Shut up, for God's sake! And you, Julia, get some coffee down you and try and sober up."

Connie wiped her face with the back of her hand. "He said he's going to take me back."

Dolly shook her by the shoulders. "Nobody's going to make you do anything you don't want to do, okay? We'll sort it."

Gloria went over the grounds with the shotgun at the ready. She checked the stables, the outhouses and the yard, and even went up to the woods, but an owl suddenly hooting gave her the willies, so she quickly scuttled back to the front door of the manor. It was ajar and she pushed it slowly. "Anyone here?"

Dolly stood there with her hands on her hips. "Yes. Me, you fool. Did you see anything out there?"

"Nope. Maybe he saw us and decided to piss off."

"Let's hope you're right," Dolly said, shutting the door.

Ester drove into the underground car park of the Club Cabar. She'd been to three other clubs and this was her last hope: it was Steve Rooney or back to the Grange. She locked up the Range Rover, checked her hair and make-up, pulled her black dress down a bit further to show off her shoulders and tits and changed her driving shoes for spiked heels. "Right, gel, let's do the business."

She walked in casually, full of confidence, toward the private lift to the club. The car park was used by a number of offices in the day but taken over by the club at night so they had their own small lift leading directly to their reception. As the grille slid back, a muscle-bound bouncer in an ill-fitting evening suit nodded at Ester.

She gave him a cursory wave. "Is Steve in?"

"Yeah, he's wiv someone. But I'll tell 'im you're 'ere."

"Thank you," she said crisply, heading toward the main room of the club. Its small sunken dance floor was empty but you could hardly see your hand in front of your face for the blinking neon strips. At least the ornate, over-brassy bar was well lit and the row of red velvet-topped high stools had only one male occupant: a swarthy, fat little man, drinking from a long glass with a profusion of fruit and paper umbrellas sticking out of it. He was surrounded by a gaggle of sexy blondes with tight mini-skirts and tied blouse tops showing a lot of cleavage, tottering on heels even higher than Ester's. They were giggling and whispering to each other as the poor sucker with the paper umbrella almost up his nose slurped a drink that had probably set him back a tenner. The girls would make sure he was parted from a lot more than that before the night was out.

Ester perched on a stool as far away from the fat man as possible. The barman was doing an impressive performance with his Martini shaker to the deafening, thudding rock music that made it impossible for anyone to have a conversation.

"Hi, Eth-ter, how ya doin?" the barman lisped.

"I'm doing fine. Gimme a Southern Comfort, lemonade, slice of lemon and crushed ice, easy on the lemonade." She lit a cigarette as she spoke, but he knew what she liked and was already searching through the array of bottles. He shimmied up and down the bar and then whisked out a paper napkin and a bowl of peanuts before placing her drink down with a smile.

"On the house."

"Cheers." She sipped, then winced. He'd overdone it with the lemonade. In the mirror she saw Steve Rooney talking to the bouncer, who gestured toward the bar. Ester turned and Rooney held up his hand to indicate five minutes.

A few more punters arrived and wandered around. Ester signaled for a refill, then grabbed a handful of peanuts. It was strange. She'd been out of the business a long time, and didn't know any of the girls now. She hated the whole scene, which was why she'd moved to the Grange, but for a while she had been coining it. Rooney tapped her shoulder and pointed at his office, interrupting her thoughts. She slid off the stool, drained her glass and followed, shooting a look at the little fat man. "I'd get out while you're still on top, fella."

Rooney perched on his fake antique desk. "So, how's tricks, darlin'? I just hope you've not come to touch me for a few quid. As you can see, it's Friday night and we're not exactly filling the joint."

"It'll pick up, it always used to."

His polished Gucci loafer tapped the side of the desk. "What do you want, Ester? I know you've schlepped round a few places tonight."

"Warned off me, were you?"

He smiled. His eyes were pale blue behind tinted glasses. "You're not still wheeling around in that Range Rover, are you?"

She flicked her lighter and lit a cigarette.

"You really are stupid, you know that, don't you? You tried it on with the wrong people, Ester. They got a lot of dough and they'll use it to find you."

"No kidding. Doesn't scare me."

"It should. That was a stupid move. They paid out a lot of cash for you, and what do you do?"

"I did three years and I kept my mouth shut. They ripped me off."

"No, they didn't. How were they to know you had a string of offenses as long as both arms? They paid your taxes and your lawyer, and you come out, try to nail them for more cash, then nick the kid's motor."

She stubbed out the cigarette. "They got enough of them. What's one little Range Rover?"

"It wasn't what it was, it was you doin' it. It was stupid."

Ester shrugged. "You seem to know a lot about my business."

Rooney sighed, picking a bit of fluff off his Armani jacket. "Because I supply them now, okay? I'm not gonna hide anything from you. It's not as if I nicked your clients. You were inside."

"Yes, I was, and now I need a job, Rooney."

"Well don't look in my direction. I'm not going to put myself out for you, Ester. You never gave me a leg-up when I needed it."

"But I sent a lot of clients your way, you cheap shit."

His face tightened and Ester would have liked to smack him. Rooney had once been a barman she'd hired for special parties, back in the old days when she ran a house for two major club owners. They'd have the clients drinking and eating at their respectable joints and when they wanted a girl Ester supplied them. She kept ten good-looking tarts, and they were always busy. There were private parties for movie stars, MPs, titled perverts; in fact anyone the club owners gave membership to would at some time or another end up at the Notting Hill Gate house . . . until it was busted. Ester had served a few years back then, and when she came out of prison she had been determined that the next place would be her own. So she turned tricks solo for four years, working the main hotels until she had enough to put down on Grange Manor House. Rooney had learned fast, and soon after her bust, which he was never questioned about, he had gone to work for the club owners.

It had been Rooney who had sent her the Arab clients for the manor, and he'd taken a cut. But, just like her bust at Notting Hill Gate, when it went down at the Grange, Rooney's name was never mentioned. Rooney had even suggested to her that, if she played her cards right, she might even earn extra by making a couple of videos of certain clients at the manor. He had sold a few for her, just light porn stuff, but when she told him about the tape she'd made of his Arab clients' kids, he had walked away. He told her that if she had any sense she would as well. A couple of movie stars caught with their pants down was one thing but not the so-called flowing-robed royalty: that was asking for trouble.

"You don't know how to say thank you, do you?" she said curtly.

Rooney leaned close. "Sweetheart, I owe you fuck all. You done nothing for me. Whatever I done, I done all by meself."

She laughed. "You're still an illiterate shit."

"Maybe I am, but I'm a fucking sight richer than you are and I don't look for trouble. That's why I'm in business and you're nowhere."

She was about to remind him who gave him his first job, but there was a rap at the door and Brian, the bouncer, appeared.

"There's a party of six kids, they said to ask for you. None of them are members but they look as if they got a few readies."

Ester stood up, smoothed down her dress and saw the car keys on the desk. She whipped them up fast and then picked up her handbag. "Well, I'll be going."

Rooney asked her to go out of the back entrance. "I don't want any aggro, Ester. I'm sorry."

She pushed past him and he looked at Brian. "If she's in that fucking Range Rover, get it."

Rooney closed his office door and headed into the club's reception.

Ester went out through the kitchens, down the fire escape and into the car park. She was searching in her bag for the Range Rover keys when she saw Brian stepping out of the lift, accompanied by another equally heavy-set bouncer. They walked nonchalantly toward the Range Rover and leaned against it. "This isn't yours, is it, Ester? Give me the keys, darlin'."

"Piss off."

Brian made a grab for her but she quickly twisted the keys into her fist, jabbing hard at his face. She caught his right eye a beaut, and he backed away. Ester felt her hair being torn out by the roots by his friend and screamed, hurling the keys at him. But Brian was back, slapping her hard across the face. Ester fell onto the dirty garage floor and tried to crawl away, but they kicked her in the head, the ribs and the groin. She curled up in a tight ball to protect herself, but they kept on kicking until she half rolled beneath a car.

She stayed there, wedged under it, as they threw her belongings onto the ground before driving the Range Rover out of the car park. She moaned, gingerly feeling her ribs and her face before searching for her handbag. Finally she pulled her body upright. It was agony.

When she pressed the alarm on the keys she'd taken from Rooney they lit up a brand-new Saab convertible and, as sick as she felt, she couldn't help but smile. It was beautiful. She was just about to drag her belongings together when she heard the lift opening. Rooney slid back the gate. "I'm sorry about that, Ester, but I've got to take the Range Rover back and if you've got any sense you'll take that tape back as well."

She picked up her case. "Thanks for the advice."

Rooney peeled off two fifty-pound notes and tossed them toward her. "Take a cab."

She wouldn't let him see her grovel and pick up the notes, so she stood there until the lift had disappeared, then picked up the money, wincing in pain, and opened the boot of the Saab, tossing in her case.

"Fuck you, Rooney." She got in and drove out fast, smiling.

Gloria had all the guns laid out on the kitchen table, and it was a formidable collection. She was in her element as she handled them expertly, showing them off as if they were fashion accessories. Kathleen hung back, eyes popping. She wouldn't go near them. But Julia was brave enough to reach out and touch the barrel of the Hechler and Koch machine gun. "My God! You had these stashed in the house?"

Dolly wasn't happy having such heavy-duty weaponry in the house, but at the same time knew she was looking at cold, hard cash. "What are they worth, did you say?"

"Thirty grand at least," Gloria said, beaming.

Dolly nodded. "Well, the sooner they're out of here the better. You tell that husband of yours I want a cut, fifty percent. If he doesn't like it . . ."

Gloria sniggered. "He can't really do a lot about it. He's doing eighteen, Dolly."

"I know that," Dolly replied. "I just don't want him sending any goons round. So get a contact and get rid of them—fast."

Gloria began to roll up the shotguns in their padded cloths. She obviously knew what she was doing and Julia couldn't help but be impressed. "Do you know how to use them?"

"Course I do. I belong to one of the top gun clubs in the country. You got to know what you're sellin' or buyin.'" She picked up a .45 and held it out in front of her at arm's length as if she was about to take aim.

Dolly turned on her angrily. "Just put them away, Gloria!"

"Right, right." As Dolly walked out, Gloria grinned at Julia. "You know, they say Hitler's mistress never died in the bunker with him. That one, dead ringer for Eva Braun."

Julia smiled, and put the kettle on.

Angela was sitting holding Connie's hand. She was still scared, jumping at every creak in the house, and sprang up when Dolly walked in.

"I'm going to bed. Julia will stay downstairs just in case he comes back but I think he's gone."

Connie stammered, "He'll be back, Dolly. He'll never leave me alone."

Dolly didn't want to hear it all over again. "How did he know you were here?"

Connie paused. "I might have mentioned it, I don't remember."

"Well, then, you got nobody else to blame, have you? Goodnight, Angela love."

Angela shut the door and went back to sit with Connie. "Why don't you tell the police about him?"

Connie sniffed. "Don't be stupid."

"Well, he can't just knock you around and get away with it."

"He can't? Who're you kidding?" Connie wiped her nose with a sodden piece of tissue. "All my life I've been on the end of a fist. First my dad, only he did a lot more than knock me around. My poor mum was so scared of him she used to lock herself in a cupboard. Even when she knew what he was doing to me, she didn't stop him. It meant that it wasn't *her* getting a beating and . . . Every man I've been with has been the same. I dunno why but I always thought Lennie was different. I really thought he loved me."

Angela slipped her arm around her.

"Can't hide out here forever though, can I?" Connie continued. "Because he'll come back. He thinks I'm his property." Angela did sympathize with Connie's situation, but to be honest, she was getting bored with Connie going over and over the same ground. "If I could get an agent, a decent one, I know I could make a living doing proper modeling, I know I could. I can't do anything else, that's for sure."

"How old are you?" asked Angela innocently, and was taken aback when Connie turned on her.

"Mind your own fucking business."

* * *

Ester kept her foot pressed to the floor. She hit a hundred and twenty, passing everything on the road, and then suddenly felt sick and quickly veered over onto the hard shoulder. She only just got out before she vomited, sitting with head bent, the driver's door open, as she waited for the dizziness to pass.

Julia saw the headlights and went to the window, wishing she had one of Gloria's guns. But then she heard the clip-clip of high heels coming toward the back door.

Angela woke and sat up. Connie was by the window. "I just saw a car drive up."

Angela listened. She heard a door open and close. The next moment there was a light tap and Gloria appeared at the door with a loaded shotgun. "Did you hear someone?" Angela nodded. "Right, you lock the door and stay put. I'll see to him."

Gloria crept down the landing and almost blasted Dolly. "Cor, you give me a fright!" she exclaimed.

"What you think you're playing at? Put the gun away," snapped Dolly.

"Somebody come in the house, we all heard it. Shush, listen." They could hear a chair scraping and then Julia talking. They inched down the stairs together, Gloria in front with the shotgun.

Julia examined Ester's ribs. They were cracked, she reckoned, beneath the deep purple bruising.

"I just pranged the car—steering wheel hit me," Ester said, gasping with pain.

Julia produced a large bandage and had just begun to wind it around Ester's midriff when the door burst open. Ester jumped out of her chair, flinching, as Dolly and Gloria marched in.

"Oh, it's you," Gloria snarled.

"Yes. Sorry about this, Dolly. I had a bit of an accident in the car. Is it okay if I just stay for a night or two?"

Dolly folded her arms. "An accident? Who you kidding?"

Ester turned her bruised face away, changing the subject fast. "Whose is the flash Porsche parked down the lane?"

Julia looked at Dolly, then back at Ester. "Our lane?"

"I passed it on my way in."

Gloria ran upstairs to ask Connie what car Lennie drove. She was back a moment later. "It's his."

Julia helped Ester to bed and then joined Gloria and Dolly to search the grounds. This time Dolly carried the shotgun, making Gloria hold up the flashlight. They toured the stables, the outhouses, and saw Ester's Saab.

"Where did she get this?"

Julia said Ester had told her she'd traded the Range Rover in.

"Did she?" Dolly said, already suspicious. They walked together round to the front of the manor, getting more and more anxious as they began to wonder if Lennie was hiding in the house. The beam of the flashlight moved slowly over the grounds, the overgrown bushes and hedgerows, and then swept across the swimming pool.

"Wait! Move it back, down the deep end of the pool." Dolly was squinting in the darkness, trying to work out what she had seen. They walked slowly toward what looked like a bundle of rags but as they moved closer, it was obviously the body of a man.

Lennie was lying face down, his arms floating in the stagnant water in front of him, one leg caught round some old rope.

Dolly hesitated only for a moment. Already there were guns in the house. A body was all they needed. "Get him out."

Julia stared at her. "Are you crazy?"

"No. We get him out and bury him as fast as we can. It's almost dawn."

"Don't you think we should call the police?" Julia asked.

"No, I don't. What do you think the social services would make of it? Get Connie and Angela—we'll all have to help drag him out. We'll put him in the back of Gloria's car."

"I don't think that's a good idea," Julia said, and Dolly turned on her, her face like parchment in the dim light.

"Fine. You take care of it, then," she said coldly, walking away.

Gloria went and fetched Connie, then waded into the filthy water with a hook, to pull the body closer. "Is it him?"

Connie broke down, sobbing that she didn't do it, she never even touched him. Dolly re-joined them, standing slightly apart.

"Well, look at the gash on his head. He must have cracked it on the side of the pool. Nobody's accusing you of doin' anything. So stop howling." Gloria waded in deeper, drawing the body closer to the steps.

It took three of them to drag him out of the pool. Julia had pulled a big sheet of polythene from the roof of the house and they heaved the body toward it. They turned out his pockets as Gloria drove the Mini round, then they rolled the body in the polythene and lifted it into the back of the car. "Now what?"

Gloria asked. Dolly checked the time: it was almost five o'clock and the builders would be starting at seven. It didn't give them enough time: and they couldn't dump it in broad daylight.

"Drive it back to the lean-to and we'll leave it there until tomorrow night."

"What? In my car?"

"Yes, Gloria, unless you can think of somewhere better," Dolly retorted.

By the time the others had returned to the house, Dolly had a pot of coffee on the stove and some toast made. They trooped in and started to wash their hands, all suddenly quiet.

Ester walked in. "Everything okay?"

"What do you think? We got her bleedin' boyfriend stashed in the back of me car and a kitchen full of guns," Gloria said angrily.

Connie broke down into heaving sobs again and this time Dolly turned on her. "*Shut up*, all of you. Now sit down and listen." They sat like kids, seemingly grateful that she was taking charge. "You, Connie, go out to his car. Here are his keys and wallet. Any money we take, but burn his cards. You then drive the car back to London, go to his flat, get the log book." She proceeded to give Connie directions to a garage she knew in North London. She was to sell the car after cleaning it of all fingerprints, leave notes canceling the milkman and newspapers, and make it look as if Lennie had gone away. Then clean any fingerprints from the flat and return to the manor.

Connie nodded dumbly, not really comprehending.

"Go on then, get started. Get rid of that car as soon as possible." Dolly spooned sugar into her coffee. "Right, Julia, and you, Kathleen, go through the local papers, find out when the next funerals are going to be, then check out the grave in the cemetery."

"*What?*" Julia was about to laugh, but again she was thrown off balance by the coldness in Dolly's eyes.

"Best way to get rid of a body. Find a dug grave and dump him. Now Ester, that car out back. Is it hot? How did you get it?"

"I bought it. Well, it's on the never-never in part exchange for the Range Rover. It's not nicked, if that's what you're thinking."

"Okay. Gloria, you go and see Eddie. The sooner those guns are out of here the better."

Angela had remained silent throughout. Dolly patted her shoulder. "I'm sorry to get you involved in this, love, but I think it's the best thing for all of us and with you driving the car that took out Jimmy Donaldson, I just think the less we see of the filth the better."

Suddenly hearing the name of the man she had run over made Angela's whole body tremble. "I won't say anything," she said.

Dolly frowned. "Well, I hope not, and that goes for everyone here. Now I'm going to have a couple of hours' kip."

She walked out. They were impressed by her—but a little afraid of her coldness.

Kathleen swallowed and nudged Gloria. "Thank God she's not found out about that business down the sauna. I think she'd bloody kill us."

CHAPTER 10

The Mini remained in the lean-to, pools of water slowly forming under its wheels. Julia and Kathleen checked the newspapers and then went to the cemetery. Connie was already driving to London to sell the Porsche and clean Lennie's flat. She parked it a good distance from his block, and set about finding the log book. Having so much to do calmed her.

Ester stayed in bed with some aspirin. Her ribs hurt and she felt dizzy if she so much as sat up. Dolly slept, the only one of them able to do so. Gloria caught the train to London and went to Brixton to visit Eddie.

Angela cleaned the kitchen; she was worrying herself into a panic about Jimmy Donaldson. As she cleared the dirty crockery, she saw the big bags of guns left by the kitchen cabinet.

Mike listened impatiently to his mother fretting because she'd missed her flight so she now had to rearrange her trip to Spain.

"You have to get out soon, Mum, I mean it."

"I will, Mike, but I got to pack the whole place up, you know. At least it's over, love. She took the cash, said she didn't ever want to see me again."

He hung up and the phone rang again immediately. Mike swore when he heard Angela's voice and was about to slam it down again when she whispered, "Guns." She was hysterical, and he had to calm her down before he could piece together what she was saying: Dolly Rawlins had bags full of weapons that belonged to Eddie Radford in the manor.

Ester walked slowly down the stairs and stopped when she saw Angela furtively hunched over the telephone in the hall.

"I'm positive, I got to see you."

"Who you calling?" Ester asked.

Angela whipped round, dropping the phone back on the hook. "Just my mum. I'll get you some breakfast."

Ester continued her slow progress down the stairs; she felt terrible. She felt even worse when Norma drove into the yard, tooting the horn to herald her arrival. "Get rid of her, Angela."

Norma was hauling out some bags of feed for the horse and smiled as Angela approached. "I was just passing so I thought I'd drop this lot off."

"Everybody's out," Angela said lamely.

"Oh well, can you give me a hand then?"

Angela helped her take a sack out of her Land Rover and into the stables. She could see Gloria's Mini out of the corner of her eye.

"Say hello to Julia. Tell her I'll maybe drop by later, see if she wants a ride."

Dolly felt the blood rush to her cheeks as she read the letter. Her application to open Grange Manor House as a children's home had been turned down. She walked stiffly into the drawing room as Ester appeared.

"Just a word of advice. That little Angela's making secret phone calls."

Dolly nodded, not listening. Ester shrugged and went back to bed.

Angela came in a few moments later with a cup of tea. "That Norma brought feed for the horse. She even looked right at the Mini—I was scared stiff."

Dolly roused herself and sighed. "I've been turned down."

She showed the letter to Angela. "But they don't even say why. Why don't you call them on Monday?"

Dolly considered. "Yeah, I got a right to know why they rejected me."

Connie drove Lennie's Porsche across the river and to the small garage Dolly had told her would buy it without asking too many questions. She was calmer now as two mechanics looked it over. She'd told them it was her boyfriend's and he had just got a job abroad. They continued checking the engine and left the cash negotiation to Ron Delaney, the garage owner, a young, flashy, overconfident man wearing a tracksuit and heavy gold chains. He didn't waste much time: if he had any suspicions about the car he didn't mention them but offered a cash deal price well below the "book." Connie accepted twelve thousand pounds in fifties and twenties, eager to get back to the manor.

Gloria waited to be searched before entering the visitors' section at Brixton. When her name was called, she hurried over to Eddie, who was already sitting at the table. He looked her up and down. "You look different," he said nonchalantly.

"Yeah, it's all the fresh air."

"What you brought me?"

"Nothin'. I didn't have any time and I've not got any cash."

"Every time you come you got a line of bullshit, Gloria. Last time you said—"

"I know what I said. It all went wrong, there's no pay-off."

"No? What about the diamonds?"

"Fakes. So now I got to sell the gear, Eddie. I'm flat broke and I got to pay the rent. There's no need to flog the lot but if you got a contact then . . ."

"No way."

Gloria leaned closer. "Eddie, I got them at the manor. We've already had one bleedin' search—if they come back and . . ." Eddie peeled off a cigarette paper. Gloria bent closer. "Eddie, she'll have to have a bit of a cut."

"Who?"

"You know who. Dolly Rawlins. If it wasn't for her they could have arrested the lot of us. It's only fair."

"Is it?"

"Oh, come on, Eddie, just gimme a name, I'll do the business. You know me, you can trust me."

"Can I?"

Gloria pursed her lips. "What's the matter with you?"

Eddie opened his baccy tin. "That stash is mine, my insurance for when I get out. Now, if it was just you, maybe I'd be prepared to—"

"What you mean, if it was just me? Of course it is."

"No, it isn't. Now you want to give her a cut, next she'll want more, so if she wants to make a deal you tell her to come and see me. Maybe I'll do a deal with her, maybe I won't."

"She won't come in here, Eddie."

He fingered his tobacco carefully, laying it out on the paper. "Tell her she got no option."

Dolly listened as Julia described the cemetery, where the recent burials were, and explained that graves already dug and waiting for funerals were at the far side. Connie returned with the money and handed it over to Dolly. She had seen no one at Lennie's flat and she had done exactly as Dolly had told her. She was rewarded with a frosty smile. Gloria arrived back later that afternoon and told Dolly what Eddie had said.

"He wants me to go and see him in the nick?" Dolly was livid. "No way. I'll sort something. He won't be out, Gloria, for a very long time. In the meantime they're here, in the house, and I don't like it. The sooner we're rid of them the better."

Tommy Malin wanted a fifty percent cut. He agreed to arrange a buyer and they would make the exchange that night. Gloria was furious—Eddie would go out of his mind. Why pay some bloke fifty percent? It was madness.

"We pay because I want cash and I want to get rid of them," Dolly said.

"Then go and talk to Eddie."

"No. I can trust Tommy."

"You sayin' you can't trust Eddie?"

"Can you?"

Gloria was gobsmacked.

"He's in the nick. Who knows who he'll hook you up with. We do as I say. We sell the guns to Tommy Malin's contact."

"We could bleedin' sell them to the Queen Mother for a fifty percent cut," stormed Gloria, but Dolly walked out. Conversation over.

Mike ran along the stone corridor and up the stairs to Audrey's flat. He banged hard on the door and she opened it with the chain still on. "It's me— come on—let me in."

She looked at him fearfully. "What's happened?"

"I want you to put in a call for me. I just got a tip-off about something. Maybe we'll get her after all."

"Who?"

"*Who the hell do you think?*"

"Dolly? What do you want me to do?"

"Call my governor. I know he's at the station so we'll go to a pub and you put in a call."

"Why me?"

"You won't say your name, for Chrissakes. I just want you to tip him off about something."

"What?"

"Guns. Dolly Rawlins has got bags full of guns stashed at the manor."

DCI Craigh replaced the phone. He was working overtime and was in a foul mood, but he had come in because Traffic reckoned they had now traced the vehicle used in the hit-and-run that killed James Donaldson. The car was registered to a hire garage called Rodway Motors, but what interested Craigh was that the garage was in the Aylesbury area—not far from Grange Manor House.

Craigh was about to leave his office when his desk phone rang. He reached out for it just as DI Palmer walked in.

"We might have got a trace on the vehicle," Craigh said as he answered the phone.

Audrey had to cover one ear because of the racket in the pub. She turned to Mike, just able to see him sitting up at the bar, watching her. He gestured for her to hurry up and make the call, then checked his watch. When he looked at her again, she had already dialed. Audrey asked if she was speaking to Detective Chief Inspector Craigh. When he confirmed that she was, she said her carefully rehearsed speech. "Dolly Rawlins is holding a stash of weapons owned by Eddie Radford. The guns are at Grange Manor House in Aylesbury, and worth at least thirty thousand pounds." Then she replaced the receiver and went to join Mike at the bar.

"What did he say?" Mike asked.

"Well, nothin'. You told me to just say what I had to then put the phone down."

Mike downed his pint. "I'd better get back home in case he calls me there."

"What do you want me to do?"

"Just leave, like you were planning to."

Audrey sipped her gin and tonic. "I got to wait, Mike. I've missed my flight again, so I'll have to go back to the travel agent. You know, you could come with me, all of you, Susan and the kids."

Mike shook his head. "No way. You don't seem to understand. I like my job, and I don't want to lose it."

Mike had only just walked into his own home when the phone rang. It was DCI Craigh, and he wanted him back at the station.

"What's up?" Mike asked innocently.

"Just get in here fast as you can," Craigh said.

"Okay, I'm on my way." Mike hung up as Susan and the kids came into the hall.

"Are we going to the swimming pool, Dad?" his youngest boy said excitedly.

"No, I'm sorry. I just got a call—they want me in."

"But it's Saturday," Susan said, frowning.

"I know, but . . . I got to go."

Susan didn't believe him. She stared at him, her face tight. "Oh yes? Well, I hope they're paying you overtime—you seem to be on duty all hours lately. You sure you're not just going off with that girl?"

Mike sighed. "Sue, don't keep on about that, all right? You want to call the station and check? Go ahead, but this is getting me down. You question every bloody move I make."

She pushed the kids to the front door. "Maybe you give me reason to."

DCI Craigh told Mike about the car. "We're going over there to check it out. And there's something else. I got a call, a woman—she may have been your contact but she asked for me. Guns. Come on, I'll tell you in the car."

The builders finished early as it was the weekend. The coast was clear. Dolly ordered a disgruntled Gloria to start loading up the guns. They would use Ester's Saab to deliver them to Tommy Malin.

Ester was uneasy. She knew just how hot the car was. "I can't let anyone drive it, Dolly. I'm the only one on the insurance."

Dolly fixed her with a look. "So you can drive. Gloria will go with you—unless you're planning on leaving?"

Ester said nothing and Dolly took her silence as confirmation that she agreed to help them out. "Pack them up, go on, get started. Julia, Kathleen and I will do the graveyard shift."

"What about Connie? She got us all into this mess with her ruddy boy-friend, why can't she help bury him?" Kathleen moaned.

"Because Connie will be doing something else." Dolly walked away before they could argue.

Connie was lying on her bed reading a magazine when Dolly entered. She didn't bother to knock. "That builder bloke, the one that took you out?"

"What about him?"

"Well, you go out with him again, make him happy, understand me? I owe him, but I don't want to fork out all the cash we got, so you go see him, give him a few more grand, and tell him the rest will be coming soon."

Connie hesitated. "What about all that cash from Lennie's car?"

"I need to pay off electricity, phone connection and keep a bit back for emergencies and groceries. Besides, I think you should earn your keep after all we're doing for you." Dolly stared coldly at her.

"Okay," Connie agreed. "He said I could go to his gym with him. I'll give him a call."

"Good. Oh—this gym. Do they have lockers, ones you can keep the key?"

"I dunno."

"Check it out when you call him, ask about membership and if you can leave your gear there."

"Why?"

"Don't ask questions, just do what I tell you to."

Connie turned away. Dolly had a nasty way of lowering her voice when she was angry.

DCI Craigh drove into Rodway Motors' car-hire section and he and Mike went into the reception while DI Palmer walked over to the main garage. Craigh showed the receptionist his ID and waited as she thumbed through the log book. She then looked up. "It was hired by a Mrs. Gloria Radford."

Craigh flicked a glance at Mike, then turned back to the receptionist. She pushed the log book toward him and he read that the Volvo had been hired for one day only, the same day James Donaldson was killed. Mrs. Radford had listed her address as a flat in Clapham.

Craigh nodded to Mike. "She was at the manor, wasn't she? The night we busted it?"

Gordon Rodway, the owner of the garage, walked in, followed by Palmer. The car had been returned, no damage recorded, and it had subsequently been hired out again. It had also been through a carwash three times, polished and hoovered.

"I want no one near it. I'll have my people check it over," Craigh said, none too happy as they all followed Rodway back to the garage. The Volvo was still on the ramp where a mechanic had been checking the exhaust. "What's the interest in this car, then? We recorded the mileage, if that's any help."

Mike walked round to the front bumpers: no dents, no paintwork scratched, it looked immaculate. But the Forensic boys would be all over it with a fine tooth comb; if this was the car that ran over James Donaldson, they would find the evidence.

Dolly looked at Connie in her skin-tight leotard. "Well, do they have lockers?"

"Yes, and it's a hundred and fifty quid for membership."

"Good. Join up, and when you get there tonight, put this in the locker and bring me the key." Dolly handed her a bag, which weighed a ton.

"What's this?"

"Just some personal things of mine—call them a safeguard. But not a word to any of the others. Just make John nice and happy. You don't have to screw him, I wouldn't ask you to do that, just string him along."

Connie went out to the front pathway to wait for John to collect her. It was just growing dark but not dark enough yet to move the body.

Angela was cleaning the kitchen when Dolly came in. "Julia's looking for you, she's out in the yard," she said.

Dolly opened the back door. "Julia?"

She came out of the stables and joined Dolly on the kitchen doorstep. "Yeah. Look, I don't think it's a good idea for Kathleen to come along tonight. She's getting all twitchy, says she doesn't want to be a part of it."

Dolly sighed. She touched Julia's arm lightly; she liked her, she was straightforward, you knew where you were with her. "Right, you and me will sort the body, Kathleen can stay here with Angela."

"What about Connie?"

"She's doing something else. Are the guns all loaded up?" Julia nodded. Dolly glanced at her watch. "They should get moving, Tommy said his contact will be there about ten. Ester's all right to drive, isn't she?"

"I think so."

"Is she staying on?" Dolly asked.

"I don't know."

"If she isn't, does that mean you won't?"

Julia flushed. "I guess so, but I don't think she's got anywhere to go. She's got a big mouth but . . . well, maybe you should talk to her yourself."

DCI Craigh got back into the car. Palmer was at the wheel. "Gloria Radford hasn't lived there for a few weeks. Flat was taken over by the council but she returned to collect something from out in the back shed. I had a look round and it's mostly filled with junk. Maybe she took the guns and stashed them at the manor."

Mike leaned on the front seat. "What are we waiting for, then? If your tip-off was right and there are guns at the manor, why don't we just bust the place?"

Craigh looked directly ahead. "We already made ourselves look like a bunch of arseholes, Mike. This time we do it by the book. We cover ourselves and check out the fucking information first—and apart from that I'd like a day off. That all right with you, is it?"

Mike sat back, knowing not to push it. He stared out of the window as they drove down the road. Palmer looked back at Craigh. "So far they've found nothing on the vehicle, Gov."

Craigh lit a cigarette. "Let's see if we can have a chat to Eddie Radford on Monday. He might have some information. That suit you, Mike?" he said sarcastically.

"Whatever you say, Gov. Just, why wait twenty-four hours? They could shift her guns."

Craigh checked his watch. "Okay—we go see Eddie Radford. Then we call it quits."

Ester eased herself up and winced. The last thing she felt like doing was driving back to London. She wondered if she could get out of it when Dolly walked in, closing the door behind her.

"How did you get the beating, Ester?" She sat on the dressing-table stool and waited.

Ester was about to lie, but didn't have the energy. "Okay, last time I got sent down I also got a raw deal. When I was busted, a couple of my clients got scared—you know, that I'd plead not guilty and they'd have to prove it and name my clients. They got my little black book—well, it wasn't little, it was a whopper, and I got K for kings, P for princes, no kiddin'. I was coining it, specials laid on for this Arab royal family. I was told that if I pleaded guilty, my fine would be paid, my back taxes paid and I'd get a few quid on top. I was assured I'd not be sent down. Well, I was. I got five years. They paid my legal costs, a percentage of my taxes and then walked away. Not one name was mentioned. So, I got pissed off."

Dolly fingered a perfume bottle, then looked up. "Go on."

"I used to make private videos which clients would take after the show. I never made copies but on the night I got turned over, I stashed one and it was never found. When I got out, I went to them straight, said I felt I was owed some dough. They threw me out, told me that if I showed my face again I'd be sorry. I then called them and said they would now be very sorry, that I had a video and I was gonna expose them." Dolly tutted. Ester looked at her. "It's not even that bad, just a few slags rolling around with them, but you know how Arabs are. I asked for five hundred grand."

"And?"

"Next thing they got some punk after me with a fucking price on my head. I mean, they're all crazy! So I kind of hid out here. They won't leave me alone and the result is what you can see. They beat me up and I ran like hell."

"Back here?"

Ester nodded. "Yeah, but I won't be staying long, just enough time to get my face healed."

Dolly stood up. "Okay, at least you told me the truth. So, go do the business with Gloria and you can stay on here until you're recovered, then you do whatever you want . . ."

Ester smiled, instantly regretting it because of her cut lip. "Thanks."

Eddie Radford was really edgy. He knew word would be out he'd been lifted and that he was having a talk with the filth. Every prisoner there would know within an hour or so—word travels fast in the nick—and he didn't like it, didn't like anyone even thinking he could be grassing.

"What's all this about?" he snapped.

DCI Craigh drew up a chair. Mike stood leaning against the wall as Craigh offered a cigarette.

"I don't want a fag. I want to know what this is about," he repeated.

"You know someone called James Donaldson?"

"No."

"Dolly Rawlins?"

"No."

"Gloria Radford?"

Eddie looked at Craigh, shrugged. "Yeah, she's my wife."

"She holding something that belongs to you, is she?"

"I dunno."

"You're in for dealing in guns, armed robbery."

"Yeah, that's right."

"Eighteen years."

"Great, you can count."

"Can you, though? That's a long time, a very long time, Eddie. Be better spending time in an open prison—lot cushier than this dump," Craigh said softly.

"Thinking of taking me out to Butlin's, are you?"

Mike changed his position, staring hard at Radford. Craigh flicked his cigarette packet over. "We think your wife was driving the car that killed Jimmy Donaldson, Eddie."

"Oh yeah? Well, she was never a blinder behind the wheel."

"You know about it, do you?"

"Look, I dunno this Donaldson, I don't know what you got me up here for, I want to go back to my cell."

"But she could be charged with murder, Eddie."

"Tough luck. I want to go."

"If she's picked up, who's gonna flog your guns, Eddie?" Eddie frowned. "They're being held for you at Grange Manor House, aren't they?" Eddie chewed his lower lip. "We know they're at the manor so if we arrest Gloria you're gonna lose your pension fund. All I need from you is confirmation that they're there and in return, well, we can talk to people, recommend you get moved. We can't make promises but we can certainly talk to the right people."

Eddie shifted his weight on the chair and reached out for Craigh's cigarettes. "I dunno anythin' about this Jimmy Donaldson bloke or whatever Gloria's done. I dunno anythin' about that."

"But you know about the guns, don't you, Eddie?"

Eddie removed a cigarette, lit it, and let the smoke trail from his nostrils as he decided what he should say. He knew they were worth thirty grand, but what good was that if they were sold by that cow Dolly Rawlins? What good were they to him if he couldn't get his hands on them? What if they were gonna arrest Gloria?

"I want to be moved," Eddie said quietly.

Craigh smiled. "Open prison, swimming pool, tennis courts and, like you said, Eddie, some nicks are better than Butlin's . . ."

Eddie flicked ash from his cigarette and rested both elbows on the table. "She's staying with her, with Dolly Rawlins."

They were surprised at how quickly he'd given her up, but he didn't seem to give a damn about his wife or her possible arrest. All he seemed to care about was the money he was going to lose.

"They're worth thirty grand," Eddie said, hardly audible.

The same figure the anonymous caller had given to Craigh. He now reckoned the call was on the level, the tip-off legitimate. His weekend was well and truly blown. He knew they would have to act on the tip-off now.

Dolly and Julia drove to the cemetery. It was pitch dark and Julia drove without headlamps, guided by the white tombstones as they moved slowly down the dirt-track road toward the recently dug graves. Flowers and wreaths were still strewn across the ground. They parked as close as they could, then took out the spades and zigzagged their way through the tombstones toward the freshly dug grave. It was all ready for its occupant, the trench dug, boards placed across the gaping hole.

Julia carefully moved aside the wooden planks, and said, "Let's get on with it."

They began to dig, making the hole even deeper so they could bury Lennie's body and cover him up without anyone noticing the grave had been tampered with. The coffin would then be placed on top of him at the funeral. Goodbye, Lennie!

It was not too difficult because the earth was so fresh and they worked in silence. Only the swishing of the spades could be heard in the quiet of the cemetery.

While Dolly and Julia were at the cemetery, Ester and Gloria headed for London's West End to fence the guns. Gloria squinted at the *A to Z*. Ester had insisted they cut across London by various back streets and they were now somewhere in Elephant and Castle but neither had any idea exactly where.

"Wait a minute, go left, first left," Gloria muttered.

Ester drove on and turned left, then swore. No entry. She sighed and snatched the book from Gloria. "Let me see."

"It's not my fault. Why you had to come your route I dunno. I mean, we been going round in circles for over an hour now."

Ester squinted at the small squares on the map. "We don't want to get stopped with what we've got in the boot, do we?"

"Gettin' lost with them's not a brilliant move neither," Gloria retorted.

"Okay, I got it, we're not too far." She began to do a U-turn, when, caught in the headlamps, they saw a police officer examining a locked gate. He turned and watched the car bump onto the pavement.

"Oh, bloody hell. Do you see what I see?" said Gloria.

Ester looked in the mirror. He was walking toward them. She turned off the lights, gunned the engine, careered up the road and screeched round the corner.

"Well, that was fucking subtle," muttered Gloria.

Julia was waist deep and still digging.

Dolly peered down. "Okay, just drop him in and cover him. It's deep enough, isn't it?"

Julia started to climb out. "Yeah, the maggots'll have a field day."

"Let's get him out of the car," Dolly said as she chucked her spade aside. Julia stuck hers into the ground and followed. The body was wrapped in an old carpet and polythene sheeting. They dragged it toward them and, between them, eased it from the rear of the Mini. It was too heavy to carry easily and they resorted to dragging it across the uneven ground toward the grave.

"One shoe's missing," Julia whispered.

"Shit! Go and see if it's in the car."

Julia searched the car but found nothing. "Maybe it's still in the pool," she said, as she helped roll the body down into the grave. They began to shovel the earth back into the hole, both working flat out, as slowly, bit by bit, Lennie was covered up. Dolly stamped the earth down on top of him before clambering out, and Julia dragged the planks back to lay across the grave.

Gloria was furious. She found it hard to believe Ester could be so stupid but at least she now understood why they'd kept to the back streets.

"Hot? This bleedin' car's hot and you been driving it around London, almost ran over a bloody copper. I'm tellin' you, Ester, you need your head seeing to. If Dolly finds out . . ."

"Oh, shut up. We're here now. Go on."

Gloria got out of the car and knocked on a small door built into the big yard gates. It was opened by Tommy, who had a whispered conversation with her, and then the main gates eased back. Ester drove in, and Tommy and his contact began to unload the guns, carrying them into the warehouse.

Gloria had never met the buyer before, a small, softly spoken man wearing a camel coat, a good suit and pinkish-toned glasses. His expert began to check over each weapon as Gloria placed them on the desk. A large space had been cleared, the blinds had been drawn, and they quietly got on with the business in hand.

Ester was surprised by Gloria, who proved adept at handling the guns, making a convincing sales pitch with each piece. The weapons consisted of two 9mm Browning pistols, semi-automatic, four .38 Smith and Wessons, three .35 Magnum colts, two .44s, two .455 Webley's specials, collector's items, with boxes of ammunition, two Westley and Richard rifles, 26-inch barrels, bead foresight and stands, two Hechler and Koch machine guns and four Kalashnikovs.

While Gloria was doing her business, Ester was selling Tommy the Saab for cash. She admitted it was a bit "iffy" but not too hot. Tommy raised an eyebrow.

"Come on, man, you know it's a great deal. You can switch the plates on it and get it out of the country within twenty-four hours."

"Okay. I've got an old van you can take in part exchange."

Tommy glanced over at the gun dealers, then at Gloria who was searching one of the big bags. "Ester, a minute," she said, and Ester went to join her. Three shotguns missing. "You know anything about that?"

Ester shook her head and whispered that Tommy was interested in buying the Saab.

"Good, I'm not driving around in it anymore." Gloria returned to the dealers.

"No shotguns, sorry, but I got a desert Eagle that's the gun to have right now. You want to see it?"

The officers in the patrol car received the information that the Saab was stolen; the owner had reported the theft two nights ago. The beat officer had succeeded in taking the Saab's registration number and had flagged down the patrol car, whose window he was now leaning against. "I thought it might be. They drove off fast soon as they saw me, heading back toward Tower Bridge, but they could have turned off anywhere. Lot of old warehouses round that area."

The patrol car moved off. As the officer watched it disappear, he turned to continue his street patrol. An old, green-painted van passed him but he didn't give it a second glance. Inside, Gloria was counting the money, licking her fingers to flick through the notes. "Ten grand! What a bleedin' rip-off. I couldn't believe the cheap bastard."

"Well, we made up for it with the Saab."

"Yeah, but that's not the point. I hate being skinned. They got a lot for their dough, you know. They were worth at least thirty grand. I mean, two of the rifles would cost you seven big ones alone."

Ester headed over Tower Bridge. "Well, I'll split the money from the car with you. Dolly needn't know."

Gloria smirked. "You mean about it being nicked?"

"Yeah, we just divide the cash between us."

"No way. She gets the lot because she'll be on the blower to Tommy checking it out, you know her. And besides . . ."

"Besides what?"

Gloria stuffed the money up her skirt, wriggling it into her panties. "Somebody kept those shotguns—and you never know . . ."

"Never know what?"

"Maybe she's got something in mind? I mean, she's pulled a couple of blinders, hasn't she? Way I see it, let's keep her happy, see what's going on in that old brain of hers."

Ester laughed. "Why not? In the meantime, you keep that cash warm."

"Better to be safe than sorry," Gloria said, as the wad of notes eased round her panties. "They got bastards holding up motors in traffic jams to nick handbags now, you know. They push a gun into your face and nick your wallet. Shocking world nowadays."

DCI Craigh, DI Palmer and Mike headed toward Grange Manor House, accompanied by twelve local officers from Thames Valley along with a search warrant, this time not for diamonds but weapons.

Julia and Dolly had carried the spare earth to the hedges and scattered it around. They were filthy dirty but the job had been done. They were just putting the spades back into the car when they heard the noise of engines. They froze, looking toward the lane as a police car drove past, followed by two more vehicles.

"What was that about?"

"I don't know and I don't care, just so long as they're not coming into the cemetery," Dolly muttered.

Julia walked round to the driving seat. She got in and turned to Dolly.

"Connie really owes us a big favor."

"Don't worry, she'll pay it back," Dolly replied as they drove slowly out of the cemetery and onto the lane. "Anyway, enough excitement for one evening. Let's go back to the house."

CHAPTER 11

DCI Craigh gave the signal and all vehicle lights went out as the convoy moved slowly down the drive to the manor. The cars stopped and six men moved quickly to the rear of the house, while six more positioned themselves around the front. Craigh, accompanied by Palmer and Mike, walked up the front steps. He tapped lightly and called quietly that it was the police. Receiving no reply, he stepped back, and Palmer hit the lock on the front door with a sledgehammer. At the same time, the men at the rear of the house got a radio message to enter via the kitchen.

The sound of the forced entry echoed like thunder inside the manor. Down came the front door as the back door splintered.

Kathleen was putting coal into a scuttle when she heard the crash and the voices shouting: "*Police! Police!*" She threw the scuttle aside, drew open the cellar window and climbed out.

Angela almost had heart failure. She was caught midway up the stairs and started screaming in terror.

Connie was the first to return. Big John had dropped her at the manor gates. She was picked up as she walked down the drive, two uniformed officers holding her between them as they pushed her toward the front door. By now every light was turned on, the place seemed to be swarming with police and she was as terrified as Angela. She thought they were arresting her because of Lennie, while Angela thought they had come for her because of James Donaldson. They were questioned, asked for their names, dates of birth, and shown the search warrant: neither said anything.

Kathleen was equally terrified and, once out of the cellar, made a run for it, heading toward the woods. Two officers gave chase. By the time she was brought back, gripped tightly by two police officers, she was sobbing hysterically.

Ester and Gloria drove in just as Kathleen was being escorted from the woods. Both women were asked to step out of their vehicle, place their hands on the top of the car and stand with their legs apart. Gloria was yelling her head off, demanding that a female officer search her, as Ester shouted that she wanted to know what the hell was going on. No one answered. They were shown the warrant as DCI Craigh walked out of the house. He instructed his men to run checks on all the women.

"What you talking about?" Gloria demanded.

Kathleen stood by the patrol car, head bowed, still crying.

"What you think we are? Bleedin' IRA? I'm from East Ham, she's from Liverpool, you got this all wrong." Gloria was yelling while Ester nudged her to shut up. "I want to go to the toilet," Gloria shouted.

Ester warned her again to shut up but Gloria hissed back, "Have you forgot I got the dough in me knickers?"

The police received information that Kathleen O'Reilly was wanted for absconding from a magistrates' court; there was an outstanding charge of fraud and kiting against her. She was ushered into the patrol car.

As Dolly and Julia drove up to the manor, they gaped at the scene: Ester and Gloria, spread-eagled over the van, Kathleen sobbing inside the patrol car, and everywhere uniformed officers carrying big-beamed torches.

"Shit, now what?" Dolly exclaimed.

"Will you get out of the car?" DCI Craigh gestured for more officers to assist in searching the new arrivals.

The women were herded into the house and taken into the drawing room where Connie sat with Angela while the room was searched by a uniformed officer. Dolly looked over the search warrant and then handed it back to Craigh. "You mind if I make a pot of tea?"

He shook his head. If that woman had a stash of guns inside the house she was acting very cool about it, but he wasn't about to call the men off, far from it. They would comb every inch of the house and grounds.

The dawn came and with it better visibility. The search continued, both inside and out. The women sat drinking tea, eating sandwiches, but did not offer either to the police.

At half past eight on Sunday morning, Craigh gave up. He returned to London with Palmer and Mike. They had found nothing and all they had to show for eight hours' work was a missing felon, Kathleen O'Reilly.

Dolly examined the smashed doors and broken banister rails. She began making up a list of damages and she would make damned sure they paid through the nose for them. She was angry, not just because of the warrant and the search but because it was obvious they had a tip-off from someone. The question was, which one of them was it? She knew they had been very lucky: a few hours earlier and they would have been caught not only with the guns but with a dead body. The women were all on edge, waiting for the police to leave. They couldn't talk, too scared they might be overheard. By one o'clock the remaining police called it quits and left. As soon as the women saw them moving out, they all began to talk at once.

"Eh! Dolly, what about Kathleen?"

Dolly frowned. "I don't know what to think."

"I can't see her being a grass," Gloria said as she hitched up her skirt.

"Somebody is, though," Dolly said.

Gloria pulled the money from out of her panties. "There you go. I had it stashed in me drawers—about the only thing I've had in them for a few years."

Dolly arched an eyebrow. "No need to be crude."

They counted the money, discussed the sale of the car and then Dolly looked at her watch. "Right, I'm going to have a sleep, then I'm going to church."

They were astonished. She yawned, asking if the boiler was on as she needed a bath.

"Church?" Gloria asked.

"Yes, church. I want the locals to trust me—I've got to if I'm going to open up this place." Dolly paused. "Even though they turned me down, I'm not finished yet. I knew it wasn't going to be easy but—"

"Why don't you be realistic, Dolly?" Ester said. "You don't stand a chance in hell. As if they would let kids come here." She yawned.

"Why not?" Dolly persisted.

"Because you're an ex-con, darlin'. Now maybe you'd stand more of a chance if you applied for teenagers—better still, ex-cons, young ones coming out. They all need a home and—" Suddenly Ester laughed and clapped her hands. "I tell you something, with my contacts, if you got a houseful of young girls we could open this place again. Coin it in! What a perfect cover."

"Run this as a brothel?" Dolly asked, not believing what she was hearing.

"Why not? It ran before and, like I said, I have contacts. Put in the cash we got from the guns, from my car—we've at least got a kick-start."

Julia turned on her. "Use poor kids coming out of the nick? Is that what you'd do, Ester?"

"Why not? We've already got a couple of tarts here for starters."

"Who you bleedin' callin' a tart?" Gloria snapped.

"Oh, come off it. You and Connie have been turning tricks and Angela's done a couple. All I'm saying is be realistic."

Julia was furious. "Well, before I'd get kids on the game, I'd pull a robbery. You make me sick, Ester."

"Do I? Well, maybe we should think about pulling a robbery, then. What do you say, Dolly? You know this will never get opened as a foster home so what about it? You got any ideas?"

Dolly moved slowly to the door. "The only thing I've got on my mind right now is trying to find out which one of you shopped me. Somebody here did—one of *you* did—and after I sort that out I'm going to bloody well open this place up, whatever anyone thinks."

They waited until the door closed behind her, then started looking from one to another: was one of them a grass?

Gloria sighed. "What about Kathleen, then? She was the only one of us the filth had anything on. Maybe she was scared and wanted to make a deal."

"I told you, Kathleen's a lot of things but she's not a grass," Julia said.

"That leaves one of us in here, doesn't it?" Gloria said, looking at Ester.

"It's not fucking me," Ester snapped.

Julia opened the door. "This is ridiculous. We're all knackered. Why don't we do what Dolly's doing and have some kip? We've been up all night."

Dolly could hear toilets flushing, baths running. She was wide awake, couldn't sleep. Ester tapped lightly on the door and peeked in. "Dolly, can I have a word?"

Dolly lay back on the pillow. "Sure, sit down."

"Look, I'm sorry if I spoke out of turn down there but I was just tired and right now I need a roof over my head."

Dolly nodded. "Sure. Anything else?"

"Maybe check out Angela. She's been making phone calls." Ester backed out and closed the door.

Dolly sat up and thumped her pillow. Next to turn up was Connie. She wanted Dolly to know that she believed in the project and was sure it would work, she loved the old house. "It wasn't me, Dolly, I wouldn't have told any-one about the guns, I mean, I wouldn't, not with Lennie here, now would I?"

Dolly smiled ruefully. "No, love, but Lennie could have got us all in hot water."

Connie was near to tears. "I know, I know."

A while after she left, Gloria tapped at the door. One by one they came, just to make sure Dolly knew it wasn't them.

The only one who did not appear was Angela.

She was lying wide awake in her bed, and jumped when Dolly walked in and closed the door behind her. "I want to talk to you, Angela, and I want you to be honest with me. Who have you been calling?" Angela burst into tears and Dolly came and sat on the edge of her bed. "Now don't cry, just tell me. We all know you're always making phone calls."

"My mum and—"

Dolly listened as Angela blurted out how frightened she was about being arrested for running over Jimmy Donaldson. Between sobs and gasps she told Dolly about her boyfriend, who was married with kids, and now didn't want anything to do with her.

Dolly patted her hand. "Well, maybe it's best that you're here."

"I'm pregnant."

She cradled Angela in her arms, comforting her, asking if she wanted to keep the baby. When Angela sobbed that she didn't know, Dolly assured her that, as long as she was at the manor, she and the baby would have a home.

When Dolly came out Connie was passing Angela's room.

"She's pregnant," Dolly said.

Connie looked at the closed door, then back at Dolly. "So that's why she's been on the phone, is it?"

"Don't tell the others. She doesn't want anyone to know."

Connie scooted down the stairs and into the kitchen. Gloria was sitting with Ester as Julia washed up.

"Okay, this is what we've decided, Connie," Ester said.

Connie's eye was caught by a stack of bits and pieces of jewelry.

"We're all giving up what we can, you know, just to make it look like we're really behind this foster home crap. We don't think Dolly stands a chance in hell but . . ."

Connie pulled out a chair and sank into it. "I got a few pieces I can give."

"Good. It's just that she's got to trust us, Connie. We think she may be coming up with something. We don't know but Gloria said three shotguns are missing."

"Yeah, I took them into the gym, they're in a locker there."

Ester turned to Julia. "See, what did I tell you? I knew she was planning something."

Julia was putting away the dishes. "So we all make out we love this place, is that right?"

Connie pouted. "But I do."

"So do I," said Julia.

"Yeah, well, that's 'cos of that bleedin' horse. You're never off the friggin' thing."

Julia glared at Gloria. "Okay, so I love Helen of Troy, but I also like this place."

Ester slapped the table. "For Chrissakes, can we get done with *The Sound of Bleedin' Music*? All I am saying is she doesn't trust us."

"Well, *I'm* not the fuckin' grass," Gloria said angrily.

"I think it's Angela," Ester said.

"No, she's not, she's pregnant," Connie said, and they all turned on her. She shrugged her shoulders. "She is, Dolly just told me, that's why she's been making all these calls."

Gloria stood up. "Well, she's a bloody little liar. She's not pregnant."

"How do you know?" Ester demanded.

"Because she borrowed my Tampax yesterday." Dolly walked in and Gloria whipped round. "We think it's Angela. She's not pregnant, Dolly, she's a liar."

Dolly clenched her hands in front of her. "Is she? Well, one of you get her down here, then. Get her in here right now."

Angela was hauled out of her bed by Gloria and pushed down the stairs. She crept into the kitchen like a frightened rabbit.

"How many weeks gone are you?" demanded Dolly.

"Two months," Angela said.

Gloria pushed her. "No, you're not. Why did you borrow my Tampax if you was up the spout?"

"Because I had some blood, I did, I swear on my life."

Connie went over to her and slipped her arms around her. "Don't cry, we believe you."

"I fucking don't," yelled Gloria.

Dolly scratched her head, and then said to Julia, "Take her upstairs and examine her."

"Oh, for God's sake, Dolly, this is ridiculous," Julia said.

"Is it? Well, I want to know, because if she isn't then she lied to me and she could have been lying from day one. Somebody is tipping off the police, so examine her. Go on, do it."

Julia led Angela out of the room, then Ester tapped Dolly's shoulder. "This is for you. It's from us, all of us. We want to help out in any way we can, Dolly. Some of it's gold and—"

Gloria pointed. "That tie-pin belonged to Jack Dempsey and that Rolex Eddie gave me. It could be a fake, though," she added.

Dolly picked up pieces of the jewelry, strangely moved even as she noted that they were still wearing their best items. But it was, as the old saying goes, the thought that counted.

About ten minutes later Julia returned. "She was telling the truth. I think she's more like three months than two. You can often have a few spots, even a period, during the early months."

Dolly felt awful but she had needed to know.

"So you think it's Kathleen?" Gloria asked.

"I don't know—I just don't know," Dolly said, drumming her fingers on the table. "I mean maybe, just maybe, it's no one. Have any of you had dealings with DCI Craigh before?"

No one could recall having been arrested by him on a previous occasion. Connie said that she quite liked him, he'd been very nice to her; it was the younger bloke she didn't like.

Angela was suddenly standing like a child in the doorway.

Dolly reached for her and took her hand. "I'm sorry about that, love, but I needed to know."

Angela backed away, pressing her body against the wall.

"We're just talking about the coppers," Dolly said.

"Well, I don't like them, any of them," Julia said.

"Me neither," Gloria muttered.

"Funnily enough, I'm sure I've met that younger one, the blond-haired guy, the good-looking one," Ester said.

Ester looked at Angela and everyone followed suit.

"I don't know him!" she wailed. But she was trembling.

Ester sprang forward. "Yes, you do!"

Angela bolted, and Ester took off after her.

The rest of them followed, to see Angela running up the stairs, with Ester giving chase. Ester lunged forward and caught hold of Angela's foot. Angela fell forward, then started bumping and slithering down the stairs as Ester climbed over her, hauling her by her hair.

"Ester! Don't! *Ester, she's pregnant!*" screamed Julia.

Angela fought off her attacker, pushing and screaming, and managed to escape up the stairs, but a furious Ester pursued her along the landing and caught up with her in a couple of strides.

"You little liar! You're a bloody liar, Angela!" Ester was terrifying as she punched and slapped like a whirlwind. "Tell me the truth! Tell me the truth or I'll fucking kill you."

Angela dived beneath Ester's arm and ran into her own room, but she didn't have time to lock the door before Ester kicked it open and slammed it behind her. Dolly was first in after them, then Julia. Dolly dragged Ester off Angela, who was hunched on the bed, trying to protect her face from Ester's blows. Ester was red-faced with fury.

"Ester! *Ester! Calm down!*" Dolly slapped her face.

"You just slapped the wrong face, sweetheart. Ask that dirty piece of shit who her boyfriend is. He's that bloke that was here, isn't he? *Isn't he?*"

Angela clung to the pillow, as if it would shield her from any further onslaught.

"Is this true?" Dolly asked calmly.

Angela nodded through her tears. Crowding at the door, the other women stared at her angrily.

"You don't understand," she wailed.

"Oh, I think I do," Dolly spat, prepared to leave her to the women, just like a cell fight in the nick.

"He's Shirley Miller's brother," Angela shrieked.

Dolly froze, her hands clenched at her sides. "Get out and leave her with me. All of you, get out."

"What you think she's doing up there?" Gloria asked. Dolly had been with Angela for about fifteen minutes.

"Suffocating her, I hope," Ester muttered.

"So it was her all the time," Connie sighed.

"Yeah, the two-faced little bitch," Gloria snarled. "She could have had the lot of us sent down. Ester was right. I just wish I'd got a few punches in."

Gloria looked up. "You don't think she'd bump her off, do you?"

Angela was still red-eyed from weeping but at least she was calmer now. She had explained how she had first met Mike after Ester was raided, how he had been kind to her as she was under-age. He had been helpful in getting her social workers and it was thanks to him that she was never reported. They had then become more than friendly after Ester was sent for trial, but recently Mike had refused to see her as his wife had found out. When Ester had called, Angela had contacted him and he'd asked her to report anything she found out about Dolly Rawlins.

"What did he tell you about Shirley?"

Angela sniveled. "Only that you were responsible, and his mother . . ."

Dolly smiled inwardly. Audrey had such a big mouth but she'd kept her son's part in it very quiet.

"What are you going to do with me?" Angela asked.

Dolly opened the door and held up the key. "You can stay here until tomorrow, then you pack up and leave. I never want to see you again. You betrayed me—the only one of them I trusted. Seems I was wrong. I'll never forgive you, love, so get packed."

The door closed silently but to Angela the key turning in the lock was like thunder.

Dolly shuffled along a pew and bent to pray. Then, as the service began, she sat back and opened the hymn book. No one paid much attention to her. When the service was over, she shook hands with the vicar and made her way toward the gates. To her right was the big cemetery where only the night before she had buried Lennie. But she hardly gave it a second thought because up ahead she had seen Mrs. Tilly opening her car door. She hurried toward her.

"Mrs. Tilly!" Dolly called, and was taken aback by the cold, aloof stare she got in return. "I got a letter," Dolly said, a little out of breath.

Mrs. Tilly was in two minds whether even to speak to Dolly but her own anger got the better of her. "You lied to me, Mrs. Rawlins. When I think how much work I did to persuade the board not only to see you but make an on-site visit."

Dolly interrupted, "I'm sorry. Are you saying you've been to the manor?"

"Oh yes, we came, Mrs. Rawlins. Didn't Ester Freeman tell you?"

Gloria was looking out of the window as a stern-faced Dolly marched up the path. "Well, the church has certainly done wonders for her! She looks ready for nine rounds with Mike Tyson."

The door banged shut and promptly swung open again because of the damaged lock. The drawing-room door was thrown wide. Dolly hurled her handbag onto the sofa and threw off her coat.

"Something wrong?" Ester asked innocently.

"Oh yes, you can say that again. Now I know why they turned me down. They only came here and found the lot of you bollock-naked in the sauna."

"Oh, come on, we weren't all naked, Dolly," said Julia.

"You, Julia, shut your mouth because you and that bitch over there were, and I quote, 'in an obvious sexual embrace.' I presume that was before you turned the hosepipe on the chairman of the board."

They hadn't got any excuses, not that she gave them a chance to make any as she paced up and down. "All of you knew you'd blown my chances and not one of you had the guts to tell me what you'd done. Eight years I planned this, eight years I waited and now you've ruined it. You've destroyed any hope I had of reversing the rejection. Well, the lot of you can pack up and piss off with Angela."

She slammed the door so hard that the chandelier shook dangerously.

"Oh, bloody hell," muttered Gloria. "I knew it'd come out. How do we get round this one?"

Ester was up and heading for the door. She turned and winked. "Leave it to me."

Dolly banged the kettle onto the Aga as Ester walked in with her hands up as if at gunpoint. "Just let me tell you something, okay? Don't shoot."

Dolly was not amused. She threw tea-bags into the pot.

"Listen, Dolly. There may, just may, be a way round this."

"Like what?"

"Just listen. That bloke who came with them, beaky-nosed, bald fella with a few hairs combed over the top of his head."

"Mr. Crow. He's chairman of the board."

"Ah, crow by name, crow by nature. Well, Dolly, I recognized him and maybe one of the reasons why the board turned you down, or he did, was because—"

"You were all frolicking naked in the sauna?"

"No. He used to be a regular. I'm sure he wouldn't want that known, would he? You could pay him a private visit. Maybe *he* can do something for you."

Dolly put her head in her hands. "He was one of your clients?"

"Yeah. Work him over, Dolly. Make him sweat. It's got to be worth a shot."

Mike was watching TV when the phone rang. He watched Susan jump up to answer it, making no effort to take it himself. He was sick and tired of being monitored.

Susan called from the hall. "She wants to speak to you."

He didn't know if she was referring to Angela or his mother. "Who is it?"

"She said her name was Dolly Rawlins."

Mike was half out of his seat when he fell back, his face drained of color.

"Mike? She said it's important."

Audrey was booked on the first flight to Spain on Monday morning, her third attempt to leave. She opened the door to Mike, all smiles, thinking he had called to say goodbye, but one look at his face made her step back, afraid.

"What's happened?"

He walked into the living room and threw himself down on the sofa.

"Dolly Rawlins just called my house."

"Oh God."

"She just wanted me to know that she knows about my involvement with the diamonds, with everything."

"What's she going to do?"

"I don't know but I'm in deep shit because if she goes to my governor, I'll be arrested. So will you."

"She wouldn't do that. It'd implicate her."

"I know. That's what I'm banking on."

"What do we do?"

Mike sank lower into the sofa cushions. "Well, maybe you should leave anyway."

She went to him and put her arms around him. "Come with me, love, you and the kids and Susan. We just up and run for it."

He pushed her away. "I can't do that."

"Why not?"

"I can't do anything that'll throw any suspicion on me. Don't you understand? I'll just have to wait, see what she wants."

Audrey broke down and sobbed. "It's not fair, is it? Some people get away with murder. You know she killed that poor Jimmy Donaldson, just as she as good as killed our Shirley."

Mike swung round and grabbed his mother's arm. "I don't want to hear her name again. If it wasn't for Shirley I'd never have got into this mess. I mean it, Mum! And I don't want to see or hear from you either. You got me involved in this, Mum, and I got to get myself out of it, so leave, go away, get the hell out of my sight."

He was almost at the car when he stopped and leaned against a brick wall. He started to cry—he couldn't stop the tears. He hadn't meant to say all that about Shirley. He sniffed, wiped his face with the back of his hand, then forced himself to get angry.

She was to blame, whatever way he looked at it, whatever guilt he felt. She'd married that cheap villain Terry Miller, she . . . Shirley was dead and buried, he had to get his life sorted, he had to straighten things out. He was losing it, he was blowing everything that was important to him and if he didn't get hold of himself there was no one else to prop him up.

By the time he got into his car he was calmer and in control. He didn't look back to the lit-up window of his mother's flat. He really never wanted to see her again.

Audrey was all packed. She'd earmarked a few items for shipping out but now she was taking down the little personal items, the photographs from the gilt mirror above the mantel. She read her younger son Gregg's last postcard, looked at the stupid kittens, and sighed. Well, he'd just have to ask around to find out where she was. They would tell him down the market. She tossed the card into the bin. She didn't have the energy to worry about Gregg, or anyone but herself. Now she could even blame Dolly Rawlins for her son walking out on her. Everything was Dolly Rawlins's fault and Audrey felt the anger boiling up in her. But then she straightened herself out: she'd be in Spain this time tomorrow, with a villa and a few quid in the bank. At least she'd beaten that bitch over the money. At least she had something to show for poor Shirley. She turned toward the sideboard as if to confirm everything was all right but she'd already packed Shirley's photograph: there was nothing there, no sweet, smiling, beautiful Shirley. Audrey felt the tears, not of anger or fury or revenge: tears of guilt because she knew she had thought about and cared more for Shirley after she was dead than when she was alive.

CHAPTER 12

Dolly was directed to sit on a row of chairs in the drafty town hall corridor. Mr. Crow's secretary walked out of his office without even glancing in Dolly's direction. Dolly stood up, watched the squat-legged woman disappear, carrying a thick file, then quickly tapped on the door of Mr. Crow's office and walked in. She was through with waiting.

Mr. Crow looked up, frowning when he saw her close the door behind her. "Mrs. Rawlins, did my secretary tell you—"

"Yes, she said I could have a few moments. It won't take any longer."

He pursed his lips and put his hands together, as if he was praying. "I am a very busy man."

"I'm busy too but, like I said, this won't take a moment. I've come about the letter."

"Mrs. Rawlins, the decision was unanimous. Obviously you can take private action if you wish, that is entirely up to you, but as far as I am concerned I do not at this stage feel you would be advised to proceed."

"All I want is to make a home for kids without one."

"I am aware of that, but it is my job to make sure any child placed into care will have not only the right supervision but also a suitable environment."

"Is it my criminal record that went against me?"

"Obviously that was taken into consideration, and we are also aware that you have been questioned by a DCI Craigh regarding—" Again he was interrupted.

"You referring to the warrants? The house was searched, the police found nothing incriminating and—"

Mr. Crow sucked in his breath. "Mrs. Rawlins, under the circumstances, and with reference to an on-site visit to your property, it was decided that—"

"You didn't really need one, though, did you?"

"I'm sorry?"

She leaned forward. "A visit. You already know the Manor House well, don't you? According to Miss Freeman you were a regular visitor when it was a brothel. Isn't that right?"

Pink dots appeared on his cheeks. "Just what are you inferring, Mrs. Rawlins?"

"That perhaps you had an ulterior motive for rejecting my application, that had nothing to do with me or my criminal background."

"Be careful what you are insinuating, Mrs. Rawlins. You are, I am sure, fully aware you remain on license for the rest of your life and—"

"I'm just stating a fact," she said quietly.

"Then please, Mrs. Rawlins, be careful. I have told you this was a unanimous decision by all members of the board. We do not feel that you would be the right person to be given access to young children. We do not feel that the Manor House would be suitable accommodation. It is my only intention to make sure any foster carer recommended by the social services department is both mentally and physically—"

She stood up, this time leaning right over his desk. "You know, my husband said he could never go straight because people like you, like the police, would never allow him to. Well, now I know about you."

Mr. Crow stood up, the pink blobs spreading, no longer with embarrassment but with anger. "I'd like you to leave my office now."

"Oh I'm going, and I won't come back. I waited a long time to make a home for kids a reality but it was stupid, wasn't it? I never stood a chance. Don't worry, I won't let on that you're a two-faced bastard."

She left, closing the door quietly behind her, and he could hear her footsteps on the marble corridor outside. He was shaking with anger but he was now confident that he had made the right decision. He would add to her report that she had lied to the board. Contrary to Mrs. Rawlins's denial, Ester Freeman was still resident at Grange Manor House.

Dolly drove back to the manor. She had to wait at the level crossing for ten minutes. This time she couldn't be bothered to talk to Raymond Dewey who sat, as usual, on his little trainspotter's stool, jotting down his times and numbers. He waved at her but she turned toward the lake and the small narrow bridge the railway crossed. She got out of the car and walked a few paces, still focusing on the bridge. Then she turned round, toward the station and the signal box. She sauntered over to Raymond and gave him a forced smile.

"Hello, Raymond, how are you today?"

"I'm very well. This is the twelve fifteen from Marylebone."

"Is it? You know every train, do you? All the right times and the delays?"

"That's my job."

"I bet there's one train you don't know the times of."

"No, there isn't one. I know every train that passes through this station, how long they take to go over the bridge and—"

"So you write them all down, then?"

"Yes," he said, proudly proffering his thick wedge of school exercise books. "Each train has its own book."

Dolly took one of the books with his thick scrawled writing across the front. "Mail train." She flipped over the pages. He had listed every delivery, time of arrival at and departure from the station, plus delays at the crossing.

"You're very thorough, Raymond," Dolly said, as her eyes took in his dates and times. She then shut the book and passed it back to him as the lights changed and the train went by. As the gates opened, she returned to the Mini.

"Thank you very much, Raymond." She smiled and waved as she drove past him. She felt strangely calm, almost as if it was fate. Had she been sub-consciously thinking about it? It seemed so natural. It certainly wouldn't be easy but, then, she had always liked a challenge. This would be one—a ter-rifyingly dangerous one.

A few minutes later, Dolly parked the car and walked up into the woods. From there she had a direct view of the station, the bridge, the lake and the level crossing. She spent over half an hour carefully checking the lay of the land. She could tell with one look why the police had chosen this specific station to unload the money from the road onto the train. There were only two access roads, both very narrow, and room for only one vehicle at a time. Anyone attempting to hold up the security wagon as it delivered the money to the train would be cut off. The station could easily be manned by four or five police officers and no one could hide out there. If they did, if they hit the train standing in the platform, they wouldn't have a hope in hell of transporting the money by road as there was no access for the getaway vehicles. The tracks were lined with hedgerows and wide-open fields, not a road in sight.

Dolly studied the bridge. Fifty-five feet high, the lake beneath, no access either side of the tracks, just a narrow walkway. Surely it would be impos-sible. How could you hold up the train on the bridge and get away with heavy mailbags on foot? It couldn't be done. She looked down at the lake, then back to the bridge. If you got a boat, you'd still have to reach the shore, and no vehicles could get down there. Again, there were no roads, just fields, hedges and streams.

Dolly was so immersed in her thoughts that when she heard twigs cracking she spun round in shock, her heart pounding. Julia appeared, riding Helen of Troy.

"Sorry if I made you jump. I did call out!"

Dolly covered her fright, smiling. "I didn't hear you—I didn't even see you, come to think about it. You been here long?"

"No, I just rode up, cut across the fields." Julia dismounted and tied up the horse. "How did it go at the social services?" she asked.

"It didn't. It's finished."

"I'm sorry."

"So am I. Are they easy to ride?"

"Yeah. Why, you thinking of taking lessons?"

Dolly moved tentatively toward Helen, putting out her hand to stroke her nose.

"She won't bite you. Be confident, they know when you're nervous." Julia moved to stand beside Dolly, putting an arm round her shoulders.

Dolly petted Helen's nose. "That Norma . . . she said this horse was police-trained?"

"Yep. She's very solid, nothing scares her. As Norma said, she's bomb-proof. Be good for kids to learn on."

Dolly withdrew her hand, her face drawn. "Yes, well, there won't be any kids to teach. I'll see you back at the house."

She trudged off as Julia unhitched the reins and got back into the saddle. She rode away, unaware that Dolly had turned back to watch her as she cantered into the fields.

There *was* a way to get to that train. Julia was now galloping, disappearing from sight as she jumped the hedges.

DCI Craigh and DI Palmer looked over the forensic reports taken from the red Volvo. There was no indication that the car had been involved in any accident, no trace of blood, or body tissue. They didn't have enough to bring charges against Gloria Radford and, even if she had hired the car, they had no evidence that she had run over James Donaldson. In other words, they had fuck all.

"Now what?"

Craigh looked at Palmer and shrugged. "Well, we're up for a hard rap around the knuckles from the Super, and that's just for starters, unless we can iron this out somehow."

Palmer looked over their reports and noted the vast amount it had cost Thames Valley and the Met to mount the searches of the manor, together with the surveillance. And all they had to show for it was one arrest: Kathleen O'Reilly.

Craigh sucked his teeth. "I'm going to interview O'Reilly again. So far she's not said a bloody word, but you never know."

"Bring her in, shall I?"

Kathleen had been taken to Holloway. She would stand trial again for the previous charges of fraud and kiting but she insisted she was just staying at the manor and that Dolly Rawlins had no knowledge of her previous record or that she was on a wanted list. All she did was pay Rawlins rent.

Mike appeared and Craigh fixed him with a stare. "I'm going to talk to O'Reilly again but the word from the Gov is to stay well clear of Rawlins. We got to get ourselves out of this mess so you make sure your reports are tight as a nut."

Mike hesitated. "What about my sister?"

"Less said about her the better. We're in enough trouble as it is so just get on with the backlog of work on your desk." Craigh glared at him. "This isn't over yet, son. We could all be in trouble. We never found any diamonds so at least that's been sorted, understand?"

"Yes, sir."

Mike sat down at his desk. His heart was thudding in his chest. Had he got away with it? Or was that call from Rawlins going to turn into a real threat? He felt sick to his stomach and when he reached for his files his hand was shaking. If Rawlins put him in the frame, he was finished.

Kathleen was as unforthcoming with Craigh as she had been the night she was arrested. She didn't know anything about any diamonds or guns; all she did was rent a room from Dolly Rawlins.

"What you think she is? Some kind of female Al Capone? Why don't you leave her alone? All she's doin' is tryin' to open a home for kids and you're just harassing her."

Craigh thanked her for her observations and turned on his heel. Maybe she really didn't know anything about Rawlins and maybe, he began to wonder, they had been pressured into the searches and warrants by Mike Withey because he had personal motives. The more Craigh thought about it the more he made up his mind that if the Super tapped on his shoulder he'd point the finger at Mike. He wasn't going to take the fall.

Dolly sat with a mug of tea. She was deep in thought when Ester walked in. "Angela's still in her room. Gloria took up a coffee at breakfast time, told her to get packed, but she's still in there."

Dolly got up and poured the dregs of the tea into the sink. "I don't care, just get rid of her. I got to go up to London, have a word with Kathleen."

Connie walked in with three sheets of paper. "Dolly, you wanted John to give estimates for the damage when the police raided the house."

Dolly inspected the figures and smiled. "These are good. Oh, Connie, can I have a word?" She turned to Ester. "Can you leave us for a minute?"

Ester sloped off, and Dolly washed and dried the mug carefully, placing it back on its hook. "There's a signal box at the station, young bloke on duty—I think there's two of them. Can you get to know them a bit? Find out what time they come on duty, when they're off and who does nights, that kind of thing."

"Why?"

"Because I want you to." Connie pulled a face and Dolly moved closer. "This time, Connie, if needs be you fuck them, because I want that information. I want you to know that signal box layout better than the back of your hand, understand me?"

Connie stepped back. "Yes . . . all right."

"Good—but don't tell any of the others, just get on with it."

Dolly went out of the back door and called Julia, who was leading Helen of Troy back into the stables. "A minute, love."

Ester caught Connie as she went up the stairs. "What was that about?"

Connie looked back down the stairs. "She said not to tell you."

"So, what did she want?"

Connie repeated what Dolly had told her then carried on up the stairs. Ester was about to go into the kitchen when she overheard Dolly talking to Julia. "You go and see Norma; try and find out about the security at the station."

"Why?" Julia asked as she pulled off her boots.

"Don't ask questions, just do it. If she doesn't know, then fine, but test her out."

Julia felt uneasy but Dolly didn't seem to be in the mood to take no for an answer, so she kept quiet.

Dolly walked into the hall. She saw the drawing-room door closing. "Ester?"

Ester popped her head out, acting surprised. "Oh! What do you want?"

"That kid, the trainspotter. He's got books, train times and—"

"We can get you a timetable, you know, Dolly."

Dolly's mouth was set in a thin tight line. "Yes, I know, but I want the times and details of one specific train. The mail train. Get his book off him but do it without him knowing."

"That shouldn't be too hard—he's mental anyway."

Dolly picked up the phone and began to dial. Ester hovered a moment before she went into the kitchen.

Julia was still there, drinking a cup of tea. "She's planning something, isn't she?" she said.

Ester nodded. "Yeah. I knew it. I always knew that if she had her back to the wall she'd come up with something."

"Yeah, but what is it?"

Ester leaned close, one eye on the door. "I think it's the security wagon that delivers the money to the mail train."

Julia let out her breath. "Jesus Christ."

Ester kept her eye on the door, afraid Dolly would walk in. "She held back three shotguns from Gloria's stash. She reckoned she was going to do something. Well, she was right."

Julia rubbed her arms. "Do we really want to be involved in it, though?"

Ester nudged her, grinning. "What do you think? Let's just play her along, see what happens. In the meantime, we got this place, we got bed and board, so why not?"

Dolly drove into George Fuller's car park. A clever, iron-faced man employed by many top-level crooks, he was the lawyer who had represented her at her trial. He was expensive but he was as tough as he looked and even when he smiled he seemed to be sneering.

"Hello, Dolly, good to see you. Sit down."

She perched on a chair in his immaculate office and passed over the estimates from the builders. "I'm being harassed. I want them off my back, George."

He nodded, then lifted his briefcase onto the desk. "Right. We can go there now and you can fill me in on the way. I'm in court at two so we've not much time."

Dolly stood up. She liked the way George got straight to the point.

They drove to the police station in Fuller's immaculate green Jaguar and Dolly told him exactly what had occurred since she was released from Holloway. She also asked if he would take on Kathleen O'Reilly's case as a favor to her. He inclined his head a little, and then gave that icy smile. "If she can meet the fees, then yes."

"She can't but I will."

Ester and Julia had already left to begin their assignments. Julia was calling at Norma's cottage and Ester went to talk to Raymond Dewey. Connie was already at the station, watching the man in the signal box. He had a pot belly and she had a feeling he would have bad BO. She shuddered. But then, crossing to the signal box, she saw the pleasant-faced young man who had given her a lift the day she arrived. She saw him walk up the steps as the pot-bellied man came out.

"You're late again, Jim."

"Sorry, Mac, got held up."

"Oh yeah? Who was it last night, then?"

Jim chuckled as he entered the signal box. Connie waited a moment and then ran out, colliding with the fat man. She was right. He was a walking deodorant advert. "Oh, I'm sorry," she gasped as she fell forward and then yelped. "My ankle, oh . . ."

It didn't take long for Jim to come down the steps with a glass of water as Connie sat at the bottom. She sipped the water and then tried to stand but had to sit down again.

"I'm sorry, love, I just didn't see you. Do you need a doctor?" Pot-bellied Mac looked down at her with concern.

"I'm all right, just a bit dizzy."

Jim helped her up and looked at his mate. "You go off, Mac, I'll take care of her. Maybe she should just sit here for a while."

Mac muttered that he just bet his mate would take care of her, and shuffled off toward his beat-up Ford Granada. "See you tomorrow, Jim."

But Jim wasn't listening. He was supporting Connie, his arm around her.

"Lucky sod," mused Mac as he drove out. He wouldn't have minded taking care of her—she was a cracker.

DCI Craigh stared at the estimates then at George Fuller and at the impassive face of Dolly Rawlins. He didn't really look at them properly—he was too edgy. Fuller declared that on her release Rawlins had, in his opinion, been harassed. If it was to be made public, not only the waste of public money but also that a woman who had served her sentence and been released with every good intention of building a home for ex-prisoners had been picked on, it would not look good for the force. Craigh tried to interrupt but Fuller was in full flow and wouldn't let him get a word in.

"We obviously know that a Mrs. Kathleen O'Reilly was arrested at Mrs. Rawlins's establishment but she was unaware of any of the outstanding charges leveled at Mrs. O'Reilly and all the women resident at the manor are, as you must be aware, ex-prisoners. As Mrs. Rawlins was attempting to open a home to give these unfortunate women a chance to straighten out their lives, then it is only to be expected that residents would be, like herself, ex-prisoners. To my mind this has been a flagrant misuse of police resources. If it were to get into the papers, I'm sure it would cause an outcry."

Fuller hardly drew breath. His quiet, steely voice firmly hammered home each point until finally he dropped in his ace. "Also, it is possible that one of the men in your team, Detective Chief Inspector, has a private vendetta against Mrs. Rawlins. Not to mention the fact that you have accused Mrs. Rawlins of being associated with a James Donaldson, who, I understand, recently died while in your custody."

Craigh felt the rug being pulled from under him but he remained calm. His hands tightened into fists on the desk as he gazed ahead at a small dot on the wallpaper.

"So if you would please give the estimates your due care and attention, I would be most grateful if Mrs. Rawlins could receive payment for the damage to her property as soon as possible."

Fuller rose, and gestured to Dolly to accompany him to the door.

"Thank you for your time, Detective Chief Inspector." Fuller closed the door after him. Craigh ground his teeth; it had been tough keeping his mouth shut. He would have liked to punch the bastard. He glanced down at the list of damage done to the manor during the two raids: deep freezers being turned off, banisters and rails damaged, the front door, the rear door. Then his jaw dropped as he read the total figure.

Ten thousand quid? *Ten grand?*

Dolly was rigid as she waited for Kathleen to be brought into the visiting section. Coming back inside made her feel ill, the hair on the nape of her neck standing up as she kept her eyes down, refusing to look in the direction of any of the prison officers. All she wanted to do was to say what she had to say to Kathleen and get out.

Kathleen was led through the door from the prisoners' section. She was wearing a green overall, her own shoes, and an Alice band that someone must have given her to keep her curly red hair off her face. She looked tired, defeated and bloated.

Dolly reached over and held her big raw hand. "Hello, Kathleen love."

Kathleen smiled ruefully. "Well, I'm back. I knew it'd happen one day but you know I just hoped we'd make some cash so I could get me and the kids to Ireland. It was just a dream, really. I should have known I'd be picked up. I'm just sorry it was at your place."

"So am I, but I've got you books and there's money between the pages. Give a few quid out to some of the girls, ones that knew me. Rest you use for whatever. I got George Fuller taking on your case, I'll find the money to pay him."

"I never said nothing, you know, Dolly."

"I didn't think you would, Kathleen."

"I'm no snitch."

"It was Angela. We found out she'd been knocked up by that young copper."

"The bastard."

"She's no better. We've chucked her out on her ear."

Kathleen flicked through the pages of the paperback novel, seeing the neatly folded fifty-pound notes. She suddenly looked at Dolly, her eyes dead. "I could have said something, though. I could have said about the diamonds, even the guns, but I didn't."

Dolly waited, knowing she was going to be hit for more money. It just surprised her that Kathleen would try it on, after she'd hired her a bloody lawyer.

"I'll get at least five this time," Kathleen said without any emotion. Dolly made no reply, waiting as Kathleen fingered the paperback. "I want my kids taken care of, Dolly. Sheena, Kate and Mary. They're in a convent but they'll be split up soon, I know it. Not many places can take three kids, three sisters, they'll split them up, so . . ."

Dolly looked at her, hard. "So what, Kathleen?"

"You take them, Dolly. I've written to the convent, made you their legal guardian. You just got to sign the papers. I want you to look after them until I get out."

"I can't do that," hissed Dolly.

"Yes, you can. You wanted kids in that place—well, now I'm giving you mine. You take them, Dolly, please. Please don't make me talk to the coppers about you, just take my kids." Kathleen bowed her head, as big tears slid down her pale cheeks. "I was a lousy mother but I'd turn grass for them. I would, Dolly. They're all I've got that's decent. Please, take them, keep them together for me."

Dolly gripped Kathleen's hand tight.

Just after Dolly had left the manor, Gloria marched up the stairs and banged on Angela's bedroom door. "Oi, what you doin' in there? We want you out. Come on. Angela?" She tried the door. It was locked but the key was not on the outside.

"Angela?" She banged on the door, turned the handle and pushed hard, but it was securely locked from the inside.

Gloria darted out to the stables and picked up a hammer. Connie appeared and asked her what she was doing.

"That Angela has locked herself in so I'm gonna break down the door and drag her out by the scruff of her neck."

She went back upstairs and hit the lock hard, while Connie pushed. It eventually gave way and they stumbled into the little box room. Angela was lying on the floor by the bed, face down. Beside her was a bottle of bleach. When the two panic-stricken women turned her over her face was blue, her mouth burned—but she was alive.

Julia was walking up the driveway when Gloria screamed at her out of the window to hurry. She raced up the stairs three at a time and burst into the bedroom. They'd lifted Angela onto the bed.

Gloria hovered. "She's drunk bleach, Julia," Gloria said quickly. "I dunno how much but look at her mouth!"

Julia barked orders, to call an ambulance, get jugs of water, then pulled Angela into a sitting position, feeling inside her mouth as Gloria and Connie hurried out, glad to be told what to do.

"Angela, can you hear me? Angela? It's Julia."

The girl lolled forward. Julia tested her pulse, which was very weak, and began to pour water down her throat from a jug Connie had brought in.

Dolly was shown into the Governor's office. She was freaking out: being in the visitors' section was bad enough, but this was terrifying. All she wanted to do was leave.

Mrs. Ellis had tea brought in and Dolly sipped from her cup, unable to meet Mrs. Ellis's eyes.

"Do you have a job?"

"Not easy at my age but I've got a few things I'm working on."

"I know about your application to the social services. Dolly, to run an institution requires training and people with qualifications."

"It was just a home, Mrs. Ellis. This place is an institution. But it doesn't matter now, I was rejected, they didn't think me suitable, and if you don't mind I don't want to discuss it further."

"If you need any help in the future . . ."

"I won't, thank you."

"You know, Dolly, it isn't wise to keep up some of the friendships you make inside. It's much better to make a clean break."

Dolly put the cup and saucer back on the desk. "Thank you, and thank you for the tea, but I've got to go."

Mrs. Ellis stood and put out her hand, but Dolly was already at the door.

"Will we be seeing you again?" she asked, still trying to be pleasant.

"No, I won't come back. Goodbye."

Mrs. Ellis sat back in her chair. Dolly had looked well, but there was a brittle quality to her every move, and she had not smiled once. An unpleasant woman, Mrs. Ellis mused, but then her attention was drawn to other matters and Dolly Rawlins was forgotten.

The ambulance rushed Angela to hospital. Julia accompanied her all the way to the emergency department but, once she'd been wheeled in, there was nothing more she could do. By the time Julia returned to the manor, Gloria had got over her shock at finding Angela half-dead on the floor, and sympathy had been replaced by anger. "She could have got us all arrested," she was telling Connie.

"She's only eighteen," Julia snapped.

"Yeah, so was I when I first went down but I still never grassed anyone. She's got no morals, coming here, playing us for idiots."

"The way we all tried to play Dolly?"

"No, we fucking didn't," Gloria spat.

"Yes, we did," Connie said.

"Well, it's all going to change soon, isn't it?" Julia said quietly.

"What you mean?"

Julia sat down. "We think she's planning a robbery."

Gloria gasped. "I knew it—I fucking knew it. Soon as those shotguns went missing I said to Ester, I said to her, 'She's got something going down,' and I was right."

Connie shifted her weight to the other foot. "I wish to God I'd never come here. I never done anything illegal in my entire life." Gloria snorted. "I haven't! I'm not like you, Gloria. We all know what you are."

"Oh yeah, what am I? You tell me that."

Ester had come in, unnoticed, and answered, "A loud, brassy tart. So what's all the aggro?"

"Where've you been?" Gloria asked.

Ester took off her coat and chucked it over a chair. "Talking to that half-wit Raymond Dewey. Dolly wants to know the times of the mail train."

Gloria's jaw dropped and she drew a chair close. "Is she gonna hit the security wagon, then?"

Julia crossed to the back door. "If she does, it's madness. According to Norma they have the place sewn up. The local police come out in force, cut off the lanes. There's no main access, we'd never get a vehicle near, never mind one that'd carry anything away." She pushed at the broken door and sighed. "This is crazy, you know, even discussing it."

Ester looked at her. "No harm in it, though, is there? Unless you'd prefer to talk about Norma. Do you want to talk about Norma?" Ester repeated the name with a posh, nasal twang. Julia pursed her lips. "Oh, have I hit a sore point? Don't want to talk about Noooorma, do we?"

"No, I don't. And stop being childish."

"I'm not being childish. It's you that's got all uptight. All I'm doing is making conversation about Norma."

Julia glared, then half smiled. "Jealous?"

"Who, me? Jealous? Of what? Norma? Oh please, do me a favor. I wouldn't touch anyone with that arse."

Julia opened the door. "You don't have to, but it's quite tight, actually." Ester's face twisted in fury. "She has a very good seat, as they say in riding circles."

Julia was out of the door, shutting it behind her, before Ester could reply, and smiling to herself. Ester's jealousy was proof that she cared.

* * *

Dolly parked outside Ashley Brent's electrical shop. She squinted at the meter and shook her head with disgust: twenty pence for ten minutes—it was a disgrace! She walked to the boarded-up door of the shop, rang the bell and waited. Eventually she heard a voice from behind the door.

"Who is it?"

"Dolly Rawlins."

There was a cackle of laughter and the sound of electronic bolts being drawn back before the door opened. Ashley Brent stood in the center of his shop floor, arms wide, his glasses stuck on top of his bald head. "As I live and die. So you're out then, gel. Give us a hug. You're looking good, sweetheart. How long you been out, then?"

"Oh, just a few months. Takes a bit of getting used to, especially those ruddy parking meters."

"Don't tell me. I mean, in the old days you could find a broken one, use it for the day. Now they tow you away if it's busted, tow you if you're a minute over, tow you for any possible excuse. What they don't do is tow the fuckers that block off the traffic. I'm telling you, everything nowadays is geared to get the punter, Doll. You're screwed in this country if you got a legit business, taxed, VAT . . . It's like we got the Gestapo after us for ten quid rates due but then you hear of blokes coining it on social. Makes you sick."

Ashley was a man who had verbal diarrhea and it was always the same: he hated the Conservatives, hated the Liberals, the Labour Party, the blacks, the Jews. In fact, Ashley was a man who lived on his own venom and it was rumored that, when he went down for a short spell, his cell-mate had asked to be moved because Ashley even talked in his sleep. He offered tea, then more verbals about the council estate across the road and, lastly, his thankless bastard kids. Dolly looked over the equipment in the little shop, while pretending to listen.

Ashley was an electronics genius and ran a business loosely labeled as security devices and trade equipment. In fact, he sold bugs, receivers, transmitters and microphones. You name it, Ashley had it in his well-stocked shop and workroom. He ran a strictly cash business for those wanting certain items and kept no record of their purchase.

Dolly spent three hours with him and left with a briefcase and a small carrier bag. He had taken time to show her how to handle the equipment. It was mostly quite simple but a few items were more complicated. He was patient and gave good advice, but never asked what the items would be used for. Whatever else Ashley was, he was totally trustworthy. But you paid for that. Dolly gave him ten thousand pounds cash.

Susan Withey opened the door.

Dolly smiled sweetly. "Hello, I'm Mrs. Rawlins."

Susan hesitated. "Mike's not here."

"Ah, pity. Well, could I come in? I want to talk to you."

"I don't think so, actually."

"I do. It's about Angela, your husband's little girlfriend." Susan stepped back and Dolly pushed past her. "Oh, this is very nice. You do the decorating yourself, did you?"

Susan shut the door and followed Dolly into the sitting room.

It was after seven and they were all still waiting for Dolly, not sure whether to start supper without her, and wondering what she'd been doing all afternoon.

"There's a car coming up the drive now," Gloria said, "but it's not Dolly. Looks like a flash Mercedes or somethin'."

Ester ran into the hall and looked through the broken stained glass in the front door. She raced back.

"Get rid of them. They'll want me. You tell them I don't live here anymore. Get rid of them, Gloria."

"Why me?"

"Because you're so good at it." Ester shot into the kitchen, pushing Julia back just as the doorbell rang.

Gloria opened the front door. Standing there was a swarthy, handsome-ish man, with dark heavy-lidded eyes, a slightly hooked nose and thick oiled-back hair.

"Yeah?"

"Ester here?"

"Ester who?"

"Freeman."

"No. Sorry."

Gloria tried to shut the door but he kicked it open. "Hey! What you doing?" Gloria shrieked.

"I want to speak to Ester."

"She don't live here, well, not anymore. She sold this house."

Gloria was lifted off her feet and hurled against the wall. She screamed as he gripped her face between his hands and pushed her head hard into the wall three times until she was too stunned to scream any more. She just stared wide-eyed.

"You tell Ester we need to speak to her, understand?"

Gloria nodded as he slowly released her and then as if to make sure the message was understood he slapped her with the back of his hand and she fell to the floor. She didn't try to get up until the front door closed behind him. Then she slowly staggered to her feet as Ester peered out of the kitchen.

"Well, thanks a fuckin' bundle for that," said Gloria, touching her nose. "He whacked me into the wall, whacked me in the face and you friggin' let him do it."

"Was it Hector?" Ester asked as she peered out of the broken window.

"I dunno who it was—he was too busy whacking me to give me his fuckin' name. Look what he done to me face."

Julia held Gloria's face between her hands and pressed her nose. "It's not broken."

"Oh, great, I should be grateful for that, should I?"

They all jumped as a car tooted and Ester shrank into a corner. "Shit, are they back?"

Connie went over to the door.

"*Don't open it,*" Ester hissed.

"It's Dolly," Connie said. "She's driven on round to the back yard."

"Don't say anythin' about this, Gloria," Ester pleaded.

"Well, she might just notice me nose is red and bleedin' and me blouse torn," Gloria retorted furiously.

"Look, they want money. I haven't got it so just cover for me—you know how she can get."

Dolly called out, and they all turned toward the door. They couldn't believe their eyes.

Kate and Mary were twins aged nine and Sheena was five. They all had bright curly red hair like their mother, round white faces with blue eyes, and were dressed in an odd assortment of charity-shop clothes. They were sullen-faced, as if they had been crying, and clung tightly to each other.

"These are Kathleen's kids. They're moving in." Dolly held up her hands. "Don't anyone say anything. They're here, there was nothing I could do about it, so let's make the best of it. Can someone get a room or two ready? Do you want to sleep together?"

The three little girls nodded in unison and clung even tighter together. "Right, let's get your coats off. Connie, bring their cases in from the car and someone put some supper on and get a room aired . . ."

Gloria turned away. "I'll do it. I just fell down the stairs and hit me nose so I need to go and wash me face."

Mike charged in. Susan was sitting on the sofa, clutching a handkerchief.

"Has she left?"

"Yes. I went into the hall to call you and when I went back she just said she had to leave."

Mike paced up and down. "What did she want?"

Susan stood up and slapped him hard. "She told me about you and that Angela. She's pregnant, did you know that? That bloody tart you've been screwing is pregnant."

Mike closed his eyes and sank down onto the sofa.

"Well? Don't you have anything to say to me?"

"What else did she want?"

"*Isn't that bloody enough?*"

Mike leaned back. At first it was just sticky mud he'd felt round his ankles, then it felt like cement. Now it felt like someone had fitted him with a straitjacket. Susan waited but still he didn't say a word. She stormed out, slamming the door behind her, and he stayed there, eyes closed, head back, trying to assimilate everything, sort it out in his head. What did Dolly Rawlins want? He never even gave Angela a thought—he was too concerned with himself.

Beneath the coffee table, which was placed against the wall, was a 13-amp adaptor. A table-light plug was fixed into one but in the other socket was a plug, not connected to any electrical appliance. The switch was turned on. The plug was a transmitter, that Mike was even paying for. Not that he ever imagined anyone would be bugging him. But Dolly was. She had inserted the plug the moment Susan had left the room.

"Neat, isn't it?" Dolly said, as she showed the women the second 13-amp adaptor she'd bought. She then showed them two pens that were also transmitters, pens you could even use to write with. They stared like a group of kids at all the equipment: the tiny receivers, the black box and, lastly, the briefcase that would enable Dolly to open up three electronic channels and record anyone she had bugged.

"What's all this for?" Ester asked.

"What do you think?" Dolly said, as she studied the leaflets.

"You planning on bugging us?"

"Don't be stupid, Connie. I'm going to put these to good use."

Dolly glanced up at the ceiling as she heard a soft cry. She said to Gloria, "I thought you told me they were asleep."

"They were last time I looked in but it's a strange house, Dolly, and, well, they're scared."

Dolly hurried upstairs and along to the room set aside for the kids. She eased open the door and could see them lying huddled together. The twins were sleeping but little Sheena was mewing like a kitten. "What is it, darlin'?"

"Dark," came the whimpered reply.

Dolly fetched her own bedside lamp, and covered it with a headscarf. "There, how's that, then?" Sheena's eyes were wide with fright. "Would you like me to read you a story?"

The little girl nodded, so Dolly opened one of the cheap plastic suitcases and took out some dog-eared books.

"Which one is your favorite?"

"*Three Little Piggies*," Sheena whispered.

"Okay, *Three Little Piggies* it is. Oh, you're all awake now, are you? Well, cuddle up and I'll read you a story."

Dolly read until one by one they fell asleep. Even so, she went on until she'd finished the book then whispered, "No one will blow my house down, no big bad wolf. This is my house."

Downstairs, Gloria picked up a transmitter. "She's obviously serious about it. This gear must have set her back a few quid."

They heard Dolly coming down and started to make conversation.

"What time did Angela leave?" Dolly asked as she walked in.

"She went out in style," Gloria said, then told her what had happened, and Julia added that she had called the hospital and Angela was off the danger list. They were unsure, however, if the baby would be all right.

Dolly sighed. "You go and see her tomorrow, Julia, take her a few things. Just check on her."

"You won't get me bringin' her in grapes; she deserves all she gets, the nasty little snitch," Gloria said.

Dolly yawned.

Ester sat next to her. "So, you gonna tell us what all this gear is for?"

"It's the train, isn't it?" Connie said.

Dolly slowly got up. "Yes, it is."

"The mail train?" Ester asked, springing to her feet.

"That's right."

Julia was resting one foot on the fireguard. "You'll never do it, Dolly. I spoke to Norma. She said the security for the drops is really tight and there's no access by road. You'd never get a truck or a car up there without the cops knowing. That's why they chose this station: for its inaccessibility."

"We wouldn't be doing it by car." Dolly was on her way to the door.

"On foot? How the hell could we carry big fat mailbags?"

Dolly cocked her head to one side. "We wouldn't carry them and we wouldn't be going by car, or on foot."

Ester smirked. "Helicopter, is it?"

Dolly opened the door. "We hit the train on horseback." They fell about laughing. Gloria snorted like a braying donkey. Then they saw that Dolly wasn't smiling. She looked from one to the other, her voice quiet, calm, without any emotion. "Julia gave me the idea, so from tomorrow we all start learning to ride. Every one of us. If we can't do it, then we look for something else. There's a local stable within half a mile of here. They've got eight horses. We're all booked for the early-morning ride so I don't know about you lot but I need to get some sleep. Goodnight."

She shut the door behind her.

"I've never been on a horse," Connie said lamely.

"Me neither—well, nearest I got was a donkey ride on Brighton beach," Gloria said.

"It's bullshit, isn't it, Julia?" Ester said flatly. "She's joking."

Julia prodded the fire with the poker. "I don't think so. One, she's laid out for all that equipment; two, she was up by the woods, checking out the station. I think she's serious. That's why she's made Connie, me, even you, Ester, start checking it out."

Overhead, the chandelier creaked as Dolly paced the floor above them. Long shadows cast from the fire loomed large across the big dilapidated room. One after another they opened their mouths as if to say something but nothing came out. They were all thinking the same thing. Was Dolly serious? Was the robbery for real? But it was Julia who broke the silence, laughing softly. "She's pulling our legs. Let's have a drink."

CHAPTER 13

Angela was lying curled on her side, a sodden piece of tissue in her hand. She had cried herself into exhaustion. She didn't look up when the door opened, thinking it would be a nurse. She knew it couldn't be her mother—she hadn't called her. She felt so sick and sad; she had never meant to hurt the baby but now it was too late. She was no longer pregnant; she had miscarried early that morning.

"There's grapes and some clothes to change into."

Angela recognized Dolly's voice but was afraid to look at her so she just curled up tighter.

"I know you lost the baby, Angela, and I'm sorry, sorry for what you've done to yourself." Dolly laid out the things she had brought. She stood near to the bed, but not close enough to touch Angela. "It won't seem like it now, but maybe it's for the best."

"You'd know, would you?" came the muffled reply.

"No, I don't really know at all. I ached for a baby, Angela, all my married life, so no, I wouldn't know what it feels like to lose one."

Angela sobbed. Dolly was so cold and hard and she so badly needed someone to put their arms around her. "Please be nice to me, Dolly, *please.*" Angela turned and held out her hand to Dolly.

"Come to the house and . . ."

"Can I stay? I'll cook and clean for you."

". . . pack the rest of your things. That's all I came to tell you. You have to leave but we'll keep your things safe until they release you from here. And you should eat those grapes, almost eighty pence a pound."

The door closed behind her and Angela fell back onto her pillow. She wished she'd killed herself properly, wished she had never woken up because she had nothing to live for, and no place to go.

* * *

Dolly walked into the kitchen through the back door, the smell of burning bacon making her wrinkle her nose.

"Oh, sorry, Dolly, it's me. I can never get the hang of this Aga. I dunno whether to put stuff in the oven or stick it on the top there." Connie shoveled charred bits of bacon onto a piece of paper towel, dabbing the fat off it.

"I been in to see Angela. She lost the baby."

"Julia told me. She's just bathing the girls—they've had their breakfast."

Ester appeared. "Serves the little cow right. Any breakfast going?"

They came in in dribs and drabs but no one seemed inclined to start up a conversation about the proposed robbery. "You all got boots, jeans to ride in?" Dolly suddenly asked.

Gloria looked down at her wellingtons. Julia arrived with the three children, who hung back shyly at the door. Seeing her, Gloria asked, "Will these do?"

Julia shook her head. "No, but there's no point in wasting good money if you're only going to go once. Might as well wait and see, right, Dolly?"

Dolly was eating scrambled eggs and burnt toast. "I'll need to borrow a pair of trousers. You girls are going to be left alone just for a while, but I got some things for you to do." They were sitting at the big kitchen table as Dolly laid out drawing pads, crayons and picture books. "Now you be good, stay put in here and wait until we get back. Don't leave the house, and I'll know if you do because I'm gonna ask the builders to check on you."

"They not comin' today," piped up little Sheena.

Dolly patted her head. "Ah, you don't know, they come and they go. Just be good girls and watch the clock. When the big hand gets to—"

"I can tell the time," said Kate, one of the twins.

"Good, then you stay put for two hours in here and I don't want to have to tell you again!" Dolly was trying her best but she wasn't used to handling little kids, as well as a houseful of adult ones.

Julia fitted her out in an old pair of her jeans which were too tight and the flies were gaping, but as Julia said, why waste money? They piled into Gloria's Mini, all five of them, and headed for the local stables.

"I see they bleedin' downed tools again," Gloria said as they drove out of the manor.

"They'll pick them up again as soon as they get paid," Dolly replied.

"I thought our Connie was supposed to be keeping him happy," Gloria sniggered.

"I'm already workin' on him and the bloke in the signal box. I don't intend to get through all the ruddy workmen, too. *You* do it."

"Don't mind if I fuckin' do!" Gloria hooted.

Dolly closed her eyes. "I wish you'd watch your mouth, Gloria, now we got the girls living in. And that goes for us all. Cut down on the swearing."

"Well, excuuuuuse me for livin'. I can't help bein' the way I am, it's called frustration. I see her getting her leg over at every opportunity and—"

"*Shut up!*" roared Dolly.

"It's the truth! I've not had a good seeing-to in years and it's not for want of trying, lemme tell you." Dolly knew it was pointless attempting to change Gloria. "Mind you, this horse ridin', they say it gives you a climax, did you know that, Dolly? I'm lookin' forward to it."

When they got to the riding school Sandy, a young stable girl with a high-pitched Sloane Ranger voice, began to bring out the horses, all shapes and sizes, as her assistant saddled them up. Julia began sorting through hard hats, which were compulsory, and they switched them round and tried them all on. Sandy kept on taking sly looks at the group of women and couldn't help tittering as they appeared to be first-timers, apart from Julia. Just getting them mounted took considerable time, and when Julia left they all looked petrified, including Dolly. When her horse suddenly bent his head to eat some grass, she almost came off with a high-pitched "Help!"

They had a two-hour lesson and at the end of it they could all mount and dismount, knew how to use the reins, and had been led up and down the field. Gloria wandered into the stables, beaming from ear to ear as if she had just won the Grand National.

"It's quite easy really, isn't it?"

Sandy smiled. "Yes, if you're a natural."

"You think I am, then?"

"We'll see. You haven't really been riding yet."

"Course I have. We been round the field ten times."

"There's more to it than that, Gloria."

By lunchtime none of them could walk. Their thighs were on fire, and everyone was moaning. But Dolly had booked them in for another lesson in a second stable twenty miles away, so reluctantly they squeezed into the Mini again.

"I don't think this is a good idea, you know, Dolly," Gloria gasped. "I mean, I'm knackered after just two hours—and my legs! I think I've done myself some serious damage."

Julia waved them off and decided to take the little girls out for a walk, but before she could set off, Big John arrived and said he needed to speak to

Mrs. Rawlins. Julia told him she was not at home but asked if she could help. "Well, it's just that she's supposed to pay me the second installment. We're behind now, and she did say today. I've got the lads on another job until she pays, but this scaffolding needs finishing and we got all that cement ordered and the sand."

"I'll tell her to give you a ring."

He looked unconvinced. "This was a cash deal and she's put me in a very difficult position."

"She'll call you," Julia insisted.

He hung about a moment, then asked, "Connie here, is she?"

"She's out."

He returned to his truck; he was determined that until he saw the color of Mrs. Rawlins's money he was not going to finish anything off or order another bag of cement. The reality was that he had been so desperate to get his firm off the ground that he'd stretched himself to the limit. He had a nasty feeling that his inexperience was going to teach him a hard lesson.

The afternoon riding session brought grave doubts that any one of them would ever be let off a leading-rein. Out of the four Connie was the best and the most confident, Gloria the worst. She yelled and shouted abuse to the embarrassment of the others and the prim stable girls. When they returned to the manor, Dolly was certain she would have to think about another way.

She made the children their tea, then sat with them and read them a story. For half an hour Dolly lost herself in the story and in the warmth of the three little girls. They were gradually becoming less fearful and more open. Dolly constantly repeated that the manor was their home, and no one could take it away from them; their mummy knew where to write to them and when she was back she would know where to find them. That was why she had brought them here.

Early next day Dolly drove into the village, toured the second-hand shops, and returned laden with hacking-jackets, jodhpurs, second-hand riding boots and two men's riding coats. Some of the clothes were in good condition, some not so good, so she laid them all out, choosing the best for herself. That morning the lesson was booked for ten and, creaking in agony, the women argued and fought over each item like ten-year-olds. Gloria stuffed two pairs of thick woolen socks inside a pair of men's riding boots as they were far too large; before Gloria could grab them Connie squeezed into a pair that were too small but highly polished. They didn't look any more professional—on the contrary, they were like something out of a Thelwell cartoon and their riding was no better.

Sandy the stable girl led them all into the field connected to the stables and they proceeded to learn how to trot with gritted teeth and loud moans.

Julia remained at the house with the children, cooking breakfast and taking them on a ramble around the grounds. They shrieked with excitement when she brought out Helen of Troy and they each had a turn at being led round the yard. None of them had been in the country before or ridden a horse, and their excitement touched Julia. As a child she had wanted for nothing, she even had her own pony, and it made her realize just how wonderful a place the manor could be for kids like Kathleen's.

It was early afternoon by the time everyone had cleaned themselves up, and the washing machine creaked under the weight of all their dirty clothes. The boots were lined up and the little girls given the task of cleaning them for fifty pence a pair. Soon Sheena seemed to be getting more boot polish on herself than on the boots, but, seeing they were happy, Dolly said nothing and called all the women into the office.

They stood around, waiting, as Dolly closed the door and crossed to her desk. She picked up a small black notebook and sat down. "Right, it's obvious we're gonna need two lessons a day."

Gloria leaned on the desk. "I got to be honest, Doll, I'm not cut out for this riding business. It's me size, you see. Being small I can't get me legs round the horse."

Dolly frowned. "We'll get you a small horse, then."

Gloria pulled a face. "You're payin'."

"Yeah, I am paying for everything, so shut up and listen, all of you."

Julia stood by the window. "The builder was here, Dolly. You know he's got a delivery of bathroom equipment arriving and he's a bit sore. He could start causing trouble."

Dolly moistened her lips. "Yes, I know. We'll start with him."

Dolly pointed at Connie and told her to keep Big John happy, to see him as much as possible and give him five grand that evening.

Gloria pouted. "All right for some. I wouldn't mind keeping him happy—got a nice arse."

No one paid her any attention; they were listening to Dolly as she described the old cesspit half a mile from the house. "I need to get it cleared, see how deep it is, so this afternoon, Gloria and Julia, that's your job."

"Oh, great! I just got meself cleaned up," moaned Gloria, but no one took any notice.

"Connie, when you see John, I want you to order through his firm, without him knowing, about twenty kilo-bags of lime."

"Why? What do we need them for?" Connie asked.

"To fill the pit," Dolly said patiently.

She jabbed a finger at Ester. "You have an assignment. I want you to find out just how tough it is to unhitch a train carriage."

"Oh, sure," Ester said, smiling as if it was as simple as buying groceries.

"I'm serious. The mail carriage is in the center of the train, it's an ordinary carriage. I want to know how you can unhitch it."

"How the fuck do I find that out?"

"You've got a big mouth, Ester. Use it. Off the top of my head you can go to the railway museums, chat up a guard, *not* at the local station—any way you think—but I need to know if it's done manually or—"

"Fine, I'll do it," Ester said.

Dolly made a tick in the notebook, turning a page. "Tonight, Connie, you go and see your boyfriend in the signal box. This time you find out the layout, how many alarms there are, how long it takes to get the law to the station."

"You must be joking," muttered Connie.

"No, love, I'm not. We have to know exactly what goes down when that mail train arrives, what he does, what—"

Connie broke in, "How do I do that?"

"Find a way, love."

"Well, one minute you're telling me to be with the builder, then the signal-box guy. I can't do both of them."

"Yes, you can," Dolly snapped, and then looked at them all. "You have to do just what I tell you or this is finished before it's started. I don't want any arguments."

"Can we ask what exactly you're planning?" Ester leaned forward.

Dolly closed her book and stood up. "I'm going to London so I'll need the car. I don't want the kids left alone so one of you bath them, feed them and put them to bed. I might be late."

She walked out and they watched her go, no one saying a word until the door latched. "She's nuts, you do know that, don't you?" Ester said angrily.

"But you're still here," remarked Julia tartly.

"Yeah, but not for long if she carries on like this. We got a right to know what she's doing."

Gloria heaved herself out of the chair. "Well, like she's always saying, she's paying, so let's get on with it. I mean, I'll do your job if you wanna do the cesspit."

There was no way Ester was going to dig shit. She was still in agony from the ride. "I can't. I'm injured."

"Well then, we just do what the boss says," Gloria sighed.

Connie said, "Okay, but I'll never be able to get that information, you know. I'm not supposed to even be in the signal box."

"Take him a bottle of wine," Julia said, and stroked Connie's shoulder. "One for the builder as well." Connie shrugged her away.

"Right, let's get on with it," Julia said, and one by one they went to do their allocated jobs.

Angela left the hospital, caught a bus and then made her way down the lane to the manor. No one was in sight so she pushed open the front door.

"Hello? Anyone home?"

Ester appeared on the stairs and glared at her. "Just stay put, no need to come in."

"I've come for my gear."

Ester disappeared along the landing. The three girls peeped out from the kitchen.

"They're Kathleen O'Reilly's kids," Ester called down.

Angela smiled. "Hello."

"Hello," said Sheena.

"How ya all doing?"

Before they could reply, Ester returned with a suitcase which she practically hurled down the stairs. "There's your gear. Piss off and don't come back."

Angela was near to tears as she picked up her case. "I got no money."

"My heart bleeds. Go on, get out."

Angela walked back down the drive, dragging the suitcase, sniffing back the tears. She didn't see Gloria and Julia way in the distance, digging and clearing the cesspit. Both wore thick scarves round their faces to combat the awful stench. They heaved bucketload after bucketload, chucking it into a wheelbarrow.

"This is making me sick," said Gloria, retching.

Julia heaved up the wheelbarrow. "Keep at it. We've only cleared a quarter of it."

"It's not on, you know. This could give us a disease, it's disgusting. I mean, this is—this is old shit, you know that, don't you?"

Julia paid no attention as she wheeled the thick, stinking mud over to a pile of old bits of furniture and junk. She tipped out the barrow and stood away from the noxious fumes. She turned back as Gloria peered down into the pit.

"Now what? I can't reach in any further with the bucket," she yelled.

"We'll have to get down into it, then," Julia said.

"I'm not gettin' in there," shrieked Gloria.

"Well, one of us has to. We'll toss for it." Julia picked up a rake and asked whether Gloria wanted the rake or flat side. Gloria bellowed she wanted the rake side. Julia tossed the rake into the air and it came down flat side.

"You bloody did that on purpose," Gloria yelled. She looked down into the pit again and back to Julia. "I got an idea. Why don't we get the kids to do it?"

Connie breezed into Big John's yard. He was sitting on the steps of his little hut.

"Hi, how are you?" She beamed as she walked over.

He didn't return her smile. "Look, Connie, this has got nothing to do with you but that Mrs. Rawlins is making me bankrupt."

Connie sat next to him and passed over the envelope. "Here you go, and there's more coming in a day or two."

John opened the envelope and then stood up. "I'd better go and divvy this up with the men."

"Oh, right now?"

He looked into her upturned face. "I got to. When they finish the job they're on, they'll be on their way. If you want that roof done at the manor, I got to pay them."

"How long will you be?"

"Ten minutes."

She slipped her arms around him. "Then I'll wait, but only ten minutes, and we can have a . . ." She kissed him and he gasped for breath when he broke away from her. "Don't be long," she whispered, biting his ear.

He blushed, glancing toward the gates then back to the small wooden makeshift hut. "You know, anyone can walk in here, Connie."

She giggled. "Exciting, isn't it? Besides, you can lock the main gates, can't you? But I think it'll be more fun if they're open and we screw knowing somebody'll walk in any minute. And look, I brought us a bottle of wine."

He was all over the place, kissing her, groping her breasts, and then he sprinted to his truck. He shouted back that he would be no more than ten minutes.

She was still standing there on the steps of his hut, blouse open, as he clipped the gatepost in his haste to get out. She didn't even wait for the tail end of the van to disappear before she shot into the hut and began to sift through all his papers until she found some order forms. She called a trade supplier and ordered the bags of lime to be delivered directly to the manor for a cash payment. She gave John's firm's reference and as soon as she replaced the receiver she hurried out, picking up her bag with the bottle of wine. Next stop, the signal box.

Mike had just finished his lunch and was about to go back to the station when the call came. He was eager not to let Susan answer it in case it was Angela again. They almost collided in the hall, they were both so desperate to reach the telephone first.

Mike snatched it up. Susan stood with her hands on her hips.

"Hello? Who is it?" Susan said petulantly.

"It's my governor." He glared at her so hard that she turned away and stomped into the kitchen.

"What do you want?" he said quietly, afraid Susan would still be listening.

"Need to see you, love, it's urgent. I'll be at the Pen and Whistle pub, the one on the corner by your mother's flat, in the saloon bar, six thirty."

"I can't—I can't see you."

"I think you can, Mike. Six thirty, just be there."

The line went dead. He stood there, holding the receiver, and then quickly dialed his station. He was put through to the incident room and he told them he was not feeling too well so he would be in a bit late. Then he looked toward the kitchen. He was sure that Susan was listening. All his anger and frustration welled up as he dropped the phone back down.

Ester, being lazy, called a number of railway museums first but was not getting the information she needed. She then tried another tactic, saying she was making a documentary film for the BBC and asking if she could she speak to anyone working at the museum who could assist her. She was given various numbers to call for permission to interview railway technicians and started working her way through them. Permission was not granted by British Rail, so she was now contacting the private railways, saying the BBC documentary had the full backing of the Transport Ministry, who were co-financing the film.

She looked at the list of essential items listed by Dolly: size and weight of the train compartments, couplings and sidings. Underlined was how long it would take to unhitch one carriage from another. She sighed: this was going to take forever.

Big John had only been gone twelve and a half minutes, more or less flinging the money at his men and racing back to his yard. He quickly ran a comb through his hair, wishing he'd got a spot of cologne, then locked the big double gates before running over to his hut. He threw open the door, his heart pounding.

Connie had left, no note, nothing. She'd even taken the bottle of wine.

Still carrying her suitcase, Angela walked along the road toward Mike's house. It was growing dark and it had taken her hours to hitch a ride from the manor. She saw Mike's car parked outside his house and was in two minds whether or not to go and ring the doorbell. She wanted to confront him, tell him about the baby, but the nearer she got the more her confidence dwindled. She definitely didn't want to see his wife. She sat down on a wall, wondering if he would come out.

Inside the house, Mike and Susan were having one hell of a row. She was demanding to know all about Angela, the phone calls—everything—and he was refusing to answer. "You stay out all night, and don't speak to me. How do you expect me to feel?"

Mike clenched his fists. "Susan, I've told you, there is nothing—*nothing* between me and this girl."

"Then why does she keep calling you? Why was that Mrs. Rawlins round here? Is it true that she's pregnant?"

"Leave it alone, Susan. I mean it. Just shut up about it. You're driving me nuts."

"And *you're* driving *me* nuts," she said in a fury, watching as he grabbed his coat. "Where are you going?"

"Out. I can't stand it here."

"One of these days you're gonna come back here and the locks will have been changed."

He sighed. "Sue, listen, give me a break. I've got a lot on my plate right now and I just can't tell you about it."

"Try me, go on, try me!" she shouted.

He ran his hands through his hair. He didn't even know where to begin. How could he tell her about his mother, the diamonds, the trouble he was in at work? He knew she wouldn't be able to deal with it. Right now, Angela was the least of his problems. He was afraid of what Dolly Rawlins wanted, scared he was heading into even deeper trouble, but he couldn't tell anyone, especially not his wife. Susan broke down in tears as he walked out. She ran up the stairs and was about to open the window, call out to him that they had to talk, when she saw Angela.

Mike yanked open the car door and then suddenly Angela was there. "We got to talk, Mike."

"No, we haven't. I got nothing to say to you, Angela, just go away from me. I don't want to see you. Stay away from me and my house." He got in and slammed the door shut. She rapped on the window and when she wouldn't stop he wound it down.

"I lost the baby, Mike."

"I don't care, Angela, you hear me? I *don't care.*"

She was sobbing, looking like an orphan with her suitcase. "I got no one to help me, Mike," she wept.

He dug into his pocket and pulled out his wallet. He took all the money he had and held it out. "Here, take this, *take it,* it's all I got on me."

"I didn't come for money," she wailed.

He pushed the money at her. "Take it, Angela. I can't see you, so please stay away from me. *Just go away, Angela!*" He threw the money onto the pavement, and started the car. It was six fifteen, and although he was afraid to meet Dolly Rawlins he was more afraid not to, so he drove off.

Angela picked up the four twenty-pound notes, unaware that Susan was watching from the bedroom window, crying just as hard as she was, and wishing she had enough money to get the locks changed there and then.

Gloria and Julia were both deep in the cesspit, clearing away the filth. Their heads appeared at the lip as Ester carried out two mugs.

"All right for some," moaned Gloria, accepting the tea.

"Blimey, it's deep, isn't it?" Ester remarked.

"I'd say this is for the mailbags," Julia replied. "What do you think?"

"I dunno—who knows what the old bat's doing? But as long as it's not for us, who cares?" Ester set off back toward the house.

Gloria looked at Julia. "What if she's got us diggin' our own bleedin' grave? She shot her old man, remember. I wouldn't put nothing past her."

Connie was perched on the counter in the signal box, a chipped glass of red wine in her hand, which she clinked against Jim's mug. "Cheers."

He moved closer. "You could get me the sack you know, Connie."

"Who's gonna know I'm here?"

"Well, anyone passing can see us."

She slithered off the counter to sit on the floor. "Now they can't." She began to run her hand up his trouser leg.

"Hang on a second—lemme just sort this out. It's the six o'clock, then we got fifteen minutes."

Connie watched as he pulled levers and answered the phone. She began to ease down her panties. She held them up, waving them. "Can I have another drink down here?"

Jim began heaving the rail levers faster than he ever had before while Connie crawled across the floor and started undoing his flies. By now she had a good sense of where the phone connection wires ran but she didn't have any knowledge of the alarms. All she knew was that it was going to be a very long night.

Dolly sipped the lemonade, flicking through her little black notebook. Mike stood over her as she looked up, smiling.

"Nothing for me, but do get yourself a drink, love, if you need one."

"I don't." He sat down, having a good look around the bar. "What do you want?"

Dolly shut the book, had another sip. "Some information—sort of like a trade."

"What information?" he asked, his heart pounding. He knew something bad was coming but when it came it left him shattered. "I can't find that out! That's classified!"

She leaned forward and tapped his arm. "Yes, you can and you will, otherwise I will have to inform your superiors about those diamonds, about your mother, everything. It's up to you, Mike. Tell me now if you don't want to do it. You must have some old friends from your Army days—they might be helpful, but if you don't want to do it . . ."

"I've just said I don't."

"Oh, I know you did, but you see, Mike, that's because I don't think you really believe that I'd be prepared to go back to prison. But I would, and I wouldn't be on my own. You'd be sent down as well, and they might even haul your mother back from Spain. So let me ask you again—can you get the information I need?"

He shuffled his feet, took another look around. "How long have I got?"

"Two days, no more." She drained her glass, placing it carefully back on the beer mat. "I'll call you, don't you call me. Two days."

He sat, head in his hands, as she walked out. The cement was drying, up to his chest now. He didn't know whether to throw the table through the pub window or do as she had asked: find out how much money the mail train was carrying, and if they were going to continue using the same route. He looked at the slip of paper she had passed him with the name of the security firm on the side of the vans she'd seen outside her local station. It was a reputable firm and he didn't know if he'd be able to get any information from them. He needed a drink, a large one. No way would he be able to go in to work. He really did feel ill.

Dolly drove back to the manor and as she turned into the drive the headlamps picked out the large rubbish tip still burning. She got out, leaving the lights on, and walked past it to the cesspit. She nodded to herself, satisfied it was big enough and, most certainly, deep enough.

When she got in she found the kitchen in a mess: dirty soup plates, mince in a pan, dried-out baked beans in another, stacks of used cups and mugs. Every surface was food-stained and filthy. She pursed her lips and dumped her handbag, throwing aside her coat. She found Ester lying stretched out on the sofa with a glass of wine, reading the *TV Times*. Julia was asleep in an easy chair, the television on in the background. Neither heard Dolly. She walked up the big staircase and looked into Connie's room, but it was empty. Then she went up to the second landing to the children's room.

The last person Dolly expected to see was Gloria, wrapped in an old dressing gown, sitting with Sheena on her knee. The other two were fast asleep in the big old-fashioned double bed. "Oh, said the little pig. What will the big bad wolf do?" Gloria rocked the child, stroking her hair. "Well, he'll huff and he'll puff and he'll blow the house down."

Sheena lifted her tiny hand to Gloria's cheek. "You're not our mummy, are you?"

Gloria shook her head. The little girl's question touched her heart—so many different homes, so many different foster carers, the little girl was completely confused.

Gloria kissed her. "No, I'm not your mummy."

"Doesn't she love us anymore?"

"Yes, of course she does. But you know, Sheena, a long, long time ago I had a little girl, just like you, and I had to go away, just like your mummy has had to go away. My little girl never had a nice house to live in and I couldn't ever see her again but you will. Your mummy being away doesn't mean she doesn't love you. She does. And she's arranged for us all to look after you until she comes back. Do you understand?"

"No." Sheena yawned.

"My little girl never understood but then it was too late, you see, I couldn't see her. But you'll be able to see your mummy. One of us will always take you to see her so you won't forget who she is, and in the meantime we'll all be like extra mothers. How's that?"

Sheena was asleep, and Dolly stayed where she was, looking at a Gloria she hadn't known existed, a sad, lonely Gloria who was being so gentle and caring, so unlike the hard, uncouth harridan she showed to them all. They all had secrets, all had hidden pain. Somehow she had not expected Gloria to have so much.

CHAPTER 14

Connie was doing up her blouse and Jim had just finished zipping his trousers as he hurriedly closed the gates for the nine thirty express to pass through. John stood at the level crossing, annoyed that he'd just missed the orange light. As it turned to red, he looked at the signal box, as if to blame it for his being held up, and saw her, laughing, her arms wrapped around the attendant. He was stunned. That wasn't his Connie up there, was it?

Connie skipped down the steps, looked back and blew a kiss, then hurried toward the taxi rank. She was in the cab heading for the manor when the gates opened and she didn't see John charge up the steps to the signal box.

"Connie here, is she?" John blurted out, when Jim opened the door.

Jim acted dumb. He didn't know who the big broad-shouldered bloke was, but he was pretty sure that if Connie had been caught in there with him he'd have been in serious trouble.

"No, nobody here but me, why?"

John looked past him into the signal box. "No reason. Sorry, mate. Sorry to bother you."

Jim knew he'd have to ask Connie about the angry bloke but only when the time was right. They'd not even been out on a proper date yet. Half of him still couldn't believe what had taken place—he'd never experienced anything like it. Blown in his own signal box! As if to assure himself that it had really happened, he pulled Connie's lacy panties from his pocket.

"Shit, I forgot me knickers," Connie said as she walked into the house, slamming the front door. She hurried into the kitchen and began to draw on the back of an envelope everything she could remember. She was just finishing when she heard the doorbell ring.

Ester came in, looking perplexed. "I didn't hear a car, did you, Connie?"

"No. Who do you think it is?"

Dolly appeared on the landing. "Just answer it, Ester."

Ester pushed Connie forward. "You answer, just in case."

Dolly thumped down the stairs as the bell rang again. She went for the door and swung it open. Angela stood on the doorstep. "I'm sorry, I got no other place to go—I thumbed a lift back."

"Well, love, you can thumb one right out again," Dolly replied.

Connie felt sorry for Angela. "Ah, let her stay for just one night."

Ester scowled. "You joking? No way! Chuck her out, Dolly."

"Oh, please don't! I'll cook and clean, I promise," Angela begged.

Dolly opened the door wider. "Right, one night. Go up onto the top floor. Your old room's gone so use another, then come down and clean up the kitchen and make us some dinner."

Angela almost kissed her hand but Dolly stepped away, letting the door bang shut.

"You must be mad," Ester said, going back into the drawing room.

Connie smiled at Angela but got pushed into the room by Dolly. "Give us a call when it's ready, will you, love?" Dolly said as she went into the drawing room.

Gloria clattered in a few minutes later. "I don't fucking believe that girl's cheek. I just seen her making up her bed."

"Just for tonight," Dolly said.

"What? Are you crazy?"

Julia yawned. "Well, the kitchen's a mess, the kids' room's a mess, we need somebody to cook, do all the ironing and washing, plus she's going to cook dinner so that should keep her occupied for one night, anyway."

Dolly sat down, took out her notebook, and flicked through it.

"Bit bleedin' risky, isn't it?" Gloria said, warming herself by the fire. "That boyfriend of hers—what if he's sent her?"

Dolly shook her head. "He's not made any calls to his station about us. I think we got the bloke by the balls."

Dolly took out a tape and slipped it into the small cassette player.

"You got him taped?" Ester said.

"Didn't I tell you? Have a listen."

"What about at the station?" Ester asked and Dolly frowned, knowing she really needed to do that, too.

They sat round listening to Susan and Mike arguing, with his kids yelling in the background. They all laughed, apart from Ester, as if it was all a big joke. Dolly left them to it, and went to the kitchen to have a private confab with Angela.

Angela was working herself into a sweat, washing dishes, scrubbing the floor, cleaning all the surfaces, as if to prove she was worth her keep.

"You want to stay on, do you?" Dolly asked, as she drew out a chair to sit at the kitchen table.

"I'll do anything to make up for what I done, anything. I know you won't ever forgive me but . . ." Angela sat down opposite Dolly and started trying to explain about the baby and Mike, but Dolly took her hand.

"Shut up. Now, are you still seeing him?"

Angela shook her head.

"I see. Well, you might have to prove yourself, Angela—not just to me but to the others. Does he know you were driving the car that killed Jimmy Donaldson?"

"No! I hate him, Dolly, really, I wouldn't help him. I swear on my life I wouldn't."

Dolly propped an elbow on the table. "Well, you remember this, Angela, because if you betray me again, if I find out that you're grassin' back to him, then you'll go down for murder and I'll make sure of it. You understand, don't you?"

Angela nodded. In truth, she didn't have anywhere else to go—even her mum had refused to let her stay. "I'll make it up to you," she said, clinging to Dolly's hand. "I swear I will. I'll do whatever you want."

"Good girl. Now I want you to keep house, feed us and take care of Kathleen's girls. And I will need you to do a few other things for me."

The women had obviously been talking about Dolly because when she returned they fell silent. She picked up her notebook.

"Dinner's not ready yet so let's get this sorted before we eat." She asked each of them about their day, making copious notes, frowning at Ester who, she felt, had not done enough. She was told to go out the next day and get more information on the carriage links.

"Good work on the cesspit, Gloria and Julia."

They felt a little like schoolgirls and didn't enjoy it.

Dolly then turned her attention to Connie. She was happy that the lime was on its way, but Connie's hastily drawn diagrams were not yet good enough, and they still needed details of the alarms and codes used to contact the local police. Connie said she would have another evening with Jim—even spend the afternoon with him because he wasn't on duty until four thirty.

"That's not written down here, Connie," Dolly said sternly.

"Well, I just told you."

"That's not good enough. I need to know everything. Is that understood?"

Dolly turned to Julia. "Do you think you could get hold of Norma's police cape and, if possible, her hat?"

"We could hire some," offered Julia.

"Yes, we could, and be seen doing it. I've seen them in the back of her car. Go and keep her friendly, just like Connie's doing with the signal-box guy. Plus, Connie, keep your eye on those shotguns at the gym."

Dolly continued down the list.

"Who's looking after the kids?" Julia asked.

"Angela—and don't argue. Until I say different, she stays. Somebody's got to look after them."

"I think that's a mistake," said Ester.

Dolly's voice was icy quiet. "You want to question me, Ester, then you can pack your gear and leave right now. Either we do this my way or we don't do it at all."

Angela tapped on the door and peeped round. "Dinner's on the table," she said meekly, and scuttled out.

They all started to head for the door, but Dolly caught Ester by the arm. "Just a second, love, I want a word." The others left the room.

Ester stood, hands on her hips. "Don't get me wrong, Dolly, I'm not questioning who's the boss. I just have a few more brains than some of the others."

"Do you?" Dolly sighed. "I don't call wheelin' around in a hot car very clever, and I don't call having blokes arrive and knock the hell out of Gloria very clever either."

"So what do you want me to do?" Ester said angrily.

"I want you to sort out this blackmail business. We can't afford to have loose ends. Take it back, Ester, or the whole thing is off. I mean it. Something like this could bring us all down."

"Oh yeah? And what about you and this copper? You must have something going on with him. That's why you got his home bugged."

Dolly rubbed her eyes. "Just sort out the tape, Ester. Tomorrow."

Dolly and Julia walked in darkness up through the woods and down to the railway line. "Bring her up to the line, Julia. See if she really is as bomb-proof as that Norma said."

"Okay," Julia replied, not sure why Dolly had brought her along.

They looked down the railway line to the small bridge, the lake, and back to the level crossing. They said nothing but both their minds were racing. Dolly was trying to visualize step by step how she intended holding up the train. Julia could see only disaster. She reckoned that with or without the horse it was going to be impossible.

"I think we'll need a boat—that's another expense," Dolly said, almost to herself.

Julia looked back at the lake, trying to read Dolly's mind. *Surely* she wasn't going to hold up the train on the bridge? But if she was, why were they learning to ride?

The following morning Julia couldn't stop sniggering. They were worse than she had anticipated—even with more than eight hours of lessons they were incapable of cantering and all still seemed very ill at ease. They were still on the leading-rein, none good enough to ride alone.

Julia rode toward Dolly and said quietly, "I hope you've got a plan that now excludes the horses, Dolly, because none of you could make it across the fields. There's five sets of hedges to jump and—"

Dolly pushed her horse past Julia. "I'll tell you when I've changed my mind and instead of laughing at how bad we are, why not start helping?"

Dolly wobbled precariously in the saddle as she spoke, but Julia didn't laugh. Dolly had that dangerous look on her face.

That afternoon Julia took over the lesson and proved to be a much better teacher than the stable girl. She decided to be tough, and not let them get away with a thing, and soon had them cantering—even Gloria, who fell off but got straight back on after Julia screamed at her.

Angela had hot soup ready and waiting. The children had been given their tea and were outside, brushing and clearing the yard for more fifty pence pieces. When they were halfway through their soup, the telephone rang and Ester, as always, dived out first to see who it was. "It's for you, Julia," she shouted before going upstairs for a bath. She leaned over the banister as Julia went to the phone. "It must be your mother—she asked if you were in surgery!" She laughed.

Julia picked up the receiver, but it wasn't her mother at the other end of the phone. It was the housekeeper: Julia's mother had had a stroke, and was very ill.

"My mother's ill," Julia said unemotionally. The women all looked at her. "A stroke. I'll have to go and sort it out. Can I use your car, Gloria?"

"No, you can't," Dolly said, clearing the bowls.

"Well, I'll take the truck."

Dolly turned and smiled. "Why not ask that friend of yours, Norma? Maybe she'll drive you over—be a good chance to talk to her."

Julia shrugged. "Okay, but I don't know if she's around. She may be on duty."

Dolly ran the water in the sink. "Don't forget we need the riding cape and her hat."

Norma opened the front door with a smile and Julia explained what had happened. "You're in luck, I'm off for two days so it's no problem."

"I really appreciate this," Julia said, taking a step into the neat cottage hallway while Norma picked up her coat and car keys. "Just one thing, Norma, about my old lady. She doesn't know I was in prison, she still thinks I'm a doctor."

"Fair enough." Norma turned into the main road and they drove off. "I hear you had another visit from the locals?"

Julia gave her a sidelong look. "Yeah, that's right. First they thought we were hiding some diamonds, then guns. It was a ridiculous."

Norma nodded. "Mrs. Rawlins has quite a reputation."

"Oh, have you been checking up on us?"

Norma swore as they drew up by the level crossing. "Oh, bugger it. Let's hope it's not the mail train."

They sat in silence, watching the gates clang shut, and then Julia leaned back in her seat, slipping her arm behind Norma. "They have a lot of security on for the mail train?"

Norma pointed along the road. "Yes, but as you can see, it's quite simple. That's why they pick on this station, no easy access for any car coming up either side of it and they'd never get as far as the motorway, the place is alarmed all along the track, with a special link to the police station. They can be here in under four minutes."

"Really?" Julia said, trying not to sound too interested.

"You know why they use the security vans?" Norma continued.

"No?"

"Because of the vulnerability of the big stations. Last big robbery was at King's Cross, so now they have armored trucks and a police escort to an out-of-the-way station like ours, then they put the bags on board and it's a clear run through all the stations. Train goes at around eighty miles an hour."

Julia began to massage Norma's neck. "Well, thankfully it's not the mail train today, and no coppers but you!" She leaned over and kissed Norma, only stopping when the gates opened again and they continued on, passing Raymond Dewey on his little stool. He waved to Julia and she waved back.

"Poor sod, what a life," she said.

"Oh, he's happy enough," Norma said, and then touched Julia's hand lightly. "I'm glad you called."

"So am I," Julia replied, then stared out of the window. She really did find Norma irritating. It was going to be a long drive.

Dolly asked Connie to come in for a chat. She closed the bedroom door. "You're seeing that signal-box bloke tonight, aren't you?"

"Yes, I told you."

"Where's he taking you?"

"Dinner at his place."

"Good. Slip him a couple of these sleeping tablets. You can have a good search around his place. Maybe he's got papers or something that'll give us the alarm codes."

Connie took the two tablets wrapped in a bit of tissue and slipped them into her pocket. "I'll be down the gym first, check on the shotguns."

"Good girl."

"Thank you, Dolly," she said without a smile.

As she was walking out, Dolly caught her hand. "Something bothering you?"

"What do you think? But, like you said, I owe you for Lennie so I'll do whatever you say."

"You make sure you do."

Connie wouldn't meet her gaze as she closed the door behind her. Dolly rubbed her eyes, and pinched the bridge of her nose. God, they infuriated her. She was always having to check up on one or the other of them—it was like having a house full of kids. She would have to start thinking about what she would do with them after the robbery.

Angela was in the kitchen when Dolly came in. "Want to go into London, love? Only I got to drop Gloria off for her usual visit with her husband so you might as well keep us company."

It was not until they had left Gloria at a tube station that Dolly told Angela what she wanted her to do. She said it so quietly that Angela didn't get nervous or even ask too many questions; she simply said yes. Not that she wanted to go into the police station, but she didn't really have any choice.

Angela asked at the desk to speak to Mike Withey. The duty sergeant asked her name and then called the incident room. "What did you say your name was, love?"

"Angela Dunn."

When Mike was told she was waiting in reception he marched straight out to her, grabbed her by the arm and pulled her out onto the street.

"I told you I didn't want to see you again."

"Please, Mike, I just want to talk to you, just for a minute. Look, I bought you a present. Please don't be angry."

"I don't want anything from you, Angela."

Angela held out the slim little box but he turned away so she took it out and showed it to him. "It's a pen."

"Great, Angela, just what I needed." She slid it into his top pocket, and he turned away from her. "I don't want it."

"Please, just give me a few minutes, please, Mike. I got to tell you something—it's important." He rubbed his jaw. "Mrs. Rawlins said she'll call you tomorrow morning, she wants to know what would be a good time."

Mike faced the wall, feeling as if someone was about to ram his head into it. "What else did she tell you?"

"Nothing, just that she would be in touch but for you to tell her what time."

He bit his lip. "Tell her I've nothing for her, not yet, but I'll be at home—say in the morning about ten."

Dolly sat in the car, the briefcase open on her lap. She adjusted the channel and could soon hear Mike as clearly as if he was sitting next to her. She had to know if she could trust him—and Angela, for that matter. So far she had said exactly what she had been told to say, and the added plus was that they were even in sight. She hadn't reckoned on them coming outside to talk.

Angela watched him hurry back into the station before she headed toward Dolly. She could see the aerial stuck on the side of the car. "Was that okay?"

Dolly beamed. "Yes, love. Get in, I've a few things I want you to do for me. Can you stay at your mother's?"

"Why? Can't I stay on at the manor?"

"Yes, but I want you to do a few things for me first thing in the morning. Have you got a passport?"

"No."

"Well, first thing tomorrow I want you to get one and I want you to take mine, with this letter. I'm the girls' legal guardian and I want them put on my passport, just for a holiday. Then you come straight home. And, Angela, you don't say a word about this to any of the others or they'll go ape-shit—you know the way they feel about you."

"What are you going to do?"

"Oh, drive around a bit. Go on, off you go."

"My mum won't let me stay, Dolly."

Dolly counted off some twenty-pound notes. "Well, here's money for a hotel—just the one night, love, then you get yourself home."

Dolly watched her walk off down the street, then noticed the channel light blinking in the briefcase and put in her earplug. Mike was making a phone call. She smiled to herself as she listened to Mike arranging to meet someone, and the more Dolly listened the more she smiled. She was sure she was right. She'd got the smart little bastard right by the balls. But better to be safe than sorry.

Gloria saw that Eddie was in a bad mood the moment he was let through the gate to the visiting room. She'd brought a few odds and sods for him, not much, and fifteen quid. He took them without so much as a thank you.

"So, how you keeping?"

"Oh, I'm havin' a really good time in here, Gloria."

She had known it would start then.

"You look different," he muttered.

"Yeah, well, it's all the fresh air."

"So you're still at the farmhouse then?"

"It's a *manor* house, Eddie, and yeah, I'm still there."

He began to roll a cigarette.

"Anythin' gone down there?" he asked nonchalantly, keeping his eyes on his roll-up. She sat back, watching him, and then he looked up, all innocence, and in that moment she knew she was stronger than him. Maybe she always had been.

* * *

Mike had no notion that he was wired up and Dolly Rawlins was taping every word he said. It was as if she was on his shoulder when he went to visit an old mate from his days in the Army, leading her directly to the security firm that handled the money for the mail train.

He had brought a bottle of Scotch and was shown into the security firm's office. His friend Colin had been a bit surprised to hear from Mike as it had been quite a few years and he wondered what he was after. But Mike soon got over that, saying he was putting out feelers for work if he was to leave the police force and a friend of a friend had told him that Colin had a cushy number going.

Dolly had to hand it to Mike. He was quite a smooth operator. She listened as he chatted on about his Army days, about how badly he was paid and how, with a wife and two kids to keep plus a mortgage to pay, he was getting sick and tired of the Met. She was parked fifty yards from the security firm's main depot and would have remained there if she hadn't seen a police patrol car cruise by. She did one slow tour round the block and then she was out of range of the transmitter. She decided to call it quits for the evening. Most important was that she felt confident that if anything was to go down from Mike's place she'd be ready for it. She headed home, everything she was planning playing over and over in her mind. It was all coming together, and yet as the miles clocked up she became more uneasy. Was she in over her head? Did she really believe she could go through with it? Just thinking about it exhausted her. Had it been like this with the widows?

Then he began to talk to her. It didn't take her by surprise—Harry's voice often came to her, not like some whispered menace, nothing like that. In fact, it was the normality of the sound of his voice in her head that had often soothed her. She used to talk to him, silent conversations as if he was in the room with her, his deep, warm tones as clear as if he was sitting in their old drawing room in their house in Totteridge. He used to sit up late many nights. Sometimes she'd take him in a warm glass of malt whisky with just a sprinkling of sugar.

"You all right, darlin'?" she'd ask him.

"I am, sweetheart, but I just need to make sure I'm covered back, front and sideways, because there'll be nobody else looking out for me."

Harry never told her exactly what he was working on so diligently. But she would sit close and ask him if he wanted to talk about it . . . how she loved those times. Harry would sip his drink and rest a hand on her shoulder.

"Well, darlin', I got this tricky little situation. Not sure who to trust with an important delivery and it's only tricky because it could have repercussions."

She never asked names but in a roundabout way he would tell her who he mistrusted and why, and what he considered the best way to ensure they became trustworthy.

Still driving, one part of her mind concentrating on the road, the other listening to Harry, it wasn't until Dolly stopped at a garage to fill up with petrol that his voice started to fade away. The last thing she heard him say was, "Cover your backside, Dolly, your sides and your front, before you make the next move."

Mike remained with his pal Colin as they drank their way halfway down the bottle. He had not asked about the type of work Colin did, taking his time so as not to create any suspicion. Colin was a little ill at ease in case he was caught drinking: as he was the foreman he could get into trouble. But Mike laughed—he was, after all, a copper. Just in case, Colin slipped out to check no one was around to disturb them.

As soon as he left, Mike looked over the time sheets on the desk, and the lists of officers' names, but found nothing pertaining to any mail train pick-up or delivery. It was a big firm and Mike was about to try one of the drawers when Colin returned.

"You're gonna have to go, the night staff'll be on duty any minute and we're not allowed to have anyone in here."

"Okay. When can we do this again? Only—if I leave the cop shop, I don't want to walk out to nothing. Is the pay decent?"

They talked about the money and Mike brought the conversation gradually round to what kind of work he would be looking at, asking if it was boring and involved just driving around the country. Colin grinned. "No way, this is one of the top companies, we don't deal in small stuff—this is big. That's why they like us Army boys, you know, men that can handle themselves. We're shifting big loads of money."

"Oh yeah? What you call big, then?"

Colin gave a shifty look around and leaned in close. "Come and have a look out in the yard, see the new vans. They're all armor-plated, blow your mind, all work on timers, high-tech stuff. We do the Royal Mail deliveries."

Mike looked suitably impressed and followed Colin into the yard where he was told in an awestruck whisper just how much money the security firm carried, before Colin hustled him out. They arranged to meet for a drink the following night. By then Colin would have made inquiries to see if there were any openings for someone with Mike's experience.

Dolly switched off the lights and got out of the car. It had been a long night and she was exhausted. She couldn't wait to get to bed but as usual she toured the house first, checking who was in and who wasn't. Julia was still out, so was Connie, and Ester was watching a late-night movie.

"Julia called, said her mother was really bad and that Norma's staying over with her."

Dolly smiled. "Well, that's good, give them time to talk."

Ester made no reply, eyes on the film.

"You've still got to sort out those carriage links, you know, Ester."

"I'll do it tomorrow, after the morning ride."

"Okay—and at the same time sort that business out with the tape."

Dolly was about to go up to bed when Ester asked, "Where've you been, then?"

She swung the door back and forth. "Checking out that copper. I think we can trust him."

Ester turned from the TV set. "Well, I hope you're right."

"So do I." The door closed silently behind her.

Ester went back to watching the film, but she was angry that Julia was with Norma, and couldn't really concentrate on what was going on.

"She's back, then," Gloria said as she walked in.

Ester switched off the TV. "She's driving me nuts, wants to find out how to unhitch a train carriage."

"Well, that's easy." Gloria yawned. "Get some Semtex and blast them apart, that's what I'd do. She's got a screw loose if she thinks you or me or all five of us could lift one of them heavy links. All you need to do to get a carriage loose is blow it apart, never mind farting around trying to unhitch it."

Dolly listened to them, hearing every word. She wondered if Gloria was right, if they should use Semtex and where they could get hold of some. Then she sat on the bed looking at her notes and plans for the robbery, laid out just like Harry used to do it. She took out the small earpiece and tossed it onto the briefcase, no longer interested in the conversation below. Maybe they were right: maybe she did have a screw loose, because she had now decided that the best place to hold up the train was dead center of the bridge.

Dolly heard Gloria's bedroom door bang shut. After a few moments she got up off the bed and, pulling her own door slightly ajar, listened. She could hear muffled weeping. She went out into the corridor.

Gloria had her face buried in the pillow, trying to make as little noise as possible. She hadn't expected it to hurt so much. She suddenly jerked back when Dolly touched her. "You go creepin' around like that you'll gimme a bleedin' heart attack," she said, shrugging Dolly's hand away.

"What you crying about?"

Gloria shook her head. "Sad movie on the telly."

"What happened with Eddie, Gloria?" Dolly sat down on the side of the bed.

Gloria sniffed, wiping her face with the back of her hand, and then decided there was no point in lying. "He knew the guns was here and he said the filth paid him a visit, said they was gonna book me on murder, like they knew I was drivin' that fuckin' car. They told him about Jimmy Donaldson."

Gloria pushed her head into the pillow. "Well, it wasn't me, an' if they come after me for that then I'll tell them it was that cow Angela. I'm not taking the rap for that."

Dolly straightened the candlewick bedspread. "They got nothin'. If they had, love, they'd have sorted us out—and fast. They got nothin' on that car."

"And you'd know, would you?" snapped Gloria.

"Yes, I'd know. So, go on about Eddie."

Gloria suddenly deflated and the tears started to fall. "He grassed us, Dolly, he told them about the guns. He admitted it."

"I see," Dolly said softly.

"No, you don't see, Dolly, you don't see at all. He's my husband and he stitched me up. All the years I stood by him, probably would have waited, you know—I mean, he's not much but he is my husband." Gloria sniffed again, and then shrugged her shoulders. "Well, now you know, do you want me to pack me bags? I'll understand, I don't wanna walk but I reckon you got a right to kick me out."

Gloria didn't expect the gentle embrace, and it made her want to sob even harder. Dolly held her a moment, stroking her bleached-blonde hair, and Gloria could hardly make out what she said, she spoke so softly. "'S'all right, love, I understand. You stay on here because I understand." Dolly took out a crumpled tissue and handed it to her. "You're hurting now, probably always will, but it gets easier, believe me, it gets easier."

"You're all right, gel, you know that?" Gloria whispered as Dolly left the room.

Dolly washed her hands and face, wiping the tissue across her cheeks. There were no tears, she didn't think she had any left, but she'd felt that hurt, that pain inside, like a knife. She saw his face again, saw him standing waiting for her in the darkness, the lake behind him as dark as the night. And yet his face was so clear, as if lit by a pale flickering light.

"Hello, Doll." He had lifted his arms to embrace her and she had moved that much closer. She hadn't wanted to miss. She'd wanted to shoot him in the heart.

CHAPTER 15

Jim hugged Connie tightly. He was feeling very drunk but not as drunk as Connie had hoped. He'd had three pints in the pub and one and a half bottles of wine at home, plus two of Dolly's sleeping tablets, and he was still going strong, his face flushed, his eyes unfocused, but no way was he about to pass out.

"I love you," he said, hanging his head.

"I love you too," she lied.

"You do? Is that the truth?"

"Yeah, I love you, Jim."

He stepped back, arms wide. "I don't believe it. You love me?" She was getting really pissed off with him. Then he got down on his knees in front of her. "Listen, I know we haven't known each other very long but I own this house, I mean, on a mortgage, right? But I own it and my car and . . . you really love me?" He kissed her hand, getting a bit tearful. She passed him another drink and he gulped it down. "I need a drink to do this, I never thought I would, okay, give me another . . ." She poured the remains of the bottle into his glass and he swallowed that too, still on his knees. "Will you marry me?" He looked up into her face as he slowly fell forward, his arms clasped around her legs, unable to keep himself upright.

"Jim. Jim?" She squatted down beside him and gave him a shake but he was out for the count. She slipped his duvet around him and put a pillow under his head before searching his pockets and looking through his wallet. Connie then searched every drawer and closet as he snored away, now curled up on his side. She was about to give up when she saw a small diary at his bedside. She flicked through it: just the odd memo about dental appointments and mortgage payments but listed at the back was a neat row of numbers. She jotted them down, not knowing if they meant anything or not, then turned off the lights and let herself out.

Connie waited for the late-night bus and still had a long walk home at the other end. It was raining and she got soaked, so by the time she got to her bedroom she was in a foul mood. She couldn't sleep straight away because she still felt angry; she was being used, she told herself, almost as much as when she was with Lennie. Well, she wasn't going to take much more of it. Let one of the others get pawed all over, she was well and truly sick of it. She even felt a bit sorry for Jim, who'd obviously fallen hard. She wondered if he'd remember asking her to marry him in the morning.

Connie tossed and turned, and then felt terribly sad. She realized Jim was the only man in her entire life who had asked her to marry him. She gave up on trying to sleep and decided to make herself a nightcap.

Connie was surprised to see Ester sitting in the kitchen in her dressing gown, her hands cupped round a mug of hot chocolate.

"Can't sleep either, huh?"

Ester shook her head. She hated to admit it, but she couldn't sleep for thinking of Julia being with Norma. "You have a good night?" she asked.

"Depends what you mean by good," Connie answered, leaning against the Aga. "I found some numbers in his diary. They may be the codes, they may not be, I dunno. He asked me to marry him."

Ester looked up. "What?"

"Yeah, funny, isn't it? He's a nice guy, and so's the builder bloke, but all their niceness does is make me miss Lennie."

"What?"

"I can't stop thinking about him." She fetched a mug and spooned in some Horlicks.

"Well, you'd better stop bloody thinking of him. Especially after what we all did to get rid of his body."

Connie poured hot milk into the mug and stirred it, then joined Ester at the kitchen table. "Why is it I go for the bastards of this world and not the nice blokes?"

"Because, sweetheart, you're a sucker."

"I am not."

"Course you are. Lennie beat the living daylights out of you."

"He loved me in his way."

"What way? Who you kidding? He had you on the game and you call it love? He's not worth even thinking about—no pimp is."

"He wasn't my pimp."

"Pull the other one and grow up. He wanted you back on the game. That's why you ran off and left him, so don't start fantasizing that it was all lovey-dovey and he'd have you in a cottage with kids and roses round the garden gate. He was a piece of shit."

"You didn't even know him," Connie retorted.

"I didn't have to. Know one, know them all. And you got so used to being his punchbag you—"

"I wasn't!"

"*Yes, you were!*" Ester pushed back her chair and took her dirty mug to the sink, slamming it down on the draining board. "You got loving all confused with being smacked, sweetheart. Wallop, I love you. Beat me up and it means you love me even more—but then, when he's got you on all fours, crawling like a dog, he'll give you one last kick and you're out, used, abused and your head fucked up."

"You'd know, would you?"

"Yes," Ester hissed.

"That why you go with women?"

Ester whirled and slapped Connie's face hard. "You don't know anything about me. But lemme tell you, I know men, know them better than you or anyone else in this house ever will. You make me sick, moaning about that two-bit punk. Instead of bleatin' on about how much he loved you, you should thank Christ he's out of your life."

Connie put her hand to her cheek. "Oh yeah, my life's so much better now, is it?"

Ester shrugged. "It might be. I guess it depends what happens." Then she walked out.

Norma took her time washing up the supper dishes, feeling awkward in the strange, old-fashioned house. Julia's mother was very ill; the stroke had robbed her of speech and movement, and she lay in her bed, her eyes open wide, as if she was staring at the ceiling.

Julia had been shocked to see her so immobilized and, as a doctor, she had quickly assessed her condition and known instantly she would need round-the-clock nursing. It would be impossible for her to remain alone at the house, even with a housekeeper. She had sat beside her mother for most of the evening. She had a lot to say to her, but they had never really talked and now they never would. Her mother would never speak again. Julia even had to change her as she was incontinent, had washed her as if she were a baby, cleaned the bed and tidied her thinning white hair. She had not said a word but Norma thought her gentleness was touching. Now Julia sat staring at the silent figure, knowing a home was the only option left to her as a nurse was out of the question financially.

Julia held the frail, bony hand. "Oh Mama, we should have talked. I'd have liked you to know who I was but, well, it's too late now."

Norma peeked in. "I've cleared the dishes and cleaned the kitchen a bit. It was a bit grimy."

"Thank you."

Norma could tell Julia didn't want to talk to her, that she somehow resented her presence. She crept to the bed and looked at the old woman. She made not a sound, didn't move a muscle. There was just the vacant stare.

"You can share the bedroom with me," Julia said quietly.

Norma whispered that she would go downstairs and watch television, and crept out again. Norma was trying her best, but all this creeping around made Julia want to scream.

She began to pack her mother's nightwear, hairbrush and toiletries into a small bag, ready for the move. She would check all the homes that would take her and arrange a private ambulance in the morning. She opened and shut drawer after drawer as quietly as possible so as not to disturb her mother, carrying the garments back and forth to the open case on a low bedside chair. She thought she should perhaps put in some bed jackets or cardigans and started to search through the dressing-table drawers. She saw the newspaper-clippings, hidden beneath a fine wool shawl. At first she didn't think anything of them but then, as she removed the shawl, she couldn't help but notice the headline: "Local Doctor in Drug Scandal."

Julia's heart pounded. She sat down on the dressing-table stool and got out the neat stack of clippings. They detailed her arrest for possession of heroin, the charges for selling prescriptions and her trial and sentence. The secret she had so painstakingly kept from her mother, all the years of lying and frantic subterfuge had been a waste of time because all along she had known.

She screwed up the clippings into a tight ball and hurled them into the waste bin but it was a while before the anger rose to the surface, and she turned to the silent figure in the bed.

"You knew! You knew, all those years, and you never told me, you never *talked to me!*"

In the drawing room below, Norma heard the banging and scraping and quickly ran up the narrow staircase. When she got to the bedroom, she stood at the doorway, frightened, as Julia shook her mother's bed until it rattled, until the old woman seemed about to roll out of it.

"No, Julia! No, stop it! For God's sake, *stop this!*"

Julia then turned her fury on Norma. She was ready to lash out at her, at anyone who came near her, but Norma was quite able to take care of herself and gripped Julia tightly. "Julia, it's me, it's Norma, stop this . . ."

"She knew, Norma. All the years I've broken my fucking back keeping it away from her, and she knew."

Julia stormed out of the room. Norma didn't understand what she was talking about but she quickly settled Mrs. Lawson back on her pillows and tucked in the bedclothes. She leaned over the bed, touching the frail, wrinkled hand. "It's all right, she'll be fine."

Norma felt such sadness as the mute figure's helpless fingers tried to hold on to her and tears rolled down her cheeks. "Don't worry, you'll be taken care of, Mrs. Lawson, and I will look after Julia."

Only the tears indicated that the old lady understood.

When Norma went into Julia's room, she found her lying on her bed, the bed she had used as a girl, with fists clenched, cursing her own stupidity.

"You shouldn't have done that, upset her like that," Norma said quietly.

"What do you know?" Julia spat angrily.

"Well, maybe she can't talk but she can hear, Julia."

"I don't give a shit."

Norma began to massage Julia's back. "I understand."

"No, you don't," Julia said, her face buried in the pillow.

"Try me," Norma said softly.

Julia rolled over and looked up into her face. "This was my bedroom, and you know something? I knew I was gay when I was about twelve or thirteen. She was a stable girl at the local riding school and we came back and we did it in here, then Mother served us tea. We laughed about that." Julia sat up and leaned against Norma. "I wanted to make her understand . . . I wanted her to know who I was, Norma, but all she wanted was for me to be married and have kids. She still asks . . ." Julia mimicked her mother asking if she had a boyfriend and then she bowed her head. "You know, maybe she's always known I was a lesbian but could never bring herself to talk about it."

"So what are you going to do?"

"Get her into a home tomorrow, sell this place and that's it. There's nothing for me here. Maybe there never was." She sounded resigned.

Later that night Norma washed Mrs. Lawson. She kissed her and switched off the light before going up to bed with Julia. They made love and then Norma fell asleep.

Julia crept out from under the covers and slipped from the room. She removed Norma's police riding cape and hat from the Land Rover, closing the back as quietly as she could. She packed them into a case and left it in the hallway before returning upstairs. But she did not go back to bed immediately. Instead she inched open the door to her mother's room: she had not moved from the center of the bed, seeming somehow trapped inside the tight sheet across her chest. She appeared to be asleep.

Julia stood staring at her for about five minutes, and then silently left the room. She no longer felt anger, just utterly drained, and it was then she remembered. Her pace quickened as she went into the bathroom. She had to lie flat on the tiled bathroom floor as she unscrewed the cheap Formica surrounds of the bath, pulling them away and reaching around until she found the tin medical box. Only after she had re-screwed the panel into place did she open the old battered white box with the scratched red cross in the center. She sighed: there was the rubber tube, there were the hypodermic needles, the tiny packets of white cocaine and one small, screwed-up, tin-foil square of heroin.

The following morning Julia made a list of items she wanted from the house. She had arranged for a local estate agent to come in and had also found a home that would take her mother. It was expensive and Norma suggested they ring round a few others. "Nope. With the money from the house I can pay for it."

"Are you okay?"

"Yes, I'm fine. Just got a lot to get sorted."

Norma couldn't quite understand Julia's attitude. She was unemotional, all business. She simply put it down to her way of dealing with the situation and never thought for a moment Julia was high.

Julia didn't see her mother again. Norma got her ready for the ambulance. Julia refused to help when the ambulance arrived, remaining in the drawing room when they took her away. She was still making phone calls, canceling milk, papers, and the housekeeper.

"She's gone," Norma said sadly.

"Okay, we can leave in about half an hour." Julia continued writing, calculating how much the house would be worth. As it had been re-mortgaged three times, there would be little or nothing left from the sale. She was going to need money more than ever, and if it wasn't from the robbery, she would have to find some other means to finance her mother's stay at the home.

Norma did not notice her hat and cape were missing until they left. She didn't seem unduly worried, blaming herself for forgetting to lock the car. "Probably be some kids. It's a wretched nuisance because I'll have to fork out for the replacements but at least they didn't nick the car."

"Yeah, that's good," Julia said, picking up the small case she was carrying out to the car. "Just a couple of things I thought I'd take back with me."

Norma started the engine. "Well, if you need storage space, I've got a huge barn, and your mother has some nice pieces of furniture, antiques even."

As they drove off, Julia didn't look back. The house and her mother were in the past now. Her mother was as good as dead and at least there would be no more lies. She stared out of the window. "Stupid woman. Why did she never tell me she knew?"

Norma said nothing, knowing that Julia wasn't expecting an answer. They headed back to the manor and Norma wondered if Julia would thank her for being with her, for caring, for loving her. "I love you, Julia," she said softly.

Julia continued to gaze out of the window, not hearing, wondering if Ester was missing her. Then she began to think about the train hijack and started to smile: maybe it was the drugs, maybe it was just the thought of doing something so audacious, so crazy that lifted her spirits.

"Feeling a bit better?" Norma asked.

"Yeah, I'm feeling good, really good!"

Dolly was in a ratty mood. She was running low on cash and John was standing in her office, refusing to budge.

"I just want to know what's going on. If I lay the men off, I won't get them back. You got half a roof, scaffolding up, I got cement and sand out there. I've laid out for the equipment, Mrs. Rawlins. I've kept my end of the bargain."

"Look, I'm sorry about this but there have been a few problems. If you give me another day or so—"

"But you say that every time I come here."

"I know, but I can't help it if people don't pay me. It's not that I like doing this to you."

"The place is unsafe, Mrs. Rawlins, and you got kids running around."

Dolly opened a drawer and took out the last of the cash from the sale of the guns. Five thousand pounds. Now she was almost cleaned out. "Look, do what you can. If you have to lay a few of the men off then you have to do it but this is all I've got right now."

John counted out the money, then stashed it in his pocket. "Okay. At least I'll finish the roof," he said as he walked out. She scratched her chin. The idea of the robbery was fading fast. They couldn't manage the horses, never mind hold up the train.

Gloria yelled from the yard for someone to get Dolly as the truck arrived with the bags of lime. More money had to be paid over to the driver before he would even lift one of the twenty-kilo bags down from the back of the truck. Dolly then had to pay out for the skip that she had ordered. Money was always going out and nothing was coming in.

"What we gonna do with all this lime, then?" Gloria asked, prodding the bag.

"Tip it into the old cesspit."

"Oh yeah? Well, who's gonna do that?"

"All of you. Get them out there."

"Bloody hell," moaned Gloria.

Dolly clenched her hands. "Just get on with it!"

Connie, Ester and Gloria changed into old clothes, put on big thick gloves and scarves to cover their faces, and began to slit open the bags and tip them into the pit. The lime clouded and burned their eyes, making their skin itch, so there were further moans and groans. Julia returned, bright and breezy as she stood looking at the three figures resembling snowmen.

"It's not funny! You get changed and give us a hand," Ester snapped.

As Julia walked off, Connie called after her, "How's your mother?" and Julia shouted back that it was all taken care of. Ester then hurled a sack aside and followed Julia. "Did Norma stay with you?"

"Yep, and I got her hat and cape." Julia held up the case cheerfully.

"Well, you keep her away from here," Ester said, and Julia smiled, happy that she was still jealous.

In the kitchen, she found Angela giving the three girls some lunch, and Dolly sitting moodily at the end of the table with her notebook open. She looked up as Julia walked in. "How was your mother?"

"Mute," Julia said, and then leaned close to Dolly. "Got the hat and cape."

Dolly nodded, then looked to the three girls. "I don't want any of you going near the big pit out at the back. If you do, you'll get a very hard smack and you won't be allowed to ride Helen of Troy, do you all understand? I see one of you even close to the pit and I will make you very, very sorry."

Their expressions were glum, and Angela poured another cup of tea for Dolly.

"What's in the pit?"

"Mind your own business, Angela. Take the girls for a nice long walk up to the woods."

Dolly didn't touch the tea and instead went out to see how the others were doing. She stopped off at the stables to fetch an old canvas bag and walked over to the "snowmen." "When it's finished put this in, see how long it takes to disintegrate. Then fetch some corrugated iron. Take it off the stables roof at the back, and put it over the pit."

Gloria saluted stiffly but Dolly was not amused and walked off round to the front of the house.

"She certainly doesn't get her hands dirty, does she?" Connie said.

Julia poked at the canvas bag with a rake. The bag was disintegrating fast. "Look, Ester, it works. How was the riding this morning?"

Ester threw her gloves into the pit. "We're bloody useless. Gloria almost fell off."

"I didn't," Connie said proudly.

Julia slipped her arm round Connie's shoulder. "That's because you, my darling, have a good seat!"

Ester stared hard at Julia. It wasn't like her to be so jolly. "You been drinking with Norma?"

"Nope." Julia then single-handedly lifted one sheet of the corrugated iron and dropped it down over the pit. "Just feeling good, Ester."

Mike knew something was going down when he saw Craigh and Palmer having a confab in the corridor. As soon as they saw him, they turned away.

"What's going on?" Mike asked casually.

DCI Craigh sighed. "A lot, mate. Seems the ruddy estimates that bitch Rawlins sent in are now with the Super and he's gone apeshit."

"Shit," Mike said ruefully.

"You said it, and it's all over us. We got to get it sorted and, Mike, don't expect to get off with a slapped wrist because I'm not covering for you and nor is he." He jerked his thumb at Palmer. Palmer gave an apologetic shrug.

Mike hesitated. "What if I'd got a tip-off about—"

"We don't want any more of your fuckin' tip-offs, we got enough problems." Craigh prodded Mike with his index finger. "You sit at your desk. This Rawlins business has left us with a lot of aggro and there are old cases that now take precedence. But if there's to be an internal investigation, I'm warning you, I'm not taking the rap."

Craigh stormed off down the corridor and Palmer looked after him, then back at Mike. "Super's in with the Chief now so we just have to wait. Maybe it'll all blow over."

Mike could feel the pit of his stomach churning. He felt trapped and he couldn't see any way out of it. When he got to his desk there was a message to call Colin. Mike held the slip in his hands, half of him wanting to come clean, to tell Craigh everything. He wanted to tell him about Angela and about his mother, but the more he thought about just how much there was to confess, the more he panicked. He was trapped, all right.

Mike took the pen Angela had given him out of his pocket and sucked at the end of it. Then he looked at the clock. He had another couple of hours' work before he could skive off. Maybe the best plan of action was to see how things played out, go and see his mate again, go and talk to Rawlins, and then make the decision as to whether or not he should spill the beans.

While Angela was putting the children to bed, the women came in to see Dolly as she sat behind her desk. "Shut the door," Dolly said quietly.

They lined up, sensing something was going down. Dolly tapped the desk with her pencil, flicking through the little black book. She pointed at Connie. "You. We have to find out if the numbers you got from the bloke at the signal box are the coded alarms."

Connie chewed her lip and sighed. "How do I do that?"

"Get in the signal box and, I dunno, switch on the alarm, see what happens."

Gloria sat down. "Well, we really are professionals, aren't we?"

Dolly glared at her. "I want you to scout around under the signal box, see where their main electrical and phone cables are, see if we can cut them."

"Then there's this." Dolly took out the pen and opened it, slipping in the small batteries. "Connie, give this to the bloke in the signal box. This transmitter you place somewhere inside the box. The tail wire, make sure it hangs loose so we get a clear reception. Shove it on a shelf or somethin'. Shouldn't be too hard, it's only just bigger than a matchbox. I've got one under the signal box already but the batteries need changing."

"We got anything from the signal box?"

Julia snorted. "Yeah, we know when they eat, fart and go home."

Dolly was surprised at Julia—she wasn't usually so crude. "What's the matter with you?"

Julia wiped her nose on her sleeve. "Got a bit of a cold coming on. Apart from that I'm fine. How are you?"

Dolly raised an eyebrow. "I'm fine, Julia, but we don't want you in bed sick if we got to ride with you."

Ester propped herself on the desk. "Dolly, when are we gonna be told just how we go about the whole thing? I mean, you're a great one for giving orders but we don't really know what we're doing all this for."

"I'll tell you when I'm ready or when I think you're ready. Now get on with your jobs, all of you."

Julia sniffed and looked at Ester. "What do you want us to do?"

Dolly jerked a thumb toward the receiver and the headphones. "You take it in shifts to listen in at the signal box."

"Who's listening in to the copper?" Gloria asked.

"I am," Dolly said as she picked up her briefcase and walked out.

Ester nudged Julia. "You think she's listening in on us?"

"Put money on it," Gloria said.

It was a long night, Julia and Ester taking it in shifts, boring hours of listening in at the signal box. It only became interesting when Connie turned up. She hitched up her skirt as she perched on the table and crooked her finger at Jim. "I got a present for you."

Jim was hungover and feeling a bit sheepish. "Look, Connie, about the other night."

"Forget it, you said a lot of things that maybe you didn't mean."

"No, I meant every word, I just didn't mean to pass out."

She wound her legs round his waist. "Here, this is for you." She unwrapped the pen and slipped it into his top pocket. "Keep it close to your heart."

Ester looked over at Dolly as she walked in. "He's got the pen. It was a bit distorted to begin with but now we can hear them snogging clear as a bell."

Dolly glanced at Julia, who had the earpiece in. "I'm off, be back late. I'm taking Gloria's car."

Julia beckoned to her and she moved closer. "I think they're having it away, lot of heavy breathing, you want to hear?"

"All I want to hear is the code for those alarms."

Connie pulled down her skirt and stepped out of her panties as Jim closed the gates for a passenger train. He didn't mess around when it came to his work, even when Connie nuzzled up behind him and wrapped her arms round his chest.

"Just stay off me a second, I got work to do, darlin'."

Connie sighed, moving close to the alarm box and special telephone. "If something went wrong on the rail, Jim, what would you do?"

"Get the sack if they found you here." He looked toward the station as the train chugged up the tracks.

"I mean if there was an accident," she asked, sliding down so she couldn't be seen from the station.

"Well, with the alarms I got a direct line to the local cop shop, fire brigade and ambulance. They can all be here within four minutes."

She watched him as he went about his business, pulling the levers down, moving backward and forward across the hut.

"What about the live-wire cable?"

Julia switched on the main speaker and she, Ester and Dolly could hear the train thundering past the signal box. Then they heard something else, a third voice.

John had been playing detective, and now he knew his suspicions were right. He was standing at the gates, his car engine ticking over, when he looked up at the signal box. He knew it was her right away. As the gates opened and the train passed, he saw her more clearly. She was laughing and chatting away. He drove into the yard beneath the box and ran up the wooden steps, then banged on the door.

"Connie, I know you're in there. *Connie!*"

He burst into the signal box, and Jim whipped round.

"What you think you're doing?" John yelled at Connie.

"Seeing an old friend," she shouted back.

John turned toward Jim. "She's my girlfriend."

Jim looked at Connie in confusion. "What's going on?"

"Nothing!" she shrieked, pushing John back.

"You liar! This is the second time I've seen you up here! I'll get him the sack, that's for starters. You shouldn't be up here."

"I can go wherever I like, it's no business of yours."

"Yes, it fucking is!"

John threw a punch at Jim who ducked, looking down at the station, terrified someone would be watching. He backed away.

"Look, mate, I dunno who you are but you'd better get out of here."

John grabbed Connie. "She's coming with me."

"I am not! You don't own me," Connie yelled, kicking out at him. She was close to the alarm switch, just inches away.

Dolly put her hand over her face. "One of you had better get up there, get her out."

The alarm went off. Julia winced, the sound so loud it screamed through the room. "Jesus Christ, it's the fucking alarm!" Ester yelled.

Jim's face drained of color. He shouted for Connie and John to get out as he dialed the station to report a false alarm. Connie saw him punch in each number and then closed her eyes, trying to fix the order in her memory as John tried to haul her out. They could hear somebody shouting from the platform below. "Get out of here!" Jim roared. He knew if they were discovered in his signal box he'd lose his job for sure.

By now a passing patrol car had heard the alarm and was already heading toward the station, siren blaring.

John dragged Connie down the steps and had only just shoved her into his van when the patrol car hurtled into the yard. The two uniformed officers got out as Jim appeared at the top of the steps. "It's okay, no problem. It was just a routine test."

The officers hesitated, one continuing up the steps while the other crossed over to John.

"What you doing here?"

John grinned. "Sorry, mate, just having a quickie with the girlfriend when it went off—talk about being caught short."

The officer nodded, looking into the van. Connie tittered nervously.

"Well, you shouldn't be in this area, so go on, on your way."

John drove out, Connie sitting as far away from him as possible. "You had no right to do that, you know," she said. "I don't belong to you. I can have as many boyfriends as I like. You even live with a girl and I don't get uptight about that."

"I don't live with anyone anymore."

"Well, don't blame it on me."

John slammed on the brakes. "I thought you were serious about us."

"Oh, do me a favor."

"I just did. You could have been arrested for being up there with him, you know, and he'll probably lose his job."

"Only if you rat on him."

John clenched the steering wheel till his knuckles turned white. "I don't understand you, I thought—"

"You thought what?" she said, her face red with anger.

"That maybe you . . . well, I made a mistake."

"Yes, you did, John. I don't like being told who I can go out with by you or anybody else. If I want to screw—"

"Stop talking like that."

"Talking like what?"

He turned on her. "A cheap tart."

She slapped his face, almost wanting him to slap her back, but he shook his head and turned away.

"I'll take you home."

He started the engine, feeling sick. "Why did you lead me on?" he asked softly.

She gently touched his shoulder. "I'm just not ready to get serious about anyone, not yet."

He shrugged her hand away. "It's not as if you're any spring chicken. How old are you, anyway? You carry on like this and no decent man'll want you."

Connie felt as if he had punched her, harder than Lennie ever had. "I'm twenty-five."

"Well, you got a good figure but I don't think you can count, sweetheart. You're not twenty-five."

She didn't know what to say. She just felt the tears welling up, trickling down her cheeks. She was only thirty-five but he made her feel as if she was old and worn out. She snuffled as the van turned into the lane by the manor.

"Just drop me here," she said quietly.

He stopped the van sharply, then leaned across her to open the door for her.

"Jim asked me to marry him," she said as she climbed out.

"Well, he's a sucker. He can have you and don't worry, I won't rat on him. He's gonna need every penny he can get keeping you—unless you do more of those films you told me about."

She slammed the door hard and teetered off along the uneven road in her stilettos. John watched her perfect arse as she sashayed along. Then he drove off, wondering whether or not he could make it up with his girlfriend. Maybe he should even ask her to marry him. She was a decent girl. Sometimes it takes a piece of trash like Connie to make you come to your senses, he thought.

Julia passed him on her way back to the manor. She pulled up alongside Connie and wound down the window. "I was sent out to see if you needed any assistance."

"I obviously didn't," snapped Connie, continuing toward the front door. She watched Julia drive round to the stables before she let herself in, and ran up the stairs, trying to avoid seeing anyone else, but Dolly caught her halfway. "You get the alarm codes? You set it off, didn't you?"

Connie sniffed, refusing to look at her. "Yes, I got them, but right now I want to be alone."

"Come on now, Connie love. Come back down here and tell me all about it."

"Just stop telling me what to do, I done what you wanted, now leave me alone." She went on up the stairs.

Dolly looked at her watch and then back to the drawing room. She was tired herself but she had to make sure Mike wasn't setting them up. It was in danger of all falling apart and it seemed, at times, that she was the only adult amongst them. Maybe she should call it all off, and just get rid of the lot of them. She smiled, imagining pushing each one of them into the lime pit.

Connie sat at her dressing table, studying her face in the mirror. "Maybe you are old," she whispered, and then quickly did a movie-star pout. "Gonna be rich, though, and then you'll always be young and beautiful, and . . ." For the first time she knew for sure she would go through with any robbery Dolly Rawlins had in mind. She stopped making her Marilyn

Monroe face, and the real Connie appeared, the other side that she always hid away, the angry, bitter, tough little Liverpool tart that'd give any lad a backhander, just like her dad gave her, like every man seemed to think he could. She'd taken the punches, taken the shit, all her life, but she wasn't going to take any more. She closed her full, sexy lips in a tight line. "Fuck you, Marilyn."

Connie breathed on the mirror and, with the tip of her finger, traced the numbers. Now, thanks to her, Dolly had the code for the alarm. Connie beamed: she wasn't as dumb as they all made out, but, as the numbers faded in the mirror, she began to panic, searching for something she could use to write them down. She found her black eyebrow pencil and a piece of tissue, then closed her eyes, replaying in her mind the moment Jim, in his panic, punched in the numbers. She might be no good with words, for reading and the like, but she'd always been able to count. No punter ever short-changed tough little Connie Stevens by a penny.

When Dolly appeared, she asked her twice if she was sure she had the right code, staring at the tissue with the childish figures.

"Yeah. If the alarm goes off, we call that number."

Dolly gave that odd smile. "You did good, darlin', very good." Connie felt good, but there was no further praise as Dolly left the room, folding the tissue and putting it into her pocket.

Dolly went out alone later that night. If Jim had just used the telephone, then the wires had to be beneath the hut, and all she had to do was cut them because the alarm would also be connected to the central box. She used a map-reading torch, inching her way beneath the signal box, to check for herself. And, sure enough, in the area marked "No Admittance," was a large, secure BT fixture, similar to those in residential areas, the ones an engineer sits by with hundreds of tiny wires, and you pass him by wondering what the hell he is doing. Dolly could just make out that she would need some kind of sledgehammer to pry it open. It didn't matter which wire belonged to which telephone; she'd simply slash her way through the lot of them.

Dolly enjoyed the walk back to the house in the darkness. The air smelt good and clean, a light rain had fallen, the ground sparkled in the moonlight, and she smiled to herself as Harry talked to her in that low soft voice.

"Check everything out for yourself. Never leave anything to chance or to anyone else. Remember, Doll, look out for yourself." Dolly stopped and his voice died. It was strange, because a new thought dawned on her. What if it had been *her* voice that Harry had listened to? Maybe it had been Dolly who had quietly pushed him in the right direction. She had just never been given the credit. At least, not until it was too late.

CHAPTER 16

Mike was having a few beers with Colin, and pushing him for more details about the "big stuff" the company handled.

Colin leaned in and lowered his voice. "We deliver the sacks to the mail trains. After they had the big robberies at the main stations, we were brought in. You know about them?"

Mike took a sip of his pint. "Nah, they'd be handled by the Robbery Squad, special division, if it's a big one."

Colin stood up, buttoning his jacket. "Well, if anyone hit what we're carrying it'd be the biggest in history."

"Oh yeah?" Mike tried to conceal the tension he was feeling.

Colin leaned even closer and whispered something as Mike looked at him in stunned amazement. "You kidding me? That much?"

Colin winked, tapped his nose. "That's classified information but that's how much."

"Shit. That's mind-blowing."

"Yeah, and so's the security. Routes change every few months, just to safeguard it ever being leaked." Colin grinned. "Think about it and we'll have that curry next week. We'll take the wives, shall we? Make a night of it."

Ester slipped her arm around Julia, drawing her close. "What are you taking, Julia?" Julia tried to move away but Ester held on tightly. "I know, Julia, I can tell by your eyes. And you get very chatty. So what is it?"

Julia shoved her away. "For Chrissakes, nothing. What's got into you?"

Ester refused to budge. "Lemme see your arm."

"No, I won't. Don't you trust me?"

Ester examined her face. "No, I don't. You've been acting strangely since you got back from your mother's."

Julia shook her off but Ester grabbed her again. "Tell me, Julia, or I'll tell Dolly."

Julia rolled her eyes. "Okay, look, I took one hit, some gear I'd left at Mother's, just the one, I swear to God. I was feeling so bad, and Norma was getting on my nerves."

Ester got out of bed and looked around the room. "I'll find it, if you got a stash here. I'll find it, Julia."

Julia reached out for her. "Darling, there's nothing, on my mother's life. There was just a teeny-weeny bit. I wouldn't get back on it, you know that."

Ester reluctantly allowed Julia to draw her back to bed. "I hope not, Julia, because if you *have* started, you're fucked. And if Dolly found out she'd kick you out of here so fast."

Julia wrapped her arms around Ester, kissing her neck. "You don't have to worry, Ester."

They kissed and then curled up together as Julia tried to think of a good hiding place for her stash and Ester wondered if she should warn Dolly. To use Julia in the robbery if she was back on junk would be madness. Maybe she should just piss off and leave them to it, before the whole thing went tits up.

Gloria felt restless. Her back ached constantly from all the horse riding and she kept thinking about Eddie, wondering how he was. Not that she missed him; if she calculated the years they had been married, the time actually spent together was minimal because he had been in and out of prison so much—and she had been inside herself on and off. It hadn't really been a marriage at all. The truth was, he was just somebody who was connected to her, for good or ill, and there was nobody else. Her kids wouldn't even know who she was by now. She wouldn't know them, either, if she came face to face with them. Maybe it was having the little girls around her that brought back the memories. She'd had her kids taken away when she first got arrested. Like Kathleen's girls, they had been shuttled from one foster home to another before she signed the adoption papers. She did it to give them a better life. She wondered if they had one, and then started to cry. She cried for the long, wasted years and eventually fell asleep.

It felt as if she'd only just dropped off when there was a loud bang on her door.

"Come on, get up! Time to ride."

* * *

That morning they had a breakthrough. It happened almost all at once: the fear left them and they went from a canter into a gallop and, at the end of the two-hour lesson, they were all beaming and patting each other on the back. The positive feeling continued as they ate the eggs and bacon Angela had prepared while Julia gave each of them separate hints on improving their performance even further.

Dolly was encouraged enough to ask Julia to find out where they kept the keys to the stable yard and how they could cover the horses' hoofs.

"What do you want to do that for?" Julia asked.

Dolly kept her voice low. "We'll make a hell of a lot of noise coming out of that stable. We got to ride down the lane, right past two cottages. We got to be silent." She went back to her coffee and was left at the table with her precious notebook as Angela washed up, while Ester and Gloria checked the tapes to see if there had been any developments at the signal box.

Like Dolly, Gloria had also been under the signal box. She had called out for Buster, a make-believe dog, and nobody had paid her any attention as she clocked the electric cables, the main electricity-power sector and the telephone wires. Gloria had also seen the large danger signs with the red zigzag. Shivers went up her spine because the voltage was so high: Connie had told them at supper one night that a dog got onto the line and was thrown up into a tree!

When Gloria got back to the manor, she didn't mince her words. "How do we get on the line? We'd get blown into a friggin' tree if any of us hit that cable." She was drawing a map of the signal box and the railway junction. "If the gates open and that train moves, it's gonna go over the bridge, right? Well, after that it'll pick up speed and no way is it gonna stop." Gloria prodded her diagram with a chipped fingernail.

Ester frowned, turning the map round. "Maybe she's gonna stop it at the crossings, then we ride up to it."

"No way. She stops it there and we're screwed. There are lanes either side of it—we couldn't stop a cop car with a bleedin' horse!" Gloria sniffed.

Julia leaned over them, arms around each of their shoulders. "Maybe she's gonna blow it up."

"Oh shut up," Ester rapped.

"We still got three shotguns," Gloria shrugged.

Ester looked at Julia. "You know, I think it's time we had a serious chat. We're all here being ordered around to do this and that and she's keeping her mouth shut, scribbling in that ruddy black book of hers. I reckon we've got to face her out, ask her just what she intends doing and, more important, how she's gonna do it."

Gloria crossed to the window and drew back the curtain. "We got a visitor. Shit! It's that ruddy cop, Angela's bloke. I told you we couldn't trust that two-faced bitch."

They huddled at the window, watching, as Dolly walked toward Mike, who was getting out of the car. "Stay put, love, let's just go for a drive, shall we?"

Mike waited for Dolly to get in beside him and then turned the car round and drove out.

"What do you make of that, then?"

Ester sucked in her breath. "Well, I dunno about you two but I think it stinks. What's she doing driving around with him?"

Dolly and Mike parked in a small turning into a field. He said what he'd come to say and then waited.

"Ex-Army bloke, is he?" Mike nodded. "You sure it's the truth?"

"All I'm saying is what he told me. Now, I done what I said I would and that's it."

Dolly pursed her lips. "How do I know I can trust you?"

Mike leaned back in his seat. "I have to trust you, that you're not going to stitch me up, Mrs. Rawlins."

"Oh, I know, love, but I've got more to lose than you."

"I got my job, my kids, my wife. Like I said, I've done what you asked me and that's it."

Dolly examined her fingernails. "Sorry, love, it isn't. I need some Semtex."

"*What?*"

"You heard."

"I can't get that kind of thing!"

"What about your friend?"

"You must be joking! He works for the ruddy security firm, I can't go asking him for bloody Semtex."

Dolly shifted her weight in the seat. "What about some of your other old Army friends? Could they get it?"

"Look, I got to go, I can't do any more." He gripped the steering wheel tightly. "Let me off the hook, Mrs. Rawlins, and if you want some advice, whatever you're planning, and I've got a bloody good idea what it is, you'll never hit that security wagon. It's armor-plated, they got a convoy, cops at the front, cops at the back, they keep right on its tail. You do yourself a favor and scrap whatever you're thinking of doing."

"Why? Because you know about it?"

"Because it's a no-hoper right from the start and—"

"And?" Dolly waited, watching him sweating.

"Look, I grass on you and I'm in the frame so hard I'd get time just for what I done to date. All I'm doing is telling you to pull out, forget it. I don't care how many blokes you're using, you'll never do it."

Dolly opened the car door and looked down at him. "Thanks for the advice. Maybe you're right."

She straightened up and could see Angela coming toward her with the three little girls. "Mike, she doesn't know anything."

"Well, at least that's something."

"Hello, my darlin's." Dolly held out her arms for the girls and they ran to her. One had been collecting some pussy-willow twigs and presented them to her.

"Thank you." She turned to Angela. "Have a word with Mike, just a few minutes, I'll wait here."

Dolly took the girls toward a hedge and began looking for a bird's nest, but she could hear what they said and she'd noticed that Mike still had the pen stuck in his jacket pocket.

Angela sat on the edge of the passenger seat, the door open. "Hello, Mike."

"Hello, sweetheart." He reached out and took her hand. "Look, I know what I said to you the other day was harsh, but I wasn't thinking. I'm sorry about the baby, I really am."

She clung to his hand. "You know I love you."

He sighed. "I know, but, Angela, you and me, it can't work. I got a wife and two kids and I've no intention of leaving them. I never had. If I led you to believe I would, then it was a shitty thing to do, but you have to know it's over, sweetheart. It should never have started."

"But it did, Mike."

"Yes, I know, and it's all my fault. But the truth is you're better off without me."

She started to cry, and he cupped her face between his hands. "I'm sorry, really sorry."

Dolly coughed. "We should go, Angela love. Say goodbye to the nice man, girls."

The three little girls waved at Mike, even though they had no idea who he was. Angela got out of the car, her eyes bright with tears. He pulled the door shut, feeling like a heel. He wound down his window. "Mrs. Rawlins, can I have a quick word?" Dolly went to the window. "You hurt her, get her involved, and I'll see you get busted."

"Will you now?"

He knew the threat sounded empty. "Why are you even thinking about it? You got those kids."

"And you got their mother banged up," she retorted. "I'll look after Angela, don't you worry about her. You just worry about me, Mike love, because remember, I know everything."

Mike felt worn out. He just wanted it to be over. But it wasn't. He had to get hold of some Semtex and it made him sick just thinking about it.

They walked down the lane, Dolly with a small child's hand in each of hers. "Don't cry over him, Angela, he's not worth it. You're gonna make your own life now."

Angela picked up little Sheena.

"You ever been to Switzerland?" Dolly asked suddenly.

"No, I never been nowhere abroad," Angela said.

"Well, as soon as you get that passport, you're gonna get us plane tickets, all five of us, with not a word to the others, because that's where we're going—Switzerland."

Dolly breezed into the drawing room and was confronted by Gloria, Ester, Julia and Connie, all stone-faced.

"We want to know what the hell is going on," Ester said angrily.

Dolly put her hands on her hips. "You sorted out that business with the video, have you?"

"You know I haven't," Ester snapped.

"Then when it's done, when I'm ready, we'll talk. That goes for all of you, all right?" She pointed a finger at Connie. "You go and get the shotguns today. You, Gloria, give them all a lesson in how to use them. Go up into the woods and don't come down again until you can all handle them."

"You know how to use them, though, don't you, Dolly?" Gloria asked sarcastically.

"My husband made sure I could always take care of myself," Dolly replied. "And you, Ester, sort that video business. You, Julia, get the muffling for the horses, and, Connie, you go to that builder, and tell him to order a leaf-suction machine. I dunno what you call them but they suck up garden leaves."

"I can't see him," Connie said petulantly.

"Why not?"

"Because I hate his guts."

Dolly turned on her, pushing her backward. "Then unhate him. Just do it. That goes for all of you. We get through today and tonight we'll talk."

She turned, calling for Angela and the girls to get ready.

"We're going on a boat. See you later." The door closed behind her.

"I think she's bats," Gloria said.

Ester shrugged. "Well, she's got until tonight and then we force her to come out with whatever she's got inside that twisted head of hers."

Dolly began to row. She had one oar, Angela the other, and they began to propel the boat slowly to the center of the small lake, the three girls perched happily on the seat at the bow.

"Look, look, it's a bridge," Sheena said, pointing.

Dolly nodded. "Yes, love, it's a bridge. Maybe we'll see a train crossing it today."

Neither Angela nor Dolly were adept at rowing, and it took them a while to get to the center of the lake where they rested as Dolly caught her breath. She leaned on the oar and looked at the bridge: there was a good twenty-foot drop down to the lake at the lowest point. She then glanced at the boathouse on the other side.

"Is this your boat, Dolly?" Kate asked.

"No, love, it belongs to an old man who lives not far from the manor, in one of those cottages. He lent it to me."

"Can we come out again?" Sheena piped up.

"Yes, we can borrow his boat any time we want."

They shouted with excitement and Dolly spotted the floating dock. "Let's go over to that boathouse, Angela, maybe we can go ashore for a little walk."

The innocent-looking boating party headed toward a small wooden jetty. Two speedboats were tied up, covered with green tarpaulins. Dolly made each girl remain in their seat until she herself had stepped ashore to guide each one out with Angela's help.

"Can we go in a speedboat?" Sheena asked.

"Not today, darlin', another time maybe."

Dolly told Angela to take the girls for a ramble, while she remained sitting by the jetty. She began to make notes in her little black book, her eyes flicking from the jetty to the bridge, from the lake to the undergrowth, and then, for a long time, she focused on the bridge.

The women lined up with their shotguns. Gloria had showed them over and over how to load and unload before she would allow them to fire. She explained the consequences of not paying attention. She held up her left hand. "See that? Did it when I was twelve. My dad was showing me at a fairground and I wasn't listening. It wasn't a shotgun, it was an automatic but it snapped back and bang, me thumb was hanging . . . off." They all looked suitably chastened. "Right, put the weight into your shoulder, left hand to steady the barrel, right index finger on the trigger, but gently, they're oiled and you need just a light squeeze, don't jerk it. They got a big kick, these shotguns, so be prepared for it. If you don't hold it right, like what I'm showing you, you'll get a bruise on yer collarbone an' it could whack into yer cheekbone, bring tears to your eyes, I'm tellin' you."

Dolly stopped rowing when they heard the shotgun blasts. She turned toward the woods and then waved to Angela to stop rowing as she took out her notebook and quickly jotted something down. *Bang!* the shotgun went again.

"Somebody's firing a gun," Angela said.

"Yeah, be up in the woods. Duck-shooting."

"What are ducks doing in the woods?" Angela asked.

"Never you mind," said Dolly, frowning. *Bang. Bang.* Damn, thought Dolly, that's loud. Some nosy parker's bound to start wondering what's going on. She started rowing. "Come on, Angela, put your back into it. We need to get back to shore sharpish."

Julia lowered the shotgun. The tree they'd been aiming at looked as if a tornado had hit it. "Maybe we've done enough for today."

Under Gloria's beady eye they unloaded and collected all the spent cartridges before they started back to the manor. The shotguns were now wrapped in their waterproof covers, and they stopped midway to stash them in the trunk of a hollow tree.

Ester had already left for London and Connie had gone to the builder's yard. Julia was sitting at the kitchen table, cutting old sacks with a knife. "I can use these with a drawstring, pad it out with some sawdust, that should be enough."

"Fine. Do it in the stables, not in the kitchen. And when Gloria comes back get her to help you."

Julia snatched up the sacks. "Right, and we got a ride booked for five o'clock. I found out their key is always left under a plant pot and . . ." But Dolly was ushering the girls ahead for an afternoon kids' program on TV, so Julia went out to the stables, closing the gate behind her. Opening one of the packets of cocaine, she took out a pocket mirror, and laid out a small amount of the powder, deftly chopping it into lines. Then she took an already tightly rolled five-pound note and snorted up each line in turn, sniffing hard, then licking the residue off the mirror. Instantly feeling better, she carefully replaced the mirror and the fiver in her pocket, then started hacking at the sacks. Stacking the squares in a neat pile at her feet, she had cut up about eight when Gloria burst in.

"Bleedin' walked to the local shop. What a load of halfwits! They looked at me like I got two fuckin' heads."

Julia studied Gloria. She was wearing a pair of jeans that were too tight, a bright purple silk shirt knotted at the waist, with her tits half hanging out from some wire contraption brassiere that went out in the Fifties. Her blonde hair was in need of more bleach, the black roots over an inch long. She was also wearing a baggy man's riding jacket. Julia laughed. "It's the wellington boots, Gloria, they're very sexy."

Gloria frowned. "Piss off. I need them, having to wade through that bloody mud lane. Them potholes get you every time." She squatted down, picking up one of the cut squares. "What're these for, then?"

"The horses' hoofs."

"Oh, of course! Any fool would have known that. What you talkin' about?"

"Dolly's orders, Gloria, so don't ask, just start sewing."

Connie leaned against the hut door and peeked in. "Hi, John, how you doing?"

John looked over, then went back to opening his bills. She strolled in and leaned closer. "You were very rude to me last night—you know that, don't you?"

He sighed. "Don't sit on the desk, it's got a wonky leg. What do you want?"

"Well, you're supposed to be fixing our roof and, like, nobody is there so Mrs. Rawlins sent me to ask when you're going to do it."

He scratched his head. "Tomorrow. I got a few things lined up for today and the men are all out on other jobs."

Connie slipped onto his knee. "Well, that's convenient, then, isn't it?"

"What do you want?" he asked again, leaning away from her.

"What you didn't give me the other day."

She took his face in her hands and kissed him, teasing his mouth open with her tongue. He couldn't resist for long and his arms were soon wrapped around her. She could feel his erection and started wriggling on his knee. "Oh, you're very easy to please, aren't you?" she whispered, licking his ear. He started to unbutton her shirt while she kept on licking and kissing, she was half-hoping someone would come in and he'd have to go. When they remained uninterrupted she knew he would screw her. Well, she'd been screwed in some worse places—but never for a machine that sucked up bloody leaves.

Ester leaned forward to the taxi driver. "Okay, I'm going in this house here. I want you to wait. If I'm not out within five minutes, will you ring the doorbell? And keep this for me." She passed over the envelope with the tape. He looked at it, then at Ester. "Five minutes."

"Okay, but that's all, no more."

They were parked outside a large, elegant house in The Boltons. Ester stepped out, adjusted her dark glasses and walked slowly up the canopied entrance. She stood for a moment on the steps, noticing the two security cameras before ringing the bell. Part of her was saying what a stupid bitch she was to come here and do what Dolly had told her, but if it kept the old cow quiet, why not?

Hector opened the door and instantly beamed. "Surprise, surprise! Ester Freeman herself!"

She stepped in and he shut the door behind her. She raised her arms as he frisked her for a weapon, spending more time than necessary patting her down. "Poor way to get your rocks off, isn't it, Hector? Here, look in my handbag. I've not got the cash for a gun, darlin'."

Hector searched it. "What do you want?"

"To get off the hook."

He smirked at her. "You got a lot of bottle, Ester. Either that or you're fucking stupid."

"Look, you prick, right now I'd go down on *you* for fifty quid, I'm that broke, so let's stop the crap and talk."

Hector ushered her along the thick-piled cream carpet into a double-doored drawing room filled with china cabinets and more Capo di Monte than they have at Asprey's. "Sit down."

"Look, I got five minutes. If I don't walk out that cab driver out there will be knocking on the door."

"That really scares me. Sit down."

She sat on a peach-silk-covered chair and crossed her legs. "I've got the video, the only copy. You can have it but I just want to know that you'll leave me alone."

Hector perched on an identical chair, twirling a set of gold worry beads round his finger. "What you done with the Saab? You nicked it, didn't you? Rooney was screaming about it."

"You must be joking. I wouldn't touch any motor of his, more than likely hot as shit. He's just a liar—but he got his heavies to give me a proper going-over anyway. He gave me the money for a taxi. That was the last I saw of Rooney."

"So what you after? If it's money, you're even more stupid than I thought."

"To give you the video of your boss's kids screwing two of my girls. You can have it back and for nothing. I just want to know that it's over."

Hector chortled. "Don't be so fucking stupid. You've been a naughty girl, and you know he won't let you off the hook. You shouldn't have been so greedy—you got paid a lot of dough."

"I also did three years and I'm telling you, you beat me up, knock me around, and I'll go straight to the cops. This time I'll give them names, all right, and he won't get off with his diplomatic immunity this time."

Hector was about to hit her when the door opened. Even though Ester couldn't see who was behind it, she knew, from Hector's face, it was the boss.

She saw the cameras at the corners of the embossed ceiling—the whole place was monitored so every word they said must have been overheard. She waited as the two men whispered outside the half-closed door, and began to get a little uneasy, afraid Hector might come back and beat the hell out of her. She was putting a lot of trust in the cab driver.

Hector gestured for her to join him. "Your lucky day. The tape."

"I'll go and get it but then it's over, Hector."

"Yeah. Like I said, it's your lucky day. Come on."

They came out just as the driver was getting out of the taxi. Ester got into the back. "Give him that envelope, love." The cabbie looked at Ester, then at Hector, and reached in for the envelope.

Hector snatched it out of his hand and pulled down the passenger window. "Ester, this had better be the only copy. If it isn't, you won't just get a rap round the head, you'll get taken out, understand?"

Ester rapped on the glass between her and the driver. "Marylebone Station." They drove off, Hector watching from the pavement, as the cabbie eased back the partition.

"I won't ask what that was about, darlin'."

"Good," she said, slamming it shut. She sat back in the seat. Maybe it was for the best. It just pissed her off that if she'd had the right back-up, if she'd been able to afford a few heavies, she could have made a lot of dough out of that video. As it was, she didn't have more than a few quid to her name. She was still in debt to the bank up to her eyeballs, but that didn't concern her—that kind of debt never did. She'd just move on. What did concern her was where she would move to. She gazed unseeingly from the cab window. If Dolly really was serious about the robbery, she would live abroad, maybe Miami. All she needed was a break and a lot of cash—she'd always needed both, but she'd never got them. When she'd had the cash she never got a break because she'd been busted so many times. Ester had spent much of her life in prison, all over the country, busted if not for prostitution, then for kiting and dealing in stolen goods. At one time her only ambition was to be top dog in prison and she had achieved it, taking more punishment or solitary than any other con.

Sitting in the cab, remembering, she decided she wasn't going to take any more of Dolly's shit. Either she came clean about the robbery, or she'd let her have it.

CHAPTER 17

Mike was late getting back on duty after the meeting with Dolly and Angela. When he passed the main desk, the duty sergeant looked up at him, wagging his finger. "You're in it, mate. DCI Craigh's been in and out looking for you."

Mike pulled a face and went into the incident room. "Hear DCI Craigh's looking for me, anyone know where he is?"

Palmer looked in at the door. "Where the fuck have you been?"

"I was at home, then I got sick and—"

"Never mind that. The Super and the Chief are in with the Gov, and they want to see me and you. I think it's coming down."

Mike slumped into his seat. "What they want?"

Palmer looked over to the door and back to Mike. "Well, that bloody ten grand claim from Mrs. Rawlins started it all. Now, well, they're digging into everything."

"Shit."

"Yeah, all over us, so get your act together."

Mike began to get out his files as Palmer was tannoyed to go to the main conference room immediately.

"Is it gonna stay internal?" Mike called after him.

"I bloody hope so," he said as he disappeared.

Craigh stood hands clasped nervously in front of him. He had been explaining why they had begun the investigation into the diamond robbery while the Chief listened, tight-lipped.

"I'm not interested in a robbery that went down eight, nine years ago. One minute you got her with a stash of diamonds, the next with weapons . . ."

"We had a reliable tip-off," Craigh insisted.

The Chief shook his head. "You call Eddie Radford reliable?"

Craigh sat back in his chair. He didn't look up, listening to the flick, flick, flick of the pages as the Chief went through one file after another, and then slapped the top one.

"You want to tell me about DS Mike Withey?"

Craigh loosened his tie. He had tried to cover for Mike, but it was pointless now.

"I am referring to the fact that his sister, a Shirley Ann Miller, was shot in the armed raid that you and your team have been trying to—"

"Sir, I have to say that at the outset of my investigation I was unaware that Withey had any personal grievances against Mrs. Rawlins. But that said—"

"That said, Detective Chief Inspector, Rawlins was never accused in relation to that robbery. She was never accused because there was never any evidence to connect her with it."

"Yes, I know, sir, but—"

"But I am suggesting that your DS, because of his personal motivation—"

"He believed that Rawlins did, in fact, have something to do with it, sir."

"Her husband might have, before she shot him, but dead men can't talk."

"Nor can dead girls," interjected Craigh.

The flick, flick, flick of the stack of files and reports continued for at least three minutes before the Chief spoke again. "There is still not one shred of evidence to link Dorothy Rawlins to that robbery, and it's verified by not one but six members of the social services that she was actually being interviewed by them at the time of this man Donaldson's unfortunate accident."

Craigh looked at his Super, who remained stony-faced with his head bent low, refusing to look at him.

"When questioned about Donaldson, Mrs. Rawlins admitted that she had made contact with him. She also admitted that he was holding certain items for her to collect on her release from Holloway Prison, and I quote, 'Mr. Donaldson was keeping two Victorian garden gnomes for me. They had been in the garden at my house in Totteridge.'"

"That really is bullshit, sir."

The Chief looked hard at Craigh. "So is most of this, but we take very seriously Mrs. Rawlins's allegations of police harassment, and we also have to take seriously her claim for ten thousand pounds' worth of damages done to her property."

Craigh knew that had been at the bottom of it all, the bloody claim for damages.

"I would now like to interview DI John Palmer. Thank you for your time, Detective Chief Inspector. That, along with a lot of money, has been wasted. I have also been discussing a backlog of work in your division that should by rights have taken priority over this entire Rawlins situation."

Craigh stood up and tightened the knot of his tie until it was almost throttling him. "Yes, sir."

Palmer took one look at Craigh's face as he walked out and hissed, "Bad, huh?"

Craigh nodded. "Look, it's no good trying to cover for that prat Withey. I'm not carrying the can for this, so don't you. They know all about his sister so just tell the truth."

Palmer would have liked more advice but he was asked to enter the boardroom by the WPC who had been taking notes throughout.

Craigh looked around. "Where is he?"

Palmer paused at the door. "He walked in about ten minutes ago, said he'd been sick."

Mike would be sick all right when they finished with him, Craigh thought, and he knew what the outcome of the internal inquiry would be: that one or other of them would be just that: finished. He just hoped to Christ it wasn't going to be him.

Half an hour later, Palmer left the boardroom. He looked even worse than Craigh had when he walked out, and he just hoped he'd not screwed himself. Mike was sitting with a plastic beaker of coffee in his hand. "How did it go?"

Palmer gave him a wry look. He went closer before saying quietly, "They don't know about the diamonds. Seems the big gripe is about Donaldson and that ruddy ten grand."

Mike exhaled and then swallowed. "What did they ask you?"

"A lot. But, Mike, they know about your sister—I mean, I never said anything, they knew already. I know the Gov wouldn't have told them so you—"

Palmer was interrupted as the same female officer stepped into the room and asked for Mike. Palmer watched him follow her like a condemned man walking to the scaffold. He took off to find Craigh and compare notes.

Mike knew it was going to be heavy but he had not anticipated the icy anger of the Chief.

"You have abused your position as a police officer. You have used personal grievances to instigate a full-scale investigation of Mrs. Dorothy Rawlins without disclosing to your superior officer your personal connection."

Mike remained with his head bowed as the cold voice continued that he had not disclosed on his original papers that his sister had been married to a known criminal and had taken part in and been shot during an armed robbery. He interrupted, "She was dead, sir. I didn't think there was any reason to put that—"

He was silenced by a wave of the Chief's hand. "There was every reason and you know it, so don't try and deny it. If we had been privy to this information, it would obviously have been taken into consideration by DCI Craigh and it would have been his decision to go ahead with the investigation without you or not."

Mike licked his lips. "I'm sorry, sir, but I feel I should mention that both DCI Craigh and DI Palmer acted with the utmost professionalism throughout, and I apologize for misinforming them as well as for not filling in the required data on my application to join the force."

The Chief nodded. "You were accepted by the force because of your exemplary Army record, and the recommendation of your commanding officers. You have proved yourself a highly intelligent and dedicated officer. I do not wish to lose you but at the same time action must be taken . . ."

Mike knew he could be up for suspension but he hadn't bargained for the fine and return to uniform for a year. That took the wind right out of him. No way would he be back with the hard hats—not after all he'd been through. Even the job at the security company would be better than that, and probably better paid, too.

Mike resigned there and then, and felt as though a great weight had been lifted from his shoulders. What his wife would think about it, what he would do, he didn't give much thought to. He just wanted to get out, have a drink and go home. Both Palmer and Craigh were waiting for him, looking really twitchy. It was Mike who smiled, lifting his arms wide in a big open-handed shrug. "Well, one of us had to go and it was my decision. I've resigned, so how about a drink?"

Craigh patted him on the shoulder, unable to hide his relief. "They didn't ask you to leave, then? It wasn't the big heave-ho?"

"No, but the 'back in uniform' did it. I'm out. Just get me to the pub."

Palmer gave Craigh a wink. Mike had let them both off the hook.

* * *

Ester took off her best suit and hung it in the wardrobe. She only had a little time before they were due out for the riding class so she pulled on her old jeans and a thick sweater and was just stamping into her right boot when Dolly came in. It irritated Ester that she was expected to knock if she entered Dolly's bedroom, even her tinpot office, but Dolly just barged in.

"Is it sorted?"

Ester stamped into the left boot and stood straight. "Yep, it's sorted. The tape's back in their hot sweaty hands."

"You're sure you haven't got any more tapes up your sleeve, are you?"

Dolly walked out before Ester could reply.

Gloria and Connie were in the kitchen getting into their riding boots. Gloria was complaining she'd cut her fingers sewing the sacks and was pissed off that no one else seemed to be doing any work but her. Connie turned on her. "What you think I've been doing half the afternoon—having a laugh? Well, if you want to take over and screw for—"

"That's enough," warned Dolly, pointing to the kids, and Connie glared back.

"The leaf machine will be delivered tomorrow morning. It costs fifty-four pounds, cash on delivery, all right?" She flounced out of the kitchen as Dolly drew on a pair of leather gloves and followed her into the hall.

"Right, we all set?" she said calmly, and walked past Ester and out of the front door.

"I swear before God I'll punch her straight in that smarmy arrogant face," Ester said quietly.

"I'll get one in before you," Gloria said as they left.

Dolly was worried the stable girl was becoming suspicious, and Julia had arranged for them to take an extra lesson at a different stable. Riding unfamiliar horses, they were unsteady to begin with but soon got their confidence back. Their instructor was an older woman who spoke in a deep, theatrical, aristocratic voice, which they all kept mimicking.

Gloria was still imitating her when they returned to the manor two hours later. They heaved themselves out of the car to Gloria's "Walk on, come along now, walk on . . ."

Julia galloped down from the wood and called out. They couldn't help being impressed by the way she neatly skirted the plants, wheelbarrows and other obstacles.

"How did it go?"

"Oh, frightfully well," shouted Gloria.

Connie smiled. "We're all joining the local hunt, don't you know, we're all so frightfully good."

Julia laughed and turned Helen of Troy toward the stables. The women followed, grouping outside the loosebox as Julia took off her saddle and carried it inside.

"You've each got to learn how to clad the horses' hoofs this evening so we might as well do it now. Practice on Helen," Dolly said, scraping the mud off her boots.

"Oh, absolutely, Mrs. Rawlins, that would be delightful," Gloria said, and Dolly actually managed a small tight smile.

Gloria had her hand under the cold-water tap; it was already swelling up. "The fuckin' thing trod on me hand." She showed it to Angela.

"I wish you wouldn't swear so much, not in front of the kids," Angela said, peeling potatoes.

"Oh fuck off," Gloria said cheerfully.

They were all famished after their successful riding session, and for the moment even Ester seemed more concerned with eating than with badgering Dolly about the robbery.

"Well, this makes a nice change from pasta," Gloria said, shoveling more potatoes onto her plate. Dolly noticed for the first time that each one of them had changed considerably. Their skins were fresher, with hardly any trace of make-up; even Gloria's usual thick eye shadow and mascara were no longer evident and Connie hadn't a false nail in sight. Ester retained a glimmer of her old sophistication, but still looked fitter and healthier. But were they up to the job? Dolly wondered.

Mike could have done with some food inside him. He hadn't eaten all day and he was soon drunker than Craigh and Palmer put together. By the time they had driven him home, he was feeling well pissed and stumbled out of the car as they parked outside his house. He leaned against the bonnet, banging it with the flat of his hand. "Thanks, see you."

"We'll talk tomorrow," Craigh said, opening the window.

Mike stepped back. "Yeah, but I'll be having a lie-in for a change. Goodnight."

They watched him stagger up his path, knocking over an empty milk bottle before fumbling his key into the lock. He lurched into the house, banging the front door closed, getting as far as the stairs before slumping down with his head in his hands, feeling sick as a dog. "Are you all right?"

"Yeah, I'm fine."

Susan stared down at him from the top of the stairs. She had just had a bath and washed her hair. "Your dinner is in the oven, probably dried to a bone, but if I'd known what time you were coming home—"

"Shut up, Sue, leave it out—just for one night."

Mike walked unsteadily into the kitchen and she returned to the bedroom. Well, he could just stay down there, she wasn't going to speak to him. She locked the bedroom door, picked up the hairdryer, turned it on full blast, and opened last week's issue of *Hello!* magazine. She hadn't planned on having an early night but she would now.

In the kitchen, Mike burned his fingers on the plate, almost dropping it, and then sat at the table, staring at the atrophied stew. He got a bottle of HP sauce and shook it, his chair scraping the floor as he got up and sat down again. He picked up his fork but suddenly couldn't face eating. Instead he sat in a stupor, wondering what the hell he was going to do with his life, how he would pay for the mortgage, the kids' schooling.

"My bloody mother, she got me into this, the stupid cow," he muttered, shoving the plate to one side.

Ester looked at the dregs of the bottle. "Well, this is the last of the wine."

Dolly put her glass down, got up and opened a drawer in the desk. She took out one of the girls' big blank-paged drawing books and a thick black felt-tipped pen. "Right, this is what I intend to do."

They sat in front of her, squashed onto the sofa with an air of nervous anticipation.

"I don't want any interruptions, not until I've finished, then you can ask whatever you want."

They all nodded, eyes fixed on the blank sheet of paper as Dolly started drawing, beginning with the manor which she marked with a big cross, and the stables, explaining how they would pick up their rides and move silently down the lane.

She drew the railway tracks, the bridge and the lake. She then marked in red the danger cables, the areas of vulnerability. No one said a word as, slowly, her plan began to take shape. It was ridiculous, it was insane. She was not even thinking about hitting the security wagon itself. She was aiming to remove the money from the train. And not, as they had supposed, at the level crossing, but *on* the bridge. "Bloody hell," Gloria muttered.

Dolly pointed at the lines depicting the rail tracks. "These are live wires, very high voltage. There's a narrow parapet right along the entire edge of the bridge, two good positions to cover us, and a big notice here." She smiled. "One that says 'High Voltage, Danger,' but it's big enough for one of us to hide behind. There's another boarding here and one on the opposite side of the lake. The railings are lower so we position two of us there." She made neat crosses and then turned the sketch round. "We've got to stop the train halfway across the bridge. We'll mark out the position with fluorescent paint. I've paced it and I reckon we can stop it almost dead center of the bridge." She continued in a quiet, steady voice, taking them through each stage of the raid. She drew the signal box, the electric cables, the telephone wires and, as her drawings began to take up one page after another, she became more animated, explaining how they would drop the money from the bridge, where the horses would be tethered. "Well, I think that's nearly all of it. I need to find out if we can get one of the speedboats, and if not, we have to find one. We also need a powerful spotlight positioned here on this jetty. It'll blind the guards but, most important, we'll be able to see the live cables, especially Julia as she is in the most dangerous position of all, right here, up ahead of the train." Dolly snapped the book closed and looked at the row of stunned faces. "So that's it."

Ester let out a long breath. "It's even more crazy than I thought. Actually, it's not crazy, it's bloody insane—no way can Julia ride her horse up onto the tracks."

Julia got up. "I can speak for myself, Ester."

Ester sprang to her feet. "But you can't take this seriously, it's impossible!"

Julia looked at Dolly. "You know how much cash is on the train?"

Dolly ripped up the drawings and threw them on the fire. "Yes. That copper found out for me."

"How much?" Connie asked softly.

"Usually between thirty and forty million."

You could have heard a pin drop. Dolly looked at their gaping mouths and that little smile appeared again as she said, "Penny for them? Well, if none of you have anything you want to say, I'm going to make a cup of tea." Still smiling, she went to put the kettle on.

Julia was the first into the kitchen after Dolly. She drew out a chair and began to roll up a cigarette. "Ester's right, you know."

Dolly rested her hands on the edge of the table. Her eyes were shining. "It may be crazy but it's also brilliant. I know it could work, I know it, Julia."

Julia licked the cigarette paper, her eyes on Dolly. "We could all get ourselves killed, just like little Shirley Miller."

Dolly froze. Julia watched her eyes narrow, her hands form into tight fists.

"So what I want to ask you, Dolly, is why? Why take such a risk?"

"Money," Dolly said simply.

"No other reason?"

"What other reason do you want? With money you can do what you like. Without it in this world you're nothing, you don't count."

Julia patted her pockets for her matches, the cigarette dangling from her lips.

Dolly turned to the teapot. Behind her Julia struck the match, still keeping her eyes on Dolly's back.

"You're sure this isn't about Harry? You're sure it isn't about emulating him? I don't want to get killed just so you can prove something to yourself, Dolly."

Dolly took out the milk from the fridge and put the bottle on the tray before picking it up. She stood poised, looking at Julia. "I killed him, Julia, I looked straight into his face, into his eyes, and I saw the expression on his face the second before I pulled the trigger. After doing that, nothing scares me. I'm not like my husband —I'm better, I always was. I was just very clever at always making sure he never knew it. Now, will you open the door and I'll take the tea in. I'm sure they've all got a lot of questions."

Julia stayed in the kitchen, smoking until the thin reed of a cigarette was down to nothing but a tiny scrap of sodden paper. She then chucked it into the sink and walked out. She needed a line; she was feeling high but she wanted to get even higher. In the dark old stable, with Helen's heavy snorting breath, Julia laid out her lines and snorted each one, and then she licked the tiny mirror and started to laugh.

"Oh man, if my mother could see me now!"

CHAPTER 18

Julia urged Helen of Troy forward. She scouted the area but there was no one in sight. They had arranged to have a ride before the stables opened for business, on the condition that Julia led them. It was not the first time that Sandy had allowed the women to ride solo with Julia, and none of them wanted her to see how accomplished they were becoming. They had their ride at six in the morning and after every lesson they returned the horses to the stable yard.

Julia and Helen of Troy continued checking the area. Their breath hung in the cold air, and not until Julia was truly satisfied that it was all clear did she lift her hand with the stopwatch as a signal to the waiting Ester, who then relayed it to the others.

The women nudged their horses forward until they formed a line over the brow of a hill, waiting for Julia to join them. Then, stopwatch at the ready, she gave the "go" signal, and they all set off at a gallop as if they were competing in the Grand National. But they weren't racing against each other; they were trying to beat the stopwatch, each rider trying to accomplish her own specific task in the allotted time. They jumped the hedges, split up, paced their positions, re-formed and started again. Eight times they timed the ride, with Julia carefully monitoring each one, shouting instructions; any more times and they'd have risked being seen.

The horses were stabled and the women drove back to the manor. Julia was waiting with the stopwatch. They were still out of breath, faces flushed, shirts dripping with sweat. Julia ticked off Connie for not being in her position on time and angrily told Gloria and Ester she had seen both of them almost come off and if they fell and injured themselves it would finish the whole caper. She didn't leave Dolly out, admonishing her for holding back too long and delaying by reining in her horse.

"Sorry, I knew I was behind." She had to bend over as she had a stitch in her side.

Not until they had discussed in detail the entire morning's exercise did they sit down for breakfast, laid out by Angela. Later, Dolly took a boat out with Angela and the little girls. They rowed across the lake and ate crisps and drank lemonade on the jetty. The girls had a wonderful time and when they went off to play hide and seek with Angela, Dolly stashed the can of petrol behind the small boathouse. She shaded her eyes to look toward the bridge and saw Julia and Ester sitting on the wall at the end. She then called the girls to get back into the boat as it was time to leave.

Gloria was out of sight at the opposite end of the bridge. She had an artist's drawing book and was sitting up on the wall seemingly intent on sketching, when the train passed in front of her. However, she wasn't looking at the blank page but counting slowly, pressing the earpiece into her ear, so she could be heard by Julia and Ester at the other end of the bridge. Connie was the only one left at the house. She was on "listening" duty, recording everything from inside the signal box.

As the days went by, the rehearsals and timekeeping totally preoccupied them. There was no time for worries about whether it could work; they were all too busy making sure they could play their parts.

But there was still one thing worrying Dolly: the stopping of the train itself. It would be done by Julia, on the tracks, with a flashlight, wearing Norma's police cape and hat. She would have to hold her position for some time, giving the driver fair warning that something was amiss. Because the train would be moving slowly, there was no chance of it running into her. The real danger was whether she could hold Helen of Troy steady, standing between the rails side-on, with a massive high-voltage cable beneath her belly.

Julia had rehearsed the sidestepping move many times. On two occasions Helen had bucked and almost thrown her off. She had not rehearsed on the tracks themselves but on mock-ups she had made from logs, and Helen was getting better all the time. What worried Julia was that when she stopped the train and it paused on the bridge what would make it stay there? If the driver felt any danger, he might start up the engine and move the train forward. "It's all very well, Dolly, marking out where it's got to stop, but how do we make sure it stays there while we get the bags out?"

"Semtex."

"Pardon?"

Dolly was listening to the tapes she had collected from Mike's house. She was now sure he hadn't grassed on her. But could he get the explosives? She still didn't know.

"Semtex," Julia repeated.

"Yeah, we'll blow it on the bridge."

"Oh, brilliant. And if it's not a rude question, where the hell are you going to get Semtex from?"

Dolly continued checking the tapes. "I'll tell you when I've got it."

Julia shook her head, almost wanting to laugh. "Oh, fine. Which one of us is going to have that job?"

Dolly packed the tapes away. "I'll let you know that an' all, but one thing I will tell you is that I'm not prepared to do anything, not one thing, until I'm sure it'll work."

Dolly felt at times as if she was a juggler trying to keep all the plates spinning on the ends of sticks, trying to keep the women focused, trying to eliminate the risk factors. Nothing could be left to chance, and if she needed a few more weeks, months even, she'd take them. She spent hours with her little black notebook, jotting down things she had to remember, crossing out others she had accomplished. Sometimes she sat in the dilapidated conservatory, wrapped in a coat, staring into space as she pictured each section of the heist. Could it work? Would it work? Was she insane? Sometimes the women seemed more confident about the plan than she was. Even Ester, of late, had simply got on with the job in hand and was no longer pushing for supremacy. Dolly surmised that would probably come. Ester was sharper than the others, more dangerous, and Dolly suspected she was just biding her time. She watched each one closely to see how their nerves were holding up. So far, so good, but it was still like a game. When it became a reality, she would see what they were really made of.

In her mind, Dolly kept returning to the bridge, the train and the damned explosives they still had not acquired. This was the most dangerous and most daring section of the entire "game," and without this piece of the jigsaw, it could not commence.

The missing piece came from an unexpected person. A call came from Mike: he wanted a meeting but not at the manor. Would this be the moment he grassed? Would he be wired up? She traveled by train to London and met Mike in a small café by King's Cross Station.

Mike was not obviously nervous but a little tense as he put down two cups of tepid tea. It took him a while before he came to the point, looking around then back to Dolly.

"What do you want, Mike?"

"I'm out. I handed in my formal resignation today. It goes without saying they've accepted it and that's thanks to you."

Dolly sipped the tepid milky tea with distaste. "So what do you want?"

"Obvious, isn't it?"

"Not really. Why don't you tell me?"

Mike again glanced around and Dolly leaned closer. At no time did he mention the train, the robbery or anything illegal, simply that he would be interested in helping her out with the business she had said she was going into, that he had a contact who might help him get the item she had mentioned.

Dolly nodded, tapping the edge of the saucer with her spoon. "You ever driven a speedboat?"

Mike breezed into the house where Susan was vacuuming the hall.

She looked at him in surprise. "What you doing home?"

He switched off the hoover. "I got something to tell you."

Susan followed him into the living room. "I just got fired."

"What?"

"I just got fired. Well, not quite, I handed in my resignation. So that's it, I'm out of a job."

"What do you mean, 'that's it'?"

"I'm out of the Met. They found out about my sister and—"

Susan sank into a chair. "Your sister? What are you talking about?"

Mike sighed. "You've seen her face often enough, the blonde girl in the photo frame at Mum's. She was my sister."

"Oh, come on, Mike! What's this all about?"

"I'm trying to bloody tell you, if you'd just shut up."

Susan leaped up. "You tell me one second you're out of the Met, next you're talking about some sister you've never talked about. How the hell do you expect me to react? What's she got to do with your job?"

"She's dead."

"I know—I know she is, Mike."

Susan sank back in the chair and closed her eyes. She was just about to say something when he continued.

"Shirley was younger than me. I'd already signed up when she was still a teenager. I had a brother in borstal so I wasn't going to lay it on the line about the antics of my family when I joined the Met. A lot of blokes have some member of their family that's a bit dodgy and Gregg's just an idiot. I never had much to do with him, even less than Shirley because he was younger than her."

Susan leaned forward. "Will you get to the point, Mike? I'm trying to follow all this, honestly I am, but I don't understand what she's got to do with your job. She's dead."

Mike put his head in his hands. "She was married to a right villain, a bloke called Terry Miller. He'd done time for armed robbery, then he was on some job, a big raid on a security van, and he . . . he got burned to death."

"What? I don't believe I'm hearing this. If this is some kind of a joke . . . You said she was killed in a car accident."

Mike snapped, "*Just fucking listen!* I don't know all the ins and outs but after Terry died, Shirley got in with some bad people and . . ." The more he tried to explain, the more insane it all sounded. He was almost in tears. "Shirley was shot during an armed robbery nine years ago."

Susan was stunned into silence. Mike's face was white as a sheet as he stumbled through the rest of the story: how he hadn't even returned for her funeral, how he had cut her out of his life and tried for years to cut out his mother too.

Susan's mouth went dry. She couldn't go to him to put her arms around him because she was still so confused. "Is this . . . this little tart you've been seeing all part of it, then? Is that why you're suddenly telling me all this?"

"No, it isn't. She's got nothing to do with it. If you must know it's Audrey, it's all down to that stupid bitch my mother. She screwed me up but I'm going to get out of it."

"Does that mean you're leaving me and the kids? Is that what this is all about?"

Mike moved to her side and gripped her arm. "Sue, listen to me. I have no intention of leaving you or the kids. I've told you that it's all over between me and Angela. It should never have even started. That was me being fucking stupid and I'm sorry I put you through it. But, Sue, you got to trust me now, really trust me, because I need you. I need you to back me up, not fight against me. It's very important I have just a few weeks on my own to sort my head out, okay?"

She pushed him away. "You *are* leaving me, aren't you?"

"No, I'm not, but I want you and the kids to go and stay with Mum in Spain."

"What?"

"Don't start with the 'what' again, you heard me. Get the kids out of school. I've arranged for you and them to go and stay with Mum."

Mike put his arms round her and although she struggled he wouldn't let her go. She broke down and started to cry.

"Don't, please don't. You got to trust me, Sue, you have to. It's for all of us. I'm going to get a job, I mean it, but I'll just need a bit of time before I can join you in Spain. I swear on my life, I'm not lying. I love you and I love my kids."

Dolly stood ten yards down the road from Mike's house. She could hear every word they said and when she heard Susan agree to go to Spain, sobbing her heart out, she removed the small earpiece and slipped it into her pocket. Now she had him exactly where she wanted him.

Dolly was in a good mood at dinner that evening and after the meal went up to read the girls a story. They had become much more open and smiled freely now. In fact their presence made the entire house more relaxed. No one ever spoke about their plans in front of them and, apart from Ester, the women had become genuinely fond of them, especially Angela, whom little Sheena doted on. They had new frocks and shoes and socks, a big room full of toys and they had even begun to use the word "home" for the manor. Having so many rooms to run free and play in, and so many adults caring for them, had had the desired effect: the little girls were happy and loved.

Angela peeped in to see Dolly tucking them in. Sheena had so many teddy bears lined up there was hardly room in the bed for her. "I got everything you told me to get so I'll be in my room if you want me," Angela whispered.

Dolly turned off the nightlight—the girls were no longer afraid to sleep in the dark—and went into Angela's room. She sat on the neatly made bed and checked all the passports. It touched her to know she really was the girls' legal guardian now.

Angela pointed to hers. "Me photo's terrible. I look like I'm scared stiff."

Dolly put them back into the envelope. "I'll keep these safe, love, and not a word to anyone or they'll all want to come on holiday with us. And if anything happens to me, Angela, I want you to promise me you'll take care of the girls. There'll be money provided for you, I'll see to that."

Angela slipped her arms around Dolly. "Have you forgiven me?"

Dolly stiffened and Angela quickly released her. "Just go about your business here, love. Don't ask me to say things I don't mean. You'll know when I've forgiven you. I need you to make up for a lot of trust you destroyed. That's hard to forgive." She opened the bedroom door. "Put your TV on, there's a good film. Don't come downstairs. I'll see to the dishes. Goodnight, love."

Angela had never known anyone like Dolly before: she seemed so lonely and yet there was something about her that made you frightened of trying to get through that barrier, of breaking the dam holding back her feelings. But Angela had begun to understand how she had hurt Dolly, hurt her more than she could have imagined, because she had shown Angela, and Angela alone, a genuine affection. She was glad they would be going away together. At least she would have a chance to get back to where they had been.

Ester was waiting at the bottom of the stairs. "You'd better come in and listen to this. It's got us all anxious."

Dolly switched on the speaker so that they could all hear the tapes from the signal box. There was a series of phone calls from the station master to Jim. The mail train was never mentioned but something referred to as the "special," due the following Thursday, was being rescheduled due to a fault with the engine. The "special" would not be arriving as prearranged but at a later time and, as Jim's colleague was unavailable, the station master wanted to know if Jim could do the late shift. Jim was heard to moan about his long hours, and then came the big worrying line:

"Well, we won't have this bloody problem for much longer. After Thursday it'll be rerouted to another station, thank Christ."

"So what time is it due?"

"Be late, Jim. Around midnight."

Dolly replayed the last line a few times and then switched off the machine. "Shit. I hope that's not what I think it is."

Ester's hands were on her hips. "You hope? Jesus Christ, if next Thursday is the last mail train through here we're fucked."

The women were tired of discussing the taped phone call from the signal box. They sat wondering why Dolly had suddenly upped and left them at eleven o'clock without a word to a single one of them.

"I'm getting sick of this," Ester said.

Julia yawned and stretched her arms above her head. "Well, she's a secretive cow, and we all know it, but maybe it's a good thing. We'll never be ready by Thursday, so my guess is it's all off and the question is what do we do next?"

"Oh shut up." Ester turned on Julia. "We've been working our butts off and for what?"

Gloria looked at her chipped nails, felt the rough skin on her hands from the horse's reins. "I can't believe it, after all we done."

Connie pursed her lips. "I never believed it anyway. I mean, I've gone along with it, like everyone, but in my heart I never really believed we'd do it. Did you? Honestly?"

Ester glared at her. "For forty million quid, sweetheart, I'd believe in anything."

Dolly was waiting for Mike at the end of the lane, sitting in the Mini, smoking. She saw his headlights flash once, twice, as he drew up and parked a few yards ahead of her. She walked over to his car and got in.

"I'm just repeating what Colin said, Mrs. Rawlins. Next Thursday he's got to be on duty so he couldn't make dinner with me, something about having problems with the engine, so instead of being back in London he was having to do a late-night drop. He never said the time."

"Midnight," Dolly said softly and Mike stared. Dolly rolled down the window. "Did he say it would be the last train coming this way? Anything about rerouting it?"

Mike bit his lip, shaking his head. He then leaned over to the back seat. "You won't be needing this, then, will you?" He unzipped the bag. "Mate from Aldershot, owed me a favor."

Dolly turned and looked into the bag and then into his face. "You fancy a walk, do you? Maybe a nice quiet row across the lake? I'll show you where I plan to blow up the train."

Mike thought she must be joking, but she wasn't. Feeling sick, he just nodded.

"Drive to the end of the lane, we'll walk through the woods."

Mike explained how dangerous Semtex was, handing her a diagram showing how it should be used. Dolly listened attentively, making Mike repeat himself a few times, then quietly talked herself through the procedures. He stressed over and over again that only a small amount was needed.

They walked on in silence until they came to the lakeside and gazed into the black water.

"You'll need money now you got no job. I might be able to get a few grand to you."

Dolly stood still as he slowly turned to face her. "Can I ask you, and I want the truth, Mrs. Rawlins, did you have anything to do with that diamond robbery? Did you set it up?"

She looked into his eyes and lied. "No, love, it was nothing to do with me. I admit I was after the diamonds but, then, who wouldn't be? Even your mother was after them." Mike kept staring into her face and she held his gaze. "I never would have put Shirley at risk. I know I've said things to you in the past, said things about her I shouldn't have but, believe me, I never knew she was on that raid. It was all down to my husband. It was Harry's doing. You think I'd have let her put herself in danger?"

Mike shrugged. "Just from what you said before, it sounded like you set it up."

"No, love, it was Harry. All I ever done was kill him. But that was a personal matter." She could feel him hesitating, and she gestured to the bridge. "You know how much is on that train, don't you? Now do you want just a few grand in your pocket or a couple of million? Take those kids and that pretty wife of yours to live in Spain forever. Sunshine, sea and sand, good for kids."

He was half in shadow, his face caught in the moonlight. "What would I have to do?"

It was after two o'clock in the morning when Dolly eventually got home. She opened the front door quietly and didn't switch on the lights, but they were not asleep and, slowly, in their dressing gowns, they all appeared on the stairs and landing.

Dolly took off her coat and hung it up, picked up the kit bag Mike had given her and walked over to the bottom stair. She leaned on the banister. "We do it Thursday. At midnight." She spoke softly but they could hear every word. "We've got two days." She looked at the mute faces. "Now, let's see who's got the bottle. Are you up for it?"

Ester was the first to say yes. The others hesitated but one by one they agreed.

"Good." Dolly said it like a schoolteacher satisfied with her pupils. "Goodnight, then."

No one could sleep that night. The job was for real and they had only two days to go. Toilets could be heard flushing throughout the night as their nerves hit their bladders. Only Dolly's room remained still and dark as she slept a deep, dreamless sleep, knowing the last piece of the jigsaw was in place. Her only worry was that it might have come too late.

Angela dished up breakfast, aware of the uneasy silence round the table. She put it down to them having had an argument about something, but none of them felt like talking now. She was cutting up toast soldiers for the little girls to dip in their eggs and told Sheena off for using her sleeve instead of the napkin to wipe her mouth. The others could hardly wait for Angela and the children to go on their morning ramble, eager to be left alone to discuss the robbery, but Dolly seemed more intent on making sure they had their wellington boots on, along with thick scarves and hats, before she waved them out of the back door.

As it closed, they all started talking at once, but Dolly ignored them and walked out into the hall. "I need Gloria and Connie this morning."

Ester threw down a half-eaten piece of toast. "That's it? Don't you think we should fucking talk about this?"

Dolly returned and stood, granite-faced, in the doorway.

"No, love. You've got your jobs. The last part is to do with Connie and Gloria, nothing to do with you. When that's done, we'll have a meet later this afternoon after the ride." Dolly left the room.

Ester glowered at Julia. "Christ, I'd like to throttle her."

"Feeling's mutual," came the reply from Dolly in the hall.

Gloria looked at the kit bag as Dolly unzipped it. "Now, you don't need much and the most important thing is to know exactly where it's got to go. I've got the instructions . . ."

Connie felt her knees go and she slumped on the sofa. Her mouth was dry. "I feel a bit faint. I think it's just the time of the month."

Gloria paid her no attention. She was studying the diagrams and then the kit bag. "I never handled nothin' like this, you know, Dolly."

"Well, you'll have to practice, then."

Gloria goggled. "Where do I do that, for Chrissakes?"

Dolly waved her hands. "We got acres of space, Gloria."

"Who gave you this?" Gloria asked.

"Mind your own business."

"Well, it is my fucking business because we're dependent on him or her knowing what they're doing for starters. I'm not playing with Lego here, you know. This is high explosives."

Connie had tried to stand up but then fell back again. She looked as if she was about to pass out.

Dolly felt her head. "You're not runnin' a temperature, are you?"

Gloria picked up the bag and looked at Connie. "I know what it is. It's called shittin' yourself with nerves. You watch her, Doll, she's a liability."

Connie struggled up. "No I'm not, you leave me alone. It's my period, I always feel like this."

Dolly gestured for Connie to come closer. She had a small, high-voltage generator on the floor. "Right, love. You get this over to the little landing-stage on the lake. I'll get one of the others to carry it with you and then we got to get the light fixed up and hidden."

Connie's face was ashen. "But do you think it's a good i-i-idea for us to be lit up? Anyone will be able to see it for miles around and—"

Dolly smiled. "Don't worry, we're not gonna be doing a cabaret act, Connie."

Ester moved closer to Julia as they stacked the bags for the horses' hoofs. She pulled away bales of straw to reveal big leather saddlebags they were going to string across the animals' flanks. She tested one. "I hope these'll hold the weight."

There was a loud *boom!* followed by the sound of breaking glass. Both women froze and Ester peered nervously out of the stable door. "What the fuck was that?"

A second boom shook the stables and Ester rushed out. Julia strode after her in a fury, almost knocking her aside. "I told her not to do it close to the bloody stables."

Ester looked back at Helen of Troy. She hadn't flinched—unlike the pair of them.

Gloria picked herself up. The old greenhouse had been completely destroyed, leaving nothing but a gaping hole in the ground. She was covered in soil and other debris, shakily holding the dustbin lid she had used as a shield.

"Are you out of your mind?" Julia screamed.

"I got to fucking practice, haven't I?"

"Not inside a greenhouse, you idiot. Look at the glass it's showered everywhere. You stupid bitch! You could have made the horse bolt—and you could have killed yourself."

Gloria dusted herself down. "I know what I'm doing."

"You could have fooled me," Ester shouted, keeping her distance. "Just go and blow something up further away from the house."

Dolly appeared to inspect the damage. "How much did you use?"

"Not that much," said Gloria. She looked ruefully at Dolly. "Sorry."

Dolly opened her notebook. "Julia reckons we'll need it at this point of the bridge, here and here."

Gloria looked at Dolly's tight, neat writing. "Yeah. We been over it day in, day out. That's the best spot, train moving slowly so it'll get the full impact."

"Just don't blow the carriage up, Gloria. You do that, the money will be blown to smithereens, too. More important, there are three guards inside that carriage, and I don't want anyone getting hurt unnecessarily."

Gloria nodded. "I'll have another go."

Connie and Julia rowed across the lake, the boat low in the water with the weight of the lamp, the cables and the battery-operated generator. Julia did most of the rowing as Connie still felt faint and couldn't stop shaking. They dragged the boat alongside the jetty and then began to move the equipment, keeping an eye open for anyone who might observe them. Julia wore leather gloves and told Connie off because she hadn't put hers on. They then dusted the lamp down just in case she had left her fingerprints on it, and stashed the gear in the bushes, with the petrol, before heading back to the opposite shore, Julia rowing again as Connie trained the binoculars on the bridge.

Susan and the kids left London the next day. It was Wednesday, and, alone in the house, Mike began to wonder if he really was going to do it the next day, if his nerve would hold. But he knew there was no backing out now and took three or four mouthfuls from a bottle of vodka to calm himself down. He had to sell his car and then rent one—there was a lot to get organized and focusing on the details stopped him thinking too hard about just what he had got himself into.

The phone rang, making him jump.

"Hello, love, it's me," Dolly said softly. "The wife and kids gone, have they?"

"Yeah, this morning."

"Good. Angela will be at your place Thursday with the girls."

"*What?*" He sounded like his wife.

"Two reasons, love. One, you got a nice alibi, just in case you're ever questioned. She'll be there all night and will say you was with her. Might cause a bit of aggro with your wife but if nothing untoward happens she won't know, will she?"

"And the second reason?"

"Because I don't want her and the kids around when it goes down. Like I said, she's not involved in this. Friday she'll get the first train back here. You just go straight to the airport. All right, love?"

His voice was even hoarser. "Yes."

There was a long pause. "Well, you keep out of sight and get on with your business. Goodbye."

"Norma home, is she?" Dolly asked casually as they drove back from their riding lesson.

"You know she isn't," Julia said flatly.

"Just checking. You got her keys still?"

Julia sighed. "You *know* I have. We've been over and over it, Dolly."

Ester leaned forward from the back seat. She looked at Dolly and then Julia. "I don't trust that Norma."

Dolly paused at the level crossing as the gates closed. "We don't have to trust her, Ester, just use her. What do you think her friends at the nick would say if they found out not only that she was a big dyke but she was slobbering all over a—"

"Shut up," Julia said.

"Yeah, leave it out, Dolly." It was Ester now, as she saw Julia's back go rigid.

"No, you leave it out," Dolly said, her mouth a tight thin line. "We need Norma. We got to use her place to stash the money, like we used her to get the cop's hat and cape. It's the only place close enough to us the cops are unlikely to search."

Ester gave Julia's shoulder a squeeze. It was funny, really, Julia being decent enough not to want to involve Norma, and yet prepared to play a major part in the robbery. It really didn't add up. Ester felt more love toward her in that moment than she had for a long time, and she liked it when Julia pressed herself closer, their bodies touching in an unspoken message.

Dolly's beady eyes missed nothing. It was good, she thought, the pair of them backing each other up, because, come Thursday night, she reckoned Julia would need something to stiffen her nerves, maybe even a snort or two.

Julia fed Helen of Troy, and checked on the sacking and bags for the umpteenth time that day. When she came back, Dolly was standing at the kitchen door, throwing half-eaten sandwiches out for the birds.

"You're something else, you know that, Dolly Rawlins?"

Dolly brushed the crumbs from her hands and then stared at them, palms upward. They were steady and she smiled. "My husband used to say that, only he always called me Doll. Funny, I hated being called that but I used to let him, nobody else."

"Gloria sometimes calls you Doll, doesn't she?"

Dolly looked up into Julia's face. She was a handsome woman and it was as if only now it struck her just how good-looking she really was. "Being in prison I got called a lot of things. Got to the point I didn't really care anymore, but I used to, in the old days."

"Prison tough for you?" Julia asked casually.

Dolly hesitated a moment and then folded her arms. "You know, I reckon there were only a few really criminal-minded women in there. Most of them were inside for petty stuff, kiting, fraud, theft, nothing big, nothing that on the outside a few quid wouldn't have put right. Everything comes down to money in the end. The rest were poor cows put inside by men, men they'd done something for."

"That doesn't include me," Julia said softly.

"You were a junkie. That's what put you inside."

"No, Dolly, I put myself inside."

Dolly nodded thoughtfully. "Maybe your guilt put you in there. You tellin' me you really needed to flog prescriptions? I reckon part of you wanted to be caught. I mean, you take how many years to qualify? Doctors when I was a kid were respected, like royalty. My mum was dying on her feet but she got up, made sure the house was clean before the doctor came."

Julia took out her tobacco stash. She began to roll a cigarette, thinking that she had never, in all the weeks she had been living with Dolly, actually talked this way with her.

"Eight years is a long time inside that place, Julia. Maybe I met only four or five women that deserved to be locked up. The rest weren't really criminals before they went in, but they were when they came out. They were made criminals by the system—humiliated, degraded and, I don't know, *defemalized*." Is that a word?

Julia said nothing, carried on rolling her cigarette while Dolly continued in a low unemotional voice.

"The few that were able to take advantage of the education sessions might have gone out with more than what they come in with but most of them were of below average intelligence, lot of girls couldn't read or write, some of them didn't even speak English. Lot of blacks copped with drugs on 'em. They was all herded in together."

Julia licked the cigarette paper. She found it interesting. The more Dolly talked, the more fascinated she became by her. The woman they all listened to, at times were even a little afraid of, Julia guessed was poorly educated, maybe even self-taught. This was highlighted by her poor vocabulary and her East End accent, which became thicker as she tried to express herself.

Julia struck a match and lit her cigarette, puffing at it and then spitting out bits of tobacco. "Out of all of us here, who would you say *was* a proper criminal?"

Dolly reached out and took Julia's cigarette, taking a couple of deep drags. "You want the truth?"

"Yes."

"Ester was first sent down at seventeen. She's spent how many years in and out of nick—a lot, right? But as much as I don't like her, I know there's a shell around her. Dig deep and you'll just find a fucked-up kid that stopped crying because there was never anybody there to mop up her tears."

Julia was surprised. She took back her cigarette and sat on the step. "What about Gloria?"

"Well, she's been in and out like Ester and, on the surface, you could say she's a criminal or been made one by her sick choice of men. But again there's pain behind that brassy exterior, lot of hurt. She's borne two kids and given them away—you never get over that. You, Julia, have got all this anger inside you, self-hate, and hate for your mother."

Julia leaned against the doorframe, wanting to change the subject now, but Dolly continued in the same flat voice. "Connie's the same. Few years on she'll be another Gloria but she's not as bright. Some man will still screw her up—it's printed on her forehead. But, you know, we all got one thing in common."

Dolly gave that cold smile and Julia lifted her eyebrows skeptically. "Come on, Dolly, you tell me what I've got in common with Connie."

"Defemalized, Julia. Not one of you could settle down and lead a normal life. Prison done that, it's wrenched it from our bellies."

Julia chuckled. "That's a bit dramatic. Speaking for myself, and being gay, I'm not and never was—"

"You're still a woman, Julia, no matter who you screw. We're outcasts—that's what they done to us, made us outcasts of society."

"But do we have to be? If every woman in our situation turned—"

"Bad?" Dolly interrupted, and her arms were stiff at her sides. Her voice was angry now. "They didn't give me a chance to be good, did they?"

Dolly's eyes were so hard and cruel, Julia stepped back, shocked.

"I reckoned there were only five real criminals in the nick with me. Well, I was number six."

"I don't believe you, Dolly. You had dreams of opening this place, of doing good, fostering kids."

Dolly smiled, this time with warmth, her eyes soft. "And with my cut of forty million quid, that's what I'm going to do. I can go down Waterloo Bridge, pick them off the street and bring them back. I won't need any social services, I won't need anyone telling me what I can and can't do because with money you can do anything. That's all it takes, Julia. Money, money, money."

Julia grinned. "Well, let's hope we pull it off, then."

"Oh, we'll do it, Julia. It's afterward we're going to have to worry about because we're gonna be hit, and hit hard. We foul up one little bit and we will go down. Every cop for miles will be round here, we'll be searched and the house taken apart. We'll be questioned and re-questioned, they'll rip the grounds up . . . They'll never leave us alone, for weeks, maybe months."

"If we pull it off," Julia said quietly, and Dolly guffawed, a loud single bellow.

"If we don't, we don't. But if we do, every single one of us can go for what we want, do what we want, be what we want."

Julia's heart began to thud in her chest. Dolly's face was radiant with unabashed excitement. "I'm not scared, Julia, not for one second. I'm feeling alive for the first time since I killed him." She lifted both her arms skyward and tilted back her head, like an opera star acknowledging the adulation of a packed house of applauding fans. Julia could see the pulse at the side of her neck beating and felt suddenly terrified that Dolly Rawlins was insane. As if Dolly read her mind, she lowered her arms and chuckled. "When we've got our hands on forty million quid—then you won't think I'm so mad."

CHAPTER 19

Angela arrived at Mike's home with the children at three o'clock, blithely unaware of the drama that was to take place that evening. Mike opened the door, immediately handing her the keys, saying he had to leave but would be back that evening. He didn't touch her, even when she tried to reach for his hand. "Just settle the kids in, I'll be back later."

She closed the front door, and went straight to the wall socket receiver as Dolly had instructed her. The girls were already playing with Mike's sons' toys and Angela had a good nose around before she started to cook spaghetti for them. They had been scared of moving to yet another home but felt better when they all called Dolly and said hello to her and were told they would see her the following day.

Mike headed for the manor in a hired car. He had plenty of time so he drove carefully, making sure never to exceed the speed limit. The last thing he wanted was anyone to remember him so he didn't even stop at a petrol station.

The women checked and double-checked everything on their lists. Julia went over the cladding and the bags, and the big machine for clearing up leaves. She tested the engine, the suction hose and the long trail of flex ending at the socket in the stables. The machine would be used to hoover up the money and they had already tested it to be certain that the suction was strong enough. Julia then went on to check the lime pit. It was ready for the mailbags to be hurled into; the lime would eat away at the thick canvas, and again it had been tried and tested. The corrugated-iron slats were standing by in position, the builder's skip was in place and already attached to the truck so it could be towed across the pit opening.

With a dog's lead, Gloria and Ester headed for the bridge, looking like innocent walkers, calling out for the fictional lost dog. They returned to the house, mission accomplished. Each reported to Dolly and she ticked the jobs as they were done while Gloria collected the shotguns and cleaned and polished them.

Gloves, hats and boots were laid out in the kitchen. Norma's police cape and hat were in readiness for Julia. The hours ticked by slowly. Eventually dusk came, and Dolly asked if anyone felt hungry. Nobody did.

Mike parked the car and eased the old rowing boat silently into the water. He was wearing a black polo-necked sweater, black ski pants and sneakers, and a black woolen hat. He had a fishing rod and a bag with him, nothing else. He rowed across the lake to the opposite side. The lake was black, the bridge in darkness, lit only by the flash of the signals as a train passed across and on into the distance. He tied up the boat alongside the small wooden jetty and crossed to the anchored speedboat. He pulled back the canopy and climbed inside, checking the ignition and wiring. That accomplished, he went into the woods and searched for the lights. His gloves were sodden but he didn't remove them. He had to pull away the bracken and twigs hiding the gear before carrying each item to the end of the jetty, where he set up the high-powered spotlight. The silence was unnerving, nothing moved and the lake remained still and dark. He could not risk testing the spotlight, just hoped to God it would work. If it didn't, there was nothing he could do about it.

By nine thirty, the women were anxiously waiting for the signal to begin. They didn't speak but the atmosphere was very tense. Connie kept clearing her throat until Gloria said she should have a drink of water as it was getting on her nerves.

"I'm sorry."

"That's all right, love. Just a sip, mind—remember what I said about you drinking." Dolly was reading a magazine.

"I hope we can trust him," Ester said for the umpteenth time. Dolly ignored her but she wasn't really seeing any of the magazine pages of knit-yourself-a-bolero or the new-fashion beachwear either. She knew Mike had a hell of a lot to lose: two kids, a wife and a future, to put it plainly, but she didn't bother saying anything to Ester. She'd said it before and knew it was just Ester's nerves talking.

Gloria crossed and uncrossed her legs, just as she had been doing for the last half-hour. They were almost at breaking point.

"Time to get dressed," Julia said, walking out. Connie sprang up and Dolly tossed aside the magazine.

"We've got a while yet, Connie, just relax."

Julia pulled on her boots, put on a thick sweater over her shirt and began to do up the big rain cape. Like an omen, there was a sudden roll of thunder.

"Oh shit," Ester said, running to the window. "That's all we need."

"Never mind the rain," Dolly said calmly. "If it's raining the cops won't hang around."

"If there's a storm the horses will freak," Julia said as she picked up Norma's police hat. "If the thunder makes them edgy, pull the reins in tight," she said, putting on the hat and turning to the kitchen door.

"Where are you going?" Ester said sharply.

"Just to take a leak," Julia said, slipping out.

"You've already been," Ester said, following.

"Let her go," Dolly said quietly.

Ester drew Dolly aside.

She whispered, "She'll be snorting coke."

"I know, but if she needs it to straighten out, then let her do it." Dolly ignored the other women's gasps, and looked out of the window. "It's coming down hard. The ground will be slippery."

"Oh Christ," Connie said, panting with nerves.

Dolly opened a bottle of Scotch and got down some mugs. "For those that need a bit of Dutch courage."

Upstairs Julia knocked back half a tumbler of vodka and then snorted two thick lines of coke, the last of it, but, then, this might be her last night. She stared at her reflection in the dressing-table mirror. She looked huge in the big cape and boots, and she put on the hat, pulling it down low over her face, tucking in her hair. She had a black scarf round her neck, and she practiced pulling it over her face. She looked at her reflection for a long time and then held out her hand in front of her. It was steady. She smiled. "Okay, you can do this."

Julia returned as the women were pulling on their boots. No one spoke. She walked through the kitchen and a roll of thunder heralded her opening the back door. They could see the rain coming down in sheets outside.

"Well, take care. Hold the reins in tight, let them know who's boss, especially over the jumps."

They all nodded, and Ester reached up to kiss her. "Take care, Julia, for Chrissakes. Take care on that live rail."

Julia smiled. "It's Helen that's got to take care. I don't want her thrown up into a tree, do I?"

Connie moaned softly. She was chalk-white but at least she'd stopped coughing. One good belt of Scotch had stopped that.

"See you later." Julia went into the stable to saddle up Helen. She was the only one not to have her hoofs clad as Julia would not be riding on the road. She was to head to the far side of the bridge over the fields. They all had their coats on when they heard Julia moving out. The clock said ten thirty.

Mike blew into his gloves. His hands were freezing and he was already sodden through from the downpour. A bolt of lightning lit up the bridge and lake for a second and he just hoped to God it had not lit him. There was still no sign of a living soul.

The convoy was halfway to its destination. The heavy rain did nothing to slow it down and the armored security wagon was sandwiched between two police cars as it continued toward the station.

Colin was at the wheel, maintaining radio contact between all three vehicles. The empty mail train had left Marylebone Station. The carriage to be used for the collection of the mailbags was at the center of the four-carriage train. It looked like an ordinary passenger train except for the blacked-out windows. The three guards sat inside playing cards, a good hour to go before they had to pick up the money bags. "I'll be glad when tonight's over. I hope to God they don't make this a regular thing, I hate getting home this late. Anyone know the next route they're gonna take?" one of the guards asked.

"No one does."

"Bloody train's clapped out. You'd think carrying this much dough they'd have some kind of high-powered armor-plated job, wouldn't you?"

The rain splattered onto the carriage windows. "Your deal, mate, and let's hope this doesn't turn into a fuckin' storm, we'll be soaked."

"I won't. I'm staying here. Let the security blokes carry the gear in. Right, aces wild, this one's dealer's choice."

His two friends groaned as they heard an ominous distant roll of thunder.

Julia moved slowly across the field, concerned to see the thick mud forming in some of the ditches. She opened two gates in readiness, pulling them out of old tractor ruts where they were stuck. She checked the time; the gates had already delayed her by three or four minutes and she'd have to get a move on.

Julia urged the horse on through the darkness. She had a long ride ahead to get back to the far end of the bridge, right round the far side of the lake and then up a dangerous high bank to take Helen onto a narrow ledge before moving down onto the line itself. The route didn't worry her—she'd been doing it for weeks—but she felt uneasy about the heavy rain. The steep bank was slippery and Helen could stumble or, worse, she might inadvertently hit the high-voltage cable.

The women parked the Mini in a narrow field-gateway. They kept to the grass verge as they headed toward the stables, passing two small cottages. Lights were on in both and they moved silently in single file: Dolly, Gloria, Ester and, coming up at the rear, Connie.

They saw no one: there was only one street-light to worry them, almost directly outside the cottages. They carried the cladding and saddlebags between them, Gloria, Ester and Dolly with the shotguns. They found the stable key and unlocked the main doors. By torchlight they began to clad the horses' hoofs in the thick sacking bags. It was eleven fifteen; they had three quarters of an hour before the train was due.

When the horses were ready, they rode out one by one, the rain still pelting down. They hoped the sacking would give them some more grip in the mud.

Dolly was first out. She walked her horse down the lane, then made for the woods. It was inky black and not a light could be seen until she broke from the cover of the trees and headed toward the railway line below. She had to cross a small bridge about half a mile from the signal box. She winced as the horse's hoofs thudded on the wooden-planked bridge. She held the reins tightly, keeping to the narrow grass verge, and started to make her way along the side of the tracks. She slipped off the horse and tied him up securely. She began to be glad of the rain as it was really pelting down and would keep potential busybodies indoors. Dolly squeezed under the protective wired fence, already cut in readiness, and moved inch by inch toward the station car park. Above was the signal box, lit up, with Jim inside. Dolly crept beneath it, taking out the wire-clippers and the razor-sharp hatchet. Now she would have to wait and hope to God nobody walked by the slip road and saw her horse tethered there. In the practice runs no one had ever passed even close to it, but maybe tonight would be the night. Half an hour suddenly seemed like a very long time.

Connie and Gloria, using a different route to Julia, also rode to the far side of the bridge. The horses slithered a little in the mud but, on the whole, were steady as they galloped. They had one riderless horse, Ester's, as she had already gone to her designated position, on the other side of the bridge. Once there, with the shotgun ready and loaded, she was to wait for the train. They were going to blow it halfway across the bridge, further down the track, the old railway sign Ester's only protection if too much Semtex was used. She prayed that Gloria now knew the right amount.

Dolly could hear the distant rumble of the train. It was still so far down the tracks she couldn't see it but she tensed up in anticipation, praying that the others were in their positions and ready.

Connie and Gloria tied up the three horses. They were a bit frisky, not liking the heavy rain. Connie followed Gloria as they passed the jetty and Mike appeared. He did no more than look toward them, signal, and start to move to the end of the jetty. He then crouched low, waiting. There was still about twenty minutes to go before the train was due at the station.

Gloria and Connie moved to the end of the bridge, along the railway line, in the opposite direction from Ester. Gloria motioned to Connie to remain behind as she bent low and, keeping pressed to the small parapet at the edge of the rail, checked that the wires and the plastic-covered packages were all intact. She worked quickly and only hesitated once as she double-checked the live and earthed wires. She had gone over it so many times she now closed her eyes tight and swore. "Please, dear God, have I got it right? Red into the right socket, blue into the left and the earth between them?" She pictured the neat drawings Mike had made that Dolly had told her to burn, wishing she still had them.

"You can do it blindfolded. Come on, gel, don't lose your bottle now."

Gloria inched her way back toward Connie, who was holding her shotgun. She whispered, "Can you see him? Is he in position?"

Connie screwed up her eyes to peer over the bridge and looked twenty-five feet down. It was pitch black. "I can see something at the end of the jetty."

Gloria nodded. They were under strict instructions not to speak, not to say one word throughout the robbery. She could just make out the outline of the tethered horses by the trees.

Julia had a tough time riding Helen down the steep bank. The horse didn't like it one bit and kicked out with her back hoofs as Julia held on like grim death. She gritted her teeth as they slid further toward the track. Helen tossed and jerked her head but they were on the narrow edge before the line itself so Julia eased Helen forward, one hoof at a time, onto the center plank.

Either side were the live cables but there was an eight-inch-high border and she began to move Helen slowly down the precarious narrow plank. Patted and encouraged, she was as dainty as a ballerina as they got closer and closer to the spot Julia had rehearsed for stopping the train. Now came the really dangerous move: she had to turn Helen to stand sideways on, blocking the entire rail. A roll of thunder made her freeze as Helen tossed her head. Not liking the narrow ledge, the horse lifted one foreleg and almost came down on the cable but Julia shouted sharply. "Still," a police command, and the wonderful old horse froze her position. Julia waited for her to settle before turning her and moving slowly sideways again.

Mike brought the boat further round. He had the spotlight switch in his hand. He could see none of the women, but knew they must be in position because the horses were tethered.

The lead police patrol car pulled into the station forecourt, and an attendant switched on the exterior lights. The platform was lit up in readiness as the train approached, the level-crossing gates clanging shut. The rear police patrol car remained just behind the security van as the guards waited for the go-ahead to begin moving the money bags onto the train. The rain was bucketing down. Two officers had not got their raincoats with them so they took shelter under the platform awning.

Jim, his hut lit up, watched the train hiss to a halt. He gave the thumbs-up to the driver who waved from the train cabin. He did not get out, simply waited in his cabin for the signal to move on.

The guards opened the central carriage, carrying clipboards and documents. Two guards from the security wagon approached and checked their documents with the other guards and, as the police formed a protective line either side of them, they opened the wagon and began to carry the bags aboard the train. They moved fast, expertly, calling the identity number as each bag went aboard. It took no more than ten minutes for the train to be loaded. As the carriage doors closed, the security guards returned to their empty wagon and the police didn't hang about either. They waited only for the signal from the signal box, and the engine hissed and began to move down the tracks, across the closed level crossing and onto the bridge.

Dolly saw the security wagon move back the way it had come and then the two patrol cars draw away from the station. She was willing them to move off, out of sight, one hand on the electric power switch for the signal box, the other clenched around the hatchet for the alarm wires. She knew exactly which ones they were because this moment, like the entire raid, had been rehearsed over and over again. The mains box opened and closed four times. But when that power went out in the box, the moment of panic for Jim was only going to last a second or two before he hit that separate linked alarm switch. If that went off, the two cop cars could turn back within minutes and they'd have major problems. She had to pull the main switch and slash the wires within seconds of each other.

The train passed, one carriage, a second, then the mail carriage, and the last one, and she said to herself, "Now, now, now."

The lights switched from red to off—perfect. The signal box went completely dark. Jim didn't panic, went toward the emergency generator but, as he was about to switch it on, he heard something from beneath him. He couldn't tell what it was, his eyes still unaccustomed to the dark.

Dolly slashed down with the hatchet. The wires frayed and two or three remained intact. She slashed again and then pocketed the hatchet before clipping at the cables. One sprang away, then the second. She had four more to go as Jim began to panic. Dolly quickly put the live wires against the generator sides. If Jim tried to switch on up in the box he'd get quite a shock—not enough to kill him but enough to stop him trying it again in a hurry.

Dolly ran under the fence, and was almost at her horse when she froze. Jim was hurtling down the signal-box steps, having almost been thrown across the signal box when he tried the emergency generator. He leaped down the steps, still semi-shocked, and fell to the ground. He moaned, clutching his ankle, rolling in the grit of the signal-box forecourt. He couldn't hear Dolly, let alone see her, as she mounted her horse and headed toward the bridge, the train moving slowly up ahead. But her horse was nowhere near as well trained as Julia's—he was nervous and skittish and no matter how much she pressed him forward, he refused to go any faster.

The guards aboard the mail carriage had no idea anything was wrong at the station. They could see nothing through the blacked-out windows. The bridge crossing was always slow, but they were moving and would soon pick up speed as usual, so there was no reason to be concerned.

The train driver didn't look back. He was used to the bridge crossing and could do it blindfolded. In fact, he looked over to the lake a moment before the flashlight swung from side to side twenty yards up ahead of him indicating for him to stop. He put his hand up to shield his eyes from the bright light. He began to brake in plenty of time, moving almost at a snail's pace as he leaned out of his cab. All he could see was a police officer standing sideways across the track.

"You fucking crazy?" he screamed. Now he rammed on the brakes but they were traveling so slowly it didn't jolt or jar the rear carriages. The train just slowly eased to a halt. He assumed something had fallen across the tracks. The interphone rang from the center carriage. He picked it up. "There's a problem on the line, let me get back to you."

He was still holding the phone as Julia carefully began to edge closer. He leaned even further out. "You're taking one hell of a bloody risk—there are live cables under you," he shouted.

Still she waited. Then she switched on the flashlight again, shining it at the driver's face as she eased the horse onto the narrow verge, moving away from the rail tracks, backing Helen precariously along the stone-flagged parapet toward safety.

"What the hell is going on?" the driver yelled again. The guards were now lifting up the blinds on the covered windows. The train had been stationary for one and a half minutes.

Julia was within six feet of sanctuary when she turned the flashlight on once, twice, three times and Gloria pressed down the detonator. They were only a fraction off-target, but nevertheless the explosion ripped through the second carriage instead of where it was meant to—between the second and the mail carriage. She swore as the carriages rocked and shuddered and the railway line buckled under the impact. Next she crawled to the second detonator and thumped it down. This time it was almost right on its marker as the rear carriage broke loose. The explosion was terrifyingly loud, echoing across the water, glass and metal splintering. There was hardly a window left intact. Inside the guards were stunned, having been thrown across the floor.

Gloria had used too much Semtex and now there was a dangerous hole in the bridge itself. But as they moved frantically on to the next stage of the operation, they didn't realize the imminent danger. Amid the chaos, Julia could hear Dolly's calm voice in her mind: "Soon as you get away from the track, you chuck this into the main front carriage, as close to the driver as possible. It'll scramble any calls he tries to make from the train to the next station. It won't give us long but it'll be long enough." Another of Ashley Brent's little toys.

Julia galloped to her next position, then collected Dolly's horse and began to drag it toward the others down below by the lake. Dolly was on foot and running toward the center of the bridge.

Ester rammed her shotgun through the carriage's broken window. The men inside still lay sprawled on the floor as two more shotguns appeared through the windows on the other side. Dolly was the one to give the order and she screamed it: "Open the doors! Out!"

Mike switched on the spotlight, turning the powerful beam a fraction to aim directly at the center carriage. He had seen the train moving off and hoped the driver's phone would be scrambled. Then he jumped into the speedboat and, with the rowing boat trailing behind, headed at top speed for the bridge. He cut the engines as he came directly in line with the spotlight. It covered the doors of the train and the path down to the rowing boat.

The dazed guards came out one by one. Dolly took up her position, screaming orders as she pointed the shotgun at them. "Lie down, face down!"

Suddenly she saw, to her horror, that the mail carriage was creaking and groaning toward the hole in the bridge. It was going to go over the side.

The guards lay down beside the track, as, unaware of the danger, Connie and Gloria went aboard. Ester walked round to the open doors. The sacks were passed out and dropped into the rowing boat, easily picked out by the beam of the spotlight. Inch by inch, the carriage kept moving closer to the hole as they worked frantically. Below, Mike stacked the bags in the boat, communicating with the women through gestures without saying a word. Dolly stood over the men, who lay face down without moving, listening to the bags crashing down and the awful sound of the carriage as it ground toward the hole.

The guards were helpless to do anything and, if they moved so much as a muscle, they felt a hard dig in the middle of their backs. The women, their faces covered by ski masks, worked on, lifting, passing, dropping the mailbags, the danger now obvious, the carriage continuing to inch closer to disaster.

Jim had limped to the nearest house and called the police. He was almost incoherent, repeating over and over the words "police" and "train" and "bombs." They would be there in four minutes.

* * *

Ester was the first to leave. She ran down to the horses and loosened the reins of her own mount, dragging him toward the water. Julia was already waiting, looking with desperation toward the bridge. Then the spotlight cut out, the batteries overloaded, leaving the bridge in darkness. "Jesus, God, they're gonna go down with the bloody carriage. It'll hit the rowing boat."

"Get out, move it," muttered Ester.

Gloria was next to leave, and the carriage suddenly shot forward by three feet, so that it hung like a seesaw over the bridge. Mike started the speedboat. He didn't care if they lost one or two bags—he wasn't going to risk being under the bridge any longer. He opened the throttle and powered back to the jetty. The next stage was hurling the bags out of the boat and into the saddlebags on the waiting horses. Mike began helping Ester and Julia. They turned and saw a mass of bricks and twisted metal about to crash from the bridge. Connie, still inside the carriage, whipped round to see Dolly waving frantically for her to get out, but she froze as the creaking grew louder and louder.

Dolly looked at the men, and back to Connie. She reached out and grabbed Connie by the arm, dragging her forward.

"Jump."

Connie pulled back, stiff with fear, and Dolly had to pull Connie to the edge of the crumbling bridge. Half-holding, half-dragging her, she jumped the twenty-five feet to the water below. The shotgun flew from Dolly's hand as she hit the water.

Connie surfaced first, gasping and flailing. "I can't swim!" she spluttered.

Mike had hurled out the last bag, unaware that Dolly and Connie were in the water and in trouble. Connie was dragging Dolly down, clawing and scratching at her in a desperate panic to stay afloat.

Julia lifted the full bags off Helen and climbed back into the saddle. "Just keep moving as planned—Ester, go on! We'll catch you up." She kicked the horse's ribs and set off into the lake, Helen not batting an eyelid as they waded deeper and deeper toward the struggling women. Connie still clung to Dolly, who tried her best to keep them both afloat, while bricks and concrete slabs began to plummet into the water around them. Then suddenly there was Julia, pushing Helen through the water and reaching out her hand, but Dolly could only grab Helen's tail, with one arm around Connie, as Julia turned in the water and pulled them back to the shore. Gloria and Ester had gone, leaving the tethered horses standing loaded with mailbags.

As they clambered onto the shore, Connie began screaming. Dolly slapped her face hard. "Get out of here! Get on your horse and get out!"

Connie, sobbing and shaking with cold, stumbled to her horse. She could hardly mount but neither Julia nor Dolly paid her any attention as they heaved Julia's bags onto Helen. They still had a long way to go before they were finished.

Mike left the boat and ran to his car. He tried to stay calm, not allowing himself to put his foot flat to the car floor. If he was caught now, he had two mailbags crammed with money in the boot. He took the route away from the station in the opposite direction from the manor.

Every police force in the county now knew that the mail train had been hit and orders went out to set up roadblocks on all major roads in the area. All vehicles were to be stopped and searched.

So far, though, no police car could get anywhere near the bridge. The guards ran down the sides of the track, their only exit, while the carriage remained precariously balanced. The police who had managed to get to the station tried to question Jim but he broke down, in a state of shock, unable to tell them anything. The three guards were in a similar state as, one by one, they were helped from the bridge. One man was bleeding badly from where the glass in the carriage window had slashed his cheek. An ambulance was on its way.

Mike made it onto the motorway before any roadblocks could be set up, but it was a long drive home and he wasn't safe yet. He wouldn't be truly safe until he'd boarded the plane.

The women were almost crying with exhaustion but not one of them flagged. They pushed themselves on. They had galloped across the fields, up through the woods, keeping to cover as much as possible. Then they galloped down from the woods into the manor grounds, slinging their bags down beside the lime pit, which was open and ready.

Julia leapt from Helen in her haste to start ripping open the mailbags. She hurled the money into the skip and threw the bags into the lime pit. Connie rode up, hurled her bags to the ground and, still sodden from the lake, wheeled her horse round and galloped off, passing Dolly, the last to return, just as she started trotting down from the woods.

Julia grabbed Dolly's bag, ripping it open and throwing the money into the skip, and then, as the pit gurgled and hissed, pressed the empty canvas mailbags down with a rake. Without pausing for breath, she dragged the corrugated iron across the pit, hooked the skip chains to the old truck and began to drag the skip across the pit, over the corrugated iron.

Meanwhile, the rest of the women re-stabled the horses, gathered up the cladding used on their hoofs and took them to the stable yard tip. The horses' tack was replaced in order. No one spoke—they could hardly draw breath from exhaustion and panic—but they were still following their plans, even down to replacing the stable keys in their hiding place. Then they went to the parked Mini, where Gloria was waiting patiently at the wheel. They almost had to haul Dolly inside she was so tired. But it was not over yet.

By the time they returned to the manor, Julia had still not finished. She was hoovering up the money from inside the skip, then emptying it into thick black rubbish bags. Gloria ran from the Mini as the others started lifting the bags and stashing them into the back of the car. They pushed and squashed them inside as bag after bag was tied off and handed over.

Gloria and Connie began a slow, careful walk, eyes to the ground, to look for a single note that might have come loose. They didn't need any torches now as dawn was breaking. The Mini full up to the roof, Julia and Ester drove out. They knew they could be stopped at any second and neither spoke, their mouths bone dry with nerves. They still had not seen a single police car as they drove round the back of Norma's cottage to the barn.

Julia forced open the door of the old coal chute, and they dropped the bags down the hole. The other end of the chute was bricked off in the cellar. They had to shove hard to get the door shut again when they'd finished and Julia applied blackened putty where wrenching the door open had left marks on the wall.

Back at the manor, Dolly now joined Connie on her hands and knees searching the ground. The shotguns had been ditched in the lake, the mailbags were hopefully already rotting, but their work was not finished—not until Dolly was satisfied they were in the clear. One note and they'd be screwed. They found four or five but kept on searching as Gloria raked over the deep tracks left by the skip. She brought stones and branches and stamped them down to cover any movement around the pit.

They didn't stop until Julia and Ester returned. Then they parked the Mini and went into the kitchen. Dolly set light to the black book in front of them and threw the ashes into the waste-disposal unit. All their equipment had already been dumped in the local tip but still they checked that there was no incriminating evidence around the house. It was almost seven o'clock before Dolly ordered them to change and get into their beds. "They'll be coming and they'll be around for a long time. We just sit tight, stay calm, and carry on here as if nothing has happened. This is the most difficult part. Any one of you can blow it so it's up to you all now, and I dunno about you lot but I'm totally knackered."

She walked slowly up the stairs and they watched her going to her room. No one congratulated anyone. Connie broke down crying and Gloria gave her a squeeze, telling her to hold it together. They then went their separate ways to bed.

Julia hugged her pillow tightly, the exhaustion still held at bay by adrenalin. She watched as Ester lay back on the pillows. "Well, so far, so good. We did it."

Ester drew up the sheets around her chin and turned away. Julia leaned over her. Ester was crying and Julia kissed her shoulder. She didn't say anything because she felt like weeping herself.

Connie cried herself to sleep.

Gloria lay wide awake, waiting for the knock on the door. She was still waiting when she fell into a deep sleep of exhaustion like the rest of them.

Dolly, in her room, couldn't stop smiling. It felt so good—*she* felt so good. She couldn't even think of sleeping, one eye on the clock, waiting to hear if Mike had made it home. In the end she felt her eyes drooping and gave in. She slept with her arms clutching her pillow like a lover.

Mike let himself into the house. He emptied the money bags, putting the cash into two big suitcases and covering them with clothes he'd already prepared. He then sat in the dining room, trying to burn the mailbags. It took a long time and a whole packet of firelighters as the canvas was supposed to be fire-resistant. In the end he poured some white spirit on top of them and they finally caught alight. He took the ashes outside and tipped them into the dustbin, then emptied more rubbish over the top.

Angela was fast asleep in his bed. He stood watching her from the doorway. She looked so young and innocent that he couldn't resist kissing her just one last time. She woke with a start.

"Will you call home and tell Dolly you and the kids are okay? Do it now, so she's not worried about you."

She yawned and sat up as he walked to the door. "I'll get the girls dressed and start breakfast."

Dolly could hardly raise her head. Her whole body felt bruised as if she'd been in a boxing match. She blinked as the phone interrupted her thoughts and she was relieved to hear Angela's voice. They were all fine and she'd get the first train back.

"Good." Dolly leaned back on her pillow. "Get a cab from the station, will you? And some fresh bread from that little corner shop." She hung up and looked at her bedside clock. Mike was home safe. He'd made it. She closed her eyes, wondering if they all would. Any moment she knew the shout would go up and the manor would be the first place they'd start. "Well, let them come," she whispered to herself. "We're ready and waiting."

CHAPTER 20

Angela, as instructed by Dolly, had got off the train at the mainline station, not the local one. Dolly didn't want her running into a swarm of cops but didn't tell her that, just that it would be too early to get a cab at the local station.

Angela arrived back at the manor at eight o'clock. The girls were about to run upstairs but she told them to stay quiet and not to wake up the house. She set about preparing breakfast, the girls helping her lay the table.

Angela hadn't known any of the women to sleep in so late and she asked one of the girls to check if Helen of Troy was in the stable, wondering if they had all gone out for an early ride. The girls stayed outside, shouting that Helen was in the stable. Angela had fried eggs and bacon, sausages and some cold potatoes. It was all keeping warm in the oven when the women came down, bleary-eyed and still wearing their dressing gowns.

"Had a late night, did you?" Angela asked as she started getting out the plates.

"Yeah, we did have a bit of a night," Gloria muttered.

"Aren't you going riding today?" Angela asked. It was unusual for them not to be up and out by now.

"No. Stables have got some kids' party so we can't," Ester said as she creaked into her chair.

"There was something going on at the station," Angela said as she served the eggs and bacon.

"Oh yeah, what was that?" Gloria asked, as she poured the tea.

"I dunno, but there were loads of police and all along the lanes more patrol cars. They even stopped us in the taxi."

Dolly walked in, her hair in pin curls. Unlike the others she was dressed. "Angela love, go and get the girls inside. They're getting filthy out there in the yard."

Angela went out without argument and Dolly sat down. She reached for the teapot, was just about to pour a cup when the sirens wailed. "Well, here they come," she said.

The front doorbell echoed through the house, and Angela opened the back door. "There's police all over the place! They're even up in the woods."

Dolly jerked her head at Ester. "Go and see what they want."

Ester hesitated only for a moment before she pulled her dressing gown round her and they could hear her slippers flip-flopping as she went into the hall.

The Thames Valley police had pulled in every possible man and were searching every house within a five-mile radius of the station, not to mention every outhouse, stable and barn, even every greenhouse. Scotland Yard's Robbery Squad was already at the scene of the raid as hundreds more officers were drafted in to the immediate area to assist in the search. No vehicle had been found, and no witness; the raid appeared to have happened without a single person seeing it.

The police interviewed the women and they all insisted they'd been at home together the entire evening, going to bed sometime after eleven. They had heard nothing and kept up a bewildered act that should have won an Oscar as they asked innocently what had happened. A murder? A rape? A kidnapping? But they were told nothing as the uniformed officers began the search. They looked through every cupboard, every chest and wardrobe, the roof, the chimneys, under the floorboards, the sauna area. The police were polite, but diligent, and staying there for almost eight hours until they had to move on. They found nothing.

By lunchtime the press were on the scene, and then it was headlines in the evening papers: the biggest train robbery in history had taken place and Thames Valley was using more than four hundred officers to comb the entire area. By now the police knew that a man masquerading as a police officer had daringly held up the train, and the robbery had been committed by possibly five or six others. They had been armed, and the public were warned that, if they were suspicious about anyone, they should act with caution as the men were deemed to be dangerous. The owner of the speed-boat had been arrested but released after questioning. The signal-box attendant, Jim, had also been questioned and released. They had, as yet, found no clues, and had no idea of the present whereabouts of the stolen money. The amount in question was not disclosed.

* * *

The women did not dare believe they had got away with it as the searches and questioning went on. Even Helen of Troy had been examined, though she had not actually been taken in for questioning, as Julia joked.

Everyone in the area who owned a horse got a visit from the police. Even the staff at the local stables were questioned and their horses examined, but in the darkness the train driver could only describe the horse that had been standing on the line as shiny and black.

Dolly knew she was a prime suspect, but they still didn't take her down to the station for questioning. They didn't take any of them in; they just continued to comb the area. Norma's cottage was the only house that was not searched. They had a look at her three-year-old hunter, but she assured them he was in no way capable of riding across live cables. She suggested they maybe try the nearest circus.

The officers had laughed. It was the audaciousness of the crime that couldn't help but hook them all in. It was called the Wild West Hold-up by the *Sun* and from then on every paper referred to the raid in cowboy terms.

In some ways Norma was disappointed that when all the excitement had been happening—a raid at her local station no less—she had been on duty outside a cinema in the West End for some big charity event when the crowd had got out of hand but nothing much had happened apart from her getting soaked as it had rained all night long. Luckily, by then she had replaced her lost cape and hat.

The police now believed that more than one horse had been involved. They had discovered the scattered hoofprints in and around the lake but, as the riding school took pony treks up that way, it became more and more difficult to ascertain how many horses there had been, let alone from which direction they had come. The women had been using the same routes as the stables so the ground was covered in hoofprints.

There still remained the fact that not one vehicle had been stopped by the roadblocks put up within ten minutes of the raid. But as the motorway was only a short distance from some of the narrow lanes, they could not exclude the possibility that the robbers had slipped through.

The village was agog, the lanes filled with sight-seeing tourists who hampered the police, as did the riders from all the local stables. The ribbons cordoned off certain areas and officers were retained on day-and-night duty, digging up wells, searching every inch of the railway lines, every tunnel and pothole, every drainpipe.

On the fourth day, Dolly almost had a fit when she saw John and his workmen filling the skip over the lime pit. They were stacking it with rubble from the old greenhouse. It remained half-filled and she just hoped that by the time it was moved the lime pit would have done its job.

The women gardened, hoed the vegetable patches, pruned trees, appearing unfazed by the continued search. But the paranoia was starting. They were worried about the dustbin liners filled with money and imagined that the police were just waiting for them to collect them.

Julia was eventually instructed to visit Norma, to ensure the safety of their precious money. She almost had a heart attack when she called on her because, as Norma opened the door, she could see three uniformed coppers sitting in her kitchen. "Hello, Norma. Long time no see," Julia said breezily.

"I meant to call you," Norma said, stepping back. "Come on in, coffee's on."

"No, I won't. You've got company." Julia remained on the doorstep but gave a little wave to the men who clearly recognized her from their stints searching the manor.

"Don't be stupid, come on in."

"Another time," Julia said, but the officers began to file out, thanking Norma for the coffee. As Julia hesitated and then went into Norma's hall, Norma hurried past her down the path. The officers stopped, as she called after them, "It's just a thought, but have you searched my barn?"

They grinned. "Why? You telling us you got the money, Norma?"

"No, I'm serious." Norma kept her voice low, stuffing her hands in her pockets. "That bunch from the manor, they're all ex-cons, you know. She's one of them." Norma looked back along the path. "I just remembered she asked if she could store some gear and I said she could. But I just hadn't expected quite so much. Have a look for yourselves."

Norma unlocked the barn door and opened it. The officers peered inside to see stacks and stacks of black rubbish bags tied tightly at the neck. They went in further as Norma hung back. "Look, you have a search around. I'll go back and keep her talking, just in case."

Julia moved fast, her heart pounding. She almost flew down Norma's cellar steps, checking to see if the bricked-up coal chute had been damaged. She peered into the small, dark cellar. "Stupid, don't be so bloody stupid," she muttered to herself. The end of the chute was bricked up and even had stacks of boxes pushed up against it. Just as her heart slowed down, it suddenly started hammering again as feet crunched on the gravel outside. They were standing right by the coal-chute door. Would they see that it had been dislodged and then replaced?

Julia tried to keep her breathing under control. She couldn't make out what they were saying. She went back upstairs and looked out of the kitchen window. Norma was smiling as she returned from the barn with the police officers. Julia spun round when Norma breezed in through the back door. "You want a biscuit?" Norma asked brightly.

"No thanks. I've got to get back, help out, the builders are proving a bit expensive so we're doing a lot ourselves and you know what it's like. Moan, moan, moan, who's doing their fair share becomes the high point of every meal."

Norma poured more coffee. I'm not good at lying, Julia thought, it's written all over my face. "What are you doing, Norma? Shopping me to your friends?"

Norma gave a big false laugh. "No, they just asked if they could look over the barn."

"Oh dear," Julia said. "It's still full of Mother's things."

The back door opened and one of the officers stood leaning on the doorframe. "Thanks, Norma, we'll be on our way."

Norma jumped up and hurried to the door. "Any problems?" The officer shook his head and went down the path to where his mates were waiting.

Julia pushed back her chair noisily. "Thanks for the coffee. Maybe we can have dinner one night?"

Norma flushed. "Sure. I'm back in London for the rest of the week but maybe after that?"

"Scared of being seen with me in front of your pals, are you?"

Norma flushed even deeper. "No, of course not, but right now this place is worse than Scotland Yard. Every copper in the world seems to be down here and they keep on dropping in."

Julia just stopped herself from muttering, "Two-faced cow." Despite her feelings, so long as the money was hidden on her property, they needed to keep Norma sweet. She smiled, cupping her face in her hands. "Stay cool, darlin', nobody really gives a fuck who you screw. I like you, Norma, don't turn away from me. Don't make me not trust you."

Norma leaned against her a moment, and whispered that she was sorry. "Please see me when I come back next week. Please?"

Julia was smiling as she backed down the path. "Can't wait until then. You take care now." She wanted to wipe her mouth with the back of her hand.

She hated the touch of Norma now, but at least the money was still safe, for a while.

They were all lulled into a false sense of security as the days passed and the newspapers stopped screaming out headlines about the robbery. It was now slipping back to pages five and six. They all remained at the manor, waiting. Dolly continued to make them work around the grounds and the house so they were always on show.

Gloria took more and more interest in the children. She turned out to be wonderful at making up games and puzzles. She had unending patience with them but, even so, the waiting was getting to her.

Julia rode every day and sometimes encouraged one of the others to take Helen out, but Dolly was wary of letting the police see that they could all ride so even that created arguments. Julia had started drinking heavily in the evenings. She had sold her mother's house and still had a few hundred left over after paying the bills at the nursing home. She was generous with the money and gave them all a few quid but spent most of it on vodka and always had a half-bottle close at hand.

Ester was the moodiest. She stayed in bed until midday, refusing to help out as she felt it was all a waste of time. Connie began to work out for hours in their gym. She kept well away from John and even further away from Jim. She painted her nails, bleached her hair, content to spend the time daydreaming of a successful career in the movies. She was planning to go to Hollywood with her share of the money, and the dressing-table mirror became the camera. Jim had been questioned so many times his nerves were in shreds but he never disclosed to the police that Connie had spent time with him in the signal box. He did this not to protect her but his job. In the end he had to take two weeks' leave as he was in such a state, and was given sleeping tablets by his doctor.

As the days and nights dragged on Dolly never mentioned the robbery. She was like a rock: calm and always pleasant, trying to keep their nerves from fraying.

One evening Ester freaked and started yelling that she wanted her cut now. If the others wanted to stay then they could, but she was leaving.

"You stay here, Ester, we all stay here until the cops give the place the all-clear. Whether it's weeks or months, we stay on, and we divide it up when I say so and not before." Dolly was icy calm, her eyes flicking from one woman to the other. "Let it all out now because nothing will change my mind. You knew this was how it was going to be. Just wait."

Angela loved the house. She didn't mind cooking and cleaning and enjoyed working in the gardens—and she adored the little girls, who were filling out, rosy-cheeked and boisterous, the only people unaware of the growing tension and the reason for it.

DCI Craigh and his men had read the reports on the robbery in the papers and heard more about it from mates connected to the Robbery Squad at Scotland Yard. They had tipped them off about the women straight away, especially their dealings with Dolly Rawlins. DI Palmer had actually roared with laughter as Craigh had read out the details of the robbery and wondered aloud if Rawlins could possibly have any connection with it.

"Oh yeah! she's a real *Annie Get Your Gun*, Gov. I mean, can you see that frosty-faced bitch riding a horse? That's how they reckon it was done, you know. Rawlins's got to be over fifty, nearer sixty."

Craigh pulled a face but he had sent in a report. He received no feedback so presumed Dolly must have been questioned and dismissed as a suspect. Still, he wondered whether, even if she had not played a part in it, she knew who had, but this was not his department and he had other, more pressing things to worry about. One in particular. George Fuller, Dolly Rawlins's lawyer, having received no reply to his original letter regarding the damage to Rawlins's property, now sent in a reminder, requesting an update. Craigh was confronted by his irate chief as he, too, had received a memo from his superior. The ten-thousand-pound claim was ludicrous, and Craigh insisted that no way had they created anywhere near that amount of damage. He had hoped the claim was just for show, and it would simply be forgotten. He was told to discuss it further with Mrs. Rawlins, and if necessary get an estimate of their own. Craigh and Palmer reckoned she would probably back down if offered a deal, perhaps a quarter of the estimated damages.

It was early evening, and the girls were being bathed and changed ready for bed. The women were all watching television. They were more tense than usual because the police had returned yet again and the skip covering the lime pit had been removed, leaving only the corrugated-iron sheets in place. Gloria had eased a part of the sheet back and prodded inside. She had felt a thick lump about three feet down but she was satisfied the mailbags had disintegrated. Still, it made them all uneasy.

Out riding and not far from the bridge, Julia had seen the frogmen searching the lake and was worried they would recover the shotguns but Gloria assured her there would be nothing to incriminate anyone, no fingerprints, no serial numbers.

They all were certain they had never handled the guns without gloves and Gloria recalled that she had cleaned them thoroughly before the raid. However, the pressure of the hunt getting so close made the tension, a constant undercurrent, rise to the surface again. Dolly continued to calm them, telling them everything going on was only to be expected. But they were all volatile, tempers flaring easily, and when, two nights later, the lights of the patrol car flared across the window, they immediately tensed.

Dolly peered through the curtain and drew it back tight. "It's cops and not local. It's that DCI Craigh and his sidekick."

"What do they want?" Gloria asked. She sounded scared.

"We'll find out. All of you get in the kitchen and stay there. Let me talk to them."

DCI Craigh examined the front door and looked at Palmer. "How much did she claim for this? I reckon this stained glass was already broken."

Palmer looked at the door and stepped back. "They done the roof. The place is looking good."

"Yeah, and it'll be looking a lot better if she gets that ten grand."

Craigh rang the doorbell and the lights flooded on in the hall. He peered through a broken pane. Dolly was coming toward the front door. Just as she opened it, the children came running down the stairs in their slippers and dressing gowns.

"Come in," Dolly said pleasantly, opening the door wider for Craigh and Palmer to walk past her. They looked at Angela halfway down the stairs with a bath towel in her hands.

"I'll just say goodnight to the girls then I'll be right with you," Dolly told the policemen, gesturing toward the drawing room. She kissed Sheena and scooped her up in her arms.

"Will you tell us a story?" Sheena piped up, and Dolly said she couldn't right now but Angela would. She stood at the bottom of the stairs as they ran along the landing to their bedroom. "Night, night, Auntie Dolly."

Craigh looked around the ramshackle room. A fire was burning low in the grate. "Great old house this, isn't it?" he remarked.

Palmer looked up at the ceiling. "Yeah, needs a lot done, though. These old places always cost a bundle to fix up."

"Bloody cold." Craigh rubbed his hands. He sniffed, taking in the torn velvet curtains and the threadbare carpet. Clearly there was not a lot of cash floating around. "Whose kids were they?"

"Dunno," Palmer said, as he sat down on a lumpy old sofa. He rose to his feet immediately as Dolly walked in and closed the door.

"So, what do you want?"

Craigh looked at Palmer, cleared his throat. "It's about that claim for the damage we're supposed to have done to your property, Mrs. Rawlins."

Dolly couldn't help smiling with relief.

Ester drummed her fingers on the kitchen table, her eyes on the closed door. "What you reckon they want?"

Julia poured herself a large vodka. "We'll find out soon enough. Any of you want a drink?"

"No, and you're hitting the bottle a bit too hard." Ester pushed back her chair angrily.

"Where you going?" Gloria asked her.

"To the toilet, if that's all right with you." Ester opened the kitchen door silently and peered into the hall.

"Don't go in there, Ester," Connie said hesitantly, but she was already out, listening at the drawing-room door.

Craigh was still standing with his back to the fire, and Dolly was sitting in a big, old winged armchair. She gave a soft laugh. "So what you here for? You want to make a deal, is that it?"

Ester froze. The kitchen door opened wider and Gloria peeped out. Ester scurried back, pushing her inside. "She's making a fucking deal with them," she hissed.

"What?" Julia said in disbelief.

"I just heard her. Connie, get out the back and see if they're alone—see if they got any back-up. Go on, do it."

Connie opened the back door and slipped out. Gloria had dodged behind Ester and gone into the hall to listen for herself. Ester followed then pulled at her arm. "Go and search her room," she whispered. Gloria glared but Ester pushed her hard, pressing her ear against the door.

Dolly's voice could be heard clearly. "No way! You must be joking. I'll do a deal but not for a quarter. Let's say half."

Craigh looked at Palmer and then back to Dolly. "You'll get it in cash."

"Oh, it has to be cash," Dolly said. She got up from the chair and moved closer to Craigh. "Fifty percent."

"I can't do that," Craigh said louder.

Ester dived back into the kitchen as Gloria scuttled down the stairs after her.

"Look at this lot! Fucking passports—she's got Kathleen's kids on hers and there's one for Angela."

Julia could feel her legs turning to jelly. "Oh, shit."

Ester looked at Julia. "She's doing a deal for fifty percent of the cash, I just heard her. She's going to shop the lot of us! How much proof do you want?"

Ester shoved the passports under Julia's nose and then looked back at the closed door. "Right. We got to get that money. You, Julia, get Gloria's car, get over to Norma's, take Gloria with you."

Connie came back in from the yard shaking. "There are police in the lane with dogs and some up in the woods but they're not heading toward us, they're just sort of sniffing around as usual."

"Shit." Ester walked to the deep freeze and opened it. She delved inside, brought out a huge twenty-pound frozen turkey and carried it to the sink, turning on the hot water. Julia was putting on her coat, heading for the back door, as Ester removed a .45 pistol from inside the bird. She dug further and scooped out the cartridges.

Julia grabbed her wrist. "Jesus Christ, Ester, what *are* you doing?"

"She's selling us right down the river! What the hell do you think I'm doing? Go and get the money, as much as you can, and we're getting out of here. I said we couldn't trust her! I *warned* you! Now do it."

Again Julia hesitated but Gloria gave her a shove. "I'll come with you, let's go."

Dolly was chuckling at Craigh, and then she patted his arm. "All right, you win, gimme three grand and we'll call it quits. You should have been a market trader, you know. But it's got to be cash."

On Dolly's last line, just as she placed her hand on Craigh's arm, Ester walked in, the gun held in her right hand, her arm pressed close to her body.

Dolly turned, smiling, toward Ester, feeling buoyant because she knew now they had nothing to worry about. Craigh and Palmer weren't there because of the robbery and she couldn't wait to have a laugh about it with them all.

Then she saw the gun.

It was all over within seconds. Dolly was faster to register Ester's intention than either police officer and, as Ester raised the gun to fire at Craigh, Dolly moved in front of him, protecting him with her body as she screamed one word, "*No!*"

She felt the impact of the bullet like a stab from a red-hot poker, her blood splattering Ester's face. DCI Craigh took a step backward, arms up to brace himself against the next shot. Palmer sidestepped at the same time, Dolly's blood speckling his shirt. Ester's body was rigid, her teeth clenched, her arm still outstretched. She pulled the trigger again. The second bullet spun Dolly a half-step backward and everything began to blur. She could hear a distant, distorted voice and then saw her own face.

"I have never committed a criminal act in my life." The social services board looked toward the straight-backed Dorothy Rawlins.

Ester fired the third bullet.

"No, I killed someone who betrayed me, there's a difference, Julia."

Ester pulled the trigger again.

No pain now, she was urging her horse forward, loving the feel of the cold morning air on her face, enjoying the fact that she had succeeded in learning not just to ride but gallop flat out and jump hedges and ditches—at her age.

Ester fired again.

Dolly's shirt was covered in blood. She was still on her feet, but the impact of the fifth bullet almost toppled her. The images and echoes of voices were fainter now and she could only just make out the figure in an old brown coat standing by a garden gate. "It's me, Dorothy, it's your auntie. Your mum won't talk about it but that young lad, he's no good. You got a good life ahead of you, grammar-school scholarship and everything."

With the sixth bullet, her body buckled at the knees, her hands hanging limply at her sides. "I'll always be here for you, Doll, you know that. I'll always love you, take care of you. Come on, open your arms wide and hold me, hold me, sweetheart, that's my girl. Come on, come to me, it's all over now."

At last she lay still. In death her face looked older: there was no expression—it was already a mask. Her mouth hung open, and her eyes were wide, staring sightlessly. It had only taken Ester a few moments to fire six shots at point-blank range, but in those seconds Dolly Rawlins's life had flashed from the present to the distant past. She had died a violent death like her beloved husband. Like him, she had not been expecting it; she had been confident, proud of herself and looking forward to the future, looking to make her dreams of a children's home come true. Maybe that had all been a fantasy, maybe this was how it was meant to end. Fate had drawn these women together, and it was fate that it was Ester who killed her, Ester, who she had never really trusted. She had taken such care of them all, checking her back and sides just like Harry had done. And like him, she had faced death straight on, face forward.

Now her cheek lay on the old, dirty, stained carpet, blood trickling from her mouth and her body lying half curled in a fetal position. Her death had been as ugly as her husband's, the only difference being that she had never betrayed anyone.

The sound of the shots brought the officers in the woods running toward the house, shouting into their radios as the others in the lane turned back toward the manor. A patrol car had already received the call and they in turn radioed for further assistance.

Within minutes, the manor was surrounded. Gloria and Julia were hauled out of the Mini, Connie was arrested halfway up the stairs, and Ester was handcuffed by DCI Craigh. She said not one word but stared vacantly ahead, her face drained of color.

One by one the women were led to the waiting patrol cars and taken away. They were in a state of shocked confusion. None of them spoke or looked at each other.

Dolly Rawlins lay where she had been shot, a deep, dark pool of blood spreading across the threadbare carpet. She had been covered by a sheet taken from the linen closet and the blood was soaking through it. Angela sat huddled with the little girls. They had heard the gunfire but did not understand what had taken place. For the time being, Angela was allowed to remain upstairs with them while the rest of the house filled with more police, plainclothes and uniform, and the women were led out.

Dolly Rawlins's body was removed, after a doctor had certified she was dead, and taken directly to the mortuary. Angela saw the stretcher from the little girls' bedroom window. They stared down, not understanding, and then Sheena asked Angela if she would read their favorite story, The Three Little Piggies.

"The big bad wolf huffed and he puffed but no matter how hard he tried, he could not blow the house down." The tears trickled down Angela's face as she closed the book. It was the end of the story.

The old coal chute at Rose Cottage was never opened by the police. Its black-painted door remained a charming, old-fashioned feature of the "olde worlde" cottage. So no one discovered the sixteen heavy-duty black bin liners tied tightly at the neck, each containing several million pounds in untraceable notes.

Readers' Club

If you enjoyed *She's Out*, why not join the
LYNDA LA PLANTE READERS' CLUB
by visiting www.lyndalaplante.com?

A MESSAGE FROM LYNDA LA PLANTE . . .

Dear Reader,

Thank you very much for reading *She's Out*. *Widows*, as many of you may know, was my first ever TV show. It was commissioned by one of the first female television producers in the UK, Verity Lambert of Euston Films for Thames Television and it remains a special favorite of mine. In the wake of the phenomenal TV success—it became one of the highest rating series of the early 1980s—I turned the screenplay and script into a tie-in novel, which was first published in 1983. The original *Widows* ran to two series on ITV and went on to have a sequel set ten years later—*She's Out*—the book adaptation of which you have just read.

When award-winning film director Steve McQueen chose to use *Widows* for a major movie that was released in November 2018, I decided to edit and reshape my original novel of *Widows* for a new audience. I loved doing it and both the reworked novel and the film were a huge success, so I went on to do the same with the second book, *Widows' Revenge*, and now with *She's Out*, a book which sees Dolly ten years after the events of *Widows' Revenge*, where she has just been released from prison.

It's always wonderful to revisit my characters. Dolly Rawlins was the first of my heroines to emerge into the limelight on screen and on the page. She was followed by, among others, Anna Travis in *Above Suspicion* and, most famously, Jane Tennison in *Prime Suspect*, who was portrayed brilliantly on screen by Helen Mirren. My book series about the young Jane Tennison, who goes on to become the heroine of *Prime Suspect*, follows Jane as she starts out as a police detective on the streets of London. The first five books in the series—*Tennison, Hidden Killers, Good Friday, Murder Mile* and *The Dirty Dozen*—are all available now. The newest of these, *The Dirty Dozen*, is set in 1980 and sees Jane as the first female detective posted to the Met's renowned Flying Squad, commonly known as "the Sweeney." If you enjoyed *She's Out* and the other *Widows* books, do look out for the Jane Tennison series.

I am also very excited to announce that in March 2020 I will be launching a new series, the first of which is called *Buried*. It is set loosely around the *Widows* world, but with a present day setting and a brilliant new protagonist,

Jack Warr. Jack is a young DCI who finds himself investigating a fire at a cottage where a body has been found, along with stacks of charred bank notes. Adopted at birth, as Jack investigates, he starts to learn more about his own identity. Soon he finds he'll stop at nothing to uncover the truth—including breaking the law himself.

If you would like to hear more about the new series, or about the Tennison series, you can visit www.lyndalaplante.com, where you can join the LYNDA LA PLANTE READERS' CLUB. It only takes a few moments to sign up, there are no catches or costs and new members will automatically receive a message from me with some exclusive insights into what I am writing presently.

We promise to keep your data private and confidential, and it will never be passed on to a third party. We won't spam you with loads of emails, just get in touch now and again with news about my books, and you can unsubscribe any time you want.

And if you would like to get involved in a wider conversation about my novels, please do review *She's Out* on Amazon, on GoodReads, on any other e-store, on your own blog and social media accounts, or talk about it with friends, family or reader groups! Sharing your thoughts helps other readers, and I always enjoy hearing about what people experience from my writing.

Thanks again for your interest in *She's Out*, and I hope you'll return for *Buried*.

With my very best wishes,
Lynda La Plante

Turn the page to read an extract from
Lynda La Plante's brand new book

BURIED

Coming March 2020

CHAPTER 1

Rose Cottage had lain empty for eight months. It was a neat, two story, white stone building with thick, black wooden lintels above the central front door and each of the five small windows—three up, two down. On the more sheltered, west side of the front wall, the ivy had completely taken over and was lifting the slate from the roof, but on the exposed east side, the stonework was bare and had been flattened by centuries of strong winter winds swirling down from the hills. From some angles the cottage looked as though it was leaning to the left.

As the cottage was rural, with stables and a hay barn, the land surrounding it had been fairly unkept even before it was left empty, but a small area directly outside the front door had been landscaped into narrow, winding footpaths circling rose beds. The wild roses, left to their own devices, were still fighting against the changing seasons, but today they looked particularly beautiful. In fact, they were the only real reminder of how lovely the cottage had once been.

Suddenly, the small downstairs windows to the left and right of the front door exploded under the immense pressure from the heat inside, sending glass and wood showering into the multi-colored rose heads. Flames quickly took hold of the black wooden lintels and, within seconds, the smoke from the fire had blackened the white stone wall.

Inside, the furniture had been moved into the center of the room, just in front of the hearth. A heavy wooden chest of drawers and two bookshelves surrounded a two-seater, horse-hair sofa, which had four occasional tables piled high on top of it. Some of the books from the bookshelves had been forced into the gaps of this makeshift bonfire, and the rest had been thrown into the hearth on top of a huge stack of paper.

The fire had taken hold extremely quickly, and the small lounge was soon consumed by flames, which rose to the ceiling beams, traveled to the wooden staircase and up the stairs. They eventually pushed their way out between the slate roof tiles from the engulfed wooden ceiling beams beneath, and it wasn't long before a spark leapt across to the hay barn, which was full of bales of hay, despite the horses being long gone. The barn went up like a roman candle and, from that point onward, there was no stopping the fire.

A quarter of a mile away, in a small housing estate, the first of the 999 calls was finally made. Neighbors watched as the dark brown smoke billowed into the clear blue sky. When the house had been occupied, the smoke from the chimney had always been the expected light gray, but this was different. It looked heavy and rancid, and just kept coming.

Speculation was rife as to how the fire had started. Was it "that bloody tramp" trying to keep warm again? Was it kids taking their games too far?

Fourteen 999 calls were made in total, sending two fire engines racing toward Rose Cottage from Aylesbury Fire Station. By the time the engines arrived, the contents of the cottage had almost gone and the hay barn was a pile of rubble and ashes. However, the stables, which were furthest away from the cottage, were still fully ablaze, with the flames heading for the surrounding trees.

When the fire brigade arrived, they split into two teams—one to tackle the fire inside, and a second on the stables to prevent the flames from jumping to the woodland beyond. The stables were easier to gain control of because, once the wooden frames had gone, there was nothing left to fuel the fire. The interior of the cottage, however, kept re-igniting as the fire found new fuel on the upper floors and from the wooden roof beams. It didn't take much to give the flames a new lease of life.

By nightfall, the grounds resembled a muddy swamp and the rose beds had been completely destroyed by four hours of torture from eight pairs of heavy fire boots walking backward and forward. Much of the furniture had been thrown into the front garden, to avoid further re-ignition inside the property, so the once beautiful rose garden looked like a fly-tipping site.

"Stop!" the Sub Officer shouted as he emerged through the hole that used to be the front door. "Nobody goes back inside!"

Sub reached for his phone and dialed Sally Bown. It was late and the phone rang for quite some time before it was finally answered. "Sal, this one's for you. We've got a body. Bring your CSI."

Fire Investigation Officer, Sally Bown, arrived at the scene at 11 p.m. From the neck down, she was kitted out in her well-worn Fire Officers' Uniform, but from the neck up, she was immaculate. Her long brown hair was in a loose, low braided bun, held in place by an antique hairpin of white beads and silver leaves, and her light makeup enhanced her natural beauty. The whole crew fancied her on an average day, so this post-bridesmaid look was definitely making their arduous night better. She didn't mind. They respected her position, so them watching her arse every now and then didn't bother her in the slightest.

"It's way better than men *not* watching my arse," was her response to any woman who objected to the glib sexism that came from the male fire fighters. And Sally looked at them, too, so she thought it only fair.

At Sally's side was a child of a CSI with puffy eyes and bed hair. He carried a case almost as big as himself, and he stuck to Sally's side like glue. He wasn't quite used to shift work yet, but if he'd been called by Sally Bown, then he was good at his job. He'd learn the rest.

In the lounge of Rose Cottage, the pile of heavy wooden furniture was now destroyed. The brass hinges and handles from the chest of drawers lay on the floor, just in front of the hearth and, on the obliterated sofa, part-melted into the springs, lay a dead body, charred and blackened beyond recognition.

"Jesus," muttered Sally, as she got out her camera and filmed the scene, starting at the front door and moving methodically toward the center of the lounge and the dead body. Her young CSI waited outside until instructed to do otherwise.

"Sally, stop!" Sub shouted. Sally stopped dead. Sub was a man of very few words and everyone who worked with him knew that he only really spoke when he had something important to say. "Retrace your steps, Sal. Now. Please."

Sally didn't question his instruction. She started walking backward, toe to heel, following exactly the same path as she'd taken to come in.

There was a deafening crack from directly above Sally's head. A hand grabbed her belt and she flew backward with the force of a recoiling bungee rope, to be caught by Sub's waiting arms. Once he had a firm hold on her, he fell backward onto the floor, taking Sally with him, and in the next split second an iron bedframe dropped through the air and landed right where Sally had been standing. A cloud of ash and debris flew into the air and took an age to come back down. When visibility returned, Sub was still seated on the floor, Sally between his legs and his arms gripped tightly round her waist. The two legs of the bed that were closest to them had smashed deep holes through the lounge floorboards, and the other two were straddling the remains of the sofa and the charred body, which was still, luckily, in one piece.

Sub momentarily tightened his grip around Sally's waist, before letting go completely. That tiny squeeze reassured her that she was safe and protected. As Sally gripped Sub's raised knees to use them as leverage to stand, and he eased her forward with his hands politely in the small of her back, she couldn't help but think to herself what a massive shame it was that he looked so like her dad.

When he arrived on the scene, Detective Inspector Martin Prescott was frustrated to be held back from entering Rose Cottage until the risk assessment had been done. He couldn't imagine three more infuriating words in the English language than "risk-fucking-assessment"!

Prescott had been Senior Officer to Sally Bown's older sister for more than twenty years, and so the families were naturally close. This was not unusual for rural Aylesbury, or for the local emergency services. Sally knew he'd be impatient, so, while the fragile ceiling and crumbling walls were shored up and made safe, she kept him occupied by showing him the video footage of the interior.

"We initially thought he could be a vagrant," Sally told Prescott.

"He?" Prescott smiled as he corrected Sally's assumption. It was very clear from the video that there was no way of knowing the gender of the charred remains at this point.

Prescott always made Sally smile without even trying. She thought his thick Yorkshire accent made him sound happy, even when they were disagreeing with each other.

"Sorry," Sally corrected herself. "We initially thought that the body could be that of a vagrant unlucky enough to have set fire to himself after lighting candles to keep warm. There's no electricity in the cottage, and we found several tea lights scattered around the lounge—on the mantel and in the hearth—but when I looked more closely at the debris on the floor directly next to the sofa, it was clear that the furniture had been piled up around him. I mean, around the body."

"So, the body was there first?"

"That's for you to decide, Martin."

"Accelerant?"

"Undetermined as yet."

Prescott was disappointed when the video footage ended. "That all ya got?"

Sally started to play a second video, which began by showing the iron bedframe sitting squarely astride the sofa. Prescott closed his eyes and sighed heavily at the sight of his crime scene being buried under a double bed. The quiet breath he exhaled formed the words, "Fuck me!"

Prescott took a moment to gather his thoughts. When he was thinking, his eyes flicked from side to side as though he were seeing the various scenarios flashing past inside his head. He appeared to be a very laid back man, but had an intensity bubbling away underneath the surface.

Sally knew that Prescott took this action because he was mildly dyslexic and, soon after joining the force, had made the decision to never write anything down in public. Instead, he had to remember everything, and in a brain that full, it could sometimes take a little longer to process what he was seeing. But Prescott was a clever man, and it was always worth waiting for him. He hid his intellect under Northern glibness, but Sally's older sister had shared all of his secrets with Sally over the years.

"Right, well, ya know the rules, Sal. It's a suspicious death, so I 'ave to assume murder till the evidence tells me otherwise." Prescott walked away from Sally before she could counter and headed for Rose Cottage to see if he could at least peek in through where the window had once been. "And if it's murder, then I'm wastin' valuable time standin' out here doing naff all!"

Sally raced ahead and stood in his way, forcing him to stop. "This may be your crime scene, DI Prescott, but you are *not* going into Rose Cottage until I say it's safe for you to do so."

Prescott looked down at Sally. She was at least four inches shorter than him, but she was a feisty woman, just like her sister, and her calling him DI Prescott instead of Martin told him that she wasn't going to back down.

"And anyway . . ." Sally added, ". . . I hadn't finished." Sally fast forwarded the second video, stopping it at seven minutes and thirty-two seconds. On the wall above the hearth the word PERVERT could be seen scrawled in red paint. It was mostly covered in a thick layer of black soot, but the letters could still just be made out. "It looks like you could have a dead sex offender. And I doubt he got here on his own."

Prescott got his vape out of his left-hand jacket pocket and said, "See, I know that should make me feel better about havin' to wait to gain access to me crime scene. I mean, a dead perv 'int supposed to be as bad as a dead anybody else, but it just annoys me more. I don't know if that word relates to this dead body or not, do I? So now I'm more frustrated than before you showed me." He dragged on the vape, but couldn't for the life of him get it to work. He put it back into his pocket and, from the other jacket pocket, he got a packet of cigarettes and a lighter. "You follow ya rules and get that place scaffolded up asap and I'll be over 'ere shortenin' me life."

Six hours had passed and Martin Prescott had been donned in a blue paper suit and shoes for the last fifty minutes. His white paper face mask sat round his neck as he watched Sally pointing at the partially collapsed roof and muttering to Sub. Sub nodded and Prescott immediately put on his mask. The man of few words had spoken.

Inside Rose Cottage, scaffolding held up the charred ceiling beams and the loose stones from the walls had been removed, leaving behind a relatively solid and safe structure. Visually, the scene was as Prescott expected, based on the preview he'd got from Sally's videos, but nothing ever prepared him for the smell of a body. The stench of burnt flesh and bones overpowers every other sense and, even through his face mask, he could smell and taste the distinctive miasma of "long-pig."

"Long-pig is what cannibals call human beings," Sally had explained on their first ever meeting, more than fourteen years ago. "By all accounts we taste like barbequed pork and, as we cook, we definitely smell like it."

"Fuck me," Prescott had mumbled through his face mask. "No wonder you're single." And from that day forward, Prescott and Sally had got on like the proverbial house on fire.

Prescott and Sally paused just inside the jagged hole in the wall that used to be the front doorway of Rose Cottage and watched the dog handler lead her spaniel through the rubble. The dog wore tiny red canvas boots, velcroed in place around the ankles and with thick rubber soles that protected her paws from smoldering embers and sharp debris, allowing her to work safely and comfortably. The single repeated command of, "Show me, Amber," was all that could be heard inside Rose Cottage.

Amber's handler kept her off the sofa, as the charred body was still there. The dog worked hard, sniffing and moving around the remnants of furniture. Her tail wagged, her tongue lolled, she jumped and rummaged, but she didn't make one single indication that an accelerant was present.

"Maybe the fire burned intensely enough to destroy any accelerant?" Sally speculated. "Or maybe a less common one was used. The dog only knows the most common ones, such as petrol or household flammables. Your Forensics people might still find accelerant on the items you collect."

"I'll make sure I've got a tennis ball in me pocket if they do." Prescott signaled for his blue suited CSIs to descend on the scene. He pointed at the sofa. "There's a body in there, fellas, but it's goin' nowhere, so don't rush and don't compromise evidence just to get it out."

A sea of nodding blue paper heads dispersed around the room and set about collecting anything and everything that might be useful—wood, brass hinges, plaster, bed springs. All items were individually double-wrapped into nylon bags to preserve any traces of accelerant.

Now that Prescott was inside his crime scene, he had the patience of a saint. He could see the wheels of the machinery turning, see his officers working and progress being made. He followed his CSIs deeper into the mess, allowing them to clear and preserve the way in front of him, and Sally followed after. This was *his* scene now, and she totally respected the shift in authority.

Eventually, and in relative silence, Prescott and Sally made it as far as the sofa. The iron bedframe, which was now gone, had missed the body when it fell. Even so, the body was massively damaged. The face was not only burned down to the skeleton, but the cheekbones and lower jawbone were smashed and many of the teeth were missing.

"Could that damage to the skull be from falling debris?" Prescott asked.

Sally leaned in to get a better look. "The ceiling was largely gone by the time we arrived, so God knows what might have fallen through and landed on the sofa. The cleaner looking skull fractures around the temple area could be heat stress. The skull can sometimes just pop, depending on the intensity of heat the fire achieves."

"Damn shame this fella's teeth are so damaged," Prescott commented, almost to himself. Then louder, "Look at the bloody mess your lot has made of this place!"

Sally was just about to tear a strip of him when she looked at his partially hidden face. His eyes were crinkled at the edges and she knew he was smiling.

"Bloody fires," Prescott continued, avoiding her gaze. "If the flames don't destroy the evidence, the water does."

Prescott scratched his head through his blue paper hood and his eyes flicked about again as he thought through everything he was seeing. "If this is murder, we might be lookin' for someone who's savvy 'bout forensics, you know. I mean, you can't print burnt wood and you can't find shoeprints under water."

He was suddenly distracted by the contents of the hearth. The water from the fire hose on the floor in this area of the room looked like thin black paint—a result you might expect to get after paper is burned, creating a fine, soluble ash. Further back in the hearth, untouched by the water altogether, were the remnants of what looked like stacks of dry, charred paper. The paper was now nothing more than tiny fragments of its original form, but the volume was confusing.

Prescott picked up the longest of four fire pokers, and gently nudged the top layer of paper away in the hope of getting to some less burnt samples underneath. He tried not to damage any of the delicate paper. Eventually, he spotted a single, intact piece, no more than one centimeter in length, showing the instantly recognizable pale blue-green pattern from the bottom left hand corner of an old five pound note. Prescott carefully picked up this fragile piece of evidence and placed into the palm of Sally's gloved hand.

"It's cash, Sal. These stacks o' paper . . . it's all cash."

Jack Warr was a strikingly attractive man. Thick, dark hooded brows hid the deepest brown eyes. He had a cleft chin, which showed the permanent shadow of impending stubble and, when he smiled, two long dimples appeared on either side of his mouth, running from his chin to his high, pronounced cheekbones. He had an effortlessly athletic physique that looked great in anything.

Maggie, his partner, always said it was a good job that his body was so amazing as he made no real effort with the clothes he dressed it in, but she fancied the pants off him no matter what he wore. It was those eyes that had got her in the first instance, though. Eyebrows down, Jack's eyes would express such incredible intensity that if he told you he could take on David Haye and win, you'd believe him. Eyebrows up, he looked like a delicate, innocent soul that any woman would love to care for. This balance between man and boy was why Maggie loved Jack so much. He was her protector and her lover, her rock and her friend.

"Where's the jacket that goes with this shirt you've put out?" Jack shouted from the master bedroom. He liked to call it the "master" bedroom, regardless of the fact that it was exactly the same size as the spare bedroom. The view over Teddington was what made it masterful, according to Jack.

Maggie didn't answer, so Jack was forced to go into the kitchen to find her. On the breakfast bar was a bowl of cereal and a cup of tea that she'd put out for him, on the back of his chair was his jacket and underneath were his shoes. Maggie's crooked smile said, "Why do we do this every morning?"

Jack kissed and hugged her tightly. He never tired of just holding Maggie in his arms. She felt the same today as she had when they first met. Jack would maintain that Maggie's exceptional body was effortless, but she tried her very best to go to the hospital gym during every lunch break and, when Jack had the car for work, she'd leave herself enough time to walk to the hospital. For Maggie, this daily exercise was not only good for her body, but also hugely therapeutic, as it took her away from the stresses, pressures and horrors of being an F1 Doctor. Both Jack's and Maggie's jobs weren't always easy. Shift patterns and heavy workloads dictated that junk food was sometimes on the menu and, when they did get a rare day off together, they loved nothing more than going out for dinner, accompanied by casual drinking and a movie.

Maggie exercised to stay beautiful for Jack, and Jack did absolutely nothing to stay fit for Maggie. She was a health-conscious, thirty-four-year-old and he was a slobbish thirty-six-year-old. Maggie, in stark contrast to Jack's "Heathcliff" look, had blonde hair and blue eyes. Jack adored the way she looked when she rolled out of bed in the morning, with her hair ruffled and her pale, flawless skin unhidden by makeup. She was the most beautiful woman he'd ever seen, and would ever see. He had eyes for no one but her.

Maggie had just come off a night shift on the Orthopedic Ward at the New Victoria Hospital. She was three weeks into her new rotation and, regardless of always coming home exhausted, she still got Jack ready for work before she went to bed. By the time he got home that night, she'd be gone again, so this hug had to last him at least twenty-four hours. Jack nuzzled Maggie's neck. He normally hated the way she smelt when she came home from work—the horrific combination of alcohol hand sanitizer, that chemical smell that hangs in the air in hospitals, moth balls and, occasionally, vomit—but this morning he was running late, so she'd already had time to shower and, therefore, smelt of tangerines.

Fourteen months previously, Maggie and Jack had agreed that moving from Devon to London was the right thing to do for her career. His career, in his words, wasn't as big a deal as hers. Maggie knew she wanted to be an Orthopedic Surgeon, whereas all Jack really knew for sure was that he wanted to be able to go and watch Plymouth Argyle whenever they played at home. Jack wasn't lazy, but rather discontent. Restless. And, as he explained it, at a cross-roads.

At thirty-six, Jack should, by now, have been a Detective Inspector at least, rather than a lowly DC. When Maggie had asked Jack if they could move to London for her career, he'd said, "Sure. Gang wrangling will be a bit like sheep wrangling, I expect. Only with knives." Maggie had asked Jack what it was he truly wanted, and all he could come up with was "You," which, although lovely, wasn't very helpful. Then he'd answered more seriously, "I want that look I see in your eyes when you put that stethoscope round your neck. You're proud of what you do, Mags. You're excited. I want to feel excited."

London was, in fact, a huge risk, both emotionally and financially, but Jack's commitment to Maggie made it the right decision. They knew no one in the South East and, although Maggie could make a lifelong friend in a supermarket line, Jack was more standoffish. He didn't care about friends—he had Maggie—but the money was a worry. They went from having both time and cash to spend at the end of the month, to being skint ships that passed in the night. And they had to plan two months in advance for any extra expenditure—for example the car's MOT. Maggie dealt with all of this, though. She was the organizer, and she was the one who never panicked when the account turned from black to red.

Jack had agreed to make the life-changing move because he'd always known that Maggie was destined for greater things, and his indecisiveness couldn't be responsible for holding her back. As it happened, Jack's current boss, DCI Simon Ridley, had heard on the grapevine of Jack's transfer and had done a little digging. Jack's reputation in Devon was as a solid foot-soldier with an exceptional eye for detail and a natural ability to talk to people, read them and work out the best way to get what he needed from them. His interview technique was greatly admired, just never pushed to its limits in the small town of Totnes. Ridley had decided to give Jack the opportunity to find his path with the Serious Crime Squad, but very quickly worked out that Jack not being stretched in his previous role was less to do with the location and more to do with Jack's own lack of ambition. However, he was diligent and got on with his work, so Ridley had kept him on . . . for now.

* * *

It was Jack's turn to have the car that morning which, as he sat in a tail-back on the A3 near Battersea, he was deeply regretting. His work mobile danced on the passenger seat, pinging and vibrating away as message after message came through, some from the App version of HOLMES, as case related information was shared, and some from DCI Ridley. HOLMES was the Bible for the police force and was normally installed and issued on tablets for use in Court or on cases. But the technology was unreliable, so many officers invested in top of the range mobile phones and installed HOLMES on them instead. It was allowed—just about.

As the pinging and vibrating continued, Jack smiled and shook his head as he imagined Ridley's messages. They would be perfectly spelled and punctuated instructions for the day. Jack knew that Ridley was in meetings all morning, which was why being a little bit late was no big deal. Jack would make the time up at the end of the day anyway, seeing as Maggie would be on her next night shift and he'd be going home to a cold bed.

Ridley led a divisional team of twelve Serious Crime officers. The case that Jack was currently working on started out with one young dad, who happened to be an engineer, realizing that the baby monitor in his daughter's nursery was sending a signal to three devices, rather than the two he expected. The monitor had been hacked and an unknown person or persons were watching his daughter sleep.

Once the police had the geography of the rogue signals pinned down, the legwork had begun. Hundreds of hours tracing, interviewing, ruling-in and ruling-out every known pedophile and associate in the area. Over several months, they had discovered hundreds of hacked baby monitors, all within the same fifty mile radius. They visited 756 pedophiles, their friends and their families, and they narrowed the field to thirty-two. Then to one, a Donal Sweeney, who shared a cell with a man whose never-convicted pedophile nephew sold baby monitors to highstreet stores.

It was 8:45 by the time Jack walked down the battleship gray corridor toward CID's shared office. There was nothing remotely dynamic about this part of the station. He paused in the canteen doorway, inhaled the coffee-bean air and diverted inside.

Jack slowly worked his way through all of his text messages and emails over an espresso and a croissant dipped in honey. Jack only drank coffee at work, because Maggie hated the smell and taste of it when he kissed her, and seeing as kissing Maggie was more important than caffeine, Jack did without coffee when he was at home. But Jack needed caffeine to get him through this bloody fraud case.

The canteen was bustling with uniformed officers. Some ate heavy meals, some light breakfasts, depending on where they were in their shifts. As Jack made himself a to do list from Ridley's text messages, he giggled through his croissant, sending a fine spray of loose puff pastry across the table. Ridley had written:

> Laura's post-8 p.m. report overwrites yours, rather than adds to yours from yesterday morning. Please amend in the system. Print in triplicate and leave on my desk.

Ridley was the only man in the world who texted in full sentences. Jack sat back in his chair and, wiping the stubborn, buttery crumbs from round his mouth with the back of his hand, he looked around the canteen. He could hear snippets of conversations as officers talked about the cases they were on, the arrests they'd just made, the raids they were about to make. The amount of adrenalin and testosterone flying around Jack was dizzying, and hugely disappointing, because none of it was his. Jack knew that his team would be at their desks, focused and driven to find the dirty bastard who was watching other people's kids sleep. So why was he late and sitting by himself in the canteen? The truth was that, no matter how friendly and welcoming Ridley's team was, Jack still kept them at arm's length.

Jack had gone from being a normal sized fish in a normal sized pond, to being a very small fish in the hugest pond in the UK—the Metropolitan Police Force. And he was out of his depth. After fourteen months of working at the MET, Jack still hadn't found his calling, his passion, his heart in London and, as the months ticked by, he honestly feared that he never would.

When Jack finally walked into the Squad Room, he froze in the doorway. *Shit!* Ridley was *not* in meetings all morning and Jack being a little bit late was a *very* big deal.

Ridley didn't acknowledge Jack's presence, and no one in the team dared look away from him while he was talking. This was an impromptu briefing, in response to a phone call from DI Martin Prescott over in Aylesbury.

"We've just been handed a house fire, in which the charred remains of an unknown person have been discovered, together with approximately two million pounds in old money—also burned. This is being treated as murder, arson and robbery. It's come to us because it's looking like it could be connected to one of our old cases from '95—the biggest train robbery this country has ever seen. No one was ever arrested and thirty million plus vanished without a trace. We're heading to Aylesbury in twenty minutes."

Then, and only then, did Ridley look at Jack. Ridley's dark eyes were a frightening combination of anger and disappointment. "You're with me," he said, then headed into his office and slammed the door shut.

The team shuffled uncomfortably in their seats, wanting to offer sympathy but, equally, wondering what the hell Jack thought he was playing at by being so late. As Jack bowed his head in disgrace and wondered how this day could possibly get any worse, he spotted a blob of honey sliding down the front of his trouser leg. *That's fair*, he thought.

A Q&A WITH LYNDA LA PLANTE

You studied acting at RADA (Royal Academy of Dramatic Art) in London. Had you always wanted to act?

I had never really thought about being an actress, as from a very early age I had studied ballet. When I was twelve, I had a very nasty fall from a swing and injured both knees, so a career as a ballerina was no longer possible. To avoid disappointment, my mother enrolled me in drama classes. I doubt very much that I would ever have actually become a ballet dancer, but I soon became obsessed by acting and was encouraged by my drama teacher to apply for the Royal Academy.

Your peers at RADA included Anthony Hopkins, Ian McShane and John Hurt. Did you go on to act in any productions with them?

Ian McShane and John Hurt were friends of mine at RADA, but I had a much closer relationship with Anthony Hopkins. We worked together at a repertory company in Liverpool and then both starred in *La Mandragola*, a wonderful play by Goldoni. Shortly after the season, Anthony went on to join the National Theatre.

You toured with the RSC (Royal Shakespeare Company) and National Theatre, and had a successful television career. Why did you decide to give up acting and take up writing instead?

There comes a time in every actor's life when they must face the future and decide where their career is going. I had been consistently cast in almost interchangeable roles in every crime series on television. Although I had a steady stream of work, I often felt dispirited. I returned to the theater in the Royal Shakespeare Company's production of Eugene O'Neill's *Long Day's Journey into the Night*, and even starred as Calamity Jane, but the frustration was building. My first attempt at writing was *Widows*, which went on to be an incredible success and, truthfully, I enjoyed the process of writing, researching and being part of a casting team more than I enjoyed acting. I knew almost immediately that I wanted to be a writer and creator and had no regrets about not returning to acting.

You are the multi award-winning writer and creator of the television series *Prime Suspect*. How did that come about?

After the phenomenal success of the TV series *Widows* (which has continued to the present day since a major movie directed by Steve McQueen, based on the original series, was released in 2018) I had become a fully fledged writer. I was approached by the network to see if I had any new material and that material became *Prime Suspect*.

***Prime Suspect* gave Helen Mirren her first major television role, as your character Jane Tennison. What qualities did she have as an actress that made you want to cast her?**

I had seen Dame Helen Mirren on stage and admired her greatly. She is a brilliant actress and has a natural weight to her presence. She was also the right age to play Jane Tennison, which was very important to me following the research I had done, and having met detective chief inspectors working for the Met Police.

You have written a series of books based on the early life and career of Jane Tennison, which follow her from when she is a young police woman at the age of twenty, to when we meet her in the *Prime Suspect* novels at the age of forty-five. Why did you decide to write them?

I had never considered writing books about Jane Tennison's background, but at a Q and A session after a book signing event, I was asked what Jane Tennison's early life had been like. I was, to tell the truth, unable to answer the question. I know I'm not the only author who has found myself in that position, as I recall that Raymond Chandler was once asked where Philip Marlowe's character came from and he answered that he hadn't got the faintest idea. The more I thought about the question, the more interested I became in discovering where and when Jane Tennison began her career and started to research numerous female police officers. I was very impressed by their stories and interested to learn how tough it would have been for Jane Tennison to survive in this world. When we first meet Jane in *Prime Suspect* she is already forty-five years old—very accomplished, strong willed and exceptionally professional—and it continues to fascinate me to explore how she came to be this way. I am fortunate to realize that my readers are also keen to find out.

The *Tennison* books not only paint a vivid and colorful portrait of London and policing in the seventies and eighties, but they are also set at a time where forensic science is in its infancy. Was this a challenge?

As well as discovering how a young female officer survived the rampant discrimination and tough world of policing in the seventies, eighties and nineties, returning to this time means also entering a world where there was no DNA testing, no mobile phones and forensic science was in its infancy. This is not necessarily a challenge, but instead fascinating to learn how the investigations were carried out and to see the ability of the detectives when doing their jobs without advanced technology. This does, however, require a lot of work, particularly when making sure that the stories have all of the pace that readers are used to these days.

You are the only layperson to be made an Honorary Member of the Forensic Science Society. Why were you awarded this honor, and what does it mean to you?

Throughout my career in crime writing, I have been dependent on the Metropolitan Police officers, pathologists and the expertise of forensic scientists. I have never taken what is described as "dramatic license," and have instead relied on the expert advice that I have been given. My respect for the scientists and the time they have given me to make sure my books are as factually correct as possible, is incredibly important to me, and because of this, I was given membership of the Forensic Science Society. I was very honored, and it is an award that I treasure.

You have written and produced over 170 hours of primetime television. Why did you decide to produce as well as write?

I decided to produce as well as write scripts mainly through a desire to have more involvement in the finished product, which you don't always get as a writer. After one notable experience where my suggestions on a film were ignored, I felt very frustrated and therefore disappointed in the end result.

For this reason, I decided to hire experienced producers, casting directors, set designers and costume designers and worked hard on learning my profession. Only then could I truthfully say I was in total control.

Of all the books you have written, do you have a favorite book and character?

My first book, *The Legacy*, remains my most treasured novel. I know it was overly long and, in fact, so long that it had to be divided into two books, but the character of Evelyn remains my favorite. *The Legacy* follows the course of Evelyn's life over five decades, which I really enjoyed exploring, so perhaps, in a funny way, this is also one of the reasons I enjoy writing Jane Tennison so much. I like following my characters' stories throughout their lives and creating fully formed characters.

You are continuing to write the *Tennison* series (the newest book being *The Dirty Dozen*). Will there be any further *Widows* books?

I am continuing to write about Jane Tennison's career through the years and *The Dirty Dozen* sees Jane joining the infamous Sweeney (the robbery squad), a tough group whose sole job is to investigate dangerous armed robberies. However, as much as I love writing about Jane Tennison, I truthfully don't know if I can leave the amazing women from *Widows* behind. Perhaps there will be another shocking twist to their story . . .

The groundbreaking thriller from
the Queen of Crime Drama

WIDOWS

Facing life alone, they turned to crime together.

Dolly Rawlins, Linda Perelli and Shirley Miller are
left devastated when their husbands are killed in a
security van heist that goes disastrously wrong.

When Dolly discovers her husband's bank deposit box
containing a gun, money and detailed plans for the hijack,
she has three options. She could hand over the ledgers
to the detective. She could hand them over to the thugs
who want to take over Harry's turf. Or, she and the other
widows could finish the job their husbands started.

As they rehearse the raid, the women discover
that Harry's plan required four people and recruit
hooker Bella O'Reilly. But only three bodies were
discovered in the carnage of the original hijack—so
who was the fourth man, and where is he now?

Now a major motion picture
Available now

WIDOWS' REVENGE

**Dolly, Linda, Shirley and Bella are back.
And this time it's a fight to the finish.**

Against all the odds, Dolly Rawlins and her gangland
widows managed the impossible: a heist their husbands
had failed to pull off—at the cost of their lives.

But though they may be in the money,
they're far from easy street.

Shocked by her husband's betrayal, Dolly discovers
Harry Rawlins isn't dead. He knows where the four
women are and he wants them to pay. And he doesn't
just mean getting his hands on the money.

The women can't keep running. They have to get
Harry out of their lives for good. But can they outwit a
criminal mastermind who won't hesitate to kill?

Especially when one of them has a plan
of her own . . . to kill or be killed.

Available now

THE DIRTY DOZEN

The fifth book in the Sunday Times bestselling Jane Tennison series.

April 1980 and Jane is the first female detective to be posted to the
Met's renowned Flying Squad, commonly known as the "Sweeney."
Based at Rigg Approach in East London, they investigate armed
robberies on banks, cash in transit and other business premises.

Jane thinks her transfer is on merit and is surprised to
discover she is actually part of a short term internal
experiment, intended to have a calming influence on a team
that likes to dub themselves as the "Dirty Dozen."

The men on the squad don't think a woman is up to the dangers they
face when dealing with some of London's most ruthless armed criminals,
who think the only "good cop" is a dead cop. Determined to prove she's
as good as the men, Jane discovers from a reliable witness that a gang
is going to carry out a massive robbery involving millions of pounds.

But she doesn't know who they are, or where and when they will strike . . .

Available now

From the creator of the award-winning TV series
PRIME SUSPECT, discover JANE TENNISON'S story,
from rookie police officer to fully-fledged detective.

TENNISON
HIDDEN KILLERS
GOOD FRIDAY
MURDER MILE
THE DIRTY DOZEN

Available now